THE

LIGHT

OF

EPERTASE

Epertase Publishing
Second American Paperback Edition

This is a work of fiction. Names, characters, places, and incidents either are the product of the author's imagination or are used fictitiously. Any resemblance to actual events, locales, or persons, living or dead, is entirely coincidental. The publisher does not have any control and does not assume responsibility for author or third-party websites or their content.

DEDICATION

To my mother, Lillian Dove. You have always been there for me. Thank you for being such a wonderful mother.

I love you.

ACKNOWLEDGEMENTS

I want to take a moment to thank you, the reader. Whether this is your first introduction to my writing, or you have been with me since the beginning, I thank you.

A lot of readers believe that a book publisher releases a book and somehow people simply discover it. But it isn't so easy for 99 percent of the books released each year. On top of exhaustive promoting from the publisher and the author, the best way for an author's work to be read is by recommendations from those who have already found and read it. Word of mouth is crucial to an author's success and you have humbled me with your praise. So, thank you. I hope each of you continue to enjoy my work as much as I enjoy writing it.

I also want to thank my family, friends, and Columbus Fire Department coworkers. You have been so supportive, and I can't thank you enough. (Except for John Galloway.)

To Rhemalda Publishing: Thank you for your patience and dedication in putting out books that are as close to the author's vision as possible. You were a dream to work with. I wish things had worked out better for you and I will be forever grateful for your help in getting my start.

To my wife, Angie, and son, Aiden: Thank you for being my life.

To Steve Murphy: Thank you for another brilliant cover.

To Bobbe Ecleberry: I wouldn't be here without you.

To the fantastic author, Jon Sprunk (*Shadow's Lure*): Thank you for reading Epertase and gracing my cover with a quote. To my readers, I suggest you try Jon's work, too.

And now, I don't want to keep you any longer from Epertase 2. Please, sit back and enjoy *A Kingdom's Fall*.

Special note: This trilogy has been completely revised in 2020. If you purchased a copy of any of the books in this series before Winter, 2020, then there are changes to the story. While most of the changes won't be too discombobulating, there is one that will throw everything off for you. The character you know as Terik from pre-2020 copies has had a magical name change. He is now known as Atticus. This change was made to help with the confusion of having both Terik and Tevin as prominent characters. With the revisions, the story remains mostly the same, however, you will no doubt find a few inconsistencies between the new and the old. I hope you will overlook those in light of the grander story. All that said, I believe this series is immensely better and I couldn't be prouder.

INFINITE SEA

VOLCANIC REGION

Bluefields of Sorrow

Danduke River

The Lands of Muéi

RECITAR

Wastelands

Farmlands

Pataska

Havens Ravine

EPERTASE

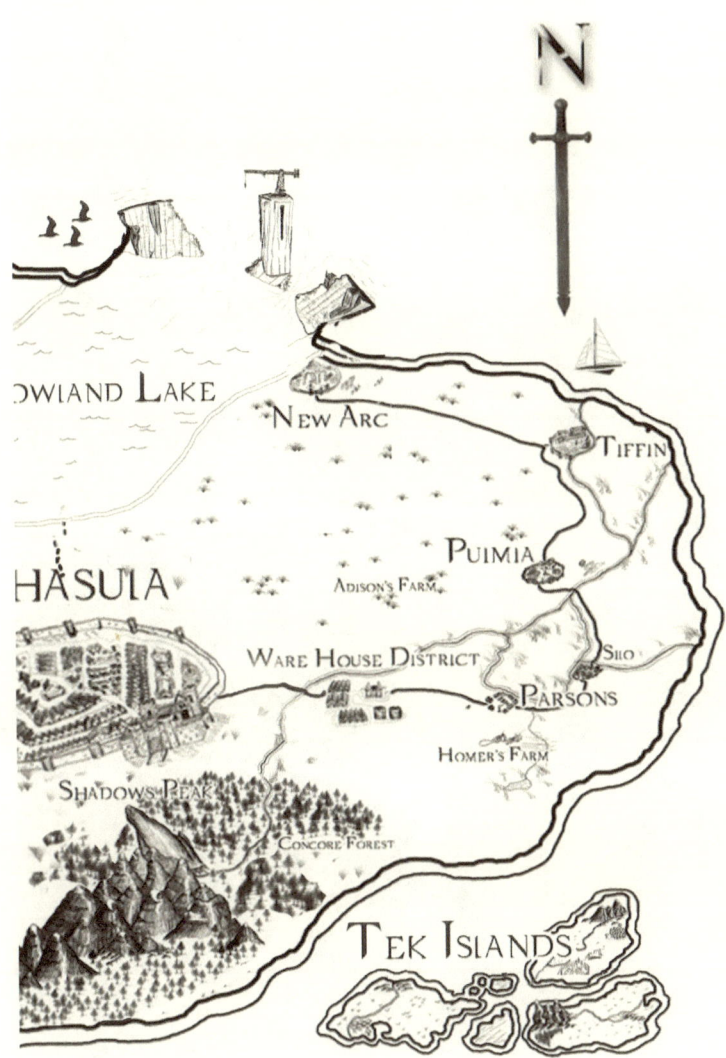

EPERTASE

A KINGDOM'S FALL
THE LIGHT OF EPERTASE
BOOK TWO
BY
DOUGLAS R. BROWN

2

That which survives the initial assault may yet die from the infection left behind.

CHAPTER 1

A DEADLY SEARCH

Most of the farmland had been churned into mud by the Tek army's boots and massive rolling machines. The farmers who had survived by hiding with their families in secret underground bunkers now worked day and night in hopes of one day returning their fields to profit and self-nourishment.

Fergus was one of those men—strong and thick from a lifetime of hard work while passive in his temperament from a lifetime of kindness. The bunkers had given him, his mother and father, two sisters, and many of their neighbors sanctuary twice in his life. The first time was when the heathens invaded years ago, and the second was more recently when the unsuspecting Teks marched over their heads.

It had been a month since the Epertasians had defeated the Teks, and Fergus had replanted most of his crops. As the full moon lifted, he wiped his brow and gazed over his field. His hard work had paid off. He looked forward to a future that afforded him more sleep.

It was nearing midnight when his father interrupted his daydreaming with frantic shouts of "Fergus" from across the field.

Fergus slowed his oxen and watched curiously as his elderly father hurried toward him, arms gyrating above his head, as if he were being chased by a dragon.

"Fergus," he shouted again, his voice shaky and strained.

Fergus started toward him, slow at first and then at a jog. "What is it, Father?" he shouted.

His answer came not from his father, but from a woman's high-pitched scream behind the barn.

His father stopped short with his hands on his knees. "Get your sisters and mother to the bunkers," he cried between gasps.

Fergus dropped the bag of seed from his shoulder and sprinted toward the house. His father caught his breath and headed for the barn. A part of Fergus wanted to go with him, investigate the screams, but he had learned over the years not to disobey, especially during times of trouble. His father's distress told him it was one of those times.

Fergus burst through the front door into the dark, quiet house. "Mother," he shouted. "Mother." He plowed through her half-open bedroom door. "Mother, wake up."

The bed creaked as she scrambled to the edge. With a groggy voice, she said, "Fergus, what is it?"

"Father said we must get to the bunkers. Get the girls and meet me out front." He raced back through the living room and onto the porch. Resting next to the steps was a wood pile with an axe wedged into the top piece. He grabbed it.

His mother and two sisters, Aeryn and Laudia, appeared at the door, each wearing nightgowns with furs draped across their shoulders. Aeryn held out an oil lamp to him. Her hand was trembling, maybe from the night's chill, though more likely from fear. Fergus snatched it from her. "Run for the bunkers." He didn't try to mask the dread in his voice for their benefit. He was afraid, and he knew they should be, too.

Before they left the porch, a chorus of odd, cackling howls filled the quiet night, freezing them in their steps. That wasn't the sound of wolves or any other creature he'd ever heard.

His mother touched his shoulder. "What's that noise, Fergus?"

He shook his head.

The howls continued, deep in pitch and broken like the rattle of a deadly snake.

Fergus looked toward the barn. The moonlight illuminated the edge of his property. The landscape danced with a sea of strange creatures galloping across the field in a sweeping wave. Their long, spindley arms acted like front legs, their two-fingered hands slamming the ground with each awkward stride. Though their movements were clumsy and stilted, the creatures were fast. Their death-pale skin was of nightmares. He glanced to the ivy-covered bunker entrance and then back to the coming swarm. It was going to be close. The creatures were crossing the fields with the speed of lions and the ferocity of dragons.

"Run," he shouted, gripping his axe so tightly his hand began to cramp.

"What are they?" Laudia shrieked.

"I don't know. Just run as fast as you can."

"What about Dad?"

"Dad will be fine," he lied, and gave her a shove.

The four ran toward the bunkers. The howls from behind grew louder. He heard Aeryn whimper. "Be strong," he shouted. He didn't look back, even as the sounds of the creatures' stampeding feet reached them.

The bunker was near.

Twenty horse-lengths.

Fifteen.

We're going to make it.

Ten horse-lengths.

Fergus inhaled through his nose, nearly gagging on the putrid stench of sulfur. And then one of the vile beasts shot past him and barreled into Laudia's back. She grunted with the impact and screeched in panic.

His mother turned toward her.

Fergus called her back. "Keep running, Mother. I'll help her."

The creatures closed in. To give his family a chance, especially Laudia, he dropped his oil lamp and turned with his axe raised. One creature immediately slammed against his chest before he could use his weapon. The air grunted from his lungs as he collided with the dirt. His axe landed just out of reach. As he tried to get up, the creature tackled him, straddling his chest. Fergus cranked his head around in time to see his mother and Aeryn tackled to the ground as well.

One of the creatures climbed onto Aeryn's chest and she cried out. The creature raised its malformed fist above its head and Fergus saw he'd been mistaken. Instead of fingers, two talons protruded from its hand. But it wasn't the two talons that told Fergus what it was. No, it was the concave bone measuring the length of a man's hand that jutted from the creature's palm. It was called a scoop-claw, and he knew what that meant.

He whispered, "By the gods. Fishers."

Fergus prayed for Aeryn to get away, knowing it was too late to help Laudia, who had already stopped screaming. The creature drove its bony scoop-claw toward her face. She shrieked once and stiffened. The fisher dug out both of her eyes and swallowed them whole. It howled to the sky. Fergus winced away. His mother's cries cut off next, though he couldn't get his head around to see her.

Fergus looked up at the rabid beast straddling his chest. It seemed patient, waiting so he could watch what happened to his family. Warm drool dripped onto Fergus's cheek. The fisher lazily raised its hand to strike.

Fergus reached for its throat, but it pushed his arm into the puddle of burning oil from his broken lamp. Searing pain climbed his forearm. When he yanked his arm away from the oil, his hand brushed the base of the lamp. He snatched it, closed his eyes, and shoved the open flame against the creature's chest. The vile stink of sizzling flesh followed a shrill yelp. Fergus opened his eyes. The fisher recoiled from Fergus's chest with blackened flesh covering its ribs.

Fergus scrambled to his feet as the other fishers gathered in front of him. They watched and waited. It was almost like they wanted him to run. Like they wanted a chase. Like it was a game to them. There must have been twenty of them with more coming in the distance. Fergus backed toward the bunker. The burned fisher crouched on its haunches and cocked its head sideways.

Fergus glanced at his family lying in the dirt with bloody, empty eye sockets. There was nothing he could do for them. His heart sank. His stomach turned and he dry heaved. With his eyes trained on the fishers' every movement, he knelt, reached into the overgrown ivy that hid the bunker door, and unlatched the bolt action lock. The creatures tilted their heads.

With a groan Fergus jerked open the hatch. Normally, two men were needed for the task, but Fergus was stronger than most men and his adrenaline was surging. The burned fisher dropped its head back and loosed a broken, stuttering howl. The others joined in and the unified screech was ear-piercing.

And then they lowered their heads and pounced.

Still clutching the broken lamp, Fergus dove through the hatch, letting it slam closed behind him, almost catching his ankle. The right side of his body struck the dirt floor. Despite the jarring thud, he held the lamp up and kept the low flame from snuffing out. He scrambled to his feet and secured the hatch with a bolt as the creatures slammed against the other side.

Then Fergus fell to his rear. The tunnel was long and dark and led beneath the other farms. Flashes of his slaughtered family streaked his mind and he pressed his forehead into the dirt. The fishers slammed against the iron hatch like their shoulders were battering rams. Each impact peppered his head with tiny chips of stone.

BAM.

Sitting and wallowing in crippling self-pity was suicide. He pushed against the grief threatening to overwhelm him and climbed back to his feet. He willed himself forward. *One step.* His chest rose and fell as fast as a hummingbird's wings. *Another.*

BAM.

He flinched with each crash of the fishers' bodies against the hatch. The darkness swallowed the light from his broken lamp as if the dim flame wasn't even there.

BAM.

Calm your breathing. They can't get through. The iron hatch is too strong.

BAM.

Come on, Fergus, you can do it.

His legs quivered as he struggled forward another step. He swallowed and took another step. And then another.

BAM.

His thoughts returned to the creatures plucking out his sister's eyes with their scoop-claws. He wished he hadn't seen such a horrible sight. He shook it away. *No. Don't think about it. Just keep going.*

A rat scurried across his foot. He found the stone wall at his side and followed it forward.

BAM.

The tunnel stank of mold and stagnant air. His small flame flickered and struggled to stay lit.

BAM.

And then his flame died completely.

He stopped and listened, hoping to hear his neighbors, especially powerful John Shaw from the next farm over. But the silence bit through him like the bitterest cold. Fergus held his breath to hear better. Where was the crashing against the hatch? Had they given up?

He took another step—a blind one. A cool breeze brushed across his cheek, raising an army of tiny bumps on his arms. He didn't need instincts to tell him there shouldn't be air moving through the tunnel unless …

No. Just keep going. He would have heard them had they gotten through the hatch. His next step fell heavy. And then a single staccato growl cut through the dank tunnel air ahead. Fergus gently lowered his worthless lamp to the dirt floor, careful not to make a sound. He pressed his body snug against the jagged wall. Maybe if he was quiet enough they wouldn't notice him. He tried to remember his father's tales of the mythical fishers from the Volcanic Region. "They see like bats," he'd said. "Only movements in the darkness." Or was that their cousins, the hylocks? Maybe it was both. He concentrated on slowing his breathing. The single growl ended, replaced by something far worse. Sniffing. Staying still wouldn't hide his scent.

His only choice left wasn't a good one. It relied on making it back through the hatch while hoping the fishers above had given up and moved on. It was possible, he told himself, since he couldn't hear them trying to get through anymore. He pried himself from the wall. With his back to the stalking fishers, he gingerly took a step toward the hatch.

Their sulfur stench filled his nostrils.

By the gods.

Though he wasn't a fighter, he wasn't a quitter either. He spun toward them. A dozen glowing orange eyes stared back.

"Where … Raahhsiiieee?" the lead creature hissed, his eyes brighter than the others.

"Rasi? I don't know."

A slight hiss drifted from behind. *Oh no.* Fergus closed his eyes. *The hatch.* A sharp pain ripped through the back of his neck before his cheek met the cold dirt floor. His legs stopped working and he couldn't feel his toes. Or his fingers.

A fisher rolled him to his back, its dull orange eyes hovering above his face.

"Iiiee want to seeeee," it said.

Beside it, another creature cackled, "Then eeeat his eyeees."

The creature slowly lowered the scoop-claw that jutted from its palm. Fergus tried not to scream. A sudden, sharp pain filled his brain. He screamed.

CHAPTER 2

A HERO COMES HOME

Rasi hoped his return home to Puimia would be uneventful, if not unnoticed completely, despite word of his coming surely preceding him. He was nervous and excited to see his parents again, having shed many tears since last he saw them.

At Puimia's western border he flung his hood over his head, allowing the fabric to droop over his brow and hide his face in shadow. The seven symbiotic tentacles that had long ago melded to his back curled close to his body beneath his bulky cover, lulled to sleep during the previous night's journey. The early suns burned away the dew on the grass, though they had yet to warm the air enough to hide his breath.

He rode his gift from the kingdom of Epertase, a black stallion he had named Shadow in honor of Shadows Peak, the mountain that had been his home for many years before its mysterious ruin. He guided Shadow through the outer fields until he reached a familiar dirt path atop a familiar hill. In his mind, he pictured his hometown just beyond the crest, as vivid in memory as it was on the day he'd left as a teenage boy.

At the top of the hill, beside a thick patch of overgrown bushes, he locked his eyes on his hometown with a stare that bordered on hypnotic. Little had changed, which surprised him. Puimia was everything he remembered. Maybe his home wasn't rich or filled with modern fancies like Thasula, but the warmth of the townspeople radiated beyond the boundaries, more than erasing any dinginess or poverty that strangers may see at first.

He was in such awe that he didn't notice the rustling overgrown bushes at his side until his tentacles—or straps, as he called them—started to uncoil, breaking his trance.

"It's him," the bushes whispered with another rustle. Shadow danced to the side. Rasi steadied his steed with a soft caress. His straps weren't as easily calmed and they shrugged his cloak from his back onto Shadow's hindquarters. His blood thirsty appendages shot into the air like deadly snakes poised to strike.

Eaaasy, he whispered in his head. *There are no threats here.* He brushed his right palm along the leather-wrapped hilt of his sword just in case. The bushes violently shook again, and two young boys sprang onto the dirt path. Their faces bore the same dread as boys caught stealing from a market. They righted themselves before Rasi. Rasi watched, amused.

With their eyes to the ground, one of them said, "Don't hurt us, Mr. Rasi. We only wanted to see you for ourselves." Rasi wondered how long they'd been hiding in the bushes and whether their parents were conducting frantic searches to find them at that very moment.

His straps relaxed, flopping down his back, over Shadow's hindquarters, and to the ground.

The boys lifted their gazes. Their expressions, so full of dread a moment before, changed in a blink to wide eyes and wider smiles.

The taller of the two shoved his friend. "See, I told you he was coming. My father heard so at the store."

His friend shoved him back and then ran down the hill toward town. The taller one gave chase.

Rasi chuckled, fascinated at how quickly their terror had turned to excitement. If there were anyone who didn't know he was heading home before, they surely would now. He retrieved his cloak and wrapped it around his shoulders again, this time loosely tying the strings around his neck. With a slight jab of his heel, Shadow clopped down the hill toward the mostly slumbering town. The lack of worried mothers searching for their boys told him the two were as skilled at sneaking out as he'd been as a child.

When he passed the first home at the western edge of the village, he noticed two figures standing where the long walkway met the front porch. One of the figures was an older man wearing little more than his bright red winter coveralls and a fur wrapped around his shoulders. His similarly attired wife clung to his side. As Rasi and Shadow passed, the man nodded respectfully. His wife hesitated and then gave a shy smile. Rasi nodded in return before the two hurried back into the warmth of their home.

As Rasi neared the market square, he saw the townspeople exiting their homes and shops to line the edges of the street and await his approach. The two boys stood nearby.

Easy, he told his nervous straps once again, feeling them tensing at his back. *We are not here for combat. Those days have passed.*

He held his head low while scanning the growing crowd. A man whom he recognized from his school days as a local shoemaker began to clap, slowly at first. He was joined by another man, and then another, until everyone in the crowd was clapping. More people exited their homes and joined in the steady applause. It felt strange to be celebrated and welcomed after so many years of being hated and alone.

A man wearing a badge stepped into Shadow's path. Rasi tugged the reins, stopping short as the stranger reached up and patted Shadow's neck. The applause from the crowd died until nothing but the howl of the wind blowing between the buildings remained. Rasi waited, unsure of how to proceed.

"Rasi?" the badge-wearing man asked.

Rasi nodded once, his hand still near his sword.

"I'm the marshal here. On behalf of your hometown of Puimia, I would like to extend our heartfelt appreciation for what you have done for our country. I … I mean, we … just wanted to let you know that anything you need is yours. We are happy to hear that you have been pardoned and cleared of regicide and are honored to have you back in your rightful home."

The marshal stepped to the side and waved Rasi onward. Rasi nodded again before giving his horse a nudge with his heel. As he ambled past, children stared up with bright, curious eyes.

Such praise and admiration made him uncomfortable. Careful to keep his expression neutral, he remained alert for the possibility of something going wrong. But not a single person faltered in his or her sincerity. The men nodded, the children gaped, and the women smiled.

He wanted to tell them it was too cold to be out at such an early hour, that their gratitude was undeserved at best, but he had a feeling they wouldn't listen even if they could understand his garbled words. Sometimes more than others, he wished Elijah hadn't cut out his tongue. He nodded to them instead and continued toward his parents' farm. Though he didn't look back, he heard the pitter-patter of his youngest admirers trailing him. Slowly, their footsteps retreated as they were called back by their mothers.

The ride to his parents' farm was short and he soon saw their home in the distance. As he rode closer, he noticed the roof had been poorly patched with scrap wood. Boards covered most of the windows. The run-down appearance was a kick in his gut. He wasn't sure what he'd expected to find, but never did he anticipate his childhood home being so dilapidated and unkempt—not with his father's hard work and meticulous attention to detail.

Over his long, lonely years of living in the mountains, he'd had one recurring nightmare in which he returned home to find his parents had died. Seeing their house in such decline brought those nightmares screaming back. Moving closer, he saw the paint had peeled away and overgrown weeds crawled up the side of the house like ivy. His father's prized flower garden was little more than brush and weeds. A look into the wheat fields found them a third the size he remembered.

He hopped from his horse at the porch and stood frozen before the first step. If something had happened to them, a part of him didn't want to know. A light flickered between the boards on the front window. That a candle burned at all gave him hope. The three steps up the porch were the hardest he'd ever climbed. His fist hovered near the door. Somehow, knocking was too difficult. What if his father had died? Or his mother was sick? He lowered his hand and staggered backward a step.

As he stood staring at the door, the handle rattled slightly from the inside. He lost his breath. His heart weighed heavy in his chest. The front door slowly groaned open.

His mother stood in the doorway with a weary face and bags below her eyes. She was frail, and in her hair sparkled bits of gray. Seeing her after so many years was magical. She squinted before her eyes grew wide and bright. Her hand lifted to her mouth.

"Rasi? It is really you." She reached out and cupped his cheeks between her hands. "They said you were coming, but I didn't believe them. I've heard rumors so many times over the years that I'd lost hope."

Rasi wanted to cry, but held back the tears for her sake.

His mother, however, let them stream down her cheeks without apology. Rasi took her hands, pulled her to him, and wrapped his arms around her. She squeezed back with her cheek against his chest. His straps squirmed, brushing her arms, but she didn't acknowledge them. He pulled back and looked into her eyes.

She smiled and tilted her head. After wiping her eyes, she looked over her shoulder and shouted, "Donis."

Rasi's knees weakened. *Thank the gods.* His father was still alive.

Over her shoulder, Rasi saw a frail old man appear from the hallway. His father was a shell of his once powerful self. He held a waist-high walking stick for balance.

"Boy?" he shouted with the same authority in his voice as always. "Is that you?"

Rasi nodded.

"Well, come here then. It's been too long."

Rasi gently squeezed past his mother and shot across the room. He smothered his father in his embrace. Donis's grasp wasn't the same strong grip Rasi remembered, but that didn't lessen the joy in his hug. As he leaned back, Rasi noticed the tremor in his father's hands and the constant, rhythmic bob of his head. He must have seen Rasi's concern because he turned away.

"Don't look at me like that, boy." Rasi looked to the ground. "I'd better never see pity when you look at me again." Donis reached out to the wall for balance. Rasi reached for his arm, but pulled his hands back to avoid another scolding. His father made his way to the table. "Doc says I got that damn shaking disease. Some days it's worse than others. Today's not too bad." Donis lowered himself into a wooden chair and set his cane on the floor beside him.

His mother raced over. "Are you hungry? I was about to make your father breakfast."

Rasi nodded.

His father, never one to hold back, said, "Well, let's see 'em, boy."

Rasi cocked his head to the side with an uneasy grin.

"Come on, you know what I'm talking about. Let's see 'em."

Rasi looked to his mother, who turned from washing her hands in the sink. She nodded. He untied his cloak and shrugged it from his shoulders. His straps slithered around his waist and legs before lifting into the air, hesitant but proud. Donis leaned back in stunned silence. The dark red meat of Rasi's straps flared out, pressing against the ceiling and walls and surrounding Donis in a cocky display of intimidation.

Rasi looked to his mother, whose mouth was agape, her hand towel dangling from her fingertips.

Donis reached out to touch one of the straps as it floated past, but it jerked away. With his eyes never leaving them, he said, "Very impressive, boy. Don't you agree, Criya?"

His mother caught herself staring, blinked, and turned away, ignoring his question. "Honey, we've heard about what you've done for us—for everyone. Your father is very proud of you, aren't you, Donis?"

"Yeah, you did good, boy."

Rasi sat at the table across from him. A nosey strap prodded at the cupboard and opened it. *Get outta there,* Rasi demanded. The sulky strap withdrew to where the others had found a place to drape on the ground.

Donis leaned on the table. "Before we go any further, look me in the eyes and tell me the truth." He pinned Rasi with a cold, intense stare. "I know you've been cleared, but I need to hear it from you. You didn't kill the king and queen, did you?"

Rasi was offended that his father would ask such a thing. Without pause, he shook his head.

"And you had good reason to strike Elijah when he was a prince?"

The best. Rasi nodded.

"Good. He always was a weaselly little shit." His father leaned back in his chair. "I never for a moment believed any of it."

His mother set a plate of freshly cooked eggs and two slices of slightly stale bread on the table. She rubbed Rasi's upper arm in a loving, motherly way. "They say King Elijah took your tongue," she said.

Rasi nodded.

"I'm so sorry for how much you've suffered."

Rasi nodded again.

The three ate breakfast with few words, but plenty of his mother's loving gazes. He wished she wouldn't watch him eat since it was so sloppy. She didn't seem to care even as he used the fork to push the eggs between his teeth and some of it fell to his lap.

For the first time in many years he felt part of a family again. He spent most of the morning listening to exaggerated tales of his own adventures. He heard how Elijah had tried and failed to save his own daughter from Scorne and his band of killers. And how it was Rasi who saved her in the end. His mother spoke with confidence as though she'd been there. She spoke of rumors of Alina and Rasi's love affair with a wide smile. He listened to tales of impossible battles in which he single-handedly fought off hundreds of Tek soldiers. He continued to shake his head at the inaccuracies, but there was no hope of righting the stories. They had already grown into legend.

Her bragging was more than he felt comfortable hearing. He didn't see himself in such a heroic light. She talked of the Teks as mindless monsters while he saw them as men fighting to protect their own way of life. He squirmed as she bragged up his fantastical accomplishments while his father sat in his favorite chair, no doubt largely unconvinced of his boy's celebrity.

After having his fill of exaggeration, Rasi went to his father's desk, searched through a drawer until he found a sheet of paper and a charcoal stick, and scribbled, "Don't believe all that you hear. I did nothing that Father, or any other honorable man, would not have done in my place."

"Nonsense," his mother said. She wadded the paper and tossed it into the wastebasket. "Well, you're home now. Besides, that's all behind us. You have earned a long rest."

Footsteps on the front porch roused Rasi's straps from the floor. The room silenced. Rasi stood up, overturning his chair. Donis struggled to his feet, but Rasi was at the door before the old man could right himself. Rasi ripped the door open, almost from its hinges. A group of startled children let out a unified squeal and stampeded from the porch onto the barren front yard.

Rasi looked down at his outstretched hand; he had drawn his sword without a single conscious thought. What had he become that his first thought when children arrived was violence? His straps relaxed and he stepped into the doorway.

After the children gained enough distance to feel safe, they slowed and turned back toward the house. One of the bolder ones even climbed the first porch step. He shouted as if annoyed that he'd been chased off, "We only wanted to see if you were really here." Though he tried to portray confidence with his words, his back foot slipped to the ground.

Rasi's mother squeezed between the door frame and her intimidating son. "Now, now, children. Come on back here. You're safe."

She glared over her shoulder at Rasi. "You be nice. They're just curious, is all."

He'd seen that look on his mother's face plenty of times. He returned a stunned "I wouldn't hurt a kid" stare and quickly returned his sword to its sheath.

The kids crept closer to the porch. Rasi's mother gestured for him to come away from the doorframe as the children sat quietly in a semicircle around the steps.

"What do you want, children?" she asked in her motherly tone.

One of the children, the bold one, answered, "We want to see his monsters."

Rasi's mother peered back at him. He slouched and moved to the edge of the porch. With a playful growl, he made his straps flare around him in an explosive display of power. All the kids let loose high-pitched yelps and probably wet their trousers a little. Then their moment of terror morphed into nervous chuckles followed by outright laughter.

Rasi realized that he, too, was laughing. He had forgotten, or perhaps he never knew, the innocence and joy a child could elicit. He left the porch to kneel in their semicircle. At first they scooted away from him, but their curiosity won and they each reached for a feel. He forced his straps to relax beneath their probing fingers.

The children giggled with each twitch of his uneasy but docile appendages. A couple of the boys began an impromptu wrestling match with one of his straps. Rasi worried the strap would become agitated, but his constant mental demands for restraint, combined with the obvious playfulness of the children, seemed to put the strap at ease.

As time passed, the children grew braver. Two of them dove at Rasi, knocking him to his back. And then all the kids, eleven of them in total, piled on.

For the first time since Rasi could remember, he was having fun. He peeked from the pile at his mother, who stood proud next to his wobbly father on the porch steps. The years of sadness lifted and they appeared, if only for that moment, happy again.

Then one of the children got a little too rambunctious and bit one of the straps. All seven straps shot into the air in one defensive burst.

Eaaasyy, Rasi whispered in his mind. The children ceased their games at once and backed away. The offending child said that he was sorry, that he only wanted to see if the monsters could feel. Rasi nodded sympathetically, but it was obviously the end of playtime.

He focused his thoughts on calming his angry straps until they relaxed enough that he felt he could trust them near the children again.

With playtime ended, the children shouted their goodbyes and headed back toward town. Rasi waved. One of them turned and waved back. Rasi walked onto the porch, past his parents, and into the house.

His mother whispered, "Thank you," as he passed.

Rasi tossed and turned for most of the night, images of Scorne, Teks, and mountain creatures filling his head. He told himself again and again that he was safe, but his years of surviving in the harshest conditions haunted him. By midnight he convinced himself that his lack of sleep was the result of the comforts of civilized living and crawled onto the floor where he continued tossing and turning until morning.

Long before the light of the suns peered through his partially boarded window, the quiet tiptoe of his mother getting an early start told him it was time to get up. He stretched away his many kinks, dressed, and slipped from his room into the main living area where his mother prepared breakfast.

She jumped when he touched her shoulder, and he realized he hadn't yet lost his instincts for stealth.

"Oh, honey, I didn't wake you, did I?" she asked.

Rasi shook his head.

"I still make your father's breakfast before he wakes. Habit from when he had more fields to work, I suppose."

She glanced up from her wood-burning stove with a smile before diving back into her cooking. "Your father is very sick, you know. As hard as he tries, he can't keep up with the work that needs done. That damn disease." Her voice broke like she was about to cry, but she gathered her composure.

Rasi touched her shoulders and nudged her away from the stove. He wasn't sure if he'd remember how to cook like a civilized man, but he was determined to try.

"Don't even think about it," she said sternly. "This is my job and you are not to touch a lick of food unless you are filling your mouth with it." She crowded him away from the sizzling eggs in the skillet. "Besides, you need to get cleaned up. You smell like you haven't bathed in weeks."

She caught him off guard with her bluntness. She was right, he realized. He hadn't indeed bathed in about a week, but he'd gotten so used to his own stink living on Shadows Peak that he didn't notice it anymore.

His mother continued, "There is a warm pot of water in the washroom. You can use that, and I'll heat up another pot when your father wakes up. The new vat of soap is still soft, but there should be a bit of hard soap next to the wash pail."

Nonsense, Rasi thought. He would have told her so if his speech wasn't so garbled. He disappeared into the washroom, returned with a green glob of slimy soap thick on his fingertips, and walked to the front door with his mother shouting from behind.

"Rasi, what are you doing? It's freezing out there."

He wasn't about to let his father's bath be delayed even for a moment, so he ignored her. If he'd bathed in the mighty frozen rivers of the mountain region in the dead of winter, he could withstand a few moments of chilly well water.

He paused when he opened the door, and not because of the cold morning air. His mother must have seen the bewilderment on his face because she wiped her hands on her apron and hustled to his side.

"Well, I'll be," she mumbled.

He didn't know what to think. The front yard was littered with food baskets, bottles of homemade wine, carpentry tools, wood, and about any other gift he could imagine. There was even a slaughtered pig wrapped with a ribbon tied around the midsection. And pigs were a precious commodity.

Rasi stepped onto the porch, cautious and untrusting. He looked around for signs of a trap, or at the least a practical joke, but saw no one. His mother shoved past him to the pile of presents. She plucked a folded piece of paper from the hog's ribbon and read it aloud.

"'For all of your service to our kingdom, we, the people of Puimia, offer our gratitude.'"

Rasi grunted. *Undeserved,* he thought, and marched past the food, past his smiling mother, to the family well. He scraped the gooey soap from his fingers onto the edge of the stone well and pulled up a full bucket with the rope. Without flinching, he dumped the frigid contents over his head and then lowered it back down.

"You're not in the mountains anymore," his mother hollered, sounding a tad disgusted. Before she disappeared into the house, she added, "And you aren't an animal, either."

Once he finished his rudimentary bath and his home-cooked breakfast, he excused himself to the outdoors once again. His mother cleaned his dishes and then presumably went to wake his father.

Rasi went to the barn and returned carrying a hammer, while his straps dragged a burlap bag of spikes and a large leather bag full of wooden shingles. He studied the two-man high eaves for a few moments, dropped the tools and shingles, and took a few steps backward. With a grunt, he ran toward the wall and leaped. Two of his straps reached for a grip and hoisted him onto the roof. He then lay on his belly and guided his straps back down to his tools and bag of shingles to hoist them as well.

The roof's pitch wasn't terribly steep, though he imagined the difficulty his father would have in his current condition. With the claw end of his hammer, he ripped away several rotted shingles and pieces of patchwork wood. If his father wasn't yet awake, the pounding of spikes into the fresh roofing would surely interrupt his sleep.

At lunchtime, his mother shouted for him to come eat three different times, but he didn't have interest in stopping his work.

By his third trip to the barn for more shingles, he wondered if he should just replace the entire roof. His monotonous work allowed his mind to wander. At first, he directed his thoughts away from images of Alina, but by afternoon he had lost the willpower to do so. He wondered what she was doing and how Thasula was responding to her rule. Over and over, his mind returned to the look on her face as he'd committed his last violent act before her eyes—slaughtering the Tek soldier Rayles. As sad as those thoughts made him, he was equally stubborn in the belief that he had done what was necessary. He knew his stubbornness would probably keep him lonely for the rest of his days, but some things about a man just couldn't be changed.

He pushed away those thoughts once more and pictured Alina's bright green eyes. That made him smile, if only for a moment.

By nightfall, he had replaced the entire roof with the help of his straps. When he climbed down for the last time, his father was waiting. The two men admired his work. It wasn't the prettiest roofing job in Epertase, but it would keep out the rain.

His father pointed. "A little crooked in places, don't ya think?"

Rasi shrugged.

Donis put a hand on Rasi's shoulder. "You did good, son. Thank you." Then he staggered back into the house. Rasi followed with his head held high and his posture straight and proud, despite a new nagging ache in his lower back.

New windows and shutters from town were the next day's project.

CHAPTER 3

THE NEW DISEASE

Something about the castle hadn't felt right to Alina since her return. The décor, the people, the view, none of that had changed, but her home felt different. It *was* different. Even knowing what her father had attempted to do to her didn't lessen how much she missed him. For most of her life he had been a good father.

Another night found her jolting awake covered in sweat. The lamps she left burning by her bed so she wouldn't wake up in the dark anymore helped her orient herself and calm her jittery heart.

To Thasulans, and likely all Epertasians, the castle stood as a symbol of goodness and fairness. But to Alina it had become a cold place of death. Her grandparents, whom she loved more than words could describe, had died there. Her mother had succumbed to the sickness in her chest in the next room. But the biggest tug at her heart was how she still looked for her father to rush in and comfort her after her nightmares like he had when she was a child.

Perhaps that was the cause of her new nightmares even more than her abduction by Scorne. Knowing that the man who had always been there for her was the same man who had nearly sacrificed her for his own ambition was more than she could bear. After turning her back on Rasi, she had no one left to comfort her in the night.

As she gathered her composure and looked around, she realized she despised every part of the castle. There wasn't a room left that didn't bring her painful memories. As she sat looking at the fancy portraits on the walls, she decided that she'd had enough. With images of Scorne's hateful face still burning behind her sleepy eyes, she threw on a robe and headed to Levi's room. He was her closest adviser.

After a delicate rap on his door, he opened it, the little hair he still had standing on end. "Your Majesty?" he said while putting on his glasses and trying to decide if he were awake or still dreaming. "What is it?"

"I needed to talk to someone."

He tried to press his hair down with his hand. "Your Majesty …"

"I've told you before to call me Alina when no one's around."

"I'm sorry. Alina. I don't think it's appropriate for you to confide in me in my private room at such a late hour."

"Rubbish," she answered with zeal. "I am queen. I can go where I want, and I dare anyone to question my intentions."

He straightened his robe so as to not show anything that might be offensive, and wiped the sleep from his eyes. "Well, what is it, Your Maj—Alina?"

"I want to build a new castle," she blurted.

"Is there something wrong with this one?"

Alina crossed his room to the window with an energy she hadn't felt in a long time. "Yes … I mean no. I mean everything. This castle has served its purpose for many, many years. But I see nothing but sickness and death at every turn. Do you know that King Phillip once hanged thieves on the very front lawn for the kingdom to witness?"

"That was a long time ago."

"It might as well have been yesterday."

"What will you do with this castle if you build another one?"

"I don't care, Levi. We'll give it to the less fortunate … or the rats … or whatever. I want a place that knows no violence, a symbol of the peaceful future I hope to bring to our great people."

"If that is your wish, I say indulge yourself. But if your goal is happiness, I don't believe a new castle will suffice."

She scowled at him. "Why do you say such things?"

"I've known you since you were young and can tell when you are sad, or happy, or even hungry. A new castle will not bring Rasi back."

Alina considered brushing off his comments with a wave, but she had a hard time disagreeing. She went over and sat on the edge of his bed. "It is true," she admitted. "I miss him terribly. Why did I have to send him away? After all the good he's done, I did what everyone else in his life has done and turned away from him. I just don't know what to think anymore." She lifted her eyes to Levi's. "You know that he kept secrets from me for many years, secrets that put me in danger, don't you?"

"Maybe, in a way, he was protecting you."

She ignored his reasoning. He sounded just like Rasi. "He killed the Tek commander in cold blood, even after I commanded him to halt."

"He doesn't seem the type to take orders."

She sighed and whispered in quiet resignation, "No, I suppose not." She thought for a moment and then added, "It was still murder. The man had surrendered."

"I have no clear answers, Alina. Having said that, from what I know of Rasi I would venture to say whatever he's done, he has done with the best intentions." Levi touched her shoulder, which was a very risky act for an adviser. "Why don't you send for him?"

Alina leaned her cheek on his warm hand. "He is a hard man, Levi. At this point, he would probably turn me away."

"You'll never know until you try."

"And if he does turn me away?"

"What if he doesn't?"

"I don't know. You may be right, but I don't know if my heart could take his rejection."

"I know I'm supposed to give you advice, but this is one matter you must figure out on your own."

Resignation that she wasn't going to solve her problems in one night settled in.

Levi cupped her hand in his. "As for the castle, I say build away. I think it would be good for Thasula."

"Really?"

"Yes, really."

She smiled.

"Now, let's get you back to bed. You need your sleep."

"Thank you, Levi."

He walked her back to her room. She climbed into bed, but the idea of building a new castle was too exciting to go back to sleep. She was still awake when the suns lit a ray across her floor through the window.

By the time she had dressed, James, the aide she had inherited from her father, was knocking at her door.

"What is it?" she asked.

"Doctor Eckels is here to see you."

"Very well. Show him to my study. I'll join him shortly."

"Right away, Your Majesty."

She tidied up her desk, took a last look in the vanity mirror to make sure she was in order, and left to meet with the good doctor. As she walked through the hall, she passed a large glass display case with the Tek commander's glowing blue sword hanging within. She thought, *Yet another symbol of death to decorate this castle.*

She was happy to see Doctor Eckels again. Even after hiring him to Thasula following the war, he seemed more of a stranger than ever before. His hair was a little longer and more disheveled. Dark half-moons under his eyes showed his fatigue.

"Doctor, a pleasure to see you again. How goes the new clinic?"

"Busy, Your Majesty. How goes the ..." He looked around, leaned in, and whispered, "... the pregnancy."

"I can't complain. The royal doctor thinks I'm around three months along."

"Well, I could never tell."

She smiled. "Baggy clothes."

"So, an early spring baby, huh?"

"I suppose so. But that's not why you're here. What is it?"

"Since you hired me, and I do appreciate your generosity, I have more patients than I could have ever dreamed. The free clinics are a great service, but they are being overwhelmed and I'm having trouble with the cases I'm seeing lately."

"Do you need more nurses?"

"Oh no, no. That's not the problem at all. The staff you have provided me with is stellar and I couldn't ask for more. It's just … well … I don't know, maybe I'm not used to the kind of patients that come with big cities nowadays, but I fear I'm ill equipped to help the people I've been seeing."

"Well, forgive my bluntness, but that seems like nonsense. We have the same types of patients as where you're from."

"I respectfully disagree, Your Majesty. I have never seen such afflictions as I have since arriving here. I cannot explain. Perhaps it would be best if you saw for yourself. Would you be available to pay the clinic a visit in the near future?"

"Of course. Is now a good time?"

"Now would be fine." He bowed his head with a smile.

"James," she shouted. He appeared in the doorway. "Fetch my fur. Inform Captain Masera I am traveling to Doc Eckels's clinic and I'll meet him at the stable."

"Right away, Your Majesty."

She turned back to Eckels. "I shall meet you there, my friend."

He backed away with his head still bowed, turned, and left.

Masera and three of his top Elite Guards escorted Alina to the clinic, which was two blocks from the castle. A line of people wrapped from the entrance around the side of the building. Alina approached the rear of the line and climbed down from her horse. "Good morning," she said to the woman at the back of the line.

The woman bowed. "Your Majesty." Her hands rested on the shoulders of a young boy who stared forward as if hypnotized.

"And who is this young man?" Alina asked.

"This is Ben."

Alina knelt beside Ben and playfully offered to shake hands. He didn't react. She lifted her eyes back to his mother. "What happened to him?"

The woman shook her head. "It started yesterday. He got quiet all of a sudden, and then he just stopped responding completely."

As Alina looked along the line, she saw many children with the same blank gaze and a few adults as well. It reminded her of the Lowlands and gave her a sick knot in her stomach. She stood up and touched the woman's shoulder. "I'm sure Doc Eckels will be able to help." Then she eyed Masera, who shrugged in return.

As Alina walked along the line, she encouraged each person she passed. Near the front, two nurses rushed out to a gentleman lying on the walk. Alina hurried over. The man was pale and gaunt and wheezing. His neck was deformed with a purple, tornment-sized mass next to his windpipe. He struggled to look at her, but couldn't move his head for the tumor. The nurses struggled to lift him to carry him inside.

"Masera, help them."

Masera climbed from his horse and grabbed the man's legs. Together they carried him through the clinic doors. Alina followed. Inside, there were many more patients with tumors or blank gazes, in addition to the regular injuries and illnesses she had expected to see. The sounds of suffering broke her heart. Every bed was taken. The nurses and Masera lowered the tumor-riddled man onto a blanket on the floor. Alina rolled another blanket up and placed it gently under his head. When she stood up, Doc Eckels caught her eye. His gown was saturated with red stains, some of which glistened in the light.

She lost her words.

"I am sorry you must see this," he said, breaking her trance.

She whispered to keep from panicking anyone. "Is there a plague of some kind?"

"I don't believe so."

"Whatever you need, Doc. No matter the cost." Though Alina's first reaction was shock, her second was resolve. "What do we know about these tumors?"

His forehead wrinkled and he pressed his glasses up the bridge of his nose with his middle finger. "We don't know much, I'm afraid. From what I gather, the tumors and mutations appeared just before the war with the Teks."

"Mutations?"

Eckels motioned her to another bed that held a middle-aged man. "This is Jeffery," he said.

Alina hovered over Jeffery. He appeared normal enough except grass grew over his entire body like hair. "Good morning, my friend," she said.

He smiled hesitantly.

She reached for his arm and paused. "May I?"

He nodded.

As she touched his arm, the blades of grass parted around her finger. A couple of blades even grabbed her knuckle. It reminded her of the grass of the Great Plains in the weeks leading to her becoming queen.

She smiled warmly at him. "Doc Eckels will do everything he can to figure this out, good sir."

"Thank you, Your Majesty."

She turned to Eckels. "So, there are others like him?"

"Not exactly. Other than the tumors, I haven't seen the same mutation twice."

"I don't understand."

"This man is the only man I've seen with grass growing on him, for instance. I saw a dog in an alley the other day that had legs like a spider growing from its ribs. And a lady who had patches of thorns on her arm that moved away from my touch."

"How is this possible?"

"I don't know. It's like their bodies have become hosts to strange parasitic creatures."

Alina looked at him askance.

"Watch." He retrieved scissors from a stand and went to the grass-covered man. When he pulled a blade of grass taut and moved the scissors toward it, the other nearby blades grabbed at his hands. "Look how they try to defend themselves." He looked to the man and asked, "You're not doing that, are you?"

He shook his head.

He withdrew the scissors and the grass relaxed. "The blades have blood flowing through them, too. If I cut it, it'll bleed just as if you cut this man's skin."

"I'm speechless."

"Well, I summoned you because I think you actually may be able to help."

"Help? Me?" Alina stepped back. "I'm no doctor."

"Not with skills, Your Majesty, but with knowledge."

She squinted.

"You might not realize it, but you've seen something similar before."

"Oh?"

"Yes. Your friend Rasi."

"Rasi?" She cocked her head for a second. "You mean his tentacles?"

"Exactly. Do you happen to know how he came to have them?"

She sat on the edge of the grass-covered man's bed and handed him a glass of water. She cast her mind back to the early days of her relationship with Rasi and a story he'd told her about his past. "He killed the rashta they were attached to. He said the tentacles pulled free of the dying creature's back and attached themselves to his body."

Doc Eckels held his hand over his mouth while rubbing his cheek with his index finger. "Hmm."

"Does that help?"

"Maybe. My patients claim these afflictions began shortly after the sky fire that made you queen. The tumors began as tiny moles showing up in the days after." He turned toward the grass-covered man. "What about you, Jeffery? When did you say you noticed the grass?"

"I fell asleep in the Great Plains. When the sky turned to fire, I woke up and the grass was digging into my flesh. It was only a few pieces at first, but it kept getting worse over the weeks. That's why I finally came to see you."

Alina patted Jeffery's hand, and then she and Eckels walked away from his bedside. Eckels continued, "But Rasi had his tentacles long before the sky fire …," he trailed off in thought as they passed another woman with a discolored knot on her forehead.

Alina gave her a reassuring smile as they passed. The woman bowed her head.

Finally, Alina broke the silence. "My change wasn't the first time the skies turned to fire." Then she shook her head. "But that doesn't explain Rasi's straps, does it?"

Doc's eyes widened slightly. He bobbed his head. "Maybe it does, actually."

"I don't see how."

The words seemed to tumble out as quickly as he could think them. "Most of what I'm seeing is pretty useless. Living grass, tumors, things of that nature. But what if the stronger anomalies could endure over time? What if it was indeed your fire that caused this?"

She nodded, though still not sure what he was getting at.

"Think about it, Your Majesty. When King Matthew received the Light from his father before it was his time, the skies filled with fire, right? I mean, that's what the legend tells."

"Yes."

"What if these anomalies occurred then as well? The weaker ones, like the grass, simply died off with their hosts. But the stronger ones …," he trailed off for a moment before his face revealed that the pieces had finally fallen together. "What if the stronger ones, like the tentacles, moved from host to host? A rat to a cat, a cat to a dog, and so on until Rasi killed the rashta."

His theory didn't sound completely unfathomable. "You think Rasi's straps are over a thousand years old?"

"Maybe."

"Then what about the children outside with the vacant eyes? Are they my fault as well?"

"Don't say that, Your Majesty. None of this is your fault. And those outside are suffering from something entirely different."

A young girl sitting on a gurney at the opposite side of the room caught Alina's eye. The girl's empty gaze was trained on the wall.

Alina nodded toward her. "You know, I've seen that look before, Doc."

"You have? Well, by all means, anything you can tell me will be welcomed because I'm at a loss. I can find nothing medically wrong with them."

"I've seen an entire civilization with those blank eyes."

"Where?"

"In the Lowlands. They were controlled by King Fice. He seemed to hold a similar spell over them. Let me ask you, can that girl speak?"

"She hasn't since she's been here."

"That's odd. The Lowlanders spoke, at least."

"Could King Fice be here now?"

"I haven't heard any reports of him being in Epertase, let alone Thasula. Besides, if he were strong enough to sway Epertasians right under our noses, he'd have done so years ago."

Alina went to the girl's bed. Her father stood from the bedside chair and bowed.

Alina acknowledged his bow with a warm smile. "Have a seat, my friend."

Eckels greeted the girl's father with a sympathetic nod. "This is Abigail. Like those outside, she arrived this morning."

Alina touched Abigail's cheek.

"When did this happen, sir?" she asked.

Abigail's father answered, "She returned home from school yesterday and hasn't spoken since."

She turned back to Eckels. "How many children now have this condition?"

"I couldn't say. More and more each day. A lot of parents don't even bring their children here anymore since I have no answers for them. Abigail is here because she also has a slight fever." He put his hand on her forehead. "I think she is fighting a little bug."

"She'd been sniffling for the past few days, even before this started," her father said.

Alina considered the likelihood of Fice being in Epertase and the dire consequences if he were. She addressed Eckels. "I need to speak with Masera at once. I will send additional help and money to aid in your work." She kissed Abigail's forehead. "Keep me informed of any developments," she added before taking her leave.

On her way out, she saw the man with the tumor lying on the blanket, staring at the ceiling with death's gaze. A nurse draped a sheet over his face. Masera was waiting outside.

CHAPTER 4
SEEDS OF DOUBT

Since the war ended, Captain Jarrah had personally overseen the soldiers in his brigade as they sifted through layer upon layer of heavy rock, debris, and Tek corpses from the base of Shadows Peak. The search for Tevin the Third's remains was not going well. The size of the boulders and area to cover made it seem an impossible task. Jarrah had grown increasingly frustrated.

It was late afternoon of another long day when his lieutenant, Pierce, reported to his tent. Jarrah had just finished packing a bag of his personal belongings.

"Sir," Pierce said, poking his head through the entrance.

"Come in, Pierce."

"I'm sorry to report there's still no sign of Tevin's body. If I had to guess, I'd say we were less than halfway through the rubble, and it could be quite some time before we finish."

Jarrah rubbed his scruffy chin. "I understand. Keep working."

Pierce eyed his bag. "Are you going somewhere, sir?"

"I am. As of tomorrow, you will be in charge. This search has weighed on me and my wife heavily and I've decided to resign my post."

Pierce squinted, confused. "Sir ... You ... I ... I don't know how to respond. Since we began this operation, you've not been away from this site for more than a night. I know it's slow, but we'll find Tevin's body. I have no doubt."

"When you do, I'll be pleased to hear. For now, I have new priorities I must turn my focus to. I may have an opportunity for you in the future if you're interested."

"Of course, sir. Please tell your wife we are doing all we can and that I have faith we will find her brother soon."

"I will. Thank you."

Jarrah squeezed Pierce's shoulder. "I have an important meeting tonight. You be safe, friend."

"You as well, sir."

Jarrah left the tent and mounted his steed. He rode through the forest, across the Great Plains, and into Thasula in time for a late dinner. He waited at a small round table with two chairs for his dinner guest to arrive. His waitress, an overly friendly lady with a small gap in her front teeth which caused her to whistle when she pronounced sibilants, took his order.

"Just some soup and a tornment juice," Jarrah said, his eyes trained on the door.

"Do you know why people get that ssstrange tingle in their mussscless after drinking tornment juiccce?" the helpful waitress asked.

He was too distracted by the whistles to actually hear her question, but her tone told him it was indeed a question, so he shook his head to be polite.

"It isss a consssstrictor." Two more whistles. "Our ancccesstorss …" Three more whistles.

Shut up, lady.

"… sssaid tornment fruitsss mixssed jussst right"—four more—"were good for ssslowing bleeding in an open wound, though I've never tried it myssself."

The whistles drowned out anything she tried to say. "Yes, I've heard that. Just my order, please."

Her shoulders slouched and she huffed away, indignant at his lack of interest in her wisdom. She returned with his drink and slopped it onto the table, spilling some of it.

"Here'sss yer drink, sssir," she said with an angry tone and two more whistles.

He felt sorry for her husband, if she had one. Even when she spoke to a guest at another table, he could hear the damn whistles. It was like being stuck in a box with an annoying fly. He considered delivering a profanity-filled tirade, but his guest arrived before he had a chance.

Jarrah waved him over. He offered his hand. "Andon, good to see you. Thank you for meeting with me today."

Andon shook it. "Of course, Jarrah. What's on your mind?"

"Something not pleasant, I am afraid."

"Oh?"

"Have a seat."

The whistler came over again. "What can I get you?" she asked Andon with her back to Jarrah.

"A whiskey," he answered.

Once she was out of earshot, Jarrah wasted no time. "Did you read the official report put out by the queen about King Elijah's death?"

"Yes, I read it."

"Did you think it was as full of holes as I did?"

"Well, it was inconsistent in places, but Alina had been through a lot and being hazy on a few facts here and there shouldn't be held against her."

"I suppose," Jarrah said, looking down at his tornment juice while fiddling with his fingers.

"What's on your mind, Jarrah?"

He hesitated before answering. "What if I had reason to believe Alina wasn't as innocent in Elijah's death as she led us to believe?"

"I'd listen. But only because of our friendship."

"Did you know the criminal Rasi and our precious queen were in love for several years before Alina mysteriously disappeared? And that Rasi was there when Elijah was murdered?"

"Well, the story tells of Rasi and Elijah working together to find her."

"But Elijah hated Rasi."

Andon glowered. "Go on."

"I've wrestled with Alina's official report since the war, and I can't think of any reason she wouldn't reveal her love for Rasi in any of the reports. Can you?"

"Maybe because she was involved with a man accused of killing the king and queen."

"You don't find that pertinent in light of Elijah's death?"

"Sure, I do. But Rasi has since been cleared."

"By her. Let me tell you something else I've recently learned. Elijah found out about Rasi and Alina's affair more than a year before he died. Wouldn't it make sense that he either forbade her from seeing Rasi or threatened to hang Rasi for regicide? What would a woman do to save the one she loved?"

Andon slowly shook his head like he was punch-drunk.

Jarrah let a slight grin crack his mouth and shoved his drink to his lips in hopes of hiding it. "I spoke casually with Masera the other day, and he said before Alina even asked to see her father's body when she returned from her ordeal, she ordered Rasi's release from the prison. No trial, nothing. Just a full pardon and exoneration. It seemed, to Masera anyway, her only concern was Rasi. Did you not find it strange that once she was queen, Rasi became our commander with no input from us? The whole situation doesn't make sense."

"Are you saying Alina killed her own father to be queen, Jarrah? Because I find that a little too paranoid, even for you."

"Oh, no. I would never say that. I'm only asking what you think. Before you answer, you should take into account one other important detail. As long as Elijah drew breath, Rasi was not welcome in Epertase. I would say that puts a wet blanket on being in love, don't you agree?"

Jarrah leaned back in his chair and sipped his juice. He allowed his words to fester in the smoky air. The whistling waitress set Andon's whiskey on the table. Andon didn't reach for it or thank the waitress, and he didn't ask for his bill. In fact, he said nothing and sat with a creased forehead.

Jarrah fueled the fire. "I just think it would be a shame if all of those mighty warriors, including your brother, Dru, died because of a selfish princess's love affair." He let his words marinate before adding, "Nah. He probably would have died even if Elijah's war plan had been followed." Jarrah peered up from his drink. Andon caressed his bearded chin. "By the way, Andon, who was with Dru when he died, anyway?"

Andon's hand dropped from his beard and thudded onto the table, knocking the whiskey glass over. He didn't move to right it. Jarrah waved for the bill. Andon stared stunned at the overturned glass.

Jarrah tossed a silver bit onto the table, walked around to Andon's side, and put his hand firmly on his shoulder. "Your drink is on me, friend. It was good to see you again. Keep in touch."

Jarrah hurried out to his horse, proud of his work, leaving his friend behind to stew.

CHAPTER 5

AN OLD FRIEND

It was barely dawn when Rasi started working, as he had each morning since returning home. With his father ill and the winter wheat needing to be sewn, he immersed himself in his work. He would be lying if he said it didn't feel good to get his hands dirty with soil instead of blood for a change.

Donis watched from the porch. To him, Rasi was no hero, merely an absent son returning home to help like a good son should. Even standing on the porch, Rasi knew his father would be neck-deep in dirt right next to him if not for the shaking disease. Hell, he'd probably be complaining about how clumsy Rasi was. It'd been a few years and Rasi was out of practice. The work was hard and satisfying. It felt good to be normal again, though some would call it plain.

By midmorning he had already put in a full day's work, yet a tired look over the field told him he had barely begun. His family's longtime neighbor, Mr. Jamison, stepped from his house next door and waved, no doubt heading to town for supplies. Rasi waved back. Mr. Jamison had hardly changed, tall and broad, looking like he wouldn't even need the oxen. With his hands cupped around his mouth, he shouted, "I was going to start on your pop's field later this week."

Rasi nodded. If it wasn't for Mr. Jamison, his parents likely wouldn't have survived the last few winters. Seeing Mr. Jamison reminded him of Annie, Mr. Jamison's only child. Thinking of his childhood friend warmed his heart on such a brisk day. He felt a bit of guilt over not visiting her yet, but he'd told himself he was too busy. Replacing the windows on the house had taken two full days and plenty of curses, which was why he was just starting on the overdue wheat crop.

He looked to the enormous task ahead with little doubt of how long it was going to take—three strenuous days at best, five if rain came. But the wheat was crucial. It was all his father had to sell to Puimian shops in the spring.

By lunch, he and his oxen had found their rhythm. The animals lugged him and his plow through the hard dirt while he jammed an iron spike into the trailing mounds of soil to make holes for the seed. His straps dug seeds from his over-the-shoulder bag, dropped them in the holes, and scooped the dirt back over them. They seemed as content to be farmers as they were to be warriors, which surprised him. Then again, they were happy just being fed and adapting was what they obviously did best.

Despite his work, his mind always returned to Alina. He missed her greatly. Maybe he should contact her and … *No, no, no. Focus.* His stubbornness came from his father.

Soon, his mother trudged across the rough, uneven field with a pitcher of freshly squeezed tornment juice. It went down smooth and left a pleasant tingle on the insides of his cheeks and the part of his tongue that remained, even if he couldn't taste it. His mother's smile still brightened her face when she talked to him and showed no signs of letting up regardless of how long he'd been home. He desperately wanted to tell her how much he loved her, but he hated his mangled words, so he simply tried to show her instead. He longed to have someone to speak with again.

Alina.

No, stop it.

His mother kept him from his work, talking of the young boys who hadn't returned to Puimia after the war. "Little Josiah Tuttle died on the first day," she said, oblivious to how much her words made his heart ache. Little Josiah's death, as well as all the others, were his fault in a way. If his strategy had been better, maybe more young men would have returned. Despite the guilt, he listened and nodded, happy just to hear her voice.

She brushed damp, sweaty strands of his hair from his eyes and said, "You'd look like your father if you'd cut that dreadful hair." Her hand traveled to his cheek. "And shave that furry chin."

He frowned and shook his head.

She nudged him with her elbow and grinned. "And why would that be so bad? Your father is a very handsome man."

Rasi didn't mean it to be insulting. While she talked, her eyes drifted past him to the Jamison house. He followed her gaze.

Annie strolled along the porch with her head lowered. He hadn't seen her for nearly twenty years, not since he'd left Puimia as a teenager for the Heathen War, but he'd recognize her anywhere— her plain, withdrawn demeanor, and short, bobbed hair. She even wore the same type of long, flower-print dress she had always worn. She was much the same as he remembered, if a bit larger.

"Have you spoken to her since your return?" his mother asked.

He shook his head, slightly ashamed.

"You two were such good friends when you were younger. She's a bit melancholy these days and I'm sure she would be delighted to talk with you."

Rasi lowered his head. It wasn't that he didn't want to see Annie in particular, but that he didn't much want to see anyone besides his mother and father.

And Alina.

His mother cupped his scruffy chin, guiding his eyes back to her. "I wish you'd talk to me. I don't care how your words sound."

He wanted to, but was afraid his garbled speech would crush her. Any reminder of the terrible things that had happened to him would be hard for her, and he chose to keep those burdens to himself. It was bad enough she could sense his broken heart. Her sad, lingering stares said as much.

She patted his shoulder, leaned up, and kissed his cheek.

She shouted, "Hello, Annie," and waved. Annie shot her hand into the air and, just as quickly, yanked it back to her side and continued her lonely stroll along the porch.

Rasi lifted the reins of his oxen and fell back into his rhythm. By evening, his muscles let him know he had had a productive day as he made the trek from the barn to the house. He was starving. The smell of ham wafted to the front porch and the thought of fresh protein quickened his step.

His parents were already sitting at the table. As part of a new running joke, his father stared him up and down and grunted. "You don't look like no hero to me," he said. After pointing to the straps, he added, "Those fancy things on your back only mean you can clean the shithouse faster, is all." He chuckled.

Rasi fought the urge to roll his eyes, not wanting to encourage his father any more than he already had.

"Go get cleaned up before you eat. This ain't the mountains where you lost your manners." He hurled the same insults each night, but Rasi had yet to grow tired of them.

Though his father's muscles twitched uncontrollably and he had long lost the thickness and mule strength that his farmer body once had, his mind hadn't dulled. It was what Rasi most loved about him, his sharp tongue and unforgiving honesty.

Rasi raced to the well, dumped the cold water over his head, and cleaned off just enough dirt to pass his father's inspection.

He so wished he could taste the ham.

After dinner, he sat outside on the porch, dangling his legs over the edge as he watched the stars appear in the growing dark of night. His breath hovered like a ghost in the chilly air.

As he fiddled with a long blade of brown grass in his mouth, he wondered what Alina was doing at that moment. Was she looking at the same stars? Was she thinking of him? Not for the first time since he'd come home, he wondered if killing Rayles was the right choice.

His straps lifted slightly.

"Rasi?" a woman asked from beside the porch. He recognized Annie's soft, shy voice immediately. He smiled at his childhood friend. She stared at his straps, hesitant. He nodded and patted the wooden step beside him.

With her eyes to the ground, she maneuvered past the hovering straps and sat. For being so shy, she didn't seem to fear them. One of his straps gently brushed her cheek and she smiled. Still looking to the ground, she said, "Ever since you came home, you seem sad."

Rasi stared at his hands in his lap.

"I can tell by the way you move when you're working the fields. You rarely smile or even lift your head."

Rasi didn't deny it.

"You miss the queen?"

He looked up with surprise.

"It's no secret the two of you were in love. Everyone knows."

Rasi hesitated before nodding. Annie put her arm around his shoulder, surprising him again. Maybe she had shaken some of her shyness after all, or maybe he simply made her feel comfortable.

"Well, go to her," she said rather bluntly.

Rasi pulled away and stood up with his back to her. He lowered his head and shook it.

Annie turned him to face her. "Why?"

He wanted to tell her all the reasons, but feared she wouldn't understand. He opened his mouth slightly and pointed to his stump of a tongue.

She grinned. "Just tell me. I'll work it out."

In a voice that sounded like he had a mouthful of pebbles, Rasi said, "I'm no good."

She lifted his hand. "That's nonsense. You are good. Remember when we were young?" She looked into his dark eyes, further proving she was stronger than she used to be. "You were the one who was nice to me. Even when the other kids ignored me, you were my friend. You have a good heart. I've always known that about you."

Funny. I keep hearing that.

"Did I ever tell you that you were the best friend I've ever had?"

He shook his head.

"You deserve to be happy." Her hand moved up his arm to his bicep.

Fighting back tears, he pulled her in and hugged her. It felt good to have a friend. They sat back on the step and he stared out over the field.

She leaned against his shoulder. "You don't belong here. You know that, right?"

He side-eyed her.

"You're not a farmer anymore. I've heard the stories. You should be with the queen. Or training soldiers. Or traveling the world. Anything but this. When I told my father how sad you looked out in the field, he said that sometimes after a man sees what you've seen, he can never be content to go home again."

Rasi's head bobbed with her words. Though he had always thought he wanted to return home and take over the family farm, having no one to share it with was just as bad as life on Shadows Peak.

Annie didn't say anything else while they sat and watched the moon rise, but she didn't have to. With his arm draped over her shoulder, he leaned in and kissed her cheek. She rested her head on his chest.

CHAPTER 6

AN EYE FOR
AN EYE

Dark, turbulent clouds—the kind that looked like they might devour each other whole—rolled in overhead. Flashes danced across their bulbous undersides and highlighted dark shades of charcoal mixed with nasty purples and blues. A chill whisked through the street market, causing the patrons to go from carrying their jackets and cloaks on their arms to scrambling into them. The vendors scurried to close their booths and secure any loose items within.

Bohden led his horse past the scrambling vendors.

A plump man with a gray mustache and eyebrows to match stopped and hollered, "Better get inside, boy. Looks like this'll be a nasty one."

Bohden nodded while continuing to fight the growing wind and fleeing crowd to reach his mother's stall. Some of the vendors shouted when he passed that they were closing, as if he were there to purchase goods. He politely waved and continued on his course, wishing he hadn't left his jacket at home that morning.

He saw his mother, Annette, in the distance, frantically tying canvas ropes to stakes in the ground in a desperate attempt to prevent her merchandise from joining the debris in the wind. Bohden hurried to her.

"Mother," he shouted.

She glanced up from her work. "Help me prepare for the storm," she said. Bohden wrapped the reins of his horse around a post next to his mother's anxious mare and rushed to her aid.

With his help, the stall was secured in short order, giving his mother the chance for a proper welcome. She reached up and cupped his ears with her palms, pulled his face down to a more manageable height, and kissed his forehead.

When he started to ask why she'd summoned him, she turned away to recheck the ropes and rearranged her homemade beeswax candles. He wondered if he'd done something wrong. Maybe she was still upset that he had eaten the last dinner roll the night before after already having two to her one.

"What's wrong, Mother?" At first she claimed that nothing was troubling her, but Bohden persisted. "Is it the rolls?"

She scoffed at him. "What?"

"Is it the storm? The stall has withstood a lot worse than this."

"Damn the stall," she snapped.

She didn't usually yell at him. "Mother, what is it? What did I do?"

She sighed. "I'm sorry, Bohden. It's just that I need to tell you something of deadly importance. That's why I sent little William for you."

It started to drizzle outside. He didn't like the prospect of being stuck in her little stall for the duration of the storm. "We should get home first." He started for the exit.

She grabbed his arm and spun him back to face her. "There's no time. What I need to tell you can't wait." He'd never seen her so flustered. She was a strong woman, which was why it surprised him to see her eyes wet.

"I knew this day would come," she finally said, struggling with her words.

Bohden waited, worry turning his gut.

"I have always tried to be as honest with you as I could."

"Mom, it's getting ready to pour."

"Just listen. Over the years, there has been one subject where I have not been forthright with you, and it has eaten away at me."

Bohden checked the sky through the open front again. A heavy raindrop splashed onto the counter. "You have to tell me right now?"

"Yes."

Bohden cocked his head to the side. "All is well, Mother. You can tell me anything." In the back of his mind, the rain clock was loudly ticking. He rubbed his chilly arms.

Annette looked away as if ashamed of what she was about to say. The pause felt worse than anything that could possibly follow. After a stuttered breath, she blurted, "Honey, your father didn't die when you were seven."

He was wrong. It was worse.

His chest tightened like a horse had stepped onto his breastbone. He stumbled to the side, catching himself on the counter. She reached for his hand, but he pulled it away.

"I only told you he died because no little boy should know the kind of evil your father had become."

"I … I don't understand."

"His mind got very sick. At first, I was able to shield you from him, but he became worse with each day. When you were seven, he had some kind of a breakdown. For our safety I begged him to leave until he calmed down. I packed our things and we left before he came back. I couldn't let you see what he was turning into. That's when we moved here. Do you remember moving in the middle of the night?"

He nodded. "You said he died and that we had to start over."

"In a way, that was the truth. The father you knew did die. I have lived in fear every waking moment since that night that he may one day find us."

Bohden couldn't speak. His emotions raced from anger to sadness and back to anger again. His mother waited quietly, letting him work through his thoughts. Finally, he gathered enough strength to ask, "What happened to him? Why did he change?"

"I don't know, honey. He said he had been infected by something, and he thought the infection was eating away at his mind."

"Did you try to get him help?"

"He wouldn't go to a doctor, and when I finally sent for one he nearly beat the poor old man to death. That was the night we left."

"Where is he now? Why are you telling me this today?" The rain started to fall.

"Because I think he's found us. Someone has been leaving disturbing notes here at the stall." She pulled three scraps of paper from a small, wooden chest.

Bohden grabbed them and read the first. Blots of spilled ink surrounded tall, wobbly letters that looked like something written by a child before he started school. It read: *Slither, slither, beans and puke. Pretty hair and pretty eyes.*

Bohden regarded her. "Mom, why would you think this is from my father?"

"I got that one three weeks ago. Look at the next one. It's from yesterday."

In even sloppier letters that drifted up the page from the end of the sentence like the author had been drunk when he wrote it, it read: *Shave a face and shave a neck. Blood it deep with tastes of metal.*

"I used to shave his chin every night, son. It was our ritual." She nodded to the papers now dangling from his fingers. "The third one was here, I assume, when I opened the shop today, though I didn't see it until right before I sent William for you."

A bunch of incoherent doodles surrounded one sentence and a water stain. *Twelve years for twelve stabs. I can hardly wait.*

"I don't get it."

"It was twelve years ago today that we left him."

The pieces fell together and sent icicles under his skin. An overwhelming sense of something, some would call it honor, washed over him and he blurted, "Bring him here. I'll stay with you, Mother. I'll protect you."

"No," she snapped. "He's not a man anymore. He's dangerous. I saw evil in his eyes on that last night, and I swore to protect you from him."

Bohden stood straighter. "We'll go to my home, then. He doesn't know where I live …," he trailed off, looking for assurance that his home was safe and receiving none. His shoulders dropped and he asked, "Does he?" He wasn't sure he wanted the answer.

Her silence knotted his gut. The tiny wrinkles at the corners of her eyes deepened. "Then we'll leave. We can open your shop anywhere."

She nodded and tried to smile, though her smile was clearly forced. "I have money hidden at home," she said. "We need to go there first."

"It's not safe."

"We must. I will not start over with nothing. Not again."

They locked the stall, closed the shutters, and fastened them. He grabbed his mother's hand and together they rushed to their horses in the light rain. A crack of thunder jolted him, and he looked around to see if anyone had seen him jump. As they rode, the rain fell harder and harder as if a leaking dam in the clouds had suddenly given way.

By the time Bohden and his mother arrived at her house, they were cold and wet and miserable. Bohden didn't even try to wipe the water from his eyes anymore. He scanned the front and sides of the house for strange horses or signs that someone had broken in. Then he followed his mother through the front door and secured it behind him.

The thick clouds darkened the main room through the only window. Annette retrieved two towels from the washroom while he lit each of the four oil lamps that hung on the walls. He pulled the doors to the two bedrooms closed.

His mother handed him a towel with a forced smile. "Do you really think you needed to light all four of them?" she said.

It was a little bright.

He dried his face and hair. "Should I start a fire?" he asked.

"We won't be here long enough."

He draped the towel over his shoulders and warmed his hands over one of the lamps. His mother disappeared into her bedroom and lit the lamp in there.

Bohden went to her doorway and watched her. She crammed clothes, a couple of sentimental trinkets like the ceramic jester he had crafted for her in school, and anything else she thought important into a burlap laundry sack on the bed.

The bedroom door eased against his shoulder, nearly sending him out of his skin. His mother had been nagging him to fix her "self-closing door" as she called it. As his startled heart pounded, he wished he had done it. Another crackle of thunder nearly caused him to wet his trousers.

"Hold this open," she said, extending the sack toward him. He held it while she stuffed in the last of her clothes. Then she whispered, "I need you to go back into the dining room. Beneath the table is a loose board. I have gold nuggets tucked beneath the floor. They'll help us get a new start. Gather them for me."

Bohden nodded and returned to the front room. He started toward the table, but hesitated. A little voice in his head, that overly cautious voice most people ignore, whispered that something was different about the room. He checked the front door. Still closed and locked as he'd left it. The window was shut tight and undisturbed as well. Yet his gut warned him something was wrong.

Each creaky floorboard under his steps made him cringe. He gently overturned the table. From his knees, he traced his fingers along the outlines of the floorboards.

Behind him his mother's bedroom door squeaked until it kissed the frame.

"Mother?" he whispered.

She didn't answer. Perhaps she didn't hear him.

Just get what you came for, he told himself. His finger dragged over each nail hole in the floor until he found an empty one. With his fingernail jammed into a gap between two of the floorboards, he pulled the loosened one free. The top of a tan bag poked from the dark hole.

With his fist tight around the bag of gold, he froze. A chill ran down his spine. It was at that instant when he realized what had given him pause only moments before. He almost threw up. How could he have been so stupid? He couldn't breathe. He counted the oil lamps on the walls. One … two … three … and that was it.

The fourth oil lamp was gone—not snuffed, but gone. *Oh gods.* That little voice that had tried to warn him about the lamps now questioned why his mother hadn't answered.

He shoved the bag of gold into the front of his pants and stood up. "Mother?" he whispered again, his voice barely getting past his lips. He took a fearful step. "Mother?" he whispered again, only this time his voice was stronger, though no less quivering.

She didn't answer. The thought of someone hurting her replaced some of his fear with courage born of anger. The little voice told him to find a weapon. He kicked a leg of the overturned table, snapping it free, and gripped the wood in his hand.

"Mother?" he shouted, realizing if his father was in the house, whispering wouldn't help them. Again, she didn't answer.

He pushed her door open with his forearm and poked the table leg into the room as though the mere threat would halt any intruders.

By the gods.

His heart hit the floor. In the far corner of the room, his mother lay motionless at the feet of a hideous, frail, shirtless stranger. Long, matted gray hair hid the bastard's face. Bohden's mind raced through the memories of his father, and this monster was definitely not in them. The stranger knelt and caressed his mother's cheek, not even acknowledging Bohden as a threat. His glistening silver fingers left thin red streaks across her cheek. The missing lamp sat beside him.

"C-c-c-come in," he said without looking up. "I've b-b-been waiting for you."

Bohden raised his puny table leg, not quite sure what he was going to do with it.

"Very b-b-b-brave," the stranger said as he stood up. He cackled.

It was that laugh—actually, that smile—that took Bohden's breath away. Flashes of his father's smile washed through him, leaving little doubt that the creature before him was indeed who his mother feared. He wanted to cry, and a part of him—the weak part—

wanted to drop his weapon, race to the monster, and hug the devil out of him. He had missed his father so.

His weapon dangled by his hip. He could never strike his father anyway. Could he? His father took a step toward him. Bohden looked past his sore-encrusted thigh to his mother to make sure she still breathed. Her chest rose and fell in shallow movements. *Thank the gods.*

His father stopped within reach and tilted his head. With his silvery finger, he brushed his wet hair from his face and tucked it behind his ears. As he stared at Bohden, the hate in his soulless eyes transformed into something else. Maybe it was pity. Or even love. A metallic blotch slithered from his forehead, over his cheek, and around his chin before moving back to his forehead again.

"I missed you, Father," Bohden whispered.

Some of the metal skin slithered to his hand and formed a small point on his little finger like an extended nail. As he studied Bohden's face, he picked his teeth with it. "B-B-Bohden?" he said.

"Yes, Dad. It's me." Bohden dropped the table leg and extended his arms. If his father returned the gesture, he'd forgive everything. They could be a family again.

His father examined whatever gunk he had found in his teeth, and then wiped it onto his pant leg. He offered his hand. Bohden smiled as a tear escaped his eye. He stared into his father's dark pupils and, for a moment, thought his dad's eyes grew wet, too.

His father gently took his hand.

"I love you, Dad," Bohden sobbed.

His father loved him as well—he saw it in his face, even behind the scars and nastiness. That brief moment meant everything. But then his father's grip tightened. His weathered face darkened, and his upper lip curled to reveal his yellow teeth. The air thickened between the two men. The warmth Bohden had seen in his father's eyes turned cold again. The man no longer looked at his son, but through him.

Bohden's heart cracked. He tugged, trying to free his hand, but his father was way stronger than his malnourished body rightly should have been.

"Please, Dad."

His father hurled him across the bed where he hit the wall next to his mother. His father picked up the table leg. "Is this what you were going t-t-to use on me?"

Bohden scurried to his mother's side and wrapped his arms around her neck. If they were going to die, he would be with her when it happened.

"I am n-n-no longer your f-f-father." He stepped closer with the table leg. "I am Scorne and ..."

The faint light coming through the doorway dimmed as if the lamps in the front room had passed through an eclipse. Bohden looked past his father's shoulder as the door creaked open and the doorway filled with the largest man he'd ever seen.

Scorne continued, "... I am d-d-d—" He stopped and swallowed before trying again, oblivious to the newest arrival. "I am d-d-d—"

The beast of a man in the doorway interrupted. "I know," he snarled. "You're death to all." Scorne's eyes opened wide in recognition. Before he could turn, the hulk grabbed his shoulders and hurled him against the wall beside the window. Scorne scrambled to his back, the sick pleasure gone from his face.

"S-S-S-Simcane. How d-d-d-did you find me?"

Simcane, the unexpected angel of mercy, spoke with gritty hate. "You forget, Scorne. That's what I do." He moved closer.

Scorne stood up defiantly. But when he spoke again the confidence was missing from his voice. Not only did he stutter, which Bohden didn't remember his father doing, but now his voice quivered as well. "How's th-th-the eye?" Scorne asked, pointing a metal-tipped finger at Simcane's eyepatch.

Simcane didn't answer as he moved in and smothered Scorne beneath his mass. Scorne thrashed with his metal skin raised into blades, but Simcane was careful. He was as unfazed by Scorne's assault as a horse was to swarming gnats on a sweltering day. Simcane grabbed Scorne's head and lifted his kicking, squirming body from the ground.

While metal skin swarmed to Scorne's head to defend his skull, Simcane slid both of his thumbs over the soft, defenseless flesh of

Scorne's eyelids. The metal on Scorne's forearm lifted into a point and he stabbed it into Simcane's side, but the wound was shallow. Simcane didn't flinch. Instead, he stared at the ceiling in a trance-like state and pressed his thumbs into Scorne's eyes. Scorne flailed his feet and clawed at Simcane's hands.

Simcane's thumbs sank deep into Scorne's sockets to maddening squeals that would hurt a dog's ears. He pulled his bloody thumbs free with strings of gooey, red gore hanging from his thumbnails. Scorne's body thudded to the floor. Simcane looked down at his suddenly blind adversary flopping on the ground.

"How's the eyes, Scorne?" he said. Far from finished, he grabbed the nape of Scorne's neck with one thick hand and clutched his rope belt with the other. He lifted Scorne from the ground like he held a battering ram, drew back, and hurled Scorne face-first into the unyielding bedroom wall. Scorne's body went limp; his squeals silenced. Simcane drew back again and this time drove Scorne through the glass window into the muddy side yard.

"I'll be right back," he said to Bohden. He ducked through the door and marched out the front. Bohden watched from the broken bedroom window as the big man came around the house to stand over Scorne's limp body.

Scorne shook his head as if trying to shake his daze out through his ears. He struggled to his hands and knees and pushed mud out of his mouth with his tongue. Blindly, he crawled toward the street with his death dealer stalking him. Scorne froze and lifted his head like he'd heard something. As Simcane stood and watched, Scorne pushed to his feet, extended his arms in front of him, and staggered in a confused circle.

Simcane wrapped his tree trunk arms around Scorne's chest from behind. He lowered Scorne to the ground while still holding the murderer's arms tight to his body.

Scorne whispered something, though Bohden couldn't hear what he said. Simcane steadily squeezed before jerking one violent, bone-snapping time. Scorne grunted, stiffened, and then went limp.

Simcane dropped Scorne's lifeless body into the mud. He wrenched his head to the side, releasing a series of pops from his own spine. He extended his palms to the sky and tilted his head back. It almost looked as if he wanted the rain to cleanse his guilt over the violence he'd just committed.

Scorne's metal skin poured onto the ground and slithered toward Simcane's feet. Simcane took a step from its path. The metal slowed and then released a high-pitched squeal as though crying out in pain. It hardened on the ground and turned brown like rust.

Simcane walked back to the window where Bohden waited. "Don't touch that until it's rusted completely. Probably not until tomorrow to be safe." He looked past Bohden through the window. "How's your mom?"

Bohden looked to the floor where his mother was stirring. "Mother, are you all right?"

She rubbed her temples. "My head hurts." Her voice was groggy.

Simcane nodded. "Take her to a doctor." He turned to leave, but hesitated. Without looking back and with his head lowered, he said, "Sorry you had to see that, kid." Then he walked to his waiting horse in front.

Bohden helped his mother sit up.

Her panicked eyes flicked over the walls. "Where's your father?"

Bohden's hand found the back of her neck and he pressed his forehead against hers. "He's gone. It's over. We're safe." He propped her up against the wall. "I'll be right back. Wait here." He hurried out front as Simcane headed for the road.

"Wait," Bohden shouted. "Simcane, wait." He caught up to him in the pouring rain.

"What is it, kid?"

"What'd my father say to you?"

Simcane took a deep breath and thought about his answer. "He said he was sorry, kid."

Bohden lowered his head as Simcane trotted away.

CHAPTER 7

INTERRUPTED VISIT

Simcane made the journey to Thasula for a long overdue visit with Queen Alina. He hadn't spoken with her since the end of the war as he had been quite busy helping Homer tend to his farm. At the main castle gates, he dismounted Homer's horse, Shelby, and approached two Epertasian guards.

One of the guards asked, "Where do you think you're going, big fella?" His deep, authoritative voice sounded silly coming from such a puny physique.

Simcane sighed, annoyed. He'd been stopped at every guard post from the main gate onward and he'd grown tired of explaining himself. "Just tell the queen that Simcane is here to see her."

"How do you know she isn't busy?"

Simcane stepped into the guard's space to sap some of his overconfidence. "She'll want to see me, that I promise."

Usually men wilted beneath his intimidation, but to his surprise the guard held his ground. He didn't even waver like other men when Simcane straightened and expanded his chest.

"Wait here," the guard ordered and motioned for the other guard to carry the message. Then he lingered in Simcane's path to prove he wasn't intimidated.

Simcane wasn't interested in pissing matches anymore. He relaxed and took a step backward, giving the guard a tiny victory.

The guard stared him up and down, wrinkled his nose, and said, "Simcane, huh? No disrespect, sir. Just doing my job."

Simcane nodded. Maybe a more peaceful Simcane could catch on.

Neither man said much while they waited for the other guard to return, which he eventually did with word from Alina. "The queen wants him to come up right away." Then he whispered in a failed attempt to keep Simcane from hearing, "She also warned us to never delay him again."

Simcane smirked. "Take care of my horse." He crowded past the guards.

James met him at the main entrance with a welcoming smile and a firm handshake. With the pleasantries out of the way, the old-timer escorted him to the throne room where Alina was waiting. Her face lit up and her dimples deepened at the first sight of her extra-large friend. She was beautiful and elegant in a long lilac dress with her hair twirled and wrapped tightly to the crown of her head. She hugged him. "Sim, how have you been? Please have a seat." She directed him to sit on the large, regally adorned throne next to her own. He had never sat in a throne before and he felt uniquely out of place. He wondered if her smile would crack her cheeks, it was so grand.

"I have been well, Your Majesty."

"Please, Sim. It's Alina. You know that. What brings you to Thasula? How are Homer and Irene?"

"I had business to attend up north and figured I'd drop in before heading back to the farm. Homer and Irene are well and send their regards. You look healthy, Alina. How is running the most powerful kingdom in the world?"

Her wan smile betrayed her.

"What is it?"

"It's been difficult." Obviously trying to steer the conversation in a different direction, she said, "I have news."

"Yes? And what might that be?"

She shyly glanced down toward her feet. "I'm going to address the people tonight. I would like for you to attend as my personal guest." Her smile turned impish. "You can hear my news with the rest of them."

Simcane nodded. "I wouldn't miss it for the world. Any word from King Logan or Queen Lona?"

Her smile faded. "I'm afraid not. It seems Lithia is descending into chaos. I had hoped Epertase could help them rebuild, but it's failing too quickly."

"The Liths are good people. What is going on up there?"

"It seems the Lowlanders have moved in and have overrun the capital like a scaffe infestation."

Simcane scowled. King Logan and Queen Lona were dear friends, and he couldn't stand seeing their country go to shit so soon after the Teks had already crushed it. "Perhaps I should go search for them after I'm done here. Is it bad enough that you should move Epertase's army in and turn Lithia into a police state until its rightful rulers return?"

"I don't know, Sim. Epertase's army is still weakened from the war. We can't spread ourselves too thin."

An awkward silence hung in the air until Simcane changed the subject. "I have a piece of news myself. Actually, it's one of the reasons I came."

She leaned to the edge of her seat in anticipation. "And what would that be?"

"I was able to locate the villain Scorne."

Some of the rosy color left her cheeks. "By the gods. That is great news. Where is he now?"

Understanding Alina's compassion and strong belief in fair trials, he didn't want to burden her with the details of how Scorne had met his end. "Let's just say he's been brought to justice."

To his surprise, instead of lecturing him about mercy and the "Epertasian way," she simply said, "Maybe now I'll sleep more peacefully," and the two left it at that.

"Have you heard from Rasi?" he asked.

She shook her head.

"You should send for him."

"It's not that easy."

"It wouldn't hurt."

She glowered at him. "Have you been speaking with Levi? He's of a similar opinion."

She changed the subject again, and then they must have talked for hours because James appeared and announced that dinner was ready. Alina rose to her feet and invited Simcane to join her. He accepted, and the two had a magnificent feast of steamed duck, vegetables, and as much bread as he could eat in a lifetime.

After dinner, the crowd gathered in the Royal Garden and around the castle perimeter to await Alina's big announcement. If there was open ground to be found, it was quickly filled by citizens. Simcane followed her onto the raised platform built for such occasions and stood silently at her back. James and Levi stood to the side while Jarrah and Masera waited between her and the castle with their eyes focused on the crowd.

She peeked over her shoulder at Simcane before she began. A hush fell over the crowd. Her emerald eyes sparkled with the news she was about to reveal.

She stepped forward with confidence. "My good people," she shouted. "I have news to share with you." Her words were relayed throughout the crowd. A man with paper, ink, and a quill sat near the front of the platform and scribbled her words for the royal logbook and the morning paper which would be distributed throughout Epertase in the coming week.

"The kingdom has been through trying times as of late. You are a strong people and I am proud to be called your queen. With all we have been through together, I felt it was time for some good—"

A man in the front row interrupted, "Is this where you tell us the truth?"

Simcane was struck by the man's rudeness.

Alina hesitated, flustered by his outburst. "Excuse me, good sir?"

A woman shouted from a few rows deeper in the crowd, "Tell us how King Elijah really died."

Alina was taken aback. Why weren't the rest of the people coming to her defense?

Simcane stepped in front of her, his patience waning. "You will watch your tongues," he shouted.

Alina touched his shoulder with a calming hand. She stepped past him to the edge of the platform. "My friends, I do not know what more I can tell you. You have all been well informed of everything that's happened."

A low rumble of whispers filled the audience. Simcane had never witnessed such disrespect and he considered making an example out of someone in the crowd, maybe the man who'd started the unrest. While Simcane struggled with doing what was right versus what would simply feel good in the moment, the people near the back began to part.

"What is this madness?" Alina whispered.

From the gate at the far end of the courtyard, a towering man and a woman of nearly equal height entered the crowd.

"By the gods," Alina whispered as she backed away from the edge. Simcane recognized the dread on her face.

"Who are they?" Simcane whispered. "They look like Gildonese."

She whispered, "They are indeed. That is Fice, king of the Lowlanders, and one of his women."

Masera came to her side. The Elite Guard rushed the front of the platform and formed a barrier between her and the people.

Fice strolled through the parting crowd until he arrived at the front. His lips moved, though he didn't speak, and two of the Elite Guard stepped out of his way. The two Gildonese climbed onto the platform with one fluid step and turned to the crowd.

Masera stepped in front of Alina with his hand on his sword. "Remember, Your Majesty. Don't look them in the eyes."

The female Gildonese watched him with cautious interest. Archers with arrows trained on the two foreigners appeared at the top of the castle and in the guard towers. Fice turned back to Alina and stared at her with inky, unwavering eyes. He approached her. Simcane stepped into his path next to Masera where Jarrah should have been. Jarrah was nowhere to be seen. Even as tall as he was, Simcane only stood to the Gildonese's chest.

Atticus stepped onto the platform with his hand on his sword.

"What do you want, King Fice?" Alina asked, leaning past Simcane's bulk to better see him.

He licked his gums with a loud sucking sound. "I want the same as all of your sheep, which is merely to know how you came to power and how the mighty King Elijah fell from said power, gods rest his soul." His words were calm and smooth and spoken in a rambling manner that would frustrate most intellectuals.

"You do not care about my father," she snapped. "What is this feigned concern?" The members of the Elite Guard along the platform drew their swords.

Without looking back, Fice said, "Call off your dogs, young princess. You will not like the results if they continue on their current path." His fire-haired companion paced along the front of the platform, itching for a fight.

Alina must have known something that Simcane did not, because she waved off the guards.

Simcane stepped aggressively forward. He was in no mood for such blatant disrespect of his queen. "Why don't you move along, Gildonese," he said as more of an order than a question.

"Who is your peasant man-friend, Princess?" Fice asked without faltering.

"That's 'Queen' to you," Simcane answered before she had a chance.

Fice smirked. "It could be whore if I so determine."

Simcane glanced back at Alina, burning for the order to shut the Gildonese's filthy mouth. Masera tapped his shoulder and nodded toward his other side. Simcane looked to his left where the fire-haired bitch stood beside him with a dagger at his side. He wondered how she'd moved so close without him noticing.

Alina's soft touch on his arm eased his tension. "It's all right, Sim. Let's hear him out."

Fice half-heartedly bowed. "Thank you. As I was saying before your rude peasant here interrupted, we do not recognize you as queen any more than we recognize you as one of the gods, and I asked you once who this peasant is who feels entitled to speak in my presence. I will not ask again."

Simcane squeezed his fists at his side. He wanted to snap the twig of a man into two halves, but Alina cleared her throat. *Simcane, I will handle this,* she said in his mind.

"Simcane?" the Gildonese said with a sneer. "The one and only Simcane? You truly are a legend in these parts, and one whose head would decorate my mantle nicely. Is the one they call Rasi here as well? He would be the true prize."

Simcane's breathing deepened. If not for Alina's strong but gentle restraint, he would give the Gildonese his shot for everyone to see. After all, they were basically on a stage. His muscles tightened and his veins popped up on his arms like angry trails to his heart.

Alina nudged past him while calmly patting his chest. "King Fice, why are you here?" she asked.

"As I once warned, your snake-like tongue cannot be trusted and I still wait for our gold and my new kingdom, which are promises you have failed to make good on."

"I haven't forgotten. I just haven't had time nor been able to locate you."

"Well, which is it? Have you not had time, or have you not been able to locate me, as the two answers are very different in their meanings?"

Fice turned to address the crowd. "Your so-called queen has lied to me as she has lied to all of you about your honorable King Elijah's death and how the fugitive Rasi saved her when, in fact, it was that very scoundrel who helped her kill her father—your king."

Alina barged forward. "That's ridiculous," she shouted. "Rasi saved me. My father tried to help but was killed by the murderer Scorne."

The man from the front row shouted again, "Everyone knew your father organized a manhunt for Rasi while you were missing. He even sent his best friend, Tevin the Third, on Rasi's trail. Why would Elijah do that if Rasi was in fact helping him find you? Your story doesn't ring true."

Fice spoke before Alina had a chance to answer. "If something doesn't make sense …" He trailed off and Simcane wondered why he didn't finish the thought.

Alina shot a hateful glare toward the Gildonese. "Do not speak in their heads, deceiver."

And it all made sense. That Fice was speaking inside the people's heads while somehow preventing Simcane from hearing angered the giant even more. "Are you sure you don't want me to handle this, Alina?"

"No, no, no, Sim. It's all in hand."

The crowd's low rumbling increased in volume as they argued among themselves, Alina's unspoken announcement all but forgotten.

Fice looked at her, then at Simcane. His eyes remained as black as ink. "Be careful, my dear princess and her protector, for your kingdom is not as secure as you may believe. A lot of questions are afoot." He stepped off the platform with one effortless stride, his companion following suit. He turned back one last time. "We have taken up residence in the Lith royal castle, which is henceforth to be called Castle Fice of the legendary Kingdom of Recitar."

Alina shouted, "You do not get Lithia or its castle."

He chuckled. "My silly friend, we already have it."

Simcane used every ounce of restraint to keep from tearing Fice's head from his neck. If not for Alina, he or the Gildonese or both would die that day.

"I will get you your gold, Fice, but Lithia does not belong to you."

"I do not want your gold anymore as I now have my eyes set on a larger prize." His red-headed companion glared through Simcane before she turned and followed Fice as the people parted for him again, almost subconsciously. Even the Epertasian guards made way for their departure.

Atticus left his strategic position to the side and sheathed his sword. The crowd grew more and more agitated as the venom spewed by Fice seemed to fester unnaturally. Atticus moved next to Alina and Masera. Simcane stood at the edge of the platform, scanning the increasingly unruly crowd. Atticus whispered, "We should remove ourselves to the castle and disperse this crowd before it gets out of control."

Alina nodded.

James stepped up to address the audience, though his words were largely drowned out by the increased heckling. He shouted, "The queen will not be making her announcement this day. Please go to your homes now. We will inform you when she will speak again."

Someone threw a shoe at the platform.

Simcane shielded Alina with his big body while Atticus led her to the castle. Masera stayed with his men to start ushering the agitated citizens from the courtyard. Jarrah's reemergence to help disperse the crowd wasn't lost on Simcane.

Safely in the castle, Simcane approached Alina. "Your Majesty, I think I'll stick around Thasula for a bit longer. At least until everything calms down."

"That won't be necessary, my friend. I'm convinced that all will be back to normal by morning."

"Just the same ..."

"Sim, I'd be happy to know you're near if for no other reason than to have your wonderful company for dinner once more. I'm sure the citizens' good sense will prevail after a solid night's rest."

He leaned in and whispered into her ear, "One more thing before I go, then. You might want to keep your eye on your Captain Jarrah. I never liked him, but now I don't trust him, either."

"Nonsense, Sim. Jarrah has always been loyal."

"Just watch him, Your Majesty."

CHAPTER 8

THE FIRST BLOOD

After the activity around the castle had calmed and mostly returned to normal, Simcane traveled into town to his favorite drinking hole, Arthur's Dive. He plowed through the door like a prodigal son.

"Well, I'll be a dragon's mama," Marge said as she set her tray on the bar.

"Hey, Marge," Simcane said.

"Sim, I missed you." She turned and shouted, "Frank, come out. Look who's back." She grabbed Simcane's arm and led him to a table. "The usual, hon?"

"Nah. Just some water. My stomach's not what it used to be."

She paused momentarily as if waiting for a smile or some indication that he was joking. He held a straight face and sat at the closest table. The right armrest wobbled beneath his arm, so he treated it gingerly.

From behind the bar, Frank shouted, "Good to see you, Simcane."

"You too, Frank."

There were a few other patrons, but they largely ignored the reunion while sipping whatever libations they favored. Frank disappeared into the back before returning with a crate of supplies and then disappeared again, this time behind the bar.

Marge sat and gazed at Simcane from the chair across the table. "Where you stayin' nowadays?" she asked with an unbroken smile.

"I don't know yet."

"I have room at my place, if you'd like."

He nodded. A warm body would do him good. Even with so many new friends—Homer, Irene, and Alina—he still often felt lonely.

Never shy, Marge leaned over the table and poked his patch. "What happened to your eye?" she asked.

He realized how little he noticed his missing eye anymore, at least until stormy weather brought on the throbbing. "Evil people out there, darlin'."

An older fellow with a cane and a crotchety disposition shouted across the room, "Another ale, wench. He ain't the only one in here, you know." Evidently, he didn't appreciate Simcane monopolizing Marge's time.

In typical Marge fashion, she flipped her hand in a rude gesture toward him and continued with her visit. The old-timer mumbled curses before tilting his mug to his mouth in hopes of draining one more sip into his rotten gut.

Marge took Simcane's hand in hers. The two old friends continued talking until the other patrons angrily or drunkenly left, which probably didn't make Frank too happy.

Simcane asked, "Do you think I could go back to your place and get some sleep until you come home?"

"Of course." She dug her finger into her brassiere and retrieved her house key.

Simcane finished his water while Marge washed some of the other tables. She never did help the crotchety old man and he finally left, leaving Simcane the last patron standing. Simcane dropped a bit on the table despite water being one of the few free things left in the world. He shouted, "Thanks," to Frank, who had disappeared into the back room again. Frank hollered a farewell back.

When Simcane reached the door, a man's shrill, unfamiliar voice shouted from the street, "Siiiiiimmmmmcaaaane?"

Simcane's hand had gripped his sword before he realized it. He'd been in enough fights to sense when one was coming.

"Who knows you're here?" Marge asked.

"No one."

He stepped through the door. The street was packed with twenty, maybe thirty men dressed in rags like the homeless and wearing empty stares.

"Siiiiiimmmmcaaaane," the same stranger sang again as if Simcane wasn't standing in front of him. And then in unison they all stepped forward.

"What can I do for you boys?" Simcane asked. They didn't answer and took another step.

Marge stepped out to join him. "What do they want?"

"I don't know, but you'd better go inside."

"Come in with me."

"I will. Let me see what they want first."

Marge retreated into the bar.

Simcane marched into the street and stood chest-to-face with the lead stranger. The man's hollow stare gave him a chill. "I think you might have the wrong guy," Simcane said.

Without warning, the stranger drew back and punched Simcane in the jaw. Though it was like being struck by a child, it surprised him. Simcane planted his back foot and returned the favor. He felt the man's jaw shatter against his knuckles. The man dropped to the dirt like a corpse falling from the back of a funeral wagon.

All at once, the men swarmed him. He stumbled backward. The closest man reached for Simcane's foot and Simcane dropped him with a boot to his chin. He drew his fists back as someone else grabbed his waist. "What do you want?" he shouted, and tried to pry the man off him.

Another guy grabbed his knee. One of them dove for Simcane's head and met his fist. As he stumbled backward, they continued forward, trampling their downed fellows. Everyone Simcane struck dropped, but there were too many to drop them all. Simcane drew his fist back again. Someone grabbed his arm. One got in a lucky jab and his lower lip exploded in a crimson spray. A scrawny hand grabbed his throat, but he shook it away with ease. His back hit the bar door as they surged forward. The door cracked from the weight, but held. One of them grabbed his ear. Another one grabbed his balls. Their weight was suffocating.

"Marge," he shouted. "Open the door."

When she did, he and the mob spilled into the bar. Marge fled to the back room. The backward fall gave Simcane enough space to sit up and scoot backward.

Frank smashed a bottle on one man's head. They continued squeezing through the doorway, almost clogging the opening with their bodies.

As Simcane retreated across the floor, his hand met the leg of a table, so he hurled the whole table at them. But they kept coming. "Get out of here, Frank."

Frank ran to the back room.

Simcane grabbed one of the men holding his leg and smashed his face into the floor. That bought him enough time to get to his feet. A glass bottle shattered against the left side of his face. He wobbled. It was getting too dangerous to keep fighting. Fingernails raked his arm.

Every time Simcane sent two of the men to dreamland, three more replaced them. With no other choice, he raised his fist above his head and then drove it downward. The thunderous boom shook the walls and splintered the floor. Any attackers within a horse-length crashed against the walls.

The weight of using his gift pushed down on his shoulders. He fell to his knees.

A new wave of men poured through the door. Simcane fought the heaviness to get back to his feet. He stumbled toward the back room. Another hand hit his shoulder from behind. Pain shot up his leg and he looked down to see one of the freaks sinking his teeth into his shin. With his other foot, he stomped his attacker's head into the wooden floor.

He tried to draw back for another energy burst, but three men grabbed his bicep and wrenched his arm toward the floor. His veins bulged as he strained against them. Another set of teeth sank into his shoulder and he groaned. He squeezed his hand around whatever enemy body part was near, snapping one man's arm.

As the wave of bodies dragged him beneath their weight, Marge and Frank reappeared. Marge carried a stick as large as her arm and Frank shoved a lit torch at the attackers. They recoiled from the flames, giving Simcane a chance to escape. Marge swung the stick at them as she retreated with Simcane to the back room. The three ran through the back into the alley.

Simcane doubled over with his hands on his knees. "What in the name of the gods was that about?" he asked between labored breaths.

They headed to Marge's place. As they ran, Simcane took a mental inventory of his injuries, finding little more than a few scratches, bites, and bruises. He was solid, at least until the adrenaline died and more injuries revealed themselves.

That night, Frank headed home and Simcane stayed with Marge. When she woke up the next morning, Simcane was sitting on the edge of the bed. He felt her hand on his shoulder before she leaned her bare chest against his back.

"I didn't keep you awake with my tossing and turning, did I?" he asked.

"Nah. It was your snoring."

"I'm sorry."

"I could get used to it."

He stood up and pulled on his pants.

"Why don't you stay for a bit?" She pulled the sheet around her.

Simcane leaned in and gave her a kiss. "I can't, babe. I've got some work to do."

She didn't get out of bed when he left. He returned to the bar where there were no blank-eyed strangers in sight and, miraculously, Homer's horse was still tied to the post where he had left it.

Finally, a little luck goes my way.

CHAPTER 9

BJ THE KEEN

After the Tek War, BJ the Keen had returned to the small northern town of New Arc as a war hero. Living so close to the forbidden country of the Lowlands had always been exciting to him, but even though the Lowlands was now a lake it didn't change the fact that New Arc was his home.

Some men might have been uncomfortable with their sudden fame, but not BJ; he reveled in it. He proudly wore his metal of bravery, and when anyone asked about his mission with the legendary Simcane, he told the stories while taking most of the credit for their success.

When he'd enter bars on the seedier side of town, women couldn't help but eye him. He enjoyed their attention, sometimes deep into the night. It was the eve of his thirty-ninth birthday and he was ready for another night out. If all went well, the crowds would be celebrating his greatness by the end of the night. If all went great, so would a few ladies.

He'd become a favorite at Lucy's Tavern, where the patrons and employees alike anxiously awaited his increased inebriation. The more he drank, the more comical his tales of battle became and the looser his purse strings. He had a gift for making people laugh with his impressions of the Teks as incompetent empty suits of armor. Or when he stuffed feather pillows beneath his shirt and held a napkin over his eye while pretending to be Simcane, whom he lovingly referred to as Cyclops. That night, the ale was paid for by the owner in celebration of another year of BJ's life, which meant more tips for the barmaids, so everyone was happy.

Before the moon had reached its zenith, BJ was swaying arm in arm with the other patrons and singing rhyming songs at the top of his lungs. More ale spilled down his shirt than into his gullet, but he had no worries as his tankard was consistently and quickly refilled by the tender. It was his kind of party and he couldn't imagine being anywhere else.

He was into the second chorus of his made-up Tek nursery rhyme when two unfamiliar women shuffling through the revelers caught his eye. The women looked similar enough to be sisters with their distinctive wide yet strangely attractive mouths, and he rather liked a challenge.

"Are you BJ?" one of the sisters asked as he approached. She winked seductively when he nodded. Maybe it wouldn't be as much of a challenge as he thought.

"The legend himself," he shouted above the roar of the partiers.

When they were close enough to him, the shorter of the two sisters lifted onto her toes and leaned toward his ear. "May we speak with you outside?"

He rubbed his neatly-trimmed beard. Playing hard to get seemed the way to go. "I'm rather enjoying myself in here, my dears. But you're welcome to join the festivities."

The taller sister leaned toward his other ear. "We will make it worth your while." She playfully bit his earlobe.

Now, how did she know that was his weakness? He grinned and excused himself with a nod to anyone paying attention. His two new acquaintances grabbed his hands and led him through the crowd into the street. BJ leaned drunkenly against the taller of the two sisters and sniffed her sandy hair.

She pushed him away. Her flirty smile wilted. "We're not here for that," she snapped.

BJ regarded her, searching for a sign that she was now the one playing hard to get. "What's going on?" he asked. He turned to her sister, who had also lost her playfulness.

"We need your help," she said.

"My help? That's not the kind of game I came out here for." He turned to the pub.

"Please wait," she said, and touched his arm.

Her sister blocked the door. "Just listen to our words."

The sudden urge to piss convinced him to hear them out. He turned away, lowered his britches to his knees, and said, "You have until I finish." His drunken wobble nearly made him soil his own garments.

"My name is Kathryn," the taller sister said. "This is my sister, Maddie. We need your help, and we're prepared to pay you handsomely."

BJ peered over his shoulder, not convinced by their modest attire that they could afford his services. "Not"—hiccup—"interested."

As he squeezed out his last splash of urine, a small leather satchel landed in the puddle by his feet. Several gold coins spilled from the top. BJ righted himself; they had his attention. Again.

"What can I do for you ladies?"

Kathryn smirked. "As you may have heard, several men from town have disappeared recently. Our brother was one of them."

BJ hadn't heard. He wasn't one to listen to local gossip that wasn't about him. "I don't much care to hunt missing people who may or may not wish to be found."

Kathryn continued, "It's not just about our brother. Three days ago, his son returned home from school with a strange look in his eyes. Since that day, he hardly eats and has stopped speaking except for first thing in the morning when he recites the same passage over and over again."

BJ's interest was piqued. "What's he say?"

"He says, 'As Lowlanders you are nothing. You are worthless. You follow the great King Fice without hesitation.' There's more, but the gist is absolute servitude to King Fice."

BJ wiped his nose with his sleeve. "Sounds like witchcraft. I don't dabble in witchcraft." He paused, looked at the bag of money on the ground, and added, "I may, however, be able to help find your brother." He picked up the urine-soaked satchel of coins and stuffed it into his pocket. "But it'll cost you. Now, if you'll excuse me, there's a party going on in my honor that I must attend. Come and find me in the morning."

"How will we know where to look?"

"Follow the broken-hearted women," he answered with a sly grin.

He returned to the party and drank until dawn with the truly skilled and most dedicated alcohol connoisseurs. BJ stood on the bar, finishing his latest gut-busting story.

"And then," he shouted, "I threw my japsy weed into the pit of black blood, lighting the sky with a fireball that caused the Tek soldiers to tinkle in their britches." A couple of the more attentive patrons drunkenly giggled, despite hearing the same stupid line at least five other times that night alone. "I slayed one Tek pansy with a—"

The front door burst open, interrupting his story. Everyone not unconscious with their heads on the table and drool spooling from their mouths turned to look. BJ squinted to make out the intruder who stumbled in and fell to her knees. It was one of the sisters from earlier—Kathryn, he believed. Her face had been shaded in purple and red handprints and a deep cut traced the outline of her cheek. BJ stared for a moment, unsure of how to react.

Most of the partygoers looked to him.

A little spark of chivalry bested his inebriation and pushed him to her side. "Kathryn?" he asked, still amazed he remembered her name. "Who did this?"

He knelt beside her and lifted her chin.

She whispered, "They're coming for you."

His bravado outpaced his brain. "Let them come," he slurred. Then he paused and asked, "Who?"

From outside, a deep, crackly voice answered before she had a chance. "We are looking for BJ the Keen, as we have much pain to share with him before this day has finished." The voice was slow and smooth—almost melodic.

BJ stood, wobbled, and caught himself against a table. He groped the emptiness at his hip. *Where did I put that damn sword?* He shouted, "Hold on. I'll be out momentarily."

He scanned the bar for his weapon to no avail. He saw the tender. "Hey, Murph. Give me a sword. Quick."

The voice from outside shouted, "Take your time in finding your sword, as we will happily wait."

BJ snatched the sword from Murph's hand and barreled through the doorway. His enthusiasm drained at the first sight of his tormentors. Two figures stood in the street with their swords already drawn. They were each almost two men tall, covered with battle scars and ugly as sin. The dark-haired one spoke. "I am Ulrac and I am of the Gildonese tribe of Fice, though you have likely figured that out judging by the concern on your silly face. And if you have, then you surely know you will not survive the coming battle."

Even filled with ale, BJ knew enough not to tangle with a Gildonese. Seeing Eldon in battle was enough to tell him his place in the hierarchy of warriors. "I have no quarrels with the Gildonese," he slurred.

"That may well be, but you have been employed by the corrupt Epertasian leadership in the past and have shown your capacity to do hero work, which is why you must not continue to draw breath during the reign of the new king of Epertase."

BJ had never been one to back down from a fight, but he wasn't crazy. "I am a peaceful man today. I have no interest in causing you harm, good sir. Neither now nor in the future."

The Gildonese appeared bored, staring at his hand and picking at one of his nails. "We have spoken enough words. Raise your sword … or don't. It matters not."

BJ glanced at the sidewalk for a potential escape route.

"If you choose to flee, the bar from which you have just exited will turn into a slaughterhouse, and *then* we will still come for you, still find you, and still kill you."

BJ swallowed hard. He didn't feel like being killed by the Gildonese, but he wasn't coward enough to leave his friends to die, either. He hesitantly stepped into the street, still hoping for a miracle. The two Gildonese stepped apart and waited.

"I don't want this," he whined.

"You have stalled long enough," Ulrac said.

He could never outrun a Gildonese even if he decided to sacrifice his friends. The tavern doorway filled with curious patrons.

"Goodbye, my friends." If he was going to die, which he had no doubt he would, he was determined to do it fighting. When outnumbered in battle, he favored a specific opening strike, which in the past had never failed to even the odds. He called it the Bartholomew, since he was the one who'd developed it. BJ lowered his shoulders as if to surrender his head, and then lunged to his left while swinging his sword at the Gildonese to his right. If he was flawless in his speed, the Gildonese would be unable to elude his sword.

He was fast.

He *was* flawless.

And the Gildonese effortlessly stepped aside.

Cold steel sliced BJ's spine, spilling warm wetness down his back. With Ulrac in his sights, he swung again. Maybe the ale had slowed him, because even though the Gildonese seemed to move like a slug away from his blade, his sword never made contact. Ulrac landed a painful punch to his gut.

BJ fought to stay on his feet. Without warning, a mix of vomit and ale sprayed through his nose and clenched teeth. He collapsed to his knees. One of the Gildonese, he didn't see which, pressed a boot to his shoulder and thrust him face-first to the dirt. The blood poured from his back into pools around him. He didn't need to feel the pain to realize his wound was mortal. The two Gildonese hovered over him, waiting for his end. He fought to keep his eyes open and his head clear, but his blood poured out too quickly.

With what was left of his strength, he turned his head to the side. His medal for bravery lay partially submerged in the growing puddle of red. He reached for it, but was too weak. He tried to push to his knees.

As Ulrac walked away, he said, "Get it over with."

BJ closed his eyes.

CHAPTER 10

FORTUNES OF BLOOD

Alina had promised herself to never do what she was about to do, but the Elder Three were her best hope for learning why her countrymen had turned on her. It wasn't expressly forbidden for kings and queens to go into the lair, but it was highly discouraged because they would be left unprotected among wizards. She was fearful as she made her way down the long hallway.

As she passed the many lit torches on the wall, she wondered who kept them fueled. With each of her footsteps leaving tracks in the dust and dirt, she concluded that the flames must be magically eternal. When she approached two massive double doors at the end of the hall, they opened as if inviting her in. She entered the room and they closed behind her.

Something about the dark room soothed her nerves. A cool breeze lifted the hairs on her neck. A torch flared to life on a familiar rock wall revealing hundreds of vertical lines carved into its face. She'd recognize this place even with her eyes covered. The center of the room held a fire pit identical to the one she had sat by many times before. The flickering embers smoked as though someone had just doused the flames, yet the smoke dissipated instead of filling the room. For a brief moment and against all rational thought, she hoped he would be there.

"Rasi?" she whispered. She reached an unsteady hand toward the smoldering embers. Before the warmth could reach her, the fire pit flared into a monstrous fireball taller than most men. The shock pushed her to her rear. Then, as quickly as they had come, the flames were sucked back into the embers and disappeared. Alina looked past the fire pit.

Three separate images slowly appeared, one on each of the three opposing rock walls. The images were faint at first, but as they grew brighter, she had no doubt that they were the Elder Three. She hesitated, wondering if she had made a mistake.

"You may stand, Alina," they said in harmony.

She stood up and adjusted her dress.

"It is a privilege to meet you, Alina." The men were old, perhaps older than Epertase itself, with flawless white beards that brushed the ground. They appeared so frail that a slight breeze might topple them. "We have been waiting for you. You are puzzled by your surroundings, yes?"

She nodded. She didn't know if looking into their eyes would be considered disrespectful, so she was careful not to stare.

"You see the place with which you are most familiar or most desire." The Elders gave strange looks to one another. "Hmmm. We have seen this place before … But why?" The room grew silent while they pondered their own question with their fingers at their chins. Finally, they sang as one, "Ahhh, that is it. The one called Rasi visited here and this, too, was his vision." In slow, rhythmic movements, they gestured to her midsection. "Is he the healing boy's father?"

Instinctively, her hands went to her belly as if to protect her unborn from their gazes. Her knees went weak; her breath stuttered as she exhaled. "Boy?" she asked, almost unable to get the word out.

They looked to the ceiling with grave, contemplative faces.

Alina searched for the strength to step forward. "I'm losing my people," she said.

"Your people are already lost," they answered without hesitation.

"What? No. I can get them back. It's not too late."

"They follow another now."

"Is it the Gildonese?" she asked.

They didn't answer.

"What can I do?"

"You must hide where light grows from the ground."

"No," she shouted. "I won't hide. I'll fight for my people."

They snapped, "You will not. You must hide."

"But I have the Light. The people won't follow Fice—they must follow me."

"You are incorrect, dear Alina. With the Light, you must live, yes. But they do not have to follow. If you do not hide well, one day the Light will no longer belong to your family."

"If I capture Fice, will the people return?"

"You do not understand." Their voices grew agitated, starting as a low rumble and growing until they reached a piercing shrill. "You … must … hiiiiiiiide."

"Until when? Forever?"

"Until it is right not to hide."

"Argghhh." She turned away and stormed toward the door. She had just gained her throne and saved her kingdom, and now they expected her to simply give it away? She thought of the Lowlanders and their miserable lives. That pitiful existence could be in store for her people, and it broke her heart.

The Elder Three stopped her cold with their next words. "It's a shame about the one called Rasi, yes? He had a good heart."

"Shame?" She spun around. "Wait. Why?"

Together, they rubbed their chins again. "He may not survive this night."

She gasped. "Oh, gods. What's wrong with Rasi? What can I do?"

"Do?" They snickered as one. "You cannot *do* anything, young one. The same forces that now seek to steal your kingdom and your Light also seek to burn his veins. Many, many friends will die this night." They paused. "In fact, the death has already begun." The flames of the pit flared again, this time revealing an image of BJ the Keen lying dead in the dirt outside of a tavern. People cried around him.

BJ?

Slowly, the Elder Three shook their heads and bowed as their images faded back into the cold rock walls. Alina cried out to them, but she was too late—they were already gone. Alone again, she began to cry.

CHAPTER 11

HYLOCKS

Rasi's parents hadn't changed his room in the many years he had been away. Even the dresser with a broken leg still leaned on an old school textbook exactly as he had left it. Since the room seemed to give his mother comfort, he was careful not to change it after he returned. A hand-crafted wooden game that he had made as a schoolboy still sat in the corner, and he remembered guiding the lead balls into each of the scoring holes while his friends scrambled to block his attempts.

He lay on his side in his bed, exhausted. A few of his straps sprawled across the dresser while the others draped the floor, equally tired from farming. As he drifted into that dazed world between wakefulness and sleep, one of his straps slowly lifted from the floor. Then a second one lifted from the dresser, which pulled him from his daze. When he opened his eyes, the two straps were hovering above him. He was careful not to overreact since the last time they'd almost taken off his prying mother's head when she'd sneaked in to watch him sleep.

But it wasn't his mother this time—he could feel it. His partially open shutters revealed dancing shadows in the moonlight. He slipped to the edge of his bed. By now all his straps were flared and pressed against the ceiling. Their agitated movements told him they anticipated a fight. He slid into his pants and tied them snuggly around his waist. Quietly, he crept to one side of his bedroom window.

The sound of foreign whispers seeped through the glass. One of his straps reached for his sword, which rested beside his dresser. *Good,* he whispered in his mind. He strapped the sword to his hip.

When his fingers curled around the leather hilt, it felt right, as though the sword was a part of him and had been waiting for him to harness its power again.

A winged creature crashed through the window. Rasi ducked away from flying shards and splinters with his forearm covering his eyes. The creature landed near the door, its wings tucked against its back. Hunched over, it lifted its milky eyes to Rasi. Its puke-green, hairless skin was covered in a thin film of glistening slime. Its face was round like a man's, except its eyes were set closer to the sides of its head than the center, and its nose was little more than two slits on a small, raised bump.

Rasi's straps flexed, ready for the kill. He inhaled a deep, foul smell of rotten teeth mixed with week-old squank meat. The creature squatted and rocked from one thick, muscular leg to the other like an excited frog.

"Raaasiiieeeee?" the creature asked in a hissing, nasal voice.

Rasi cocked his head sideways. It was either a fabled fisher or a hylock, and its wings indicated it was the latter. All Epertasian soldiers learned about the creatures in their training, though none of them figured they'd ever meet one. He wondered how the creature knew his name. With his back to the shattered window, his straps snapped like whips in the air. He coaxed the hylock closer.

He had thought that hylocks were blind, but the creature's head followed him as though it could see his every movement. It was at that moment Rasi realized he stood within the cone of moonlight coming through the broken window. He had it backward. Fishers were the blind ones, and hylocks could see light and shadow.

The hylock dragged its serpent-like tongue along its fingers and razor nails. Rasi sized it up, remembering a second lesson from his studies. The creatures carried deadly venom in their nails.

And then, like a dagger to his heart, he remembered something else. Hylocks, like their fisher cousins, never hunted alone. Just then another creature burst through the window and landed on his back. He grunted, cursing himself for his tactical failure. Though he was angry at himself, he was angrier at his straps for making the same error. The creature's arms wrapped around his neck.

The first creature pounced. Two straps snatched it from the air before it could strike. One coiled around its neck and slammed it against the wall above Rasi's bed.

Rasi spun his sword and jammed it under his own armpit, but the hylock on his back shifted away from the blade. Icy cold nails raked across his forearm, leaving a deep and searing pain. Rasi muffled his moan. The sword fell from his suddenly weakened grip. He pumped his fist to assess the damage. His fingers tingled, but he was happy they worked at all.

His bedroom door swung open. Donis stood in the doorway with a rusty sword.

Rasi's eyes widened. He stumbled forward to get closer to his father. A strap shoved Donis back into the hall and then slammed the door closed again.

The hylock's deadly toenails sliced the backs of Rasi's knees. That time he couldn't muffle his moan. His legs gave way and he dropped to his knees.

The hylock tapped its feet against the floor, tucked its large bat-like wings around Rasi, and bounced backward through the shattered window. Its wings opened and before Rasi could touch the ground, the hylock launched itself into the air. Its wings beat with a sound like muffled thunder.

Rasi needed to do something quick before he got too high. Luckily, the hylock was struggling with his weight. One strap coiled around the hylock's left wing. The creature beat its other wing in a failed attempt to stay airborne. They both thudded to the ground, the hylock's grip momentarily broken. Ignoring the pain in his legs, Rasi bounded to his feet, planted himself, and commanded his straps to pull.

The hylock screeched in agony. The straps quivered as they strained. Then the hylock's wing ripped free, spraying rank, milky blood from its back. The creature collapsed to its side, convulsing.

The hylock in his room launched itself from the window. A strap caught it around its neck. With one violent jerk, the strap whipped the creature toward the ground and then stopped it just before it hit. The force popped the creature's head from its body.

Rasi looked to the dark sky where shadows flashed past the moon. His back met the side of the house. He was determined not to be surrounded.

And then his mother called out, "Rasi?" from the front porch. His heart sank.

Damn.

He quickly counted the approaching shadows—at least twenty. With his parents so close, he couldn't fight them there. Escape was unlikely; Shadow was too far away in the barn. The cover of the forest beyond his father's field seemed his only hope. If he could make it that far. The backs of his knees throbbed, but he had to push through the pain to have any chance of surviving.

The hylocks descended like eagles hunting squanks. Rasi pushed off the wall and sprinted toward the trees. A glance up told him that it was going to be close.

Come on, you bastards. Follow me.

Without slowing, they swooped past the house in single file and leveled off near the ground. Their feet lightly brushed the grass as they gave chase.

Rasi pushed his legs harder, even as venom burned into his thighs. A glance back revealed how quickly they were catching up. The lead one was already close.

He heard their grunts and smelled their stink. The lead hylock swiped at his back, but his straps swatted it away, which sent it tumbling into the dirt. He ran past his plow, left out the day before.

The hylocks howled.

The forest closed in. Another attack was answered with another successful defense by his appendages. The trees were close. His straps defended against another hylock assault. When he reached the forest, he dove between two trees, his straps cushioning his landing. The hylocks pulled up and climbed back toward the sky as if giving up on their chase. But Rasi knew better. Their initial hesitation to follow blindly into the dark forest wouldn't last, but it would give him time to put distance between them.

He knew the woods well from his childhood adventures. The small amount of moonlight peeking through the canopy was just enough to find his way. Though weaponless and drastically outnumbered, he still had a chance. It wasn't the forest that gave him hope—it was the creature in the clearing at the center.

It was risky. If the dragon was still there, she might just as easily kill him as help him. But he was banking on the hylocks appearing as more of a threat. Plus, the dragon hadn't killed him when he'd sought it out as a child.

He couldn't hear the hylocks as he ran, but he could still smell their stench. The air was saturated with it. The burning venom in his thighs moved into his groin. Almost his entire arm was numb. He stumbled like a drunken man. When the burning pain reached his gut, he doubled over. But he kept his balance and continued running.

The side of his neck above his numb shoulder started to burn with an intensity that stole his breath. He wondered why they didn't finish him while he was so weak. Then it hit him—they were waiting for the venom to work. Less risky. They were skilled hunters indeed. Rasi straightened, inhaled much-needed air, and pushed through the pain.

He stopped only long enough to get his bearings. A constellation of eight stars in the shape of a fish was framed by a gap in the treetops. The fin pointing toward the moon gave him the way. He continued running and stumbling through the trees until he saw an opening ahead. His last chance.

A bramble wall was all that stood in his way. He burst through, ignoring the thorns ripping his flesh. He looked up at the near perfect circle of scorched, cracked dirt stretching as wide as his and Mr. Jamison's farms combined.

He had made it—the dragon's den.

And she was nowhere to be seen.

It was a gamble, and he had the losing bet. Another wave of excruciating pain shot through his gut and into his chest, sending him to his knees. For the first time, he checked the wounds behind his knees. Instead of the mangled flesh he expected, there were only two small punctures on each leg. Jagged red streaks ran from the punctures and followed his veins up his thighs. They burned as though they moved fire instead of blood. He dropped forward to his hands. His groin ached like someone had kicked him in the stones. He wondered how long until the venom took him, or of more concern, how much agony he'd have to endure first.

It was over; he had fought as best he could, but they were just too deadly for him. He rolled to his back, the fish constellation twinkling down at him. He thought about his parents and how they would never know what had happened to him. He pictured Alina and longed to see her once more. His chest seized and tightened.

As he watched the sky, a high-pitched squeak from the western edge of the clearing grabbed his attention. He searched for the source through increasingly blurry eyes. For a moment, he almost forgot about his pain.

Almost.

It was the most incredible sight he had ever seen. He couldn't believe he had missed them at first. Two dragon hatchlings no bigger than horses cuddled together in a muddy pit with their open mouths to the sky.

The dragon *wasn't* dead.

She *hadn't* moved on.

She was hunting.

And it was almost feeding time.

Rasi stared in awe until another wave of pain left him gasping. Even if she saved him from the hylocks, he was still going to die by their venom. Rasi crawled toward the hatchlings. Their wings were matted to their frail sides with blood-tinged goop and a milky film covered their newborn eyes. Littered in the hard dirt around them were the broken bones of deer and buffalo and whatever else their mother had found for them to eat.

One of the hatchlings must have caught Rasi's scent because it curiously pulled away from its sibling. The hatchling crawled blindly toward the edge of its mud nest while sniffing the air. As it wandered farther and farther away from its sibling, the other hatchling whined as if suddenly lost and lonely. Hearing it, the brave hatchling reconsidered and turned back.

Another wave of searing pain sent Rasi's nose to his knees. Every muscle tightened and cramped. He tried to picture Alina's smile and perfect emerald eyes. He thought about how much she would enjoy seeing the hatchlings and wished he could bring her there.

Tree branches snapped from the direction he had come. The hylocks were done waiting. Between the rushes of pain, Rasi willed himself back to his hands and knees. Slowly, he crawled inch by agonizing inch toward the nest.

When he got to the mud, the hatchlings perked their pointed ears and stumbled toward the opposite edge. *It's all right. I won't hurt you.* As he watched them retreat, something caught his eye beyond the nest. It gave him a horribly wonderful idea, if only he could make it. Seven carriage-sized mounds of dung stood at the clearing's edge. The third lesson he remembered about hylocks was their brilliant sense of smell. He willed himself around the mud nest.

Rasi reached the bug-infested mounds. The overwhelming smell of sulfur turned his stomach. He pinched his nose, turned his head, and shoved his hand deep into the soft, warm center of one of the fresher piles. His straps hesitated.

You must, he urged.

They drew back.

Do it. Now.

The first strap plunged into the mound. The others reluctantly joined it. Once they were covered in muck, they relaxed on the ground. Rasi rolled to his back and pulled the mound over his chest and legs and even smeared some over his face. It was horrible in every way, but it would be worth it if it worked.

The hylocks burst through the brush, noses to the ground and wings tucked against their backs. They fanned out in a coordinated search, ignoring the hatchlings.

At some point the pain had stopped coming in waves and was now constant. It took every ounce of strength not to writhe in agony.

One of the hylocks swept side to side on a path toward him. Rasi bit his lower lip to keep from moving. The hylock neared the mound of dung and recoiled from the smell. Then it continued on, oblivious to how close it had come to its prey.

More creatures searched the nest, ignoring the frightened hatchlings. And then one of them stopped and raised its narrow ears. *Oh no.* Had it found him? Rasi froze, afraid to even breathe.

Then the hylock lowered its head like a beaten dog. The one beside it stopped and sniffed the air.

And that's when Rasi heard what they had heard. Faint at first, he recognized the steady, rhythmic flap of massive wings pounding the air. He slowly turned his head toward the sky.

Though he didn't see anything at first, a stunning beast soon shot past the full moon. Rasi had forgotten how beautiful she was. As he beheld her magnificence, she dove toward the nest. Just above the treetops, she extended her wings and stopped, each flap of her mighty wings swaying the tops of the trees. She took stock of the creatures near her babies. With a low growl, she landed in the center of the clearing with a ground-shaking thud. Her angry roar singed the air.

One of the hylocks cried, "You may have escaped this tiiieeeme, Rasiiieee, but the queeen won't beee so luckeee."

Almost as one, they launched directly toward the dragon's head. We're they suicidal? Though each hylock was no bigger than one of her teeth, together they seemed fearless. She lunged with her enormous snout, plucking one from the air and chewing it with bone-cracking delight. Instead of attacking as Rasi expected, the other hylocks hurled past her head toward the sky. They weren't fearless at all; they were bluffing their way past her. They wanted none of that fight, and Rasi couldn't blame them.

She lowered her head next to her spawn and drooled thick, bloody ground meat and bone into the mud beside them. Then she turned north toward where the other creatures had fled, crouched, and leaped into the air.

Rasi knew some of the creatures would likely escape her hunt, but not all of them, and he smiled despite the pain ravaging his body. As he lay helpless and dying in a rancid mound of dung, he watched the hatchlings clumsily slurp at their meal.

He wanted to sleep.

Even more than that, he wanted an end to his suffering.

With the hylocks gone, his straps shook away their shit camouflage like wet dogs, surprising Rasi that they had the strength to do so. His chest felt like the belke slug sat on it. He'd seen men die from heart attacks before and wondered if that was how the venom would take him. He no longer cared about the rank odor of dragon dung, simply wanting the pain to end. He clutched his chest, as that was all he had the strength to do.

He felt warmth on his cramped thighs and realized his bladder had let loose. Thick, frothy sputum bubbled from his mouth, choking him.

Drowning him.

Killing him.

He rolled to his side and tried to drag himself from the pile, but his seizing muscles refused to obey. His straps settled back to the ground, their brief burst of energy ended. His fingers curled and cramped into distorted claws. *This is it,* he thought. *This is how the great Rasi ends.* He chuckled at the absurdity of calling himself great.

Through blurry, watery eyes, he watched the moon lurch across the sky to be replaced by the suns peeking over the distant horizon. His straps quivered around him before eventually falling motionless. He had nothing left. He took a pained breath, hoping it was his last.

Then he saw a tiny speck in the muted orange glow of one of the rising suns. By the time he made out her wings he'd already guessed it was her. He wondered if he'd be the next meal for her spawn.

She landed with a thud next to her offspring, leaned down, and fed her babies once more. The hatchlings plunged face-first into the fresh, gooey meal.

She hovered over them while they fed, sniffing the air. Then she turned and looked at Rasi with one narrow, serpent-yellow eye.

She cautiously lowered her snout until her cavernous nostrils were within his reach had he been able to lift his arm. The air around him was sucked toward her as she inhaled. She lifted her head and tilted it to the side. He wondered why she didn't just stomp him to mush and be done with it. It was almost like …

No. It couldn't be. Could it? Could she possibly remember his scent from so long ago, even through her own excrement? It seemed impossible. Yet he was still alive and the hylocks weren't. She reached a single talon out and gently nudged his motionless body.

She held her front foot above him and dragged a talon across it until blood dribbled from the pad. The drops splashed into a puddle beside Rasi's left ear. Ever so softly, she poked a talon between his back and the ground and rolled him onto his chest with a gentle nudge.

His face submerged in the blood puddle. He took a reflexive breath in the thick liquid. It burned his throat and lungs as he gasped and inhaled more gore. He panicked. His arms trembled at his side. He was drowning and could do nothing about it. And then, when Rasi had no more fight left to give, she flicked him over onto his back.

He coughed and choked, desperately trying to take in air, but the thick blood clogged his airway. She turned her attention back to feeding her babies. As though she didn't want them to see him suffer, she carried them to the opposite edge of the clearing. That's where she watched and waited.

Rasi lay on his back and slowly drowned. His thoughts faded.
I love you, Alina.

The suns beat against Rasi's face. He squinted until his eyes adjusted to the brightness of day. With his forearm, he wiped some of the blood from his face. Dried excrement flaked away with his movements. His straps lifted from the ground. He sat up and made a fist. A look at his legs revealed the red streaks tracing his veins were gone. He rubbed his sore chest, the crushing pain all but gone. He felt stronger than he had felt in a long time.

Across the clearing, the mother dragon lay curled around her hatchlings. She rested her chin on the ground with her eyes fixed on him. He struggled to his feet, amazed he was able. It was a miracle. According to the training textbooks, no creature had ever survived such a large dose of hylock venom. Rasi crossed the clearing until he stood in front of her. With a nervous hand, he reached out and touched her between her nostrils. She didn't flinch. One of her sleeping hatchlings stretched, squawked, and rolled over in her grasp.

Thank you, Rasi projected the thought. He needed to say it whether she could hear him or not.

She lifted her head, looked away, and then rested it back on the dirt out of his reach.

Rasi stepped back. He bowed and said goodbye as best he could. His mind rushed to what the hylock had said about Alina being in danger. After a final glance over his shoulder, Rasi sprinted into the woods toward his parents' farm. He didn't slow until he broke from the tree line.

His father held court on the porch in front of at least twenty local men holding swords and axes and shields. Rasi knew a search party when he saw one. While Donis shouted them into a nervous frenzy, Rasi's mother looked toward the woods. She grabbed Donis's shoulder and pointed. The townspeople followed her gesture. Criya climbed from the porch and started into the field.

She shouted as she neared, "By the gods, are you hurt?" When she reached him, she wrapped her arms around him, saying nothing about the stink.

After hugging her back, he pulled away and took her hand. Together, they walked to the waiting crowd. Donis smiled from the porch. The crowd parted so he could join his father.

No one said a word until Donis broke the silence. "You smell horrible, boy."

He wasn't lying. Rasi embraced his father.

"I'm glad to see you safe, son."

Rasi lifted Donis's rusty sword and looked it over. Then he gave his father a scowl.

"What? I can still swing a sword if I need to."

Rasi nodded with an eye roll.

Donis jabbed Rasi's ribs. "I could still give you a beatin'."

Someone from the crowd shouted, "Good to see you back, Rasi. I've gotta get back to my fields." The others offered similar goodbyes until they had all dispersed.

Donis looked Rasi over again. "I guess I should ask: is this the kind of thing we should expect more often with you home?"

Rasi shook his head. He pointed to his own chest and then walked his fingers toward the road.

His mother deflated. "You can't leave again. You just got home."

Rasi hated to hurt her again. With her sad eyes on his back, he walked to the well and cleaned himself and his straps. As much as he wanted to spend the day with his family and talk to Annie one more time, Alina was in danger and he hadn't a moment to spare. It was a long trip to Thasula. He only hoped he wouldn't get there too late.

After dumping a final bucket of well water over his head, he dried himself with an old horse blanket and retrieved Shadow from the barn. His mother and father stood arm in arm on the porch.

Rasi left Shadow long enough to put on some fresh clothes and retrieve a coin bag—another gift from the kingdom—and his sword from his room. He hugged his mother and then pried her arms from around him. His father shook his hand and said, "I'll always be proud of you, son. Be safe."

Climbing onto his horse, he had a strange and sickening feeling that he wouldn't see his parents again, so he whispered a prayer that his instincts were wrong. As he rode past, he watched his mother's heart break and remembered the same look on her face when he had first left to serve the kingdom before the Heathen War. No son should put his mother through what he had, and here he was doing it for a second time.

He waved goodbye. His mother sobbed and his father turned away.

CHAPTER 12

CAPTAIN TATE

In the months since Captain Tate had retired from Epertase's military, he had been working for a Thasula blacksmith. Business was good. Everyone who could swing a sword seemed to want one. The Tek invasion had unsettled a lot of families, and the men and boys craved new weaponry for protection from possible future threats. Tate was never one to pass up an opportunity to make money.

He didn't miss soldiering, though he missed the regular pay. But the blacksmith business was strong, and he was a hard enough worker to make a comfortable living.

Earlier in the day, the owner of the shop had left for a fair in Tiffin to display his latest swords, knives, armor, and such in hopes of keeping up the demand for his fine work. With the owner away, Tate had the time he needed to complete a favor for his newest lady friend. With his thick gloves and a set of pinchers, he removed a rod of glowing orange steel from the fire and eyed it closely. All it needed was his talents and his hammer.

His lady friend's father had been using an ugly wooden peg for his leg after a Tek projectile blew it off beneath the knee. Tate was tasked with coming up with something more durable and refined, which his lady friend insisted would do wonders for her father's state of mind. As with all artists—and make no mistake, an artist with steel and flame was what Tate was becoming—he saw the final product long before he picked up his hammer. He couldn't wait to see the look on her face when he delivered the beautiful gift to her father. Their proud family crest etched into the steel would be the icing on the cake. And then he planned to ask her to marry him.

He rested the glowing end of the steel on his anvil and lifted his hammer above his head. He hesitated before delivering the blow. As Tate had always told himself, all good things eventually came to an end, and he sensed something had gone afoul before the bell even jingled above the shop door.

Without looking over his shoulder, he announced, "I have no more time for business today. Come back tomorrow." He brought his hammer down on the glowing end of his future father-in-law's future leg.

A man approached from behind; he saw him in the reflection of a hanging shield that had yet to be painted. The man cleared his throat. Tate lowered the hammer to his side and turned toward the intruder. "I said come …" He trailed off at the sight of eight Epertasian soldiers standing between him and the only exit. Tate didn't need experience as a soldier to know their blocking his escape wasn't by chance.

"What can I do for you fellas? Is the queen's army in search of new equipment?" He tightened his grip on his hammer.

"No, no, no, Tate," their leader said as he stepped forward. "We are simply here to talk with you. I am Cap—"

Tate interrupted, "I know who you are, Pierce. You worked under Captain Jarrah's command during the war. I see you've been promoted. Congratulations. But as I said before, I am quite busy."

"We don't mean to interfere with business, Tate. We only need a moment of your time." Pierce fiddled with a couple of hanging swords. He pulled one of them partially out of the sheath, examined the blade, and then slid it back. "Nice work."

"Thank you. Now, I don't mean to be rude, but would you please get to your reasons for being here?"

Pierce circled him with slow, deliberate steps. "Captain Jarrah asked me to pay you a visit. He wondered where your loyalties rested and if there was any room for debate."

"My loyalties rest where they always have and always will—with our queen and no other."

"Tsk, tsk, tsk. I had hoped you would say differently." The other soldiers crowded around him.

Pierce rubbed the hilt of his sword, a quiet threat that was not lost on Tate. He knew an assassination when he saw one.

"What are you up to, Pierce?" His stare narrowed. "Mutiny, maybe?"

Pierce smirked. "Hmph. Something like that." He nodded toward the man behind Tate.

Tate swung his hammer with a grunt and it connected with Pierce's jaw. The bone-shattering crack was loud enough to tell the others he meant business. Pierce dropped like a stricken bird.

The other soldiers rushed Tate. He grabbed a red-hot poker from the forge and drove it sizzling into one soldier's gut. Another soldier swung his sword. Tate ducked, grabbed an unfinished sword from the ground, and plunged the blunted point through the man's heart. He backed away until his foot met Pierce's limp arm. Pierce groaned and started to stir. Tate gave him a heel to his already shattered jaw.

Tate spun to face another attack, but he was too slow. The last thing he saw before his head went stupid was a sword hilt coming at him. He tried shaking away the fuzz, but he was already on the floor. His hand touched his forehead. Blood. Pierce lay motionless beside him and Tate took a morsel of delight in knowing the difficulty the captain would have in chewing his food for the foreseeable future. Tate lifted his chin in defiance. The battle was over—he knew it, they knew it. He had given his all, but it wasn't enough.

Another blade drove down toward his neck.

CHAPTER 13

HONEYMOON'S END

O n the outskirts of the northern town of Tiffin, the mercenary Willum worked tirelessly building a home for him and his new bride. After the Tek War, he and his teammate, Gillian, had hit it off and fallen in love. They had spent most of their payment for their mission against the Teks on a wedding and some land where he now worked to complete their dream home. When finished his house would be two stories, making it only the fourth two-story home he had ever been in. Usually, such luxury was reserved for more affluent people, but Queen Alina was very generous in her gratitude.

Only two neighbors lived within reasonable riding distance, and if not for their charitable help he would never complete his construction.

The suns were blindingly bright, though the air so close to the ocean was bitterly cold that time of year. The men raised the third two-story frame wall with the help of their oxen and secured it to the other two walls with hemp rope. Willum was pleased with their work. If all went well, the fourth wall would be erected by dusk.

His neighbor to the west was a husky fellow and as friendly as they came. Willum couldn't imagine a person had ever walked past

Franklin without receiving at least a "hello" and more likely a genuinely concerned "How is your day?" Franklin and his wife, Margaret, who was also on the rotund side and always wore her hair in a messy bun on top of her head, had been the first to welcome Willum and his new bride when they arrived. After seeing the newlyweds sleeping in a tent near the construction site, Margaret had immediately welcomed them into her home where they had been staying since.

Willum pressed his shoulder against the fourth wall. "Are you ready?" he asked.

Franklin waved from his position behind the oxen.

The other man, Sage, who was older and crotchety until you got to know him, grunted that he was ready as well. Sage had a condition that made his eyelids droop, giving the impression he was constantly drunk, though he never touched anything stronger than tornment juice. He picked up a wooden stay pole as tall as two levels.

Willum picked up another one and together they stuffed the two stay poles into notches at the top of the fourth frame wall.

After getting a nod from Sage, Franklin whipped the twin oxen with a leather strap, and they plodded forward. The two ropes that trailed the oxen and passed through the opposite frame wall went taut. The wall slid along the ground until the bottom met the base between the two side walls. Sage and Willum hoisted as the oxen strained. They pushed their stay poles with all their might. The top of the wall lifted and then butted against the rest of the frame.

"Hold tight while I brace it," Willum shouted to his friends.

Once the four walls were temporarily secured with hemp rope, the three men stood and admired their work. Willum squinted, tilted his head, and asked, "Do you think it's straight? It looks a little crooked to me."

Sage also squinted. He was gruff and a bit of a mumbler. He slurred, "It'sfine."

Franklin closed one eye, tilted his head, and studied the wall. Then he agreed.

The men worked securing the four walls by hammering wooden pegs into pre-milled holes. Then they removed the rope ties. Willum was secretly surprised the entire structure didn't collapse. With all four walls pegged together and standing on their own, the three men backed away and gazed at the first real sign that a house would one day stand before them.

Willum reached over and squeezed Franklin's shoulder. "Another good day of work, wouldn't you say?"

"That it has been, my friend."

Franklin looked out over the countryside. "You know, Willum? If I could do it all over, I'd have snatched up this spot for my own house. I didn't think I'd like being atop such a tall hill, but standing here now, I think I would enjoy the scenery."

"Well, you can come stay with us any time you'd like."

Gillian reached the top of the hill, the other men's wives behind her. She was winded and carried a pitcher along with a concerned expression.

"What's the matter?" Franklin asked.

In between breaths, she answered, "I don't think we accounted for …"—pant—"… how much work …"—gasp—"… it would be to climb this hill onaregularbasis." She sucked in two more breaths.

Willum chuckled.

Franklin jabbed him with his elbow. "Wanna trade houses?"

Gillian's eyes brightened slightly, and Willum quickly reigned her in. "Don't even think about it. We will do just fine up here. Our horses will do most of the work."

Gillian squinted as she looked at the framework. "Is it crooked?" she asked.

Franklin snapped, "It's fine."

Margaret carried three glasses. At the top of the hill, she nearly tossed them to the ground to put her hands on her knees. "This hill is fixin' to kill me." Beads of sweat peppered her forehead.

Sage's wife, Sally, was the last one up. She didn't appear as winded, but her furrowed brow revealed she wasn't happy about the climb. She wiped the sweat from her face with a handkerchief. "I'm not doing that very often," she said.

Gillian turned to the house. "It looks marvelous, don't you think?"

Willum smiled a little wider.

Sally said, "It looks great." She took another winded breath. "Though it's probably the last time I'll see it up close."

Willum half-smiled, wondering if she was kidding. Like Sage, she could be a bit gruff. When she didn't smile back, he decided she probably wasn't kidding.

The three men finished off the pitcher of water while Gillian squeezed between two studs and stood in what would become the living room of her first house. "I'm going to raise so many babies in this house," she shouted.

Sage's droopy eyes widened slightly. "You 'ear that, Willum? You'd be'er run now afore it's too late." Sally smacked his shoulder. Willum wondered how she had even understood him. He only caught every other word at best whenever Sage spoke and had to piece the sentences together just to make sense of them.

Willum shook his head. "To be quite honest, I'm rather looking forward to raising a family."

Franklin side-eyed Sage.

Willum caught their look. "I don't care what you two think. Our children are going to be model kids."

Everyone but he and Gillian had a good laugh. Willum didn't get the joke.

Gillian danced her way over to them. With a sly grin, she said, "The house seems quite breezy inside. Are you sure you know what you're doing?"

Willum grabbed her hand and pulled her in. His head nestled against her bosom. It was one of the few perks of being short. "It's not finished yet, silly."

She giggled.

Margaret asked, "With snow coming soon, will you be able to finish? It can be pretty heavy in these parts."

Franklin answered for him. "You needn't worry about us. We are skilled at what we do, and a little snow won't affect us too terribly much once the roof's on."

Sage grunted his approval.

Margaret rolled her eyes to the other women. She'd heard her share of boasting over the years. "Anyway, dinner's ready whenever you boys are."

"We're ready now," Franklin answered. They gathered their tools and headed back to his house for their evening meal.

As she had every night since they'd arrived, Gillian thanked Franklin and his wife for their hospitality. And once again Franklin assured them it was no trouble at all.

The group finished their meal, remarked how quickly morning would come, and said their goodnights. Sage and his wife headed for home while Gillian and Willum ducked into the guest room for some newlywed fun.

Willum felt like he had slept for days when Gillian violently shook him awake. Even in the dim moonlight, he could see the panic in her eyes. Like a trained soldier, he bounced from the bed.

"What is it?" he asked, rubbing the crusty sleep from his eyes. He already held his sword.

Gillian was next to him, throwing on her clothes and securing her sword belt around her hips. She tied her hair back with string. She hadn't worn her hair up since the battle with the Teks, which left little doubt in Willum's mind of her intentions.

"Someone is up by our house," she whispered. "I went out to the pisser and saw shadows running along the hilltop."

Willum sighed. "Gillian, is that all? It's probably Sage's kids. You know how they like to sneak out at night."

"No," she snapped.

Willum tugged his pants over his hips.

A flickering light through the open window caught his eye. Gillian ran over for a better look. "By the gods," she whispered with her hand over her mouth.

Willum peered past her side. The blood rushed to his face. His hard work, his new house, his future, burned with flames kissing the sky.

He shoved Gillian aside and climbed through the window. She followed him as he raced up the hill, cursing under his breath the whole way. At the top of the path, he stopped and stared in anguish. His hard work and money was on its way to becoming ash. Gillian touched his shoulder.

He lowered his head. "I will kill whoever did this if it's the last thing I do." A shadow darted across his wife's face, lit by the flickering flames. He spun toward the fire.

A woman with dragon-red hair stepped around the corner of the house. She stood nearly as tall as two men and was thin, like Eldon, leaving little doubt she was Gildonese.

"Who are you?" he shouted, his sword already extended. He struggled to catch his breath from the quick climb.

"I am Josilyn," she said, sounding rather delighted he'd asked. "You will one day know me as one of your queens. Well, that is, if you still draw breath when the time comes."

"What is it that you want, woman? Besides a fight, which you're going to get for what you've done here today."

"I have been sent by my master, King Fice, to prove my worth and, in doing so, eliminate any potential threats that may one day show their ugly faces." She paused to sneer and then added, "And by the looks of you two, I'm in the right place." She picked playfully at her teeth as if she had recently finished a meal. Then she put her hands on her cocked hips. She appeared bored. "Take your time catching your breath. I'll wait." She looked at Gillian and shook her head. "You two really should work on your wind."

Willum stood up straight. "No need. I'm good." Though he should have been terrified to face a Gildonese, he was more pissed than anything else.

She stepped toward him.

Like a good warrior, Gillian flanked her on the left, sword in hand. Josilyn followed her with her eyes, though never turning away from Willum. The scorching air turned thick with anticipation.

Willum lunged forward and then just as quickly retreated. On cue, Gillian swung her sword. Josilyn seemed to barely move, yet Gillian grunted and tumbled backward into the grass, rubbing her sternum.

Willum pounced again, this time not stopping. Josilyn twirled seemingly in slow motion, somehow striking Willum's ear with the butt of her sword hilt before he could land a single blow. He crashed to his stomach. Blood trickled into his ear canal.

Josilyn leaped into the air with the grace of a dancer. Though she moved like an elegant slug, Willum found himself unable to move from her path quickly enough to avoid her attack. She landed with one foot on his gut and the other on his chest. The air puked from his lungs as several of his ribs snapped loud enough for Sage to hear from his home.

Gillian attacked again, but Josilyn disarmed her effortlessly with an elbow-popping yank. Gillian pulled her dislocated arm away with a muffled whimper. It was the first time Willum saw concern in her face.

Willum rolled to his hands and knees, wincing as he tried to breathe through the excruciating pain seizing his chest. Josilyn's cold fingernails sank deep into the fatty tissue of his back. She hoisted him from the ground and tossed him through the air.

He landed with a thud and nearly rolled down the hill. His broken ribs squeezed his lungs with every move. He lifted his head in time to see Gillian's bloody face as she collided with him.

She moaned, barely conscious. Willum struggled to get up. Josilyn approached with the swagger of an unbeatable warrior. She drew back her arm and swung her open hand. Again, Willum couldn't move from her path. Her fingernails sent streaks of fire across his face, the impact spinning him back toward the dirt.

Before hitting the ground, he braced himself. It was his last chance, pain be damned. He bit his lip, bounced from the ground, made a fist, and took his shot. She didn't appear ready for him. He had her.

But somehow, even though he was sure he had caught her off guard, his fist never connected. Her sluggish hand struck his throat. His fist whiffed by her head, the momentum sending him to his knees. He clutched his windpipe. Even if his lungs could expand, he couldn't get air to them.

He looked up to glare into her dark eyes; it was important for him to see her when she took his head. She reached down and cupped his chin with one hand while grabbing the top of his head with her other. He had broken enough necks in the Heathen War to know what came next.

He waited to hear the snap of his own neck, but instead she pulled away and caught an arrow with her left hand. Another arrow whizzed at her from the opposite direction and she caught it with her right. A third arrow in as many heartbeats struck its mark, plowing into her shoulder. Willum fell to his rear, still clutching his throat. Josilyn howled, and he couldn't tell if it was from pain or anger or whether it even mattered.

He felt woozy. If he didn't get air soon, the darkness would still come. After a few more agonizing tries, his windpipe finally allowed wonderful air into his tight chest. He swiveled his head around to see who had come to the rescue. Sage was advancing from the east while Franklin advanced from the west. They nocked two more arrows and released them.

Josilyn dove toward the arrows, snatching both from the air and snapping them in half before somersaulting back to her feet. Instead of going on the offensive, she stood her ground.

Willum inhaled another smoke-filled but wonderful breath.

Sage and Franklin launched more simultaneous attacks. They were relentless. Josilyn backed away, catching Franklin's arrow, but missing Sage's. It landed true in her thigh. She howled again and retreated with a hiss.

Willum crawled to Gillian's motionless body. He lifted her head into his arms. She was still alive, thank the gods. Sage and Franklin raced up the hill to them. Despite the arrow poking from her thigh, Josilyn disappeared with blazing speed over the opposite side of the hill.

"Who was that?" Franklin asked.

Willum shook his head. With a raspy, damaged voice he said, "I don't know …" He paused, painfully swallowed, and then added,

"But it may not be safe for you here anymore." Sage helped him to his feet. Franklin cradled Gillian in his arms, and they struggled down the hill.

CHAPTER 14

TREACHERY

Alina surveyed the courtyard from a third-floor castle window. Her Elite Guard used their shields to hold back enraged protesters at the gates. Chants of, "Tell the truth," accompanied the waving of signs painted with angry messages aimed at her. One of the signs even called her a murderer. How could it have gotten so bad so quickly? Her heart hurt to see her people so upset and angry. That she was the object of their ire made no sense.

While she watched more of her Elite Guard pour into the courtyard, James returned from gathering some of her top captains in the war room. "They're ready for you, Your Majesty," he said.

"I'll be right there."

"Very well."

"James, has Levi returned from his furlough?"

"I'm afraid not. With the conditions deteriorating so quickly in the city, we might need to consider that he won't be able to return for some time."

She had figured as much.

"If there's nothing else, Your Majesty."

She shook her head and excused him with a wave.

She sadly watched the growing crowd for a few more minutes. Small columns of smoke lifted from different areas of Thasula and she wondered what was burning. She hoped no one would get hurt. Rocks thrown by the crowd peppered the soldiers' shields.

Having seen all she could bear, she made her way to the war room. As she passed through the foyer, Simcane came through the main entrance.

She hurried to him. "Sim, it's so good to have you back."

He gave her a solemn look. "It's getting bad out there, Alina."

"I know. Come with me to the war room. We need to plan a way to ease the unrest."

Per her orders, footmen and maids scurried around gathering paintings and other valuables to be stored in the vaults in case the castle was overrun. They stopped and bowed when they saw her. She addressed them. "Friends, let me know when everything is secured and then take your leave. Go be with your families and stay safe." They whispered encouragement and then went back to their chores.

Already sitting at the table in the war room were Jarrah, Andon, and Masera. Masera stood up when she entered. "Your Majesty? What's going on out there?"

"I don't know. I think the Lowland Gildonese might have a hand in the unrest."

Simcane stood behind her like a towering bodyguard. "I've just passed through the streets. The rioting doesn't appear to involve the majority of the people. It seems only a handful of troublemakers are whipping everyone else into a frenzy. We can squash this uprising if we act fast."

"Squash?" she asked.

"Your Majesty, quick and violent is the best way to tamp down an insurgency."

"No, Sim. That's not something I could ever do to my people."

"Most of your people hide in their homes, waiting for your protection. We can stop this now."

"Please, Sim. Be seated with the others. There's more that you don't yet know."

Simcane took the seat next to Masera's.

Alina leaned on the table. "My friends, it looks like King Fice has overtaken parts of Lithia, including the capital city. I fear many Epertasians are heeding Fice's words here as well, and I fear soon Thasula will also be lost." She looked to Simcane. "I understand your passion, but I will not hurt my own people, especially if their thoughts have been unnaturally manipulated." She turned to address Jarrah, but before she spoke, the door was flung open.

Atticus stood in the doorway with a middle-aged woman and a young man. "Your Majesty, I bring information."

She gestured him forward. "By all means."

Atticus nodded to his fellow captains and Simcane and then stepped forward. "This is Dillon and his mother, Chloe. I believe they may be able to shed some light on Fice and his cancerous control."

Dillon and Chloe knelt with their heads bowed.

Alina gestured for them to rise. "I'm pleased to make your acquaintance. I am Queen Alina. Would you like refreshments?"

Dillon shook his head and mumbled a polite, "No, Your Majesty." Chloe declined also.

With a tender voice, Alina said, "Please, tell us what you know." She took her seat at the head of the table. Atticus sat next to Andon.

Dillon was timid when he began, "Your Majesty, we come from Recitar, or the Lowlands, as you know it. Your fine commander Atticus saved me from one of King Fice's prisons during the Tek War and we have lived in Lithia since the Great Flood. We've watched as Lithia descended into the same madness that gripped the Lowlands."

Alina interrupted, "If you lived in the Lowlands, how were you able to avoid his influence for so long?"

Chloe answered, "My father once told me that our family is not as susceptible as others to what he called Fice's mental sway. There used to be more of us, but Fice executed or imprisoned anyone discovered to have a free mind. As the generations have passed, families like mine have become nearly extinct. I believe that will be his goal for Lithia and Epertase."

"What can you tell us about Fice?"

Dillon answered this time. "I've never seen him personally, but I can tell you that he's hundreds of years old at least. He and his pack are said to be legendary warriors. But something about what's happening here doesn't make sense. I don't see how he could overtake Epertasian territories so quickly."

"But my people would not behave in such ways if not for his influence."

"But influence and complete sway are two different levels of control. We've seen both in Lithia. Those who don't fall under his sway can sometimes be influenced with a push combined with a strong suggestion."

"You think that's what's happening here?"

"Yes, Your Majesty."

"So, what is he telling my people to turn them against me?"

Dillon looked increasingly uncomfortable. "I've heard the words, but I dare not say."

"I will not hold you responsible for the message you convey, my friend."

"Fice says you, with your lover's help, killed your own father to take control of Epertase."

"I've heard that one already. What else?"

"He says you worked with King Logan of Lithia to destroy his army and use the Tek invasion to your advantage."

"That's ridiculous," she huffed. "Where's the evidence to convince my people of such nonsense?"

"Fice needs no evidence," Chloe said. "Once doubt creeps in, the people are his to toy with."

Alina shook her head. "There must be more than that."

"I'm sorry, Your Majesty. As I said, the hint of doubt is all that Fice needs. His lies are like weeds. A little water and they overtake the field."

Masera shook his head. "There's no way Fice could cause all this trouble on his own. I refuse to believe he is that powerful. He would have tried this years ago if it was that easy. Maybe he could corrupt a town over a generation, but not all of Lithia. Not Thasula. Not this fast. Your people are not weak, Your Majesty."

Alina rubbed her forehead before speaking again. "Have you heard anything else about King Logan or Queen Lona?"

Dillon answered, "The rumor is that they're alive and in hiding. King Fice is actively seeking them and has offered a reward for their heads."

Simcane pushed against the table and stood up. "Alina," he said, forgetting formalities. "I must travel to Lithia. If Logan and Lona are alive, I have a duty to find them."

Alina nodded. "I understand completely."

"I can't leave you unless I'm assured you are safe, though."

"I'll be fine, Sim. I have plenty of people to look out for me." Her eyes found each of her protectors in the room.

Simcane turned to Atticus. "If this situation deteriorates, you'll see the queen to safety?"

"Of course."

Simcane glared at Jarrah and then addressed Masera. "You and Atticus are the only ones here I trust."

Masera put his hand on Simcane's shoulder. "She will be fine."

Simcane turned back to Alina. "I'm sorry, Alina, but I need to go to them. I owe them."

She nodded. "Be safe, my friend."

Alina watched Simcane leave. In his exuberance, he nearly ripped the handle from the door. She studied her men. For some reason, Andon seemed withdrawn, staring at his lap and picking randomly at the underside of the table. Something didn't feel right.

She asked Dillon to describe life under Fice's rule. Once he finished explaining how he was taken from his school before the war, Alina dismissed him and his mother with her sincere thanks.

When she turned her attention back to the men, Alina noticed Atticus whispering across the table to Andon, but she couldn't hear what he said. Andon looked away without answering.

"Is all well, Andon?" she asked.

"Everything's fine, Your Majesty."

Servants entered, placing drinks in front of everyone. A moment after they left, another servant pushed open the door.

"Your Majesty," he shouted, face pale and tight.

Atticus bounded to his feet.

"What is it?" Alina asked.

"Come quickly. Something's happened in the kitchen."

Atticus shot for the door. "You stay here. I'll go."

Alina nodded. She had something else to tell her most loyal men before the meeting ended. She felt as though she was abandoning them, but it was crucial that she heeded the words of The Elder Three.

Masera took a sip from his glass, wiped his mouth with his sleeve, and watched Alina as she paced along the front of the room. "What's troubling you, Your Majesty?"

"I'm afraid I have to leave for a while. I can't say why, and I can't say where I'm going, but you must trust me. I wouldn't leave if it wasn't absolutely necessary." She licked her dry lips and retrieved a cup of berry juice from the table. "Please know that I'm not abandoning you." She lifted the cup to her mouth.

Atticus burst through the door from the hall. "Alina, don't drink that."

She stared for a moment and then looked back to her cup before setting it on the table. "What is it?"

Somebody shouted from the hallway, "In the war room."

Atticus slammed the door shut behind him and jammed the locking rod across it. Like an experienced soldier, Masera sprang to his feet for a coming fight. He staggered into his chair, grabbed it for balance, and then he and the chair hit the floor. Atticus ran to Alina and swatted her cup from the table as he passed it. "The cooks are dead."

Her face blanched. "What?"

The doors rattled.

Atticus shoved Alina behind him and turned to Jarrah, who still sat at the table. Guilt painted his solemn face.

"It's Jarrah's man, Pierce," Atticus said.

Jarrah sighed and then stood up and drew his sword.

The door rattled again with a violent collision.

Atticus whispered, "We have to flee, Alina. From here on out, we can trust no one."

Jarrah moved to block their escape through the servant's entrance at the rear of the room.

Atticus pointed at Andon. "Remove Jarrah so I can get the queen to safety."

The door jolted again as something rammed it.

Andon sat as if frozen, continuing to stare at his lap. "I'm so sorry, Your Majesty," he whispered.

Alina cried, "Andon, not you, too."

He couldn't look at her when he said, "I've lost trust in you. I've chosen to follow another."

Atticus glared at them. "You're traitors. Both of you."

Alina choked on rising tears. "Andon, I don't understand. How have I wronged you?"

Jarrah answered, "You've wronged everyone. Where were you while I searched for my brother-in-law? You never even looked for him. You didn't care. Tevin searched for you when he thought Rasi held you captive, yet you left his body buried in the rubble of Shadows Peak, just waiting for scavengers to pick away at his flesh. I was forced to use my own men to search for him."

"Jarrah, I mourned the loss of Tevin. I sent compensation to your sister and excused your men for the entirety of the search."

"You supported the criminal Rasi more than you did your father's best friend."

Her knees went weak. "That's not true. And you fought alongside Rasi. You've seen the person he is. He saved Epertase."

"We don't know that. We never had a chance to try your father's plan."

"It was flawed, Jarrah. Surely you can see that."

The double doors shook again on their hinges.

Alina looked to Masera on the floor. Thankfully, his chest still rose and fell.

Jarrah said, "I've come across more information since the war. I don't believe your lies anymore. I know how Elijah died. And I know that Rasi was there for it." Jarrah stepped toward her. "I don't want to hurt you. Just do as we say."

Atticus shuffled between Alina and Jarrah with one eye still on Andon. "Take another step and I'll take your head, Jarrah."

Behind Jarrah the servant's door quietly opened. James crept into the room with a silver pitcher raised over his head.

Atticus kept talking. "We can work this out, Jarrah."

"It's too late for that. Open the main doors."

Andon rose, walked to the door, and slid open the lock. The room filled with a half-dozen soldiers led by Pierce, whose swollen head was swathed in bandages. When Pierce noticed James across the room, his eyes went wide. He pointed frantically and grunted through his locked teeth.

Before Jarrah could turn, James bashed his head with the pitcher. Jarrah dropped to his knees, but the blow didn't knock him out as intended. He grabbed the back of his head with a wince.

Atticus shouted, "Run, Alina," and shoved her toward James. He followed.

Jarrah dove for her feet, but Atticus kicked him in the face. James led the way through the servant's entrance. The Epertasian soldiers gave chase around the table. Atticus stopped at the door and faced them with his sword draped defensively across his chest.

Alina turned back while James tried to pull her hand. "Atticus, what are you doing?"

The soldiers hesitated. "We don't want to hurt you, Commander," one of them said.

"Well, you're gonna have to if you want past."

"Atticus," Alina shouted again.

Atticus glanced over his shoulder. "Get out of here, Alina." With his focus momentarily on her, two soldiers tackled him out of the way. Andon sprinted into the hall.

"Go, Alina," James cried. Alina started running. James pressed himself against the wall, but when Andon passed him he stuck out his foot. Andon hit the ground.

Alina closed the door to the servant's quarters behind her and ran through another door into a back hallway. *Left to the front or right to the stables?* She turned right.

Andon blasted through the door behind her. His momentum carried him to the carpet. She tried to flee, but he swatted her foot, knocking her down.

"Alina," he said, his voice not the confident voice of her friend. She rolled to her back and scooted away from his reach. He scrambled to his knees. He whispered, "I'm so sorry. They promised not to hurt you. They said they only needed you tucked away for a while."

"And you believed them? Andon, why are you doing this? You were one of my most loyal captains. You and your brother."

"It was Rasi's war plan that got Dru killed."

"You're wrong. A lot of people died. That's what happens in war. I mourn Dru every day."

"But you lied to us."

"No, I didn't."

"You did. You chose that criminal Rasi over your own father."

"I did not, Andon. You must believe me. There is a lot you don't know—nobody knows—but you have to trust me."

Andon stood up and turned his back to her. He lowered his head. "Just go before it's too late."

Alina stood up. "Come with me, Andon."

"I can't. There's more to this than what you've seen. Just go."

Alina hesitated. "What do you mean?"

"Go. I can't help you if they see you."

Someone shouted, "Andon?"

"Be quiet," he shouted back. "I'm trying to hear which way she went." With a frown matching his sad eyes, he whispered over his shoulder, "I'm sorry."

Alina turned and ran toward the stables.

He shouted, "She went to the front."

She rounded a corner and was out of sight when she heard Andon and the guards give chase in the opposite direction. She ducked into another hallway that led outside to the stables where Allusia was kept.

She was careful not to draw attention as she exited the castle, though the grounds were unusually empty. To get to the stables meant crossing more open terrain than she was comfortable with, but she had no choice. No doubt Jarrah's men would soon swarm the entire grounds.

A shabby wool horse blanket lay discarded in the dirt and she tossed it over her head and shoulders like a peasant. She started across the openness. The stable was within sight when a man's voice shouted from behind, "Hey, you."

She froze.

"Why are you out here?" the voice asked, slightly closer than before.

Alina turned, careful to keep the blanket hanging far enough over her brow to obscure part of her face in shadow. "Good sir, I am just …" She paused. "Aidric?" she asked.

"Your Majesty?"

"By the gods. Aidric." She pushed the blanket away from her face. "Please tell me you're not with them."

"With whom, Alina? What's going on?"

"Jarrah and men loyal to him are turning the people against me—against us." She wanted to hug her friend, but wasn't sure she could trust anyone anymore.

"Traitors? Jarrah?" His forehead wrinkled. "I was coming to your meeting, but I was delayed. Do you realize what's happening in Thasula? It's madness. I was lucky to get here at all."

"I know, Aidric. King Fice of the Lowlands has been working to bring about the fall of Thasula and, I fear, all of Epertase."

"Where are the rest of your captains? Where's Masera?"

"They've got him. Atticus too."

"What about Andon?"

"He can't be trusted either."

"Andon? That's not possible."

"It may not seem possible, but it is so. He's with them now. I don't know how Fice got to him, but he did. We have to run. I need to get to Allusia."

"Alina, you can't ride a horse out of here. Jarrah's men are everywhere. I saw Pierce when I was riding in. You must hide until nightfall. That's your only chance. The stables would be your best bet."

She wondered how Aidric had gotten past Jarrah's men to even reach her. She worried they might have let him through because he was part of their treachery. *No,* she told herself. She had to trust him; she had no other choice. "Yes. The stables." She ran to the horse pens and he trailed behind, still limping from wounds sustained in the Tek War.

With Allusia so near, Alina considered grabbing her reins and riding through Jarrah's men, forcing them to make their choice, but such an aggressive strategy would not likely end well.

Aidric motioned for her to stay low. "Hide here until dark. I'll see what I can learn and come back for you. If I don't return before the moon is high, you must find your own way from here."

She nodded. He had always been her friend and had not shown her any reason to doubt him. She knelt beside hay bales stacked against the wall, draped the blanket over her head, and whispered, "I'm trusting you, Aidric. Please don't prove me wrong."

"I'm with you till my death, Your Majesty."

She believed him, maybe because of the sincerity in his eyes. As she tried to get comfortable, someone outside the stable shouted, "Hey."

Aidric stepped away. "What can I do for the three of you?" he asked.

"Who are you?" the approaching voice asked.

"I'm Captain Aidric. You know, one of your superiors?"

"Right now we only answer to Captain Jarrah. What are you doing here?"

"I'm here for the meeting. I was simply stabling my horse."

"The meeting's been cancelled. We're in search of the queen. We fear her life's in jeopardy."

Please, Aidric. Please.

"Then we must find her. I've been here in the stables for quite some time and can assure you no one has been out here but me and the horses."

"Just the same, we need to search the area."

Unimaginable panic twisted Alina's gut. Her hands shook. The footsteps went in different directions as they started their search. One set came to within a horse-length before continuing past. The soldier giving the orders said, "Sir, you need to come with us."

"Of course," Aidric answered.

As the soldier escorted Aidric toward the castle, he turned back and yelled to the two men still searching the stable. "Check behind that hay and then meet me at the front of the castle."

Alina felt the blood rush from her face. Her heart pounded in her chest. She lay frozen as the footsteps closed in. Aidric shouted, "I'm telling you no one's there." Then he added, "Aw, shit."

He knocked his escort down and ran toward the one nearest Alina. "Run, Alina," he shouted as he tackled the man.

She flung the blanket from her back. As Aidric wrestled with the soldier, she grabbed a horseshoe from a crate and ran along the stable wall.

"Get her," the soldier wrestling with Aidric shouted.

Aidric shoved his face into a pile of horseshit.

The two other soldiers gave chase. One gained ground fast and grabbed her dress from behind. She spun away from his grasp and whacked him across his forehead with the horseshoe. He dropped like an anvil from a roof.

Without time to get to Allusia, she ran toward the northern wall. The other chasing soldier screamed to the guard in the tower, "Close the gate." Alina hurled the horseshoe behind her. In the luckiest throw of her life, the iron slammed his knee, sending him writhing to the dirt.

She looked to the gate.

The soldier shouted, "Thomas, close the gates." They began to close.

She looked up to her one-time friend who had allowed her passage to visit Rasi in the mountains many times. *Thomas,* she said in his mind. *Please.*

He held his hand close to his chest and gave her a slight wave. The gates halted just enough for her to squeeze through before closing altogether.

Thank you, Thomas.

You're welcome, Your Majesty. Good luck and be safe.

She ran along the fence between the castle walls and the Great Plains toward the town. Once there, she melded with the crowd of protestors before slipping into an alley and out of sight.

CHAPTER 15

STRIKE BACK

uards escorted Atticus and Masera from the castle toward the prison on the outer edge of town. Though Atticus didn't recognize three of his escorts, the fourth one he did. That guard was a young, handsome, dark-haired soldier named Christopher with whom Atticus had spoken on a few occasions. The kid was always cordial and soft-spoken and obviously bright.

Waiting beyond the fence were seven wagons modified with iron bars instead of canvas tops. Each of them was filled almost to overflowing with bound prisoners, all of whom were Epertasian soldiers. Atticus recognized a lot of them.

Christopher nudged his way closer. "Sir?" he whispered, and looked around to make sure he wasn't heard by the other three guards. Atticus lifted his eyes while keeping his head bowed.

"I'd like to help you," the kid whispered.

Atticus held his bound hands out from his back just enough for Christopher to catch the hint. If the kid truly wanted to help, there was an easy way to prove it. Like a good actor, Christopher crowded against Atticus's back as if he'd stumbled.

"Move faster, bastard," Christopher ordered.

The leather strap around Atticus's wrists loosened and tickled his calf before falling to the ground. Before backing away, Christopher slipped the dagger he had used to cut Atticus's restraints into Atticus's palm. Hidden within the group of prisoners, Atticus calmly and quietly sawed through Masera's restraints.

With both Atticus's and Masera's hands free, Atticus caught Christopher's attention with a bob of his head and a pointed look. If they had any chance of pulling off an escape, it was then, before the guards at the wagons could see. Atticus picked up a rock from the ground and mouthed, "One … Two … Three." Masera took one guard to the ground. Hard. At the same time, Christopher struck another guard's skull with the hilt of his sword. Atticus bashed the third and final guard's head with his rock.

After they freed the other bound soldiers in their group, Atticus collected the leather restraints. "What's the plan now?" one of the men asked.

Atticus pointed to the waiting wagons. He turned to his new friend. "Christopher, you've risked a lot to help us. When Alina is restored to power, I'll see to it that you're rewarded handsomely."

"I don't want rewards. Just tell me what you need me to do to help."

Atticus smiled. Masera patted Christopher's back.

All eyes of the freed soldiers fell on Atticus. "Are you with me?" he asked.

To a man, they nodded.

"Let's go free our friends."

By Masera's count, there were eight guards leading the wagons with two of them heading up the rear. "We'll take the two in the back. Christopher, you're now in charge of these men. Take out the rest of them. Try not to kill anyone if you don't have to. Remember, they were your allies just a few days ago." Atticus handed out the leather restraints.

He and Masera sneaked to the rear of the convoy, using the shops along the road as cover. Carefully, they approached the two soldiers at the rear. From behind, Atticus choked one of them unconscious while Masera bashed another in the temple with the dagger hilt. Atticus held his finger to his mouth to warn the prisoners.

Christopher and the others continued to the wagons. After a brief fight, the remaining guards were in restraints and the wagons halted. Using keys lifted from the guards, the men freed the prisoners.

After heartfelt pledges of allegiance to Alina, the men were all ears. Atticus addressed them. "We must build a counter-insurgence. But we'll need soldiers—a lot of them."

Christopher raised his hand like he was in school.

"Yes?"

"The prison. Jarrah has ordered a roundup of anyone loyal to the queen and is having them taken there."

"Perfect. That's where we'll go." Atticus looked to the wagons and an idea started to form. "You were all prisoners just a few seconds ago. Who's up for pretending to be prisoners for a bit longer?"

A smile cracked Masera's cheeks. "Atticus, if you don't need me for this mission, I can promise much of my Elite Guard are still loyal. I can gather those who I trust."

"That'd be perfect."

The freed prisoners reloaded the wagons, only this time they hid smiles instead of dread.

Masera approached Atticus. "Where will we meet?"

"Alina told me of a farm east of the Warehouse District where she recovered after her ordeal with Scorne and the symbiots. She said the couple there were sympathetic to the kingdom. We may be able to use their generosity and acreage to train for our mission. She said the owner's name is Homer."

"Ahh," Masera said with a bob of his head. "I know just where that is. Alina had me send oxen and gold to the old couple after she returned."

He turned to Christopher. "I'm putting you in charge of freeing the prison." Christopher happily accepted. Atticus mapped out the route to Homer's farm and then the men went their separate ways.

CHAPTER 16

ON THE RUN

The people swarming Thasula's main drag seemed content with Jarrah's men patrolling the street, which was further evidence that they were only coming out against Alina and not what they felt was the new authority. The soldiers' thick presence forced Alina to hide in a rubbish pile behind a local establishment. Rancid meat somewhere in the pile made her question her choice of cover, but as bad as it smelled, it kept the soldiers from searching too close. She was cold and tired and afraid.

As night approached, the soldiers carried their search farther out and the number of patrols thinned near the castle. Even the protestors grew bored and returned to their homes. Everyone except those with the dead eyes, who continued wandering aimlessly. She'd never dreamed there could be so many people already under Fice's spell.

After quietly shedding her trash cover, she crept from shop to shop, careful to keep hidden from any soldiers or overly curious vagrants. When she noticed two soldiers sharing a weed stick on the corner, she ducked between a shoe store and a jewelry shop.

Movement from inside the window of the jewelry shop startled her. She was caught. A man stood inside watching with his hands on the shoulders of a young child.

Hello? she said in his mind.

He gave a subtle wave.

Are you staying safe? she asked.

He nodded. He leaned his forehead against the window to look toward the rear of his store. He looked back. *My queen? Do you need to come in and hide?*

She sighed, relieved that he wasn't going to alert the guards. *No, my friend. Thank you so much for the offer, but I need to get away from Thasula as quickly as I can.*

I understand. He stared at her for a moment more before his eyes lit up and he held up a finger as he backed away. *Wait for a second.* He disappeared while his little boy continued to stare at her with the prettiest ocean-blue eyes. Alina tapped the glass playfully by his face, but he didn't respond. There was nothing behind his beautiful eyes. For the thousandth time that night, her heart broke.

The man returned. He opened the window enough to fit his hand through. "Something to eat," he whispered.

She took a bundle of jerky from him. "Thank you," she whispered and looked around to make sure no one heard.

Then he handed her a full waterskin. "If you're going to be hiding, you're going to get thirsty."

She was humbled by his generosity. "Good sir, you're what makes Epertase great."

"Just be careful, Your Majesty. If I had a sword and knew how to use it, I'd come with you."

She waved her hand. "No, no, kind sir. You have this little one to care for." She hesitated. "May I ask a question?"

"Anything."

"How long has your son had the stare?"

He looked down and gently brushed his child's cheek. The boy didn't react. The man frowned. "For a few moons now."

"I'm so sorry. Please know I'm doing everything I can to help. Steel yourself for a long struggle. It may turn worse for a while."

"I have faith in you."

"And I have faith in you." Alina looked up and down the narrow alley and then backed away. "Stay strong, friend."

He patted his chest twice with his fist.

The smoking guards were gone, so she continued along the boarded-up storefronts. By the time the suns had risen in the morning, she was near the northeastern edge of Thasula. She looked back one last time. Her once-vibrant city had never been so desolate and cold. She whispered, "I'm sorry," and left the city behind.

Keeping off the roads was her best option. At least until she got farther away from Thasula. An empty field seemed as good a place as any to start. Though the field took her out into the open, she could see quite far in every direction, which would give her time to hide in the tall grass if someone happened along.

Her long walk through the field gave her time to gather her thoughts. She still couldn't believe Jarrah and Andon had turned on her. Fice's mind control was the only possible answer. She chewed a piece of the jerky and rationed her water with tiny sips. All she knew about Puimia was that it was east and very far.

Puimia brought back thoughts of Rasi, though he was never very far from them anyway. For the rest of the day, she worried herself sick over whether the Elder Three's grim predictions about his fate were true. She prayed with everything she had that he had escaped the burning veins of which they spoke, and that she would find him plowing a field somewhere, oblivious to the chaos in Thasula. In addition to hoping he was safe because she loved him, she also hoped he was safe because she was convinced he was the only man alive who could help her make things right in her kingdom. As powerful as Fice was, she had yet to meet any man who was in Rasi's league. At least, that's what she told herself to push her sore feet forward. It might turn out to be wishful thinking, but without some morsel of hope, she might as well sit in the field and wait for the buzzards.

By evening, the muscles in her thighs and calves ached and begged for rest, but she had no intentions of slowing for more than a few minutes. She eventually reached a dirt road in the middle of nowhere. Judging by the sunset, the road led east, which was perfect for her journey. As she walked, she occasionally encountered a rider going to or coming from Thasula, and she'd bow her head while avoiding eye contact. Though they mostly ignored her, occasionally the men would tip their hats, or the women would say a pleasant, "Hello."

As the day neared its end, the cool breeze combined with her fatigue to make her a bit complacent. A covered wagon approached from behind while she was lost in contemplation of what to do once she found Rasi.

The couple riding the wagon broke her thoughts. "Miss?" the man called out.

She briefly locked eyes with him and quickly looked away. Did they get a good look at her? She cursed her own sloppiness. The horse-drawn wagon slowed.

"Miss?" the man called out again.

She hurried her pace, hoping he'd leave her be.

"Excuse me? Miss?" he asked again.

She waved politely without looking toward him.

His female companion spoke. "Honey, do you need a ride?" Her voice was sweet and friendly.

Alina lifted her chin to better see them. The woman, a pleasantly plump lady with gray hair, many wrinkles, and twinkling eyes clasped her hands together in front of her mouth and uttered a surprised "oh." She looked to her husband and then back to Alina. "Your Majesty?" she whispered.

The man looked like he could handle himself with his thick, powerful arms and the rough, leathery face of someone who had spent a lifetime in the suns. Dull, black stains surrounding his bushy, black-as-night mustache revealed his poor attempt at appearing young. His friendly eyes invited more of her trust than she was comfortable in giving. His voice was deep and welcoming. "My goodness. Your Majesty, what are you doing out here in the cold?"

"I need to make my way to Puimia."

"Puimia? That's quite a journey." He looked east as though he might see it from there. "Especially on foot."

The lady gathered a rolled blanket from beside her and climbed down from her seat. She unrolled the blanket and threw it over

Alina's shoulders, embraced her, and escorted her to the back of the wagon. "You look famished."

The man leaned from his bench. "We'll take you as far as you need to go," he said.

The woman helped her into the back of the wagon next to a burlap bag of grain and various farming tools. Alina looked into her kind eyes and asked her name.

"Vasha," she answered. "My husband's name is Orin. Let me fetch you a sandwich." She dug through a basket until she retrieved a grape jam sandwich. It tasted wonderful. Alina realized she hadn't eaten a jam sandwich since she was a child and made a mental note to have them more often once things returned to normal.

Orin shouted back, "Puimia, here we come."

Vasha made a pillow out of another blanket and set it behind her. "You have bags beneath your eyes, dear. You should get some rest. We will get you to Puimia."

Alina looked around. Along with the grain and tools there were several bags of clothing and trinkets. "Where are you two going?"

"Anywhere but Thasula. The soldiers burned down our home. This was all we could save."

Alina gasped. "I'm so sorry. Why did they do such a thing?"

"My husband refused them shelter. They said they were looking for you. We want nothing to do with what they're doing to Epertase. Now, do not worry about us, Your Majesty. You just get some rest." She climbed down from the rear, pulled the canvas closed, and went back to sit with her husband. The wagon jerked to a slow start.

Alina closed her eyes and fell asleep.

CHAPTER 17
A LESSON IN FAILURE

It had been a couple of weeks since Captain Pierce had failed to apprehend Alina in the castle. Frustrated, Jarrah had ordered him to lead a group of fifty Epertasian soldiers into the heart of Lithia's capital city to update King Fice on their progress in Thasula. He got the sense Jarrah was nervous to do it himself.

When Pierce first arrived, he was taken aback by the destitution of the once thriving city and wondered if Epertase's fate would be similar. But those worries were quickly replaced by Jarrah's promise of giving him Tiffin when all was finished. Life might not always be good for everyone, but as long as it was good for him, no one else much mattered.

Pierce neared the castle walls, his mending jaw—his souvenir from Tate's hammer—aching deep into his brain with each bump of his steed's gait. The Lith guards at the gates stared with empty eyes and did nothing to stop his progress through. They either didn't care or knew Pierce was expected.

A single Lith soldier approached, his eyes not as empty as the others. He ordered Pierce to leave his men in the courtyard and continue alone through the main entrance. Pierce was shocked to find the entrance devoid of any furniture or paintings or anything that suggested someone had ever lived there. The only indication anyone had been there at all were hand-painted words scrawled along the wall that read, "Die, Tek demons. There is nothing for you here." Pierce smirked at the irony of Alina's victory against the Teks ultimately leading to her own fall.

He waited in the entryway as ordered. He stood for three hours before a Gildonese descended the stairs to greet him. Pierce was stunned by his size. He'd never seen a Gildonese before, and what approached was unlike anything he'd ever imagined. The Gildonese had almost glided to the bottom before Pierce realized he was even moving. Pierce's eyes traced the Gildonese's lanky physique from his feet to his head. Though normally a confident soldier, he had to consciously tell his hands to stop shaking.

The Gildonese smirked. "You must be Pierce. I am Ulrac, second in command to King Fice, and I have been sent to escort you to our master."

Pierce reached for his sword belt with the intention of removing it from his waist. "I assume you want me disarmed?" he mumbled through clenched teeth. Every attempt at speaking was agony.

Ulrac laughed loudly and grabbed his gut. "You think a Gildonese would fear a young pissant such as yourself?" He almost couldn't contain himself long enough to finish his thoughts. "Here," he said, tossing his own sword to the ground. "Take mine if you'd like." His voice cracked from the hilarity of the thought.

Pierce felt the blood rushing to his face.

Ulrac turned his back to him as a further sign of disrespect and then led him up the stairs. Toward the middle of the long hallway beyond was a door that Ulrac motioned for him to enter. Pierce turned the knob with plenty of trepidation and stepped inside. Ulrac ducked through behind him and stood towering at his back.

"Great King Fice," Ulrac said as he nudged Pierce farther into the room.

Fice rose from a chair at a desk by the opposite wall. He wore King Logan's royal robe, which barely reached past his waist and had sleeves that stopped at his elbows. His wrists were hidden from view by seemingly every gold bracelet from there to Thasula, and his neck strained under an equal number of necklaces. If the Gildonese king weren't so imposing with his height and powerful aura, he would appear ridiculous.

Ulrac continued his mocking. "Oh great one, this is Pierce from Epertase, and he has come as scheduled to meet with you. I would be glad to leave the two of you alone, however, Pierce fears he may be too grave a threat to you, so maybe I should stay near."

King Fice didn't react to the sarcasm as he leaned his head to the side. "Thank you, Ulrac, but I believe I am quite capable of protecting myself even if this Epertasian has ulterior motives and wishes to bring me harm." He looked curiously at Pierce. "You don't, do you?"

Pierce wilted under his glare. "No," he tried to answer, but more air than sound came out. He swallowed hard and tried again. "No, sir. Never."

Ulrac snickered and said, "Very well, my king." He slipped through the doorway, pulling it closed behind him.

Fice scooted the desk chair to Pierce with one swift push of his foot. "Have a seat," he said.

Pierce hesitated.

Fice scowled. The whites of his eyes blackened, and he inhaled a deep breath. His voice lifted. "Have a seat. This will take a while if I must tell you everything more than once."

Startled, Pierce plopped down on the floor.

Fice sighed. "In the chair, you fool."

Pierce scrambled to the chair, almost knocking it over.

"You are indeed a fool, aren't you?"

Pierce didn't want to answer, but something made him bob his head like an idiot.

Suddenly standing beside him, Fice said, "You bring news, I suspect?"

Pierce couldn't nod his head fast enough.

"Well, speak."

"Your Excellence," he began. Even the smallest movements of his mouth caused his jaw to throb.

"King Fice the Great will be fine."

"I'm so sorry, King Fice the Great.

Fice rolled his hand in an annoyed, get-on-with-it sort of way. "Why do you talk through your teeth?"

"My jaw was recently broken."

"By a horse kick, I hope."

"Actually, I was struck by a blacksmith's hammer."

"Ugh." Fice dropped his shoulders. "And you are the one sent to speak with me? I hope there are no hammers nearby to cause you nightmares."

It didn't matter that Pierce could hear the disdain in Fice's voice because he could neither defend himself nor would he want to try. "Thank you for the concern," he answered.

Fice's palm met his forehead. "I should like to kill you, you feeble, stupid little man. You would be wise to say your piece now before my generosity wears thin and I am unable to keep my hands from bathing in your blood."

Pierce swallowed hard. "Of course, Great Fice King … I mean, King Fice the Great.

Fice rubbed his temples.

"The Epertasian revolt is proceeding as planned. With Alina out of power, Captains Jarrah and Andon have taken majority control of the Epertasian army."

"Finally, you have given yourself value. That is very good news. Speaking of the queen, what has become of her and her lover, the warrior called Rasi? Have they been eliminated?"

"Not exactly. The queen has escaped and Rasi's execution has not yet been confirmed, but we are actively seeking resolutions in both of those matters. I assure you they will be found. But if by some miracle of the gods they are not, we don't believe they will be much of a threat to the new kingdom."

Fice lowered his head and shook it in obvious disappointment. "And just like that, you have lost what little value you had previously gained. I grow weary of you."

Pierce sat quietly, afraid to speak again until addressed.

Fice slowly circled the room. Finally, he broke the painful silence. "Come with me, for I want to show you something I feel you will appreciate."

Pierce was terrified to go with him, but he was more terrified to refuse. He stood up on shaky legs. Fice ducked out of the room and he followed.

They walked down the stairs with Fice skipping three at a time. He led Pierce through the front doors. One of Pierce's soldiers watched from the edge of the courtyard, awaiting his next command. Without looking at him, Fice ordered Pierce to keep the Epertasian soldiers where they were. Pierce waved his hand at the soldier, telling him to stand down.

Fice and Pierce walked along the deserted street past a candy shop. "Do you like candy?" Fice asked.

Pierce nodded.

"I figured you might. You are very simpleminded."

Any citizens who happened within sight of Fice quickly knelt and pressed their foreheads to the ground until the king passed. Fice led Pierce to a schoolhouse-turned-prison. There didn't appear to be any locks on the doors or windows, yet no one tried to leave. As they reached the bottom step of the porch, the door opened and a Lith "sheriff" stepped out. He wore a childish paper badge pinned to his shirt. A middle-aged man whose hands were bound behind his back stood behind him. The prisoner was filthy, bruised, and wore the look of a man with a working brain. He stared at the ground.

Fice ordered him to his knees and shouted, "This man has been charged with treason in the eyes of the new rule of this country now known as Recitar." The man shook his head in disbelief, though he didn't dare speak. Fice continued as a small crowd gathered. "We allowed this man—this leader of revolutions—to escape when we first came to the country formerly known as Lithia, and because of our failure, he was able to infiltrate our military, where he induced several other men to believe his lies. Luckily for us, my wisdom and intelligence far exceed this former soldier's and I was able to catch him before he had an opportunity to spread his infection."

Fice slid his sword from its sheath. The man sobbed, but still didn't look up. Fice approached him. The Lith sheriff yanked the man's head backward so he was forced to look into Fice's eyes. The man pleaded his innocence and pledged allegiance to his new king and cried for his life.

But Pierce knew Fice had brought him to that place for a lesson and there would be no mercy granted. Though he pitied the man on his knees, he was happy it wasn't himself. Fice exhaled a deep breath and swung his sword like lightning. The man's throat opened at his Adam's apple. His face blanched and he made a gurgling sound as blood sprayed from his neck. Fice stared heartlessly until the man flopped to the dirt.

Pierce turned away.

Fice asked, "Do you now see the importance in capturing potential rebels before they can infect others with their promises of a different future?"

Pierce nodded, though he was barely able to hear Fice's voice over the drowning gasps of the poor man dying in the dirt beside him. Fice wiped his blade on Pierce's shirt sleeve, sheathed it, and then walked back toward the castle. He glanced back over his shoulder. "You are dismissed and may leave. Your soldiers, however, will be joining Recitar's army now."

Pierce took a final glance at the dying man and wondered if the story of his crimes were even true. Either way, he understood Fice's message.

CHAPTER 18

FISHERS

As Rasi made the long journey west, he repeatedly caught whiffs of a distinct sulfur smell. He soon realized he was being tracked. He thought it may be hylocks, but the smell was all wrong. The tension in his straps beneath his cloak told him that they, too, realized they weren't alone in their travel. He urged them to stay calm until he could figure out the hunters' endgame.

They did as he asked. Reluctantly.

The traffic on the long road to Thasula seemed thinner than what he would normally expect, even with winter coming. As the suns settled in the north, he approached the first signs of life in several miles—a covered wagon traveling east. Though the older couple hardly appeared threatening, he placed his hand on his sword just in case. The bushy-mustached man nodded as they passed. Rasi nodded respectfully back and continued on his way.

He hadn't slept much since starting for Thasula and the rhythmic bounce of Shadow's steady gait caused his eyelids to droop and his head to bob. As hard as he fought, he realized he wouldn't make the rest of the journey without some sleep.

By nightfall he had pressed Shadow as far as his steed could go without rest. He scanned his surroundings for a place to sleep. To the north, the moonlight shone down on an overgrown wheat field.

Though the field appeared unattended, its presence meant someone lived nearby, or had at one time. If they had a wheat field, they probably had a barn where he could hide for a few hours. He left the road. His path took him to a worn-out fence with missing posts and pickets. The fence bore an old wooden sign with the words "Keep Out" painted on its face, the *t* partially obscured by a rot hole. Rasi dismounted and led Shadow into the overgrown farm.

A tiny, dilapidated house stood in the distance next to an even more rundown barn peppered with holes and leaning as if it were about to topple over. He pressed his palms to his aching eyelids in hopes of keeping them open for just a bit longer. As he moved from the wheat field into the high grass of the front yard, he came across a piece of flat wood sticking up from the ground like a grave marker. Carved on its face was one word: "Wife." He reached the front of the house and tied Shadow to a wobbly porch post.

Before he reached the door, an awful but familiar stench burned his nostrils. He had smelled decaying flesh enough times to know what waited for him inside. He pulled his cloak across his nose and mouth and climbed onto the creaky porch.

The front door barely clung to its rusty hinges and he peered through the gap between it and the frame. He knocked, careful not to dislodge the door, just in case someone still lived there. As expected, no one answered. He lightly pushed on the door and it fell from its frame. A cloud of dust and stink enveloped him, and he waved his hand in front of his face.

A squank scurried across the graying wood of the floor where weeds grew between the boards, some reaching as high as his knees. A painting of an old horse standing with a plain, thin woman sat on the floor, propped against the far wall as though it had fallen some time ago. There was no furniture in the one-room home other than an overturned chair in the farthest corner with two of its legs missing.

It was next to that overturned chair that he saw the source of the smell. The decomposing body of an old man lay on the floor. Chunks of his bloated face were missing, chewed away by some hungry critter like the squank that had greeted him at the door. Maggots filled his eye sockets and crawled from his mouth.

Rasi stood over the body, saddened. *You had a long life, old-timer. Sorry it had to end with no one around.*

Rasi considered resting before giving the old man a proper ending, but he knew in his heart that leaving the man, even for another moment, wasn't the right thing to do. The man's spirit had probably been watching the decaying of his own mortal self for long enough, and he shouldn't have to watch any longer.

Rasi lowered his cloak from his nose and got to work. He grabbed under the man's arms while his straps wrapped around the man's body and heaved. The man's arm popped out of the socket and nearly pulled free. Rasi paused, letting his straps readjust their grips to relieve the tension on the man's arms, and then pulled him out the door to the front porch.

Once there, Rasi looked around for a proper way to dispose of the body. Though he really wanted to bury him next to the grave marker, he was too exhausted and too short on time to struggle with the cold, hard ground. Instead, he turned to the barn. He went to Shadow and dug some japsy weed from his saddlebag. With the help of his straps, he dragged the man through the weeds and wild grass and into the barn. After a look around at the many hay bales, he nodded. *This will do fine.*

Though the roof was riddled with holes and much of the barn's contents were wet and moldy, Rasi found enough dry hay beneath an overhang to cover the man. Rubbing his japsy weed, he lit the hay in seconds.

Rasi backed away from the entrance and watched the flames take hold. The barn filled with smoke and heat. As it burned, he said a silent prayer that the man would now be reunited with whoever waited for him on the other side. "Wife," he supposed. Soon, the intense flames forced him away from the barn and he returned to the house. He went to the wall opposite the main door, pressed his back and squirming straps against it, and plopped to his rear.

Just stay awake for a little lon... And then he slept.

A horrible screech from the tin roof interrupted his slumber. He sprang to his feet with his sword in hand, his bleary eyes fixed on the underside of the roof. He didn't know how long he had slept, but he felt refreshed.

More screeches started at the front of the house, moved up to the peak of the roof, and then down the back, as if claws raked the tin. The air was hazy with smoke from the smoldering barn and thick with sulfur stink.

Something thumped onto the porch and Rasi twirled toward the sound. Rather than wait to be surrounded, he raced through the open doorway to surprise whoever was stalking him. Shadow neighed and danced and pulled at his tie-down.

Kneeling at the edge of the porch was a creature similar in size and shape to the hylocks that had attacked him at his parents' farm, yet different in appearance. It was hunchbacked with exposed vertebrae that stood like tiny fingers from its spine. Unlike the hylocks, it didn't have wings and its pale flesh looked almost human in tone rather than greenish. Its dull orange eyes sat closer together like a man's, but they moved independently of each other. It bowed its head timidly. Rasi hesitated, waiting for the beast to attack. His straps guarded his back. He wasn't going to make that mistake again.

The creature sniffed the air and then spoke with a whine much like the hylocks. "Lord Raaasiiieee," it whispered as it cowered from him with its hand defensively in front of its face. It had two sharp, talon-like fingers and a bone jutting from its palm that was concave like a pointy scoop. The scoop part told Rasi exactly what the creature was: a fisher from beyond the Bluefields of Sorrow in the volcanic region. And it was lethal.

Rasi tightened his grip on his sword hilt. As a soldier, he had been ordered to kill fishers on sight if ever he met one, though there hadn't been a single report of the creatures in the kingdom for many a century.

Rasi snarled.

The fisher retreated a step. "You come with uuusss," it hissed.

Worse than being killed by a fisher were the rumors of what they did if they took you with them. Rasi shook his head.

A hate-filled scowl exploded across the fisher's face, replacing its previously docile demeanor. "Yes," it shouted, and lunged. Rasi stumbled back with his sword out. His straps grabbed the doorframe, preventing his fall. The fisher stopped short. A closer look at its orange eyes revealed a dull film coating them. In his training he'd been taught that fishers couldn't see well.

And he'd also been taught that they didn't hunt alone.

A second fisher dropped next to the porch. Rasi's straps lifted to the underside of the roof. He darted his eyes back and forth, cautious of being surrounded.

The fisher before him sniffed the air and backed away again. "You come with uuussss."

Rasi shook his head again, prepared for the coming fight. His eyes—and likely his life—depended on it. But instead of attacking, the fisher kept backing away while licking its lips.

"You will live with uuusss forever," the fisher said as the other one joined it.

Rasi waited. *Don't show your hand,* he told himself. *There will be plenty of time when the fighting starts.* He glanced to Shadow, who nervously danced and chewed at his tie-down. *I'm coming, boy. Hold tight.*

The fisher tilted its head back, opened its mouth wide enough that its jaw dislocated, and released an ear-piercing screech that sounded like the call of a crow, only constant and several pitches too high. At the edge of the property, near the broken-down fence, another thirty or forty fishers emerged.

By the gods. These two were just scouts.

Rasi stepped toward Shadow, his eyes locked on the coming horde. The two fishers at the bottom of the porch tracked the sound of his movements. Their heads slouched below their shoulders like cautious wolves watching their prey. Rasi took another step toward Shadow. The fishers didn't attack. Though Rasi tried to stay focused, his mind repeatedly returned to his lessons. They needed human eyes, he remembered. Taking eyes while their prey still lived allowed them temporary sight. But just as troubling, the fishers believed taking eyes after their victims were dead allowed them to see in the afterworld as well. For the first time since the war, Rasi felt the sting of fear in his gut.

Shadow had best be rested or Rasi would soon be in a fight he couldn't win. He slowly sheathed his sword, careful not to make any sudden movements.

The two fishers jerked their heads up and down in unison while making clicking noises in their throats. They didn't advance even as Rasi calmed Shadow with a gentle caress, untied him, and climbed onto the saddle. The horde approaching from the fence line dropped to all fours and galloped through the high wheat.

Rasi spun Shadow around, grunted, and with a kick of his heels and a whip of his reins sent him into a full gallop. The fishers cut through the field to give chase. They were fast, unbelievably so, but they were no match for a horse, and Rasi and Shadow soon pulled away. Shadow hurtled the broken fence without breaking stride. Though Rasi missed Salient, having a young stallion had its benefits.

Once Rasi thought the fishers were far enough behind that they couldn't catch him, he slowed Shadow and focused on calming his own nerves. Between the hylocks and the fishers, the already dangerous world had just gotten impossible.

CHAPTER 19

ADDISON

Alina startled herself awake and for a moment wondered where she was. The bounce of the wagon quickly reminded her. She parted the canvas at the front where she found the older couple's heads bent forward and bobbing in unison with the cart's movements.

"Good evening, friends," she whispered, startling the couple awake.

Orin snapped to and pretended he hadn't been asleep.

"Good evening, Your Majesty."

"How long have I slept?"

He answered softly, "Quite a while. We made a couple of short stops to let the horses rest, but you never even stirred."

Vasha nudged him with her elbow and said, "Along with a little closed eye for you, don't forget."

"Well, maybe a wink or two. Are you hungry, Your Majesty?"

She nodded. Vasha squeezed past her into the back while Orin kept the horses moving. Alina joined Vasha as the older lady dug through a bag of supplies and removed a partial loaf of bread. She cut slices for a sandwich for Alina and one for Orin. She passed Orin's sandwich to him and then asked Alina if she'd mind riding with him while she took a nap. Alina was happy to do so. After a quick stop so they could all relieve themselves behind some bushes, she climbed up beside Orin.

As they rode through the night, Alina told Orin all about Rasi and the war and what was happening at that moment in Thasula. She described Fice and talked about the betrayals. Once she had unburdened herself, the conversation shifted to less unpleasant topics. They talked through the rising of the suns and well into the day. Alina loved hearing his stories about teaching children in a local school and how ornery they could get.

When Vasha woke up, she asked Alina into the back to help her tie her dress.

"You look beautiful," Alina told her, causing her to blush.

"I make dresses. I would be honored if the queen of Epertase were to try one on."

"I'd be delighted."

As Vasha searched through her bags for just the right dress for a queen, the wagon slowed to a stop.

Orin poked his head through the gap in the canvas. "Honey?" he whispered, and nodded for her to look out the rear.

Vasha climbed to the back, peeked out, and then turned to Alina. The color drained from her cheeks. "Soldiers," she whispered, stealing Alina's breath. "What should we do, my queen?"

Alina peeked out. There were at least ten Epertasian soldiers on horseback approaching from quite a distance behind.

Orin climbed from his wooden seat into the back with her and Vasha. He said, "Your Majesty. You must flee before they get closer. They will surely search our wagon."

"Where would I go?"

"There's a field with tall grass beside the road. You can hide there. But you must hurry or they'll see you. If you prefer I try and fight them off, I will, but I don't believe I can win."

"No, no, Orin. I'd never ask that of you."

"I'll do all I can to stall them."

Alina nodded. "I can never thank you enough for what you have done."

"No time, Your Majesty. You must hurry."

Vasha gave her a hug. Alina kissed Orin's cheek and climbed onto the bench beside him. He steered the wagon to the edge of the road where the wheel touched the high grass. "Go," he said.

She climbed down and he followed. She crawled into the tall grass with the back of the wagon as cover. As the soldiers rode closer, Orin pretended to be relieving himself in the grass.

One of the soldiers asked, "What are you doing here?"

Orin cocked his head and gave him a confused look. "What do you think I'm doing with my pecker in my hand?"

"Hey. We don't need that kind of language, sir."

"Well, I just thought it was obvious."

The soldier sat back in his saddle. "Have you seen the queen?"

"The queen?" Orin laughed. "That's an even odder question."

"Just answer the question, sir. You're trying my patience."

Orin continued playing dumb until Alina was too far into the field to hear him any longer. She crawled through the grass to a tall line of brambles similar to what buffered the Lowlands, but not quite as dense. She could make it through if she took it slow. She glanced back to see two of the soldiers climb into the back of Orin's wagon, while the others waited with the couple in front.

A chill washed through her and she rubbed her arms, cursing herself for leaving too quickly to take a blanket. Her breath left her mouth in a cloud that hovered in the air. She shivered. When she parted some of the grass to go farther, she startled a nest of pheasants. With wide eyes, she turned back toward the road.

The soldiers were looking her way.

Orin screamed, "Ruuun," before something muffled his voice.

The soldiers mounted their horses and leaped into the field. She turned back to the dead-end. There was no easy way to start, so she summoned a deep breath, mentally prepared for the coming pain, and climbed gingerly into the brambles.

Her dress ripped and her skin opened to the thorns. Though the wounds were shallow, they were many and painful. She wrapped the fabric of her dress tighter against the bleeding trails along her arms. She couldn't imagine how the soldiers would follow while on horseback. If she made it through quickly, it would be her only chance to outrun them.

Mosquitoes buzzed near her ears and gnats gathered around her face, crawling across her lips and into her fresh wounds. They tickled her nostrils, and when she accidentally opened her mouth to catch her breath, they stuck to her tongue. She spat them out.

The soldiers reached the brambles behind her. They were close enough she could hear them arguing about whether they should follow. One of them answered, "Do you want to tell Jarrah you had the queen and lost her because you didn't want to get a scratch?"

His answer was a sword snapping twigs and branches. At least she had gotten a good start.

She couldn't tell which direction she was going. If not for the constant cursing of her pursuers, she might have circled right back to them.

Step by miserable step, she made it through what seemed to be the thickest part of the brambles. She saw the end of her pain in the form of another grassy field, which drove her to push harder. With one last thorn digging into the meat of her thigh, she leaped for freedom. The mosquito bites on her arms itched something fierce, but she knew digging at them would make them worse.

She ducked into the tall grass, thankful the soldiers hadn't brought dogs on their hunt. By the time the soldiers emerged from the brambles, she had crossed enough ground to stay hidden within the grass. They grumbled and complained as they swept through the tall grass until one of them, probably their commander, wised up and snapped, "Shut your mouths. She can hear you idiots."

The setting suns gave her even more cover, and soon the moon replaced them. For a moment, she wondered if she would ever find her way to Puimia even if she escaped the soldiers. Despite exhaustion and worry over what the stress was doing to the baby boy in her womb, she pushed forward. She told herself the two of them would get through it. Her family had always been fighters, and her baby's father was the strongest fighter of all.

With the moon not giving much light, she wondered if she was about to crawl off a cliff. The soldiers drifted away from her trail before closing in again. No matter how fast she crawled or how much blood her knees left in the dirt, she couldn't shake them.

Occasionally, she lifted her eyes above the grass just enough to get her bearings in the moonlight. When she did it for the tenth time, she saw something in the distance. It was a strange, white-tinted glow rising from the ground like a dome. The color wasn't right for a fire. And it was too small for a town, not that she'd ever seen such light from a town anyway. Whatever the strange glow was, it offered her a sliver of hope.

She had a decision to make. The glow was far enough away that she wouldn't make it by dawn if she continued to crawl, and the sunrise would surely give her away. But if she took her shot and ran while it was still dark, maybe she could make it. It wasn't such a hard decision after all. She breathed in deep to prepare her lungs. She whispered, "It's just you and me, son. Be strong." Then she sprang to her feet. There was just enough light from the moon that she could see the soldier's silhouettes bobbing in the field. She sprinted toward the white light.

They didn't see her at first, which gave her a great head start. But eventually one of the soldiers shouted, "There she is."

The chase was on.

Each running stride took her closer to her salvation. Even if the glow was nothing, it was everything to her now. As she drew closer, she noticed a fence surrounded the field of brightness. It was more than three men high and flawlessly white, appearing as clean as if it had been painted the day before. She had no idea how she would breach it, but figured she'd deal with that when she got there. A glance over her shoulder at her pursuers gave her hope that she could make it. As she got closer, she saw hand-painted signs spaced evenly along the fence that read: "Warning. Go no farther or die."

Alina ignored them as she reached the tall pickets. A look between the gaps held her spellbound for a second. The white light wasn't one big glow after all, but hundreds of individual stalks growing from the ground like corn. Each one shone as if hundreds of tiny white fires had been conjured by wizards.

She glanced back; the soldiers were closing in. Her foot wedged perfectly between two pickets. She could climb using the crossbeams holding them together on the other side.

"Don't let her get over that fence," a soldier shouted.

Alina climbed like her life depended on it because it did. Each crossbeam rested just high enough above the previous one for her to reach. It was as if the fence was built specifically for her climb.

By the time she straddled the top of the fence, the soldiers had reached the base. Three of them started climbing. She swung her leg over and started down the other side, meeting them in the middle.

One of the soldiers ripped away a piece of fencing and crammed his arm through, grabbing the front of her torn dress. "I got her," he said as the others continued to climb.

Alina bit his hand hard enough to draw blood and yanked away. She lost her grip and thudded to the dirt. The soldier jammed his hand through the pickets and grabbed for her foot. She kicked him away and rolled to her belly. The first glowing stalk buzzed less than an arm-length away. Curious, she raised her hand toward it.

Before she could touch it, one of the soldiers dropped beside her. His momentum carried him into the glowing stalks. They appeared to grab him and pull him tight against the one she was about to touch. His body shook violently and he let out a shrill cry. His muscles tightened and his arms drew inward against his chest. His fingers curled. His screams turned to grunts as smoke floated from the gaps between his clenched teeth.

Alina scooted away from him. And then the plant released a cracking boom that hurled the soldier's lifeless body against the fence. He hit the ground face up, staring at the moon with death's gaze.

Another soldier landed beside her, but he was careful not to tumble into the plants. "Hi, Queen," he said, and reached for her arm.

Alina dove into a narrow path between two rows of plants. The stalks hummed relentlessly.

The soldier chased her, careful in his intentions but clumsy in his execution. His hand brushed one of the stalks and the plant pulled him in. She didn't wait to see him meet the same quivering, screeching demise as his partner.

She stood up, careful to not touch any of the buzzing plants. Her hair lifted from her shoulders and stood on end as if it had a mind of its own. Every nerve in her body tingled like a feather tickled beneath her skin.

"Come out, Queeny," one of the other soldiers called.

"Come in and get me," she shouted back. She carefully shuffled along the narrow row between the plants.

The soldier continued his taunting. "We can wait you out, Queeny."

"There's nowhere to run," another one shouted.

A man shouted from up ahead, "Get off my land."

One of the soldiers shouted back, "Shut up, mister. This is none of your concern."

Whoosh. Thunk.

Alina had heard enough arrows hit their mark to know what those sounds meant.

The soldier grunted and moaned. She heard the others scrambling to climb back over the fence.

"Hey, mister, stop shooting arrows at us. We're Epertasian sold—"

Whoosh. Thunk.

"Damn it. My leg."

Another soldier shouted, "Retreat."

Whoosh. Thunk. Whoosh. Whoosh.

The soldiers' shouts grew more and more distant.

Distracted, Alina crowded too close to one of the plants and an arch of white light bit her upper arm. She recoiled with a shriek, rubbing away the sting.

"Who is in my field?" the stranger shouted, still out of sight.

"Good sir, it is I, Queen Alina, and I mean you no ill."

"Who?"

"Your queen."

"I have no queen. Show yourself."

"I'm coming, sir, but it's difficult in these strange plants."

"You mean my energy crop? I wouldn't touch anything, if I were you."

Finally, she stepped from the stalks and into a neatly kept circular clearing surrounding a tiny house with more stalks beyond. They were surrounded by them.

The old man climbed from the roof with a bow hanging over his right shoulder. He dropped to the ground with a grunt, turned, and pointed at her with a shaky finger. "What are you doing all the way out here?"

She pulled her tattered dress across her chest and held it together. "There's been a revolt in Thasula. I fled, and this is where my path has taken me."

"Thasula?" he asked.

"You don't know what Thasula is?"

"That depends. Can you eat it?"

"Why, no," she answered, not sure if his naiveté was genuine. "It is only the most majestic city in all of Epertase. Well …," she paused. "Was."

"Then, no."

"May I ask, how long have you been out here, sir?"

"Well that all depends on how old I am. And if you could tell me that, I'd be much obliged. Heh-heh-heh." He grabbed his slightly bloated belly as he chuckled, then turned and mumbled, "Come on in. Cold out here."

Alina hesitated, but then something clicked in her mind. "You must hide where the light grows from the ground," the Elder Three had said. And just that quickly, it all made sense.

She followed the old man through what she assumed was the front door, though the house had no discernible features that would tell a person which was the front or which was the back. The house appeared even smaller from the inside. A quick look told her she was in its only room. To her right next to the door sat a covered bucket with white paint caked on its sides.

The room glowed as bright as day. A small fire crackled in a fireplace on the farthest wall, it's orange flame dim in comparison.

A bed hardly wide enough for one man sat next to the fireplace, taking up the rest of the wall. There was a wash sink next to a knee-high bucket, and she could guess what was in it from the smell. The wall opposite the wash sink had floor-to-ceiling shelving covered with odd gadgets, dried food in jars, and wooden tools.

In the center of the room were a table and two chairs, one of which was covered in dust and webs, but that wasn't what drew her gaze. Atop the table stood a single stick, almost like a candle. The stick held at its point a glass globe which illuminated the entire room with that strange white light.

Alina stared in wonder while creeping closer. "What manner of sorcery is this?" she asked under her breath. She reached her hand out. "May I touch it?"

"Sure," the old man answered as he made his way to the shelving.

Alina touched the globe with her middle finger. "Oh," she gasped, and shoved her finger into her mouth. "It's hot."

"Well, of course it is," the old man said.

"Why did you say I could touch it, then?"

"You touched it, didn't you?" The old man set one of his food jars on the table. "Hungry?" he asked.

"I don't know. Will it burn me?" she said, trying sarcasm on the geezer.

He paused and looked up with a confused expression. "Hmph. Well. I don't know. It doesn't burn me." Then he went about his business.

"Please, may I have a drink of water?" she asked.

He half-heartedly nodded toward the wall to her right. There was a barrel with a crooked top sitting on the floor next to the wash sink opposite the piss bucket. Alina went to it, lifted the lid, and looked for a cup. The man continued examining his shelves, so she decided against asking him for one. Instead, she scooped the water into her cupped hands and slurped it into her dry mouth.

When she finished, she went back to the table. He poured hard, brown flakes from the jar into a pile in front of her and then another pile in front of himself.

"Have a seat," he said.

She brushed the dust and webs from the chair while still clutching her ripped dress together at her chest.

"What is this thing that produces light without a flame?"

He loudly crunched the brown flakes. "It is my light," he said, like it was the most normal thing to say in the world.

"Where did you acquire it?"

He shoved another handful of flakes into his mouth and she wished he would answer before stuffing his cheeks.

He crinkled his forehead and stopped chewing for a moment. "I built it, of course," and with the word "built," he spit crumbs across the table. He didn't apologize. "I build all kinds of stuff. That's what I do."

"And the plants outside? Did you create them?"

With his cheeks bulging with food, he tried to answer. "Are you silly, girl?" He put his open hand to his mouth, spat the rest of his partially chewed food into it, and wiped it onto his pant leg. "They are plants. They … grow … from … the … ground."

Was the old geezer mocking her? "It's just that I've never seen such magic."

He shook his head. Then he got up and went to a shelf. "It isn't magic," he said, putting on a single thick, black glove that appeared three times the proper size. He reached under the table with his gloved hand and ripped away something attached beneath it. His "light" went out. When he held out his fist and opened his fingers, a brilliant glow haloed his hand from a small acorn-sized ball.

"My crops do this. I just gave them a better way to shine."

Alina stared, amazed. She had fifty questions and picked one. "How long have you had these incredible plants?"

"I've seen many winters here and they have been here since."

Alina picked up a single flake, her eyes never leaving the old man. He shoved the ball beneath the table again and the light once more illuminated the room.

She bit down on the chip, which tasted about like she imagined tree bark would taste. "What's your name, sir?"

"My mother called me Addison until she died. It's nice to meet you, Queen." He paused as if confused. "Let me ask you a question. Is that your real name? Queen? Because if it is, it's rather silly."

She chuckled. "No. My name's Alina."

"Then why did you tell me it was Queen?"

Alina ignored his question and tried to chew. "What are these flakes anyway?"

"Tree bark," he answered in a tone that suggested eating such was perfectly normal.

She discreetly emptied her mouth into her cupped hand. "Do you know if any of the soldiers escaped your arrows?"

He pressed his lips together, lifted his eyes toward the ceiling in thought, and then said, "Probably."

"Probably? Sir, they will come back for you. A lot more of them, too."

"Well, I have a lot more arrows."

Alina knew staying was dangerous, but her body was too exhausted to travel. She asked, "May I sleep here for a bit?"

"Of course. I'm rather tired, as well. I like working at night, so sleep would be welcome." He went to his bed, apparently to clear it off.

Alina dragged her weary body to him. "Thank you, sir. I'm quite tired." She reached for the bed sheet.

The old man intercepted her with a folded blanket in hand. "Anywhere on the floor would be fine," he said, and sat on the bed to remove his shoes.

"Oh?" Alina said, slightly stunned. "I suppose we'll be fine." She rubbed her belly for emphasis.

He grinned. "I'm sorry. I didn't realize that you carried a child."

She smiled politely at him. "I understand."

He reached beneath the bed and pulled out another hole-infested blanket. He handed it to her. "Here, sleep on this. It'll be much more comfortable than that hard, old floor."

Alina accepted the blanket, at a loss for words.

Addison rolled over and pulled a sheet over himself. He was snoring within minutes.

Alina spread the blanket near the fire and lay down on it. She didn't know if it was the old man's snoring, the brightness of the room, the hard floor, or the annoying hum of his crops, but, though exhausted, she tossed and turned for hours before finally falling asleep.

When she woke up, she felt refreshed, despite the new nagging ache in her back. Addison was missing. With her blanket wrapped around her shoulders, she went outside. He crouched over a small fire with his back to her. The bitter morning air stung her cheeks.

"Good morning," she called.

Without looking up, he flung his hand in a half-assed wave.

When he finished whatever he was doing, he turned toward her. Speckles of white paint dotted his face and arms and legs. She tried not to laugh.

"Hungry?" he asked.

After the tree bark, she was afraid to admit that she was, in fact, starving. Though her mind said no, her stomach overruled it and she nodded. "Have you been painting?" she asked.

"Actually, yes. How did you know? Were you watching me?"

She didn't have the heart to tell him that he looked like his bucket had exploded.

He went back to his fire and returned with a wooden plate piled high with a steaming mound of cooked eggs. She didn't remember ever being more pleasantly surprised to have eggs. She snatched the plate away. Each bite was heaven. "These are fantastic," she said.

Addison's forehead creased. "What did you expect?" His eyes were puffy, and he yawned.

"How long have you been out here?" she asked.

"A while. Couldn't sleep. Your relentless snoring kept waking me up."

As far as Alina knew, she didn't snore. "I'm ... sorry?"

"And you must have been messing with me because every time I woke up, you stopped."

She wondered how he explained all the other times when she wasn't there and the snoring still woke him. "So, what were you doing all night?"

"The fence won't paint itself."

"I thought it looked nice already."

"Nonsense," he snapped, and she wondered how she could have offended him. "I paint it every fourth moonrise," he added.

"The entire fence?"

"Well, painting only half of it would just be silly, now wouldn't it?"

She thought better of answering.

"Then I had to go get eggs from flightless birds near Allias's farm." He pointed past his crops.

"Flightless bi—Oh. You mean chickens?"

His eyes squinted. "You are weird with your funny names." He looked up to the clouds and rubbed his shoulders. "A storm's coming."

She looked to the clear sky. "How can you tell?"

"My bones hurt."

With her last bite devoured, she was tempted to ask for more.

He took her plate. "Don't even think about asking for seconds. I gave you everything I had left." He disappeared into the house and she followed.

"Addison, I didn't see any horses outside. Do you have one?"

"Why would I have a horse?"

"I don't know. Maybe to go to town?"

"Puimia? Pfft. It's less than a day's walk away."

Her eyes brightened. "Will you take me there?"

"You'd have to walk."

"Yeah, I know."

"I mean, I'm not carrying you."

"I wouldn't expect you to." He was an odd old man. "Could we leave soon?"

"With the storm coming? Not a chance."

"But I'm afraid I need to leave as soon as possible. It's deadly urgent."

"There are much more terrifying things in the world to be afraid of than leaving."

"Then you'll take me?"

"After the storm."

"But there might not even be a storm."

"Are you calling my bones liars?"

"No. I'm just. I mean … Ugh. Forget it." She was getting a headache. "I really must go."

He watched her with the widest, goofiest smile. Then he yawned again and reached to the ceiling. "If you plan to travel, I have something to give you before you go." He went to his shelves and removed a hideous quilted blanket. It was covered in multi-patterned squares with green, black, and gold stripes. "I made this."

No kidding.

He reached into a small pocket near one edge and then removed his hand. He handed her the blanket.

It was warm, unnaturally so, and getting warmer. "What kind of magic is this?"

"Magic? No. I just made a blanket that uses my crop. It should last you the winter."

"Why, thank you, Addison."

"I wouldn't want you to freeze." He looked toward the door. "Well. Goodbye."

Alina opened the door and looked out. She turned back. "Bad storm, then?"

"I'd say yes."

"Maybe I could stay until it passes?"

"If you promise not to snore."

She didn't know how to answer, so she shrugged.

True to his bones, a nasty storm moved in by the afternoon. It was too cold for rain and too warm for snow, but just right for a mixture of both. She stood at the window and watched the crops sizzle beneath the falling sleet. While she'd never admit it to him, she was thankful she wasn't stuck halfway between there and Puimia. "What would you like to talk about to pass the time?" she asked.

Addison turned off his table light and crawled into bed. "No talking. Sleep."

Sleep? Already? It wasn't even evening yet. What was she going to do? He immediately started to snore, which woke him up. "Be quiet over there," he said, rolled over, and farted.

CHAPTER 20

THASULA'S
DARK DAYS

Rasi stared at the capital city of Thasula from atop a grassy hill east of town. It was almost dusk. Dozens of columns of thick, gray smoke billowed from burning homes and businesses throughout different parts of the city. The deserted streets and boarded-up windows resembled a town that had died of the plague more than the bustling, shining star that Thasula had been mere weeks ago. While the streets within the city were mostly empty, the roads leading away were full of townspeople carrying what looked to be all the possessions they could gather in a hurry.

Rasi pulled his hood farther down his forehead to better hide his face in shadow. As he rode toward town, no one he passed spoke or acknowledged him, which was odd. One could usually count on a nod or a wave from a typical Thasulan. Everyone kept their heads bowed. Some of the women and children cried while others kept their eyes to the ground.

When Rasi reached the edge of the city, it wasn't a Thasula he recognized anymore. Small fires smoldered on the sidewalks while trash decorated the streets. A set of eyes peeked from the second floor of a house and then hid behind the curtain when Rasi looked up.

His straps squirmed beneath his cloak. One of them snuck out and crept in front of his face despite his silent demand for it to remain hidden. He considered biting it.

A woman sat on the stoop of a burned-out house with two toddlers next to her. The puffy red rims of her tired eyes told him what she'd been doing.

"I'm hungry, mommy," the little girl said.

"I know, baby." The woman rubbed the girl's back.

Rasi stopped and climbed down from his horse. He slowly walked to her, stopping short so as not to spook her. With his hood pushed slightly back, he warmly smiled. It was important to let her know she wasn't alone. She returned his gesture with the gaze of someone who had seen what evil a man can do.

She looked back to the ground. "I know you, good sir," she whispered. "I've seen paintings of your likeness. Your name is Rasi." She paused for a moment. Then a slight spark lit her eyes when she lifted her head again. "You're here to save us like you did before."

Rasi looked away. Then he looked back and nodded, a small lie to give her comfort. He removed the last of his jerky from his saddle bag, knelt, and cautiously held it out for the little girl. She looked to her mother for approval then snatched the jerky, passed pieces to her brother, and stuffed some in her mouth.

"Why would military men do this to us?" the mother asked.

Military men? Rasi shook his head.

"My husband was a soldier. He fought for you against the Teks. They took him and burned our house."

Rasi looked toward the castle. If the military had done this, where was Alina? He said her name as best he could. "A'ena?"

"The queen? They said this was no longer her kingdom and that you and she are criminals who need to be brought to justice."

How could a great city fall so rapidly? "Where A'ena now?" he asked.

She had to ask him to repeat himself, and then she gave a sad smile. "I'm sorry. I haven't heard. I suspect she's been captured or …"

Rasi didn't need to hear the "or." He reached into a pouch at his waist and set a small stack of gold coins on the lowest step.

Before he drew back his hand, she grabbed it. "Save us, Rasi," she whispered.

He squeezed her hand then gently pulled away. In his mind he whispered, *I can't*. He climbed back onto Shadow, turned, and headed toward the castle. He felt her eyes on his back.

When he reached the business district, he was heartened to see that not everyone had lost their minds. Though flames licked the sky from an old bakery Rasi had bought pastries from many times before his banishment, townsfolk rushed buckets of water to the fire in futile attempts to save the store. Rasi hoped the kind couple who owned it was safe since he didn't see them among the bucket brigade.

Rasi sadly rode past, knowing there was nothing he could do. Seeing Thasula ravaged before his eyes turned his stomach juices into lava, the burn creeping up into his throat.

He tapped his heels lightly against Shadow's sides. The castle gates appeared in the distance. Maybe he could find some answers there. The lair of the Elder Three sat off to the right, seemingly untouched by soldiers or vandals while the buildings on either side of it were either burned or ransacked. He considered going to the wizards for answers, but their final words when he last visited squashed that idea. "Do not come back here uninvited," they had said. "We cannot promise you will survive our second meeting." He didn't care to test their threat.

He tied his horse to a post holding a sign that read in black paint: "No Loitering"

From where he stood, he had a straight view of the main castle gate. It was open. He took a couple of steps before three Epertasian soldiers appeared in the opening. They were too far away to recognize him, so he stood and watched. They escorted a man with his hands bound behind his back and a sack over his head. He limped, struggling to keep up.

A fourth man soon followed. Instead of wearing soldier's fatigues, he wore a full suit of armor; clumsy, bulky, glistening armor that left none of his flesh exposed. A chain trailed him, attached from his wrist to a collar around the neck of a hylock. Who were these people who kept hylocks as pets?

The lead soldier rang a bell as he walked and shouted something, though he was too far for Rasi to hear what he said. The straps fidgeted beneath Rasi's cloak. They were tired of hiding.

Rasi ducked to the side of a flower shop and hurried around back where he found a door. It was locked, but his foot worked as well as a key. A display shelf held three stacked rows of vases full of flowers in various stages of wilting. Rasi reached for the flowers in one of the vases. The petals crumbled and fell away at his lightest touch. He went to the storefront window and hid alongside it where he could see down the road.

The strange procession stopped on the opposite side of the street. Now he could hear what the bell ringer was shouting. "Rejoice, Epertasians, for the snake-tongued queen has fallen. She hides like a dog somewhere in your city. Bring her out for your new king and you will be rewarded greatly. Harbor her longer and you will be hanged."

New king? Rasi quietly watched even as his anger boiled over.

The armored soldier led the hylock along the storefronts, his armor clanking with each step. The hylocks nose strafed the ground. The other soldiers gave it a wide berth.

Clank. Clank. Clank.

Rasi sighed. The racket of someone wearing full armor was as annoying as a mating skree owl early in the morning. Rasi wanted to punch the soldier just for that.

The bell ringer kicked the back of the prisoner's knees and forced him to the ground. He shouted, "Alina. If you're hiding near here, show yourself now or we will kill your friend." He ripped the sack away from his captive's bloody face.

The man wore a patch over his eye. It was Aidric.

The hylock sniffed the ground in a serpentine pattern, leading its handler to the middle of the street where it paused and perked its ears. It lifted its chin high and sniffed the air. Then it turned toward the flower shop. "Raaaasiiieeee," it cried.

Oh shit.

The lead soldier lifted his eyes. "Rasi? That can't be. Where?"

The hylock's nose hit the ground again and it beelined to the front of the flower shop just outside the large display window. Only a wall separated Rasi from it.

Rasi backed through the dark shop, careful to stay out of view. When his straps met the back wall, he ducked behind a display stand. The soldier bashed in the front door before the hylock scurried inside.

Clank. Clank.

Rasi opened his cloak, allowing his straps to slither free. He told them, *Just like when we hunt game. Have your fun.* He peeked around the edge.

The hylock neared, bobbing its head up and down as if excited by the hunt. "Raasiiieee," it said again.

Yep. You found me.

The hylock's leery handler stood at the door and fed more chain from a loop in his hand.

Rasi waited for the perfect moment. Even if it wasn't one of the creatures that had attacked him at his parents' farm, he was happy to get vengeance on the species in general. The hylock paused as though it sensed something.

Rasi breathed deep before springing from the dark. Startled at his gall, the hylock fell backward a step. Rasi's straps grabbed its wrist before it could inflict its venom. The hylock lunged, but its chain went taut, jerking it backward with a grunt. Its handler tried frantically to unfasten the chain from his wrist, but the hylock's constant movement kept yanking his arm away each time he fumbled with the clasp.

Panicked, and with the strap tight around its arm, the hylock unfolded its wings and tried to drag Rasi toward the large window. Another strap grabbed one of its wings while the other wing flapped madly. Rasi strained and the strap tore the hylock's wing away, much like a child torturing a fly.

"What's going on in there?" the bell ringer shouted from outside.

The armored soldier cried, "It's Rasi. Get help." He tried to pull free again, but the struggle inside pulled him back through the doorway.

Reinforcements would be coming soon, but Rasi still had a chance to help Aidric. He leaped forward, careful of the hylock's deadly nails. With straps restraining its legs and wrists and one around its waist, he grunted. A loud pop was followed by a screech as the hylock's hip jerked out of its socket. The hylock flopped to the ground, its leg jutting awkwardly. It clawed at the floor, pulling itself toward the door. Rasi removed his sword and ended the beast's miserable existence with a plunge to its heart. He looked to the armored soldier with a hateful glare.

The soldier gave up on unhooking the clasp and opted instead for dragging the hylock from the shop. *Clankclankclank.* He wasn't fast enough, and a strap grabbed his arm. He turned and begged for mercy. Rasi gestured for him to take off his helmet. He did, and Rasi gave him mercy with his sword hilt instead of the blade. As Rasi passed by the unconscious man, he kicked him in the mouth. *That's for that damn annoying armor.*

Rasi stepped outside. The bell ringer was already near the castle gate, leaving only two still guarding Aidric. While the taller of the two tugged at Aidric's bound arms, the shorter one drew his sword. "I've always wanted a chance at the legendary Rasi," he said.

The straps swarmed him before he got close and snapped his left arm and his right leg. The soldier trying to drag Aidric away gave up and ran toward the castle.

Rasi hurried to Aidric's side.

Aidric whispered, "Rasi? Is that you?"

Rasi nodded. "A'ena?"

"She escaped when Jarrah came for her at the castle."

Rasi curled his upper lip. *Jarrah.* With a swipe of his sword, he freed Aidric's hands and helped his friend to his feet.

Aidric coughed and rubbed his wrists. "She's on the run. You have to find her."

Rasi turned to Shadow and motioned for Aidric to come with him. They didn't have much time.

Aidric hesitated. "No, Rasi. I'm too weak. I'll only slow you down. Leave me."

Rasi shook his head. If he left Aidric behind, he would only be giving him back to them. He threw Aidric's arm over his shoulder and helped him to Shadow.

As he reached his horse, an arrow bounced off the ground beside him. Epertasian soldiers poured through the castle gates. A strap plucked the next arrow from the air and snapped it in two. Rasi started to help Aidric onto Shadow when a terrible whiff of sulfur stopped him cold.

"What is it?" Aidric asked.

Rasi held up his open hand. Then he slowly lifted his eyes to the roof where a single fisher squatted, drool dripping from its jowls. "Raasiiieee," it cried.

Aidric followed his stare. "By the gods. Is that—?"

Rasi nodded. His straps snapped at the air like whips. They'd just killed a hylock; they might as well try a fisher. A quick scan of the other rooftops revealed a second cackling scout.

If there were two, that meant there were a lot more coming. Rasi looked back the way he had come. Seven panicked Epertasian soldiers on horseback entered the business district.

The closest fisher dropped to the street next to him. Shadow jerked at his tie-down and neighed. The fisher's pale eyes followed him while it rhythmically swayed as if to music. Like the last time, it didn't attack. Rasi understood the game now. If he wanted to escape again, he had to do it quickly.

While the creature crouched and watched, Rasi helped Aidric to the ground. He held up a finger and stepped back into the road toward the approaching riders. Now he could see their fisher pursuers. Dozens of them.

Another arrow ricocheted from the ground next to him, but he didn't even glance at it. Arrows were the least of his problems. The fisher stalking him turned its attention to the approaching riders. It released a clicking sound from its throat before charging them. As the soldiers blew by, the fisher snagged one of their legs and clawed its way up behind him. Then it dragged the screaming soldier to the ground.

Too far away to help the soldier, Rasi lunged at the horse with a strap and caught the reins. The horse stopped with a jolt. The soldier screamed until the fisher sank its teeth into his throat. While the soldier bled out, the fisher dug out his eyes with its bony scoop. It shoved them into its mouth and howled the most god-awful screech Rasi had ever heard. It looked up, its pale eyes now glowing orange. Disgusted, Rasi hurriedly helped Aidric onto the commandeered horse. With Aidric in the saddle, Rasi smacked the horse's hindquarters, sending Aidric from the main drag into a side street and hopefully out of harm's way.

The fisher scout still on the roof dove onto another fleeing rider, knocking him to the ground.

Rasi turned back to the trailing fishers. The horde was coming fast. Though he wanted to help the soldier, it would be at the expense of his own escape. He started for Shadow, but the soldier struggling beneath the fisher screamed, "Rasi, help. I know where the queen is."

Rasi froze. Escape meant nothing if he still couldn't help Alina. The fisher positioned its scoop-claw. Rasi ran and tackled it. He bounced to his feet and the straps grabbed the fisher, hurling it at the shop across the street. The soldier crawled to Rasi's side. Rasi side-eyed him, grabbed his leather shoulder pad, and practically dragged him to Shadow. On the way, Rasi got a better look at the soldier's high cheekbones and uneven eyes. His name was Sterik. They had met during the Heathen War.

A battle horn blared from the castle gate. Charging soldiers fill the street. Rasi grabbed Sterik's arm and shoved him into the alley next to the flower shop. He pulled Shadow's reins behind. "A'ena?" he barked.

"I don't know the name of the place, but I can take you to where we last saw her."

Rasi snarled and peeked out from the alley. The two fisher scouts met with the horde in the center of the street. Sulfur saturated the air. The fisher with glowing eyes bobbed its head toward Rasi. There was no more time for games.

It called out, "Rasiiieee. Weee're comeeeng for you. You can't hiiieeeede forever."

Rasi gave it the finger.

And then the scout turned with the others to face the approaching soldiers. It was Rasi's only chance. As Main Street erupted into chaos behind them with swords against bone and claws against flesh, Rasi and Sterik climbed onto Shadow. Many Epertasians were going to lose their eyes that night. Rasi hoped he and Sterik weren't among them.

If anyone could help, it was Atticus.

When he started for Atticus's house, Sterik protested, "Where are you going? We need to head east."

Rasi ignored him, kicking Shadow into a full gallop until there was comfortable space between them and the battle. Once they finally slowed, Sterik told Rasi about the old man and woman they'd harassed on the road, chasing Alina through the field, and the annoying old man with the arrows. He described a tall fence surrounding funny, glowing stalks that had killed two of his friends. By the time he had finished spilling his guts, they were rounding the final bend before Atticus's farm.

At the first sight of the skeletal shell of Atticus's burned-out house, Rasi's heart skipped a beat. He put his hands to his head. *No, no, no.* He looked around to make sure he hadn't taken a wrong path, but there was Atticus's barn, still standing. He kicked Shadow into a full gallop to what was left of the front porch.

The charred wood and ash were long cooled with only a few trickles of smoke still lifting from piles within the rubble. Rasi's straps ripped away the partial wall that framed a doorless opening. He dropped to his knees. His straps started digging through the debris, flipping over chunks of wood and heaving charred pieces of furniture aside. Atticus's prized desk was now little more than a couple of blackened legs propped up by a pile of ash.

His straps tried to pull him deeper into the ruins to continue their frantic search, but he resisted. They tugged again, and again he fought their pull. He bowed his head and collapsed onto his heels. *Atticus. Celia.* As much as he needed to know if they were in there, at that moment he needed hope more.

Two of his straps turned toward him and hovered in front of his face as if pleading to continue their search. He shook his head. One of them nudged his shoulder from behind. *No. There's nothing we can do even if they're here.* Another frustrated strap pounded the porch floor. Rasi pressed his palms to his forehead and dragged them down his face to cover his mouth. The smoky air singed his nostrils. He closed his eyes. He should have never gone back to Puimia.

Sterik stood quietly off the porch with his head bowed. "This is Captain Atticus's house, huh? He was a good man."

Rasi scowled. *No one said he's dead yet.* He bobbed his head toward his horse. Alina was all that mattered now, and Sterik had just become the most important person in the world. As Rasi walked from the porch, his straps sulked, dragging the ground. With one last look at the rubble, he said a silent prayer before heading into the barn. Atticus's and Celia's horses were missing, which gave him back some of the hope he'd lost. Of course, it could have been the soldiers who took them. *No. Don't think like that.*

CHAPTER 21

THE NEW RULE OF LITHIA

Simcane rode Homer's horse Shelby into Lithia's capital city of Reigal. Since no one else rode horses except soldiers, he took Shelby to a stable owned by an old friend. Though his friend wasn't home, his stable boy was. The kid's crooked teeth and slouching shoulders bore enough of a resemblance to his old friend that Simcane asked his last name.

"Martin," he answered.

"Are you Tolliver's son?"

The kid bobbed his head.

"Where's your father run off to?"

"A meeting. It's been called by the new king."

"New king?"

"King Fice."

"I've met Fice. Where is this meeting?"

"At the town square."

He started to point, but Simcane interrupted. "I know where the town square is, kid."

The kid agreed to stable Shelby for two bits and Simcane happily paid.

The streets were alive with activity, reminiscent of Thasula on Matthew's Day minus the costumes, decorations, and festive mood.

Many of the faces were vacant, much like those of his attackers at Arthur's Dive. Repeatedly, people bumped into him only to bounce off and continue toward the square as if they hadn't just struck a wall.

Not everyone in the crowd had the same mindless stares, though. Some of the people appeared to still have their wits, like Tolliver Martin's son, yet they also headed to the square with their heads bowed.

Simcane wondered how things could have crumbled so fast, and how respected leaders like Alina and Logan could have fallen from favor so quickly. Even if it was because of Fice's persuasive powers, the scale and speed at which it happened seemed unfathomable.

A teenaged girl tugged on his shirt.

"What do you want?" he asked.

There wasn't anything particularly special about her other than a look of defiance and strength in her chocolate eyes. She stared at him for a moment before dropping her gaze to the ground. She whispered, "Mister, put your head down. Don't let Fice's men see that you have your thoughts, or they'll take you like they did my father."

Simcane dropped his head. She continued toward the square.

One would think it difficult for Simcane not to stand out because of his size, but as long as he kept his face blank and his eye down, no one seemed to question him. No one except for a man on the corner who caught his eye. He didn't have blank eyes and he didn't stare at the ground. It was like he knew something no one else knew. Simcane subtly watched him. The stranger approached.

"You're Simcane?" he whispered when he reached him.

"Yeah. What of it?" He started to lift his head.

"Keep your head down. We've been watching for you. Someone needs to see you. Come with us."

Simcane glanced back to the corner where two other men wearing shadowy hoods now stood. It might be nothing, but it was the best lead he had. He nodded.

The man led him to the other two and all of them ducked into a doctor's office nearby. Once inside, the men shed their hoods and hurried to the back. Simcane waited at the entrance, wary of a trap. They shoved what appeared to be a solid wall-mounted cabinet aside with such ease that it must have been on tiny wheels. It revealed an open staircase. One of the men flicked his hand toward the opening. "Hurry up."

Simcane twice looked around for an ambush.

The man jerked his hand toward the opening again, only this time with more urgency. And then someone's head poked from the opening. "Simcane?"

Simcane whispered, "By the gods. King Logan." His face broke into his first smile in a while.

Logan pressed his finger to his lips. "Shhhh. Come down here before somebody sees your big ass."

Simcane rushed to the opening and climbed down the narrow stairs. At the base of the steps, he grabbed Logan and nearly squeezed the breath from him. He stepped back. "I knew they couldn't get an old coot like you."

Over Logan's shoulder, he saw Lona standing with a smile. "Your Majesty," he said, and shoved Logan aside. She hugged him as hard as he hugged her.

"I'm so sorry I wasn't here for you."

"Nonsense. We're just glad you're here now."

"Logan, what's happened? What has Fice done?"

"He spreads lies throughout Lithia. He moved into the castle shortly after the Teks pulled out. I couldn't do anything to stop him—I had no army left to speak of."

"Surely the people didn't accept his lies blindly," Simcane scoffed before following up with a cautious, "did they?"

"He did something to their minds. I could only watch while trying to find a force suitable to repel him, but his power is unpredictable. It was too hard to know who was susceptible to his influence and who wasn't during the earliest days. Once he gained a small army of Liths and Lowlanders, he became unstoppable. Somehow, he convinced the people that we helped Alina overthrow her father so we could steal their freedom."

"Logan, you've always been just; the people must know that."

"His lies are like a cancer. Once they begin to take hold, nothing can stop their spread. And we've heard rumors that he's had help from someone in Epertase. We plan to travel there for guidance and assistance."

"We can't. Epertase is on the brink of a revolution. When I left, Queen Alina was preparing to go into hiding until more could be learned."

Some of the eternal optimism drained from Logan's strong face. "That's a shame. If it's anything like here, I fear for the young queen. Her life will be at stake."

Simcane nodded. "What can I do to help?"

"King Fice is addressing the people in the square today. That's why we took the chance to come here. We need to know what he says."

"I'll go."

Logan was hesitant, but he knew there was no one better. He nodded once. "Simcane, old friend, I fear there's no future left for Lithia."

Simcane started to argue, but the cabinet above the opening rattled before crashing to the floor. "They're down here," someone shouted.

Logan's eyes went wide.

Simcane shoved him toward Lona. There was a tunnel behind them. "Go. I'll hold them off."

"Simcane, come with us. We can find another way to learn Fice's plan."

"No. I'll find you. Just go."

"We're hiding in the Tunnels of Eiger."

Simcane whipped his head around.

Logan smiled. "I have a few crystals tucked away that allow our safe passage." Simcane started to turn away, but Logan stopped him. "Simcane. Just remember, left, right, left."

Simcane nodded.

Two soldiers descended the narrow stairs.

"I'll find you," Simcane shouted as Logan, Lona, and their few loyal soldiers disappeared into the dark tunnel. A slight blue glow emanated from bags around their waists. Simcane folded his fingers back with several cracks. He met the first soldier at the bottom of the stairs and knocked him unconscious before he could even turn. The next soldier tried to retreat up the stairs, but Simcane grabbed his belt and yanked him down. His knuckles left that soldier lying next to his friend. Simcane climbed the stairs to where two more surprised soldiers stood.

Just don't run.

They drew their swords. Simcane drew his. They attacked with the same opening salvo that was taught to all soldiers when they joined the service, so Simcane countered with a few tricks they'd likely never seen. He tried not to kill them, but his blade went deeper than intended into one of their thighs. After incapacitating the other swordsman and depositing him down the stairwell, he went to the profusely bleeding one. The color in the man's face drained with the spilling of his blood. Simcane reached for his belt and the man flinched, though he was weakening too quickly to fight.

"Hold still," Simcane said. He unfastened the soldier's belt and wrapped it around his thigh above the spurting blood. "This is gonna hurt."

The soldier bit down on the leather wrap around his wrist as Simcane cinched the belt tight. The blood spray slowed to a trickle before stopping completely with a final yank. "You're probably gonna loose that leg, kid, but you'll live." He stood up and wiped the blood from his hands onto the fellow's cloak. "When your buddies wake up, have them get you to a doctor." He looked around the office. "Maybe even the doctor who works here, if you can find him."

At the door, Simcane lowered his head and crept into the crowded street. He followed the people to the town square where a crowd had swelled around a stage. He pushed through to get close enough to hear.

It wasn't long before three Gildonese, two males and one female, stepped out from beneath a wooden arch at the back of the stage. Simcane recognized one of them as Fice. The crowd silenced as if on cue.

King Fice stepped to the front of the stage, wearing one of Logan's royal robes, which only hung to his thighs. He shouted, "I am King Fice and I seek to bring you all prosperity and truth as long as you accept me as your new leader.

"Lowlanders, I welcome you home.

"Epertasians, I welcome you to a new life, and while I understand it is hard for you to trust anyone after the lies perpetrated by your former queen, Alina, and her criminal lover, Rasi, I assure you of a new beginning, free of such evil, lying leaders.

"And to my Liths, oh my lovely Liths. I know you feel betrayed by your former vile rulers, Logan and Lona, who supported the unjust murder of King Elijah, but I ask that you trust your new leader, as I will trust you."

Simcane bit his cheek to keep from shouting, "What kind of dragon shit is this?"

Fice continued, "Initially, some of our tactics may be difficult for such a civilized people to witness, but I assure you it will be in your best interests at the end." There was something disturbing in how he emphasized "*at* the end" instead of the more common phrase "in the end."

King Fice stabbed the crowd with his blackened stare. "Lithia's royal castle is now to be known as the Castle Fice. You have come to witness the new world order and are, therefore, forbidden from leaving. Welcome, my sheep, to Recitaaaar."

His voice rose to a crescendo. "Resistance," he screamed, his voice breaking under the strain, "will bring only pain."

A woman unable to keep up her hypnotized charade began to cry. Soldiers knifed through the crowd and removed her and her children. King Logan might have been right—Lithia was no more.

As Fice looked proudly over his new sheep, a violent commotion caught Simcane's attention near the front. A hooded man stormed the front of the stage. Before he reached the platform, several of Fice's Lith soldiers pounced, but they were no match for the dual-knife-wielding aggressor. Their blood sprayed like a fountain as they fell. He licked his bloody hands.

Fice watched with an interested smirk from his perch upon the stage. He waved off the additional guards, allowing the attacker to advance. The hooded man climbed onto the stage. The female Gildonese started to step forward, but Fice waved her off.

The lunatic closed the gap between him and Fice with a recklessness Simcane had only seen once before. As he charged, he shed his cloak, revealing a puncture scar beneath his Adam's Apple.

Simcane dropped his shoulders with a sigh. *Thairen, you crazy fool.*

Fice slid a blade that was twice as long as a regular sword from its sheath at his waist. "This is the fate of those who oppose me."

Once again, Simcane found himself in a position where he could help Thairen, but it would be at the cost of the larger mission. Maybe the crazy bastard would actually kill Fice and solve the whole problem. Thairen leaped forward, bloodthirsty and careless, just as he had with the Teks when Simcane had last seen him.

Fice moved like lightning. Every attack Thairen attempted to land was bested by a Gildonese counter. Fice laughed as he sliced open piece after piece of Thairen's flesh, but the seemingly immortal warrior continued to advance, never giving a step. Even when Fice shoved his blade through Thairen's side and yanked it free, the warrior still attacked.

Thairen was as relentless as any man Simcane had ever seen, yet he didn't land a single blow. Fice moved like poetry. And, after a few more elegant swipes of his blade, the fight was ended not by an intricate fatal blow—there had been plenty of those—but by exhaustion. It simply came to a matter of blood volume. Thairen had spilled too much to continue. He dropped to his knees.

Bored with the battle, Fice sheathed his bloody sword and waved his hand to the other Gildonese. Thairen, unwilling to concede, swung his blade limply at the female, but she was equally as fast as Fice and equally as deadly. She sliced open his chest, exposing specks of white bone through the blood. Though it wasn't necessary, she seemed to enjoy it.

Fice whispered something to a Lith guard and that man, along with three other soldiers, disappeared behind the gate.

When they returned, they carried a length of rope with a crude noose at the end.

Oh, Thairen, you fool.

Thairen struggled against the Gildonese holding him, but he was too spent. The soldiers looped the noose around his neck while he squirmed.

Thairen screamed through red, blood-smeared lips, "Free me and I'll rip out your hearts."

Fice grabbed his gut and laughed out loud at the beaten man's bravado. The soldiers hoisted the rope over the archway at the back of the stage. The female Gildonese looked to Fice for direction. He nodded. She and the other Gildonese each took Thairen's arms. With simultaneous brutal snaps, they bent Thairen's elbows backward. Thairen didn't make a sound.

Proud, the Gildonese backed away. He spat blood at them. He strained, reaching for the rope around his neck, but no matter how hard he tried, he couldn't bend his ruined arms enough to touch the noose. The soldiers heaved on the rope until Thairen's kicking feet lifted from the ground. He thrashed like a live fish thrown onto a sizzling skillet. The decent people in the crowd cringed and struggled to watch in order to keep up appearances, while the swayed looked on without emotion.

Thairen's legs and broken arms flailed until his strength was gone. Even then he refused to give up, continuing to quiver helplessly—disgustingly—from the rope. Finally, he gasped for another breath that wasn't there.

Fice stepped forward again to speak. "This is what will befall any nonbelie—"

Thairen's eyes shot open, as if he'd just awakened from an unimaginable nightmare only to find himself still in said nightmare. He thrashed again. Fice stared with amusement until Thairen slowly died for a second time. Or more likely the hundredth time in his violent life.

Fice turned back to the crowd. "As I was saying—"

Again, Thairen's eyes bulged and his feet kicked violently in the air. Fice turned toward him and sighed with annoyance. "What type of mystical spell does this peasant carry?"

Like a never-ending torture, Thairen died yet again only to awaken moments later to the same painful end for a fourth time. Fice rolled his eyes. "Enough of this. Bury him deep."

After Thairen's quivering ended for a fifth time, the soldiers lowered the rope. As they removed the noose, Thairen started laughing. "Quitters," he rasped. The two Gildonese, with three soldiers trailing them, dragged him from the back of the stage and out of sight.

Maybe there was a way Simcane could help Thairen after all. He quietly weaved through the crowd and around a few buildings until he found their trail. He followed from a distance. After stopping for shovels, the soldiers dragged Thairen beyond the outskirts of town. Dozens of mounds littered a field.

Simcane crouched next to the last empty building before the field and watched. One of the soldiers grew tired of Thairen's nonstop badgering about what he was going to do to them after his arms healed and bashed his sword hilt into Thairen's skull, knocking the warrior unconscious.

They dug at the semi-frosted ground while Thairen lay unconscious under the watchful eyes of the two Gildonese. The soldiers worked at the hard ground for the better part of the afternoon. Occasionally, Thairen would stir only to have one of the Gildonese put him out again with a well-placed kick.

Why don't they simply lop off his head? Simcane wondered.

Once pleased with the size of the hole they'd dug, they tossed Thairen into the grave. Each man spat on him and one of them exposed himself and pissed into the hole. After a good laugh, they shoveled the dirt back in. When they left, Simcane ducked into the empty building as they passed by.

Once they were out of sight, he sprinted to the grave. Like a salivating dog longing to taste a long-buried bone, he dropped to his knees and raked the dirt between his legs at a frantic pace.

"Come on, come on," he pleaded, clawing at the soil. It seemed like forever before his fingers scratched soft flesh. He dug faster and found Thairen's chest. It wasn't moving. He followed his chest up to his buried neck and clawed away until Thairen's mouth was exposed.

Thairen sucked in a deep burst of air. Simcane continued digging until Thairen could sit up. The warrior choked and coughed and spat dirt. His eyes watered. "Sim," he said as casually as if Simcane was a neighbor stopping by for a chat. "Good to see you again." He sniffed the air and scrunched his nose. "Did you piss on me?"

Simcane helped him to his feet and then lifted him out of the hole. Thairen lay on his back, coughing more dirt from his mouth and probably some from his lungs.

"You gonna make it?" Simcane asked.

"No worse than the last time I was buried. It felt horrible then and it feels horrible now."

Simcane shook his head. "Worse thing ever?"

"Worse than drowning, I suppose, but better than having my throat cut." He stared down at his awkwardly bent arms and tried unsuccessfully to bend his elbows the way they were meant to. "Uh. A little help here?"

Simcane wrinkled his forehead. "And do what? I'm no doctor."

"Straighten these things out," he said, like it was a perfectly normal request.

Simcane was intrigued. "All right."

Thairen grinned. "Anytime you're ready, big fella."

Simcane took Thairen's right wrist in one hand while bracing his bicep with his other.

"Wait. Do you have anything I can bite on?"

Simcane scanned the field for a stick or something, but didn't see anything that would work. "You could bite on my shoe, I suppose."

"Perfect."

Simcane took off his sweaty and no doubt smelly leather shoe and shoved it into Thairen's mouth, imagining how terrible it must taste. Thairen bit down and contorted his face. That might be the worst torture of all. Simcane grabbed his arm again.

Thairen grinned around the shoe.

Simcane briefly closed his eye. "On three?"

Thairen nodded.

"One ..."

Crack.

Sweat poured from Thairen's forehead, yet he refused to cry out. Simcane grabbed his other arm. "Ready?"

Thairen shook his head.

Crack.

Thairen fell to his back, writhing in the grass, but still refusing to cry out.

Simcane put his shoe back on, Thairen's crooked tooth prints now permanently imprinted on it. "How long until you heal from that?"

Thairen stopped writhing to look up. "How long would it take you to heal?" He shook his head, annoyed. "I'm not a freak." Then he got up and marched toward town as if forgetting the horror he had just been through.

Simcane hustled to catch him. "Wait. Where're you going?"

"I haven't finished with them yet."

Simcane caught himself laughing aloud. "Are you serious?" he asked. Thairen glared at him. "But both of your arms are broken."

"I'll use my feet." Thairen kept walking.

"Wait." Simcane grabbed his shoulder. "Why don't you come with me and we'll do this in the right manner?"

Thairen stopped and stared at the ground long enough for Simcane to hope he might have possibly gotten through to him.

"I know where King Logan is. Come with me. Give your arms a chance to heal properly and then we'll return with a plan."

Thairen's nose twitched and he tried to scratch his face, but couldn't bend his elbow to reach his nose. He leaned against Simcane's chest and rubbed his snotty nose on Simcane's shirt.

"Was that necessary?" Simcane asked.

Thairen grinned. "No." Then another thought grabbed him. "Oh, damn."

"What is it?"

"How am I gonna piss?"

Simcane patted his back. "You're on your own with that one."

Thairen gave a mischievous grin. "Come on, Sim. Just hold it for me." He thrust his pelvis against Simcane's leg. "You know you'd like to."

Simcane shook his head. "Stop it, Thairen. You're not as funny as you think."

"But I saw how you were looking at me."

Simcane shoved him away. "Just shut up."

Thairen stopped, shrugged, and then grinned again.

Simcane glanced over. *What is this psychopath up to now?*

Thairen closed his eyes with a look of deep concentration. Slowly, the front of his britches grew wet and the stain spread down both thighs. "Ah. Warm."

Simcane shook his head. "You're disgusting."

By then, Thairen was laughing uncontrollably. Simcane wondered aloud why he'd even dug up the nutjob. Annoyed, Simcane ignored him and led the way. Like all children, Thairen would eventually get it out of his system.

Next stop, the deadly Tunnels of Eiger.

CHAPTER 22

ONCE LOST IS FOUND

A storm of sleet followed by snow had slowed Rasi and Sterik's progress at least half a day, but it eventually passed. Though Sterik had requested to seek shelter until the storm moved on, Rasi had refused to let even a minute more than necessary pass before he found Alina, no matter how cold and wet and miserable the road got.

After rounding a bend, Sterik stopped and scanned the horizon. "I think this is it." It was the third time around the third bend that he'd said as much in the last day alone. With Puimia not far away, Rasi wondered if his guide would lead him all the way to his parents' farm before they found Alina's trail.

Sterik bobbed his head. "Yes. I think this is it." He pointed across the snow-covered field toward a thick line of snow-covered brambles. "She went through somewhere around there, I'm sure of it."

Rasi scowled.

No, I'm serious." Sterik looked the way they had come and then the way they were going and pointed. "See that bend ahead?"

Rasi nodded; he'd seen every bend Sterik had previously pointed out.

"We chased her almost directly in the middle of two bends, just like right here. Yes, yes, yes. I'm sure of it now." He smacked Rasi's shoulder and pointed toward the bend ahead. "See how you can just barely see the edge of a tree line past the hill at that next curve in the road? I remember that."

Though Rasi had doubts, it was as good a lead as any. He kicked Shadow into the field. It was slow going through the snow. He had made it about a quarter of the way across when two figures emerged from a slight gap in the brambles east of where Sterik had pointed. Rasi dropped from his saddle. The snow reached his knees. He stood and watched.

Both people wore face covers and heavy blankets wrapped around them. He didn't need to see their faces to know he had found her.

He felt as nervous as a schoolboy about to ask the prettiest girl for a dance. His stomach shifted as he waited for her to lift her eyes and see him. He would have shouted if he had a tongue. Two of his straps slithered from beneath his cloak and waved above his head.

Finally, she lifted her eyes.

She didn't move for what seemed like an eternity. Her companion tried to nudge her forward until he, too, saw Rasi and froze. Rasi took a weighted step. She dropped the bag she was carrying and plowed through the snow toward him, her companion still standing with a bow draped over his shoulder and a quiver on his back. Rasi left Shadow and stomped through the snow toward her.

They met like two colliding streams of water. He lifted her and squeezed with every ounce of love in his heart. His straps enveloped them in a warm cocoon of sorts.

"I missed you so much," she said, tears flowing down her face. She pulled her cover from her mouth and their lips met. Hers were as soft and perfect as he remembered.

I missed you, too, he answered.

"Don't ever leave me again."

He shook his head. *Never.* He pried her away from his chest and eyed the stranger still standing and watching. *Who's your companion?*

"He saved me, Rasi. He held off the soldiers and then gave me shelter and food." She waved him over, but he turned away and disappeared back into the brambles. "Ah. Well, he's not very sociable."

We should go before you get too cold.

She nodded.

Once in Shadow's saddle, they went back to the road where Sterik stood waiting. Rasi introduced him to Alina. He knelt with his head bowed.

She motioned for him to stand. "Thank you for helping Rasi."

"I'm so sorry for everything that's happened. I only hope I've redeemed myself a bit."

She smiled warmly. "You have."

"Then I'm going to take my leave, if that's all right."

"Where will you go?"

"To that town we passed a few miles back. After that, I don't know. But what I do know is I'll never fight against the Epertase that you represent again. And when you return to power, I'll find my way back to service." He nodded to Rasi and Rasi nodded back.

"Good luck to you," Alina said as he started down the road.

He glanced over his shoulder and waved. "Thank you, Your Majesty."

Rasi and Alina started toward Puimia.

I saw Thasula. I can't believe what's happened to your kingdom.

"It's horrible. It all happened so fast that I couldn't stop it. Jarrah turned on me. Andon, too."

Andon? Jarrah, he could understand, but Andon? Sterik said the Gildonese from the Lowlands are to blame. Is that true?

"King Fice's sway is strong."

How did he grab power so quickly?

"I don't know. But I've seen it firsthand. Some lose the ability to think for themselves while others, like Andon, seem to have simply turned on me." Alina looked over her shoulder at him and said, "Sometimes, I just wish we could go back to the time before the Teks. Before my father died. Back when it was just you and me in the mountains." She pulled Rasi's hand around her waist and held it on her lap. "Do you remember when we had our first kiss at the base of Widows Run?"

Of course, I remember. When I'm at my loneliest, that's where I take my mind. I'll never be far from you as long as I have that day.

"Nor I you."

They rode in quiet communion, with neither speaking for a while. The snow on the ground thinned the farther east they traveled until everything was just wet and dreary and slick.

"What's bothering you, Rasi?"

He hesitated before answering. *I've been thinking. On Shadows Peak, you once asked me to flee with you and leave Epertase. Do you remember?*

"I remember."

Maybe that's what we should do. Fice's grip can't reach the whole world. There're other lands, I'm sure.

"The only thing I want now is to be with you."

I'm tired of killing, Alina.

She squeezed his hand. He paused, another burden weighing on him. *There's something else you should know before we go much farther. Fice isn't our only concern.*

"What do you mean?"

Have you ever heard the stories of the fishers from the volcanic regions?

She shook her head.

They're extremely deadly creatures thought to be extinct for years. They're so dangerous the military still instructs recruits on how to deal with them should they reappear.

"And?"

They're definitely not extinct. And they're tracking me.

"Why you?"

I don't know. But we must stay vigilant. They're very, very dangerous.

"What will they do if they find us?"

He paused, thinking of soldiers with empty eye sockets. He kissed her cheek, already regretting the additional worry he'd just heaped upon her. *I don't want to talk about the fishers, my love; I just want to be with you.*

CHAPTER 23
THERE WILL BE BLOOD

Rasi and Alina rode into Puimia to find the town still mostly asleep. The relaxing smell of chimney smoke recalled Rasi's nostalgic memories of sitting on the floor with his parents as a child and enjoying the warmth on many a bitter night. As the smell wafted to him on the slight breeze, he longed to be snuggled in front of a fireplace with Alina. He pointed to a general store next to a diner. *That's where I had my first job.*

"You worked in a store?" She seemed genuinely surprised.

I wasn't always a soldier, Alina. When I was thirteen, my father let me work one day a week away from the farm. It was also where he'd met his first wife, Edonea, but he felt no need to mention that. It wasn't that he thought bringing up Edonea would bother Alina—he knew it wouldn't—he just didn't feel like dredging up that part of his past.

Little Jenny Taylor peeked from her parents' eatery window. Though "little" Jenny was now in her twenties, it was what everyone had called her since she'd been an annoying kid always under foot. It wasn't her fault and Rasi had always felt bad for her. When she was four, a bundle of shingles had slid off her parents' roof while her father was repairing it and struck her in the head. She'd never developed right after that and her speech was hard to understand.

Rasi hadn't thought about her since he'd left Puimia for the military. She opened the door, scanned the street, and scampered toward him.

"Rasi?" she whispered, and then looked around to make sure she hadn't been too loud. She mostly ignored Alina. Either she didn't recognize that her queen sat before her, or her message was too urgent to care. "Soldiers. Dey been akin 'bout you."

Rasi shifted forward. Alina asked, "When?"

"O'er da night. Dey gone to your farm."

Rasi's eyes lifted toward the horizon where his parents' farm waited. Smoke billowed toward the sky. His heart cratered into his gut. "Rah." He kicked Shadow into a gallop through town.

Someone in the town shouted, "Fire." Rasi had seen enough burning homes to know the bucket brigade would be more for show than do any good in this case. Every urgent clop of Shadow's hooves on the dirt road twisted Rasi's stomach even more.

When his parents' farm finally came into view, he pulled the reins and dropped them onto Alina's lap. His palms pressed his temples. *By the gods, no.*

"Oh, Rasi." Alina covered her mouth. Thick, angry smoke intertwined with flickering flames to lick the eaves through broken windows and the busted-down front door. Not a gap or opening in the house was absent of flames. The heat was so intense he could feel it from the road. If his parents were home, and he was sure they were, there was nothing he could do for them. He was helpless.

A ring of Epertasian soldiers surrounded the Jamisons' home. Rasi had seen enough to understand that the soldiers' positions were to prevent anyone from escaping once the house was set alight.

Get down, Alina.

Her eyes held him as she dismounted. She began to cry for his breaking heart.

"Rah," he grunted, whipping Shadow into a full gallop toward the soldiers. He was too far away to stop the torches from breaking the Jamisons' windows. One was tossed into the front room while another broke through Annie's bedroom window. When Mr. Jamison ran from his front door, one of the soldiers struck him with the hilt of his sword, sending him sprawling on the porch steps. Then the soldier dragged him back through the front door.

Rasi's nails dug into his palms around the leather reins. *I'm gonna kill every one of you.* He pushed harder as the soldiers, oblivious to his approach, formed double lines and marched west away from the house. Mr. Jamison's open front door spewed thick, rolling gray smoke with flashes of orange dancing within. His parents were beyond saving, but there was still a chance for Mr. Jamison. And there was still a chance for Annie.

Rasi leaped from Shadow onto the porch. The blinding, choking smoke felt like gravel being smeared into his open eyes.

His straps searched the floor inside until they bumped against a body. He yanked Mr. Jamison outside to safety. Then he covered his mouth and dove back into the growing blackness. Already, he felt starved for air. The heat pounded his shoulders and face, forcing him to his knees. He couldn't see past his tears and the burning, so he closed his eyes.

By touch, he found the hallway wall. His straps overturned a couch and panic clawed at him. *Breathe,* his lungs screamed. *No,* he screamed back. He swept the floor with his hands.

His chest ached from holding his breath. His straps scrambled along the wall in search of a window, or perhaps for a new host after Rasi took his last breath.

He found Annie's door and smashed it open with his feet. Flames trailed from a torch to Annie's dresser and up the wall.

His fumbling hands found Annie unconscious in her bed and he carried her toward the window. An ember dropped from the burning ceiling and sizzled on the flesh of his arm. He swatted it away, but not before it had left a painful mark.

The sill was within reach. He needed to breathe, but there was only smoke to take into his lungs. His mind grew fuzzy. Though he ordered his lungs not to breathe—not yet—they ignored him and took in a breath. The smoke tasted like razors. He went for the sill once again, but the poisonous smoke confused him and he got turned around. His straps lifted Annie to the sill, but they were weakening, too. He heard Mr. Jamison's throaty voice, muffled as if from a great distance. Maybe it was a dream.

"Rasi," he called.

Someone took Annie from the straps and lifted her through the window. Rasi's grip on the sill faltered. He fell back into the swallowing smoke. Then he felt a strong hand grab his wrist. "Up you get, lad," Mr. Jamison said, trying to heave Rasi to his feet. "Come on. I can't do it alone."

Rasi collected all the strength he could muster and pushed it to his legs. A shove from Mr. Jamison and his straps tumbled him over the sill into the grass. The deadly air turned heavenly as he sucked in precious lungfuls. Mr. Jamison climbed back out as the ceiling completely collapsed behind him.

Annie moaned and then coughed violently. A strap gently traced her back and then nudged her to see if she was all right. Rasi heaved thick, black-tinged phlegm into the grass. Dirty, black-speckled snot streamed from his nose and his eyes watered like the falls by Shadows Peak, but he already felt himself coming back.

His thoughts shot to the soldiers who had caused it. He pictured his mother and father going through what he had just gone through and envisioned their burned bodies melted to the floor. He wished he'd never known what that looked like, but years as a soldier had acquainted him with many forms of death. Too many. Deep, furious breaths gushed through his snotty nose. He stood up. The world tinted red around him.

Alina was there beside Mr. Jamison, but she stepped back with her hand over her chest when she saw Rasi's rage-filled eyes. In that instant, she likely saw what he truly was, and it scared her. When Annie reached a kind hand toward his shoulder, Alina intercepted it and shook her head. She knew nothing could stop him now.

A glob of drool dripped past his clenched teeth and down his chin. This was who he had tried to hide from her so many times before. This was the man he was trying to be better than. But for once, he welcomed the rage. He gripped the hilt of his sword until his knuckles cracked and turned white.

Rasi? Alina said in his mind.

He glared at her from the corner of his eye, waiting for her usual pleas for mercy.

Be careful, she said.

He let out a beastly growl.

Since Shadow was off grazing, Rasi sprinted toward the back of the line of marching cowards on foot. He passed a row of Puimians carrying buckets toward the destruction. Some of them spoke, but in his rage he didn't understand what they said. A few of them stopped and turned, likely seeing the murder in Rasi's eyes. Though it would probably be better that he didn't have an audience, there was nothing he could do about it. He drew his sword before he reached the first unsuspecting soldier. The man started to turn, likely hearing Rasi's furious approach. Rasi ran him through. The surprise and pain on the soldier's face made it even sweeter. Rasi ripped the sword free. The surprise was over.

As the startled soldiers composed themselves and grasped their weapons, Rasi took special note of the captain at the front. He would save him for last.

He danced through the men, flawlessly swinging his sword while his straps protected his back. Arms snapped. Blood sprayed. Guts spilled to the wet ground in steaming piles. He heard a hate-filled snarl and realized it was from his own throat.

With blood dripping from his face, he plowed into the last of them. They didn't stand a chance. His blade work was superb and focused, his movements precise. It was what he was made to do.

Winded, Rasi looked up from the mess he had made. A crowd of stunned townsfolk had gathered around, and he was embarrassed at what they had witnessed. The captain tried to run, but several of the Puimian men cut him off and held him. With the captain pleading for the very mercy he had denied Rasi's parents, Rasi slit his cursed throat. He stared blankly into Rasi's eyes before he fell to his side and bled out. Rasi turned back toward home. The crowd parted from his path. As he walked by, he regarded the dead soldiers, seeing them as no more Epertasian than the Tek or the heathens before them.

Alina waited next to Mr. Jamison and Annie near Rasi's parents' home. She touched his cheek and he collapsed to his knees with his arms around her waist and his cheek pressed against her hip. He was afraid she would condemn his actions, but she didn't. Instead, her hand stroked the back of his head.

Mr. Jamison and Annie quietly backed away to give them some privacy.

Alina squatted so she could see Rasi's face. He tried to look away, but her fingers guided his head back. "Rasi, it's over now. You can rest."

He shook his head. He may never rest again. *I was wrong, Alina.*

"You had to do what you did."

I don't mean about that. I mean what I said earlier. I'm sorry, but I can't flee Epertase with you. I thought I could, but I can't.

She lifted his chin. "Why? We can hide."

He shook his head. *I'm done hiding.*

"But you don't understand, Rasi. I need you now more than ever."

I thought I could be a better man, but I can't. This is who I am. As hard as I've tried, I can't change. Not even for you.

A tear ran down her cheek. She clutched his hand. "Don't do it for me." She guided his palm to her slightly distended belly. "Do it for your son."

Rasi reeled like he'd been kicked in the chest. *My son?*

She nodded, and the corners of her lips dented her tear-streaked cheeks.

He stood and backed away. "We … I …"

"I know, Rasi. It's all right." She stood and reached for his hand again. He wobbled on legs almost too weak to hold his weight.

Everything had changed. At that moment he became more confident of what he needed to do than at any other time in his life. *Alina, listen to me. I now know what I must do. I must kill Fice. I can't rest until you …,* he paused and smiled, his eyes filled with tears, *both of you … are safe.*

Either she understood and agreed or she knew how stubborn he could be because she answered, "You're right. We shouldn't run."

It was then that Rasi knew her true desire. She didn't want to flee, to leave her people. She only wanted him to be happy and was willing to sacrifice everything to that end. Her strength shone through when she spoke. "I have met King Fice and he's as dangerous as they come."

I do not fear him.

"Is there anything you do fear?"

Being alone.

"That will never happen again, I promise. We're here for you." She lifted her baggy blouse and put his hand on her slightly rounded belly and whispered, "Forever."

As they headed back toward his parents' farm she whispered, "I have an idea of who could help in our fight."

Who?

"Have you ever been to New Arc?"

He shook his head.

"I can't tell you who yet, but you must trust me."

He did trust her.

Even before they reached the smoldering rubble, he heard Annie sobbing. Rasi stopped behind her. Mr. Jamison was backing out of the ruins, dragging a body.

Alina grabbed Rasi's arm. *Rasi, don't look. You don't need to see this.* Even in his mind, her voice quivered.

But Rasi did need to see. He needed to see so he would have no doubt of what he was fighting against. He needed to see so he could say goodbye one last time. And he needed to see to give himself fuel for the coming violence and death. He wasn't a farmer anymore, if he ever was one. He was a warrior, and it was the start of a new war.

With wet eyes, Alina lowered her head and looked to the side, away from Rasi, away from the gruesome tableau before them.

Mr. Jamison dragged a second body from the ash and debris. The charred corpse was about the same size as Rasi's father. Mr. Jamison moved the body next to the other one and wiped his hands on his shirt. Rasi stood silent. Mr. Jamison removed his coat and covered the bodies as best he could. Annie sobbed even louder.

Rasi walked to him. Mr. Jamison met him halfway with a firm, caring hand on his shoulder. "Boy, you don't need to go over there. Nothing but pain and death await you."

Rasi nodded and gently removed Mr. Jamison's hand.

"I'm sorry, Rasi. I was hoping to be further along before you returned to spare you this horror."

Rasi shook his head; it was his place to bury them. Mr. Jamison started to follow, presumably to help. *Alina, tell him to stay back. Tell him I need to be alone.* She relayed his message and Mr. Jamison returned to his daughter's side.

Rasi stopped short of the coat as if held back by chains. His straps floated down by his knees. *I'll give you vengeance, Mother and Father. I'll kill every soldier in the world if I must.* A part of him knew his mother would not want to hear what he was thinking, but this was who he was, and he couldn't rest until the bastards paid with their blood for what they had done.

He moved closer and knelt next to the bodies, no longer fighting his tears. *I am so sorry. I should have been here for you.* He reached for his mother's scorched, blackened hand, which appeared permanently drawn to her chest. His own hand shook too much, and as hard as he tried, he couldn't bring himself to touch her.

He didn't know how long he had knelt beside them before he decided to move again, but his calves were cramped when he did. With a deep sigh, he gathered all his resolve and slid his arms beneath her, cradled her gently, and carried her into the field. Then he returned for his father. Mr. Jamison met him with a shovel from his barn. With utmost care, Rasi lifted his father and carried him and the shovel to his mother.

Alina, Mr. Jamison, and Annie watched him work from afar. The only thing they could do was show respect by keeping vigil for as long as it took their friend to take care of his parents for the final time.

Rasi spent the better part of the day digging in the hard ground until the graves were deep enough to keep the scavengers away. Satisfied, he jammed the shovel into the dirt and then lowered his parents into their eternal resting place. He knelt beside the graves and used his sword to cut a thick lock of his hair.

I give you a piece of my hair, so you don't have to walk the long dark road of death without me. I will forever be with you in your journey to the other side. He sprinkled the hair evenly over their bodies. *I miss you both already. Men will pay for this, again I swear.*

After filling the graves with dirt, he sat in the cold winter grass until the dark skies came. When he felt he had mourned enough that day, he stood up, said goodbye, and headed for the only family he had left.

He nodded to Mr. Jamison and Annie. Mr. Jamison squeezed his arm and sadly smiled. "I will see to it that their graves are properly marked."

Rasi nodded.

Annie gave him a hug. "You will always be my friend."

Rasi thanked her. Then he and Alina went to Shadow. Before climbing up, he embraced her and looked into her emerald eyes. *You two are all I have left. Please forgive me for what I must do next. You should know that I vow to return my parents' pain tenfold to those who ordered it ... or I will die trying.*

She kissed his cheek. "I'm sorry for all the terrible things you've had to endure. And all of the terrible things you've had to do."

I'm not finished yet.

"I love you, Rasi."

A lot of men are going to die, and I will not stop until there is no doubt of the safety of you and my son.

She nodded.

I love you, too. Now, we must leave.

With one arm tightly around her in the saddle, they started the long journey to New Arc.

CHAPTER 24
UNEASY TRUCE

During the nights, Rasi and Alina slept under the stars in empty fields far from the road. They spent the days traveling while steering clear of any populous areas. They fed on crops from the edges of farms and fish caught from streams.

Eventually, they reached the eastern edge of New Arc. Their travel through the town hardly garnered a single look from the people. The citizens of New Arc acted more distracted than as though under Fice's influence. It seemed from the way they went about their daily business that they might be oblivious to Thasula's fall. Maybe Fice's sway wasn't as far-reaching as Rasi had feared.

Who are we meeting, Alina? Rasi asked for the hundredth time.

"Someone who can help us," she answered yet again. "You must trust me."

They continued through the town as the light snow that had started earlier grew into a heavier snowstorm. By the time the two had ridden through the town, the path they needed was covered and the snow was still building.

How do you know where to go? he asked.

My friend had me memorize the way. Follow the tree line.

Alina offered to share Addison's heated blanket with him, but he declined. He still hadn't come to grips with her explanation of how the blanket worked. *Witchcraft isn't for me,* he answered. The heat from his feverish straps was adequate for him, as they hadn't reached the harshest part of winter yet.

She rolled her eyes and snuggled into the blanket.

The tree line led over hills, into valleys, and finally to an open field. *This is crazy, Alina. We're in the middle of nowhere and we've wasted a lot of time.*

"You promised to trust me. We're close." She looked over her shoulder to the hill they had just descended. Then she pointed to a gnarled, twisted, grouchy-looking tree with a deep knothole that looked like an old man's eye with rings in the bark circling it like wrinkled skin. "I think this is his land."

Whose land?

She didn't answer, only smiled.

Whoever you are taking me to see lives out here for a reason. He doesn't appear to want much company.

"He's a friend, Rasi. He can help us."

After cresting yet another small hill, their path ended at a well-kept area of brownish grass surrounding a small house in the middle of an ocean of white. Two freshly shoveled mounds of snow lined each side of the property. Whoever lived that far out seemed uncommonly concerned about the appearance of their yard.

The black shutters were freshly painted, and the roof sported new shingles. Next to the house was a barn, also well maintained. As they approached the house, Rasi noticed that the porch roof sat twice as high as a normal roof, and the entryway was twice as tall. They stopped and waited.

Soon, an unnaturally tall figure appeared from the rear of the house carrying a shovel piled with snow. He heaved the snow onto one of the mounds before turning and giving a wave.

Rasi curled his upper lip. *A Gildonese, Alina? We cannot trust the Gildonese right now. They're all part of the same pack.*

She shushed him. "I asked you to trust me. He's a friend. He helped Epertase during the Tek War, and if we're to have any hope of destroying Fice, we will need his help again."

I know who he is. I met him during the war. I appreciate what he did, but that was before his people took over.

The figure sauntered around the house with the elegant movements of a gentle breeze. "Why, Queen Alina, what a wonderful surprise it is to have you visit my humble home."

She nodded. "Eldon, my dear friend. I am surprised we got so near before you discovered we were coming."

"Oh, my dear queen. I knew someone was coming long before you arrived."

Alina was stunned. "May I ask how?"

"I have friends who tell me these things."

Alina seemed to sense Rasi's growing tension and ended the small talk. "We are in need of shelter and rest." With a wink, she added in a quiet, conspiratorial tone, "And maybe a little knowledge, if you would be so kind."

A black dog with rust-colored markings on its snout and chest, and whose head stood as high as a normal man's waist, ran from the back of the house and stood next to the Gildonese. His ears pointed like knives high on the top of his head. Eldon petted him and then approached, unfazed by Rasi's apprehension. Rasi's straps lifted from beneath his cloak.

When Eldon stopped short of Shadow, the dog sat next to him with his thick chest puffed out. Eldon got down on one knee and bowed. "The great Rasi of Puimia. I am indeed honored to be in your company again, since when last we met it was for the briefest of moments."

Tell him to rise, Alina. While I appreciate how he helped us back then, I have no need for a Gildonese to kneel before me unless it's after his defeat.

Eldon smiled. "She does not need to tell me what you project with your thoughts, Commander Rasi, as I am quite capable of hearing them myself."

And manipulating them, too, if the tales are true.

Eldon nodded and added, *I have never forced another living being to obey my will ...,* he paused. "Except in battle, that is." Eldon rose from his knee and offered his hand to Alina, helping her down from Shadow. Rasi urged his straps to stay calm.

Friendly or not, the Gildonese was the last race of people Rasi could trust at the moment. He had heard from old King Cecil, Alina's grandfather, that strange things happened to them when they gathered in numbers.

Eldon turned and reached out to help Rasi. Rasi's straps lunged at him before pulling back in a brazen show of intimidation. Eldon didn't flinch.

I can get down on my own, Rasi insisted before swinging his leg over Shadow's back.

"I do not wish you ill, Commander Rasi, and perhaps one day I can prove that to you, but in the meantime," he turned toward Alina, "please enter my home and I will make us a feast. Rasi, enter or don't; it makes no difference to me."

Rasi glared up at Eldon's cold, dark eyes, and reluctantly followed Alina toward the house.

I don't trust him, Alina.

Eldon peered over his shoulder. *Again, Commander Rasi, I must warn you that I can hear your projections.*

Rasi turned toward him. *I know. I just don't care.*

Dinner was mostly silent. Rasi studied Eldon as they ate. While living with his parents he had gotten more skilled at using utensils to push the food around in his mouth without making a scene. Though he was leery about eating Gildonese food, he was also starving. Plus, he had watched the meal's preparation without fear of offending their host as each ingredient was added to the stew. He had seen no poisonous mushrooms or diarrhea-inducing roots of calpinit thrown into the mix.

Eldon broke the silence. "Queen Alina," he said with a piece of lamb hanging from his lips, "though I had given you an open invitation to my home, I must confess to never expecting that you would actually take me up on it, but with that said, I am very pleased that you have. What may I do for you and Epertase?" The piece of lamb dropped to his lap, unnoticed.

Before she could answer, Rasi interrupted, *Are you inferring that you don't know King Fice of the Lowlands?*

"Oh, King Fice. I should have suspected he'd crawl out from under his rock with the Lowlands now a lake and all. I did not say I did not know him, good sir, since I do know *of* him and his pack. After the Tek War, I did some inquiring and must admit he is a highly powerful Gildonese indeed. Has he caused trouble for your kingdom, Your Majesty?"

Rasi grunted and turned his head. *As if he hasn't heard. We need to leave, Alina. We don't need his help.* Rasi faced Eldon. *I thank you for the meal, but I think we will be lea—*

Alina grabbed his forearm. She spoke gently. "Eldon, I am sorry for our rudeness. I believe you when you say you know not what has occurred. It seems Fice's influence has fallen over Lithia and Epertase in much the same way he controlled the Lowlands."

Eldon's face contorted in what Rasi interpreted as genuine surprise. Just the same, Rasi added, *If you're a part of their pack, I'm here to put you on notice. I will kill you after I finish with them in Lithia.*

"You are welcome to try." Eldon chuckled and hid his mouth with his hand. "I am sorry to laugh, Rasi, but you cannot defeat a Gildonese by yourself. No man can. Not to mention, Fice is over twelve hundred years old, and if he has overtaken a kingdom as large as Epertase in less than three months, he is more powerful than any Gildonese ever to live. Tell me, Alina, does Fice have a female accompanying him?"

"Yes. Two, actually. Why?"

Eldon stared down at his hands. "Two? That is not good."

Why?

"Well, Rasi, it's just that female Gildonese are independent and extremely difficult to hold sway over. Females only follow the strongest, and if Fice has managed that feat two times over, his power is great indeed."

Rasi shook his head in disbelief. *If you're so powerful, how did King Thadius defeat your people in the Great War?*

Eldon chewed a piece of meat from his stew before he answered. "Well, I was not there, but I have been told that the Epertasian numbers were too grand and that my people were unable to fend off such a large force. We are powerful, but not invincible."

Yeah? Well, I'll take my chances.

Eldon remained calm and even-tempered. "Rasi, I will make you a deal. At dawn, you and I will meet in front of my home for a duel, and if you are able to inflict any damage on me whatsoever, I will send you away with my blessings and my respect."

Now they were getting somewhere. With pleading eyes, he turned to Alina.

She shrugged her shoulders and rolled her eyes. "Whatever you men need to do to work this out, I suppose, is fine by me. Please do not hurt him, Eldon."

Rasi snorted, trying to hold back a laugh. *Hurt me?* He turned to Eldon and regarded him from head to toe. Then he turned back to Alina. *That's all I must do to prove myself, and you'll leave this place with me?*

"That is all."

Eldon cracked his knuckles and flashed a giddy grin. "Rasi, you may use your sword, a shield, a rock, your funny ...," he pointed limply at Rasi's straps while searching for the right word. "Tentacles," he finally settled on. "Anything you choose to use will be fine, but if you are unable to harm me in any way, then you will let me help you and the queen."

Rasi grinned. He couldn't wait. *See you in the morning.*

Eldon nodded and showed them to their bed. As Rasi lay down with his mind spinning through all the ways his swordplay was going to overwhelm his opponent, he almost forgot Alina was beside him.

"Good night, Rasi," she whispered, and kissed his cheek.

As he lay awake with his back to her, he dreaded closing his eyes for fear of the nightmares that had recently haunted him. Alina's breathing deepened. *Alina?* he asked, jarring her awake.

"What is it, Rasi?"

I'm sorry I woke you.

"It's all right. What's wrong? Are you worried about tomorrow?"

Tomorrow? Oh. No, not that.

"Then what?"

He felt her hand on his side. *Do you know what they call me in my dreams?*

"No, Rasi. How would I know that?"

They call me the King of the Dead.

Her hand slid up past his straps and touched his cheek. "That's awful. Why do they call you that?"

Because the people in my dreams are the people I've sent to the other side. They hate me, but at the same time fear me since I'm the one who put them there. I never wanted to be feared or hated. When I wake up, I tell myself of all the good I've done. I tell myself that the men in my dreams deserved what came to them. But that doesn't help.

"Rasi, they're only dreams."

No. They're not. At first, I tried to tell myself they were, but now I know better. They aren't dreams. They're more than that.

"What do you think they are, then?"

I know what they are, Alina. They're visions of what awaits me when I leave this world. They are my future. I am damned to be their king.

"By the gods, Rasi. That's horrible. You should never have to live with such dreams. They aren't true." She paused for a moment before asking, "Do you want to know what I see in my dreams?"

Rasi nodded with his eyes closed.

"I see you. I see the kindest man I could ever know. And it's when I wake from those dreams that I'm at my happiest. That you can bring such joy to someone counts for something. I don't know what happens when we leave this world, but I know this—the place I go will not make me lonely because you'll be there with me. Of that I am sure."

Rasi wasn't so sure. If that's what she believed, he didn't want to convince her otherwise. No, it was his burden and he was angry with himself for sharing it with her.

She leaned over and kissed him with the gentleness of a feather. He rolled to face her and took her in his arms. *I missed you.*

"No more talking," she said as she pulled him onto her and then kissed him again.

Rasi didn't sleep as he lay next to Alina on the rough bedding. By morning, he was up and ready before she stirred.

Eldon was waiting at the kitchen table with two plates of eggs. "Breakfast first?" he asked.

Rasi shook his head. *Let's get this over with so I can move on. I've got a lot of planning to do.*

"Very well." Eldon rose.

Rasi stared up at him. He had momentarily forgotten how tall his opponent was. Eldon didn't wear armor, only loose-fitting clothes, and he didn't carry any weapons as he marched through the front door. Rasi followed, anxious for the coming contest and confident of the outcome.

The suns weren't yet visible at the southern horizon. A pinch of warm coral light on the undersides of the dusty clouds did little to erase the bitterness of the morning air. Shadow's tracks from the day before had been covered by an overnight snowfall, erasing any signs that he and Alina had ever come. Despite the fresh snow, Eldon had already prepared a small clearing in the dormant grass, a battle ring of sorts. Rasi drew his sword and hopped from the porch. He and Eldon circled each other.

Eldon smiled. "Any time you are ready, Commander Rasi."

Rasi drew back his arm, lifting his blade slightly above his right shoulder with a downward slant. He turned his body to the side as his straps snapped in the air and mirrored Eldon's subtle movements. The Gildonese stepped closer, unfazed.

Rasi had no interest in drawing out the contest. In the instant it took for him to flex his arm and drive the blade forward for a game-ending blow, Eldon reached out with slug-like speed and struck

Rasi's jaw. The blow stunned him—as much because of his inability to dodge the slow punch as from the pain. Eldon stood waiting while Rasi gathered himself and wiped his swollen lip. Rasi attacked again, and again Eldon maneuvered at the last moment, this time striking him in the chest.

Rasi clutched his sword with both hands. He spun, but Eldon's fist caught him in the side. Again, Eldon's seemingly slow attack was too fast to defend. It didn't make sense.

The next blow stole Rasi's air. His straps pounced like lightning, but Eldon backed away and wove his arms in painfully slow movements, batting each strap away with ease.

Rasi had never before felt the sting of being bested so effortlessly. Each time he lunged, it was as though Eldon knew his intentions first, and though Eldon was slow in his reactions, Rasi couldn't break through.

He backed away, breathing heavier after each attack.

"Have you finished?" Eldon asked, barely winded.

Just catching my breath.

"Good, because I have just begun."

Rasi believed him. Out of the corner of his eye, he saw Alina exit the house and sit on the edge of the porch, wrapped in her heated blanket. Her presence reinvigorated him. He twirled his sword while his straps lunged at the Gildonese. He dug deep for his best moves, moves not taught in soldiering, yet each attack was met with failure and pain. He swung his sword, no longer intending to kill his opponent, but just to land any blow he could, regardless of its lethality. He attacked high and then low, spinning and weaving, but nothing worked. Desperate, he dove at Eldon's waist, but the Gildonese simply slid out of the way, leaving Rasi with a face full of snow and blood.

Eldon allowed him space to get back to his feet. Rasi staggered to the porch where Alina stood. She handed him a glass and he took a swig of water.

"Have you finished?" she asked, sounding slightly annoyed.

Why can't I hit him? He moves so slowly.

"Slow?" Her eyes widened. "I can't even see his attacks; they're so fast."

Rasi tilted his head. He handed her the glass and turned back to his opponent.

All right, Eldon. One more shot. The Gildonese gave a smug bow and a smile.

Rasi returned Eldon's smile with newfound respect. He wiped the blood from his mouth across his arm and then strutted back to the fray.

"You have much heart, I'll give you that," Eldon said.

Shut up and fight.

With the speed of lightning, Rasi drove his blade forward, parried a fist, and swung his sword again. Eldon slid to the side, hit Rasi's elbow with his open palm, and landed another bone-jarring blow to Rasi's cheek before the sword hit the ground.

Rasi's straps pounced, only to be effortlessly swatted away. Rasi drew back his left fist and hurled his other fist upward without thought. Eldon's knuckles slammed his left shoulder, but something incredible happened. Rasi's right fist—the one he had blindly thrown at the open air—struck Eldon's extended arm.

The Gildonese opened his eyes wide. He stepped back and rubbed his arm. The blow wasn't a hard one, and it wasn't damaging, but it had landed. By god, it had landed.

Rasi cracked a bloody smile. He wasn't sure what he had figured out, but he was pleased just the same. He waited on edge for Eldon to lose his temper and deliver a real beating. Instead, Eldon lowered his arms to his side and relaxed his stance.

"Very impressive, Commander Rasi."

Rasi sighed.

"Do you know what you just did? How you made contact with my arm, I mean?"

Rasi shook his head.

"I'd be honored to teach you if you are inclined to stay."

Rasi thought about the prospect of fighting several Gildonese at once, and suddenly Eldon's offer seemed more desirable. He walked toward the porch where Alina stood with an "I told you so" grin.

Hey, I hit him.

"Yes, you did, Rasi. I'm very proud of you. Are we staying, then?"

For a bit, I guess. He kissed her cheek as he passed.

Alina called the dinner that night exquisite. Rasi tried to remember the taste of pork as he bit into it. All he got from each bite was extra stinging from the cuts on the insides of his lips. He nodded and pretended it was good just the same.

"Spices," Eldon answered a question not asked.

I taste a hint of salt? Rasi answered, playing along. Alina gave him a look.

Eldon tilted his head. "Very good, Rasi. I do love to add salt."

Rasi secretly passed a couple bites under the table to Eldon's dog. *What's the dog's name, by the way?*

Eldon looked up from his meal with another hunk of meat dangling from his lips. "I call him Dog," he said, and stuffed the rest of his food into his mouth. "He is the only dog here, so I see no need to remember names. He doesn't seem to mind." Eldon rose from the table and invited Alina and Rasi to the front porch for a conversation. He said he had a lot to share.

"What about cleaning up?" Alina asked.

"Do not to worry. I will clean after you are asleep, as I don't need much sleep myself."

Alina wrapped Addison's blanket over her shoulders and snuggled next to Rasi on the stoop. Eldon stood, leaning against a porch post. He lit a long, curvy pipe and took a toke, the embers flaring orange. He offered Rasi a pipe, but Rasi declined with a polite wave.

"I feel it prudent we discuss the coming war, and do not be misled, it is war that you prepare for. This Gildonese—this Fice—will not give up power once he has dug in. If, as you say, Fice has swayed both Lithia and portions of Epertase, then your battle is no longer reclaiming the castle, but all-out war. I find it difficult to believe that six or even seven Gildonese working together could move so fast to acquire such large chunks of territory, but I have no reason to doubt what you have told me, which is what gives me great pause. I will freely join in your struggle, but you must know, a pack as old as the one which you challenge will be more than a young Gildonese such as myself can handle."

Alina interrupted, "How old are you anyway, Eldon?"

"I was born to a young Gildonese woman named Zoertha. She raised me in hiding for over a hundred years before she died of what you would call Gildonese Syndrome. Are you familiar?"

Rasi and Alina shook their heads in concert. Dog stretched out on the porch and Rasi scratched behind his ear.

"It is a disease that many believe was caused by witchcraft. It takes many years to kill its victims. My mother, for instance, over those many years, fell helpless as parts of her body slowly crumbled into dust—first a finger here and there, then a foot, and so on. Eventually, the disease infiltrated her blood until her hearts became affected, and once that happened, she screamed in pain for three days until her hearts crumbled and she died."

Alina covered her mouth. "I'm so sorry. That's horrible."

He frowned. "I am sorry as well. Even nearly eight hundred years later, I am still moved to tears when I think of her." He wiped his moist eyes and refocused on the matter at hand. "The only way you will stop Fice is to kill him, which, as you might imagine, will be highly difficult, if not impossible."

So just cut off the head? Rasi asked. *The same as any solid war plan.*

Eldon winced and inhaled between pursed lips. "Not quite. When you kill the head of a Gildonese pack, there is an immediate and subconscious power struggle within the pack. To truly end Fice's sway and restore order, his whole pack must be killed or separated before the new leader tastes power. If separated by enough distance, the pack members will simply move on, mostly forgetting their dominant desires, and live out the rest of their lives in peace. That is why, many years ago, the young Epertasian king Thadius was forced to go to war with my people.

"You have seen our sway in numbers as small as seven, so you can imagine the strength of a Gildonese who held sway over an entire civilization. I, for one, am glad of Epertase's victory all those years back, else I would be no more than a slave at the bottom of the pack. And you would all likely be dead."

How did you avoid Fice's sway?

"When he took over the Lowlands a few hundred years after the Great War, I was very young. I took a holiday to the Wastelands for a couple hundred years or so. By the time I returned, he was completely embedded in the Lowlands and wasn't looking beyond their border for others. One of my mother's last wishes before she died was that I never follow my father's footsteps into Gildonese servitude. My mother always appreciated your species and wanted nothing to do with swaying you. She knew what could happen."

Alina asked, "Has there ever been a man who could defeat a Gildonese in one-on-one combat?"

Eldon stared into the distance for a moment, pondering. Then he nodded. "I have heard legend of an Epertasian who went by the name of Mallard who could perform such a feat, but he ultimately found his demise at the hands of a strong Gildonese during the war."

"So, it can be done?" she asked.

Eldon chuckled. "My dear queen, the warrior Mallard was said to have lived with a Gildonese pack for as many as fifteen years before he was skilled enough to face even the youngest of my people." He turned his attention to Rasi. "Your time with me, I fear, will only be sufficient to teach you enough to meet your painful end. You should reconsider how soon you will attempt this fight."

My son will not be born into a world ruled by Fice. Besides, if what you say is true, the longer we wait, the tighter his grip on Epertase will become.

"That is correct."

The three continued their conversation until Alina yawned. She thanked Eldon and retired for the evening. Rasi stood as well and nodded at the Gildonese. Though trust was building, he remained cautious in case Eldon was subtly using his gift of sway. Something about the Gildonese, however, told Rasi that he wasn't.

The two men shook hands.

Eldon held Rasi's hand a hair longer than necessary. "We will begin early in the morning. Fice and his pack are deadly, and your preparation will be short in the grand scheme of things."

I'm ready to learn.

CHAPTER 25
THE TUNNELS OF EIGER

Simcane holed up in an abandoned general store on the eastern edge of Lithia. Though ransacked, there was enough food left to keep them fed until they were ready to finish the journey to the Lands of Muél. As the days passed, Thairen complained less and less about his arms. The speed at which he recovered left Simcane highly doubtful about his claims of healing like anyone else.

As they led Shelby toward the hostile, barren bit of hell known as the Lands of Muél, Thairen worked his elbows to make sure they were in fighting shape. For centuries people had given the Lands of Muél a wide berth, and there were plenty of reasons. Namely ochrids. A lot of ochrids. Hundreds of ochrids.

As they walked, Thairen asked, "Hey, Sim, why do ochrids stay so close to the Tunnels of Eiger anyway?"

"That's where the crystals are. They can't wander far from them."

"That doesn't make sense. I heard the remains of one were found by a couple hunters in the Forest of Concore near Shadows Peak a few years back."

"Yeah, I've heard that, too. There's rumors of a crystal deposit buried deep below Shadows Peak, though as far as I know no one has ever found any."

"Have you ever seen the crystal walls of Eiger?"

Simcane shook his head.

"Then how do you know that the crystals blind the ochrids to you?"

"Because King Logan's using them."

"You don't happen to have any on you, do ya?"

Simcane shook his head.

"Well, this sounds like fun then. Where do we sign up?"

"You're already signed up. We're almost there."

Before they reached the perimeter of Muél, sounds like high-pitched wheezing and pig-like snorts started to reach them. For the first time since he had known Thairen, he saw a hint of concern on the warrior's face. It would be hard to heal from being devoured.

Thairen said, "Tell me again why King Logan hides in the Tunnels."

"No one will look for them there."

"There's a reason for that. How exactly do you plan to survive an ochrid attack?"

"I don't plan to face them. However, if we're so unlucky, legend has it that the creatures have a weakness at the back of their mouth." Simcane grinned. "Unfortunately, you must get past their leech-filled tails, razor claws, and rows of fangs to reach it."

"How is it you know so much about killing these things?"

"I've heard of mercenaries testing their mettle against them."

Thairen cocked his head. "Heard, huh?"

"Well, maybe one mercenary." Simcane winked and grinned again. "Do I sense some apprehension, Thairen?"

Thairen crinkled his upper lip, showing the small gap left by his broken front tooth. "Of course not." He slid a dagger from his waistband. "I rather look forward to the challenge, actually." The nervousness Simcane had seen in the warrior quickly turned to resolve.

As they entered the Lands of Muél, Simcane didn't have to tell Thairen it was time for silence. The rocky terrain separating Muél from the rest of Lithia was difficult to traverse, especially with a horse in tow, but they slowly hobbled across. Shelby neighed and pulled at his lead. "Eaaasy," Simcane said, and petted Shelby's neck. Thairen moved ahead, ready to get things moving.

A patch of trees with the lower branches stripped bare pointed the way. The brush and grass throughout Muél were mere stubble. "Are they vegetarians?" Thairen whispered.

"Probably hunted most of the game away." As he listened to the dark, he imagined how excited the ochrids would be with meat for a change. He wondered if they'd even leave his bones. With a smirk, he whispered, "We've got two choices. We can quickly find the entrance to Eiger, or we can fight all the ochrids." One look at Thairen's eager face made him regret his sarcasm. "Let's just find the tunnel."

And then the snorts and wheezes around them stopped. The hunt had begun.

"They're coming," he whispered.

Thairen squeezed the hilts of his blades. "Time to fight?" he asked, peering at Simcane over his shoulder.

Simcane shook his head. "We'd never survive fighting more than one at a time. If we have to fight, we need to get them separated."

"And how would we do that?"

"You don't wanna know. Let's just get to the tunnels." Simcane climbed onto Shelby's back and Thairen climbed up behind. No more need for stealth. Simcane lashed Shelby into a full gallop across the field toward where the trees ended. Part of his strategy relied on luck in finding the tunnel entrance before being overwhelmed by ochrids, while the other part ... well, he was glad to have Thairen along for that.

While speeding through the scattered trees, the unmistakable sound of stampeding animals intensified behind them. Thairen began laughing. The pursuing snorts revealed the ochrids' speed advantage over Shelby, and Simcane's panic rose.

Shelby burst from the thin tree line.

"There it is," he shouted, snapping Thairen's attention to their fore. In the distance, a raised rock formation surrounded a cave that had a blue glow. "Whatever happens, get to those tunnels."

Thairen couldn't stop laughing.

An ochrid leaped in front of Shelby. Simcane flinched and yanked the reins, steering him around the beast as it pounced. It flung a leech past Simcane's head and then raced to retrieve it.

Almost there.

Another beast caught Simcane's eye too late for him to react. Simcane braced for impact. The ochrid crashed into him, and he and the creature tumbled to the ground. Simcane used the beast's momentum to hurl it from his chest. Still on Shelby, Thairen grabbed the reins and slowed the steed, looking back at Simcane.

Simcane waved him off. "Just go. Get to the cave."

Simcane barely got to his feet before the ochrid righted itself. It was missing one of its front legs. More ochrids joined the game. Simcane ignored them, focusing on the first one. *Come on, you bastard. Let's have that tail.*

The ochrid stalked him left to right. The others gathered around. Ochrids were at their fiercest against each other when their own meal was at stake. That knowledge kept Simcane focused on the first one. The monster whipped its tail forward. Simcane stepped into the path of the leech. It slapped his cheek and stuck there. He didn't pull it away as it sank its tiny teeth into his face. The ochrid kept its distance, watching and waiting for the leech's toxins to do their work.

Simcane wobbled and fell to his rear. When a smaller ochrid approached, the first ochrid spun toward it with an aggressive hiss. The smaller ochrid hissed in return. The two leaped at each other and engaged in a violent tumble of ripping claws and snapping teeth. The battle was quick and fierce. Missing a leg didn't hamper the bigger one at all. It stood over its cowering foe until the smaller creature slunk away. Another beast used the fight to sneak to Simcane's foot and quietly snatch his ankle in its teeth. The first one turned and charged. Simcane's foot dropped back to the ground as the sneaky one retreated. The others lowered their heads in submission as the big one guarded its prey. Not wanting to challenge the victor any further, and not wanting to miss out on a fresh meal, the others turned toward Thairen and galloped back into the chase.

Perfect, Simcane thought. His feet and lower legs were already numb. He lifted his hand and flopped it next to his cheek while he still had the strength to do so. He touched the leech with one finger.

And he waited.

As the muscles of his chest seized against his ribs, he waited.

As the ochrid lowered its head over his face and sniffed him from head to toe, he waited.

Even as his eyes went blurry, he waited.

His timing had to be flawless or he wouldn't survive. He had the creature right where he wanted it. The hunted and the hunter were now alone. The ochrid tilted its head back and released a victorious roar. Simcane had just enough strength to flip his hand against the leech on his face. With a pinch of what little control he had left in his fingers, he squeezed the slimy creature before it could slither away. Its guts squirted onto his hand and cheek. He tore it from his skin and dropped it.

With the leech gone, the strength returned to his arms and legs. The ochrid opened its mouth for the kill. Simcane crammed his fist into the beast's open mouth and grabbed the soft, gooey flap hanging near the back of its throat. He ripped the hunk of flesh free and threw it to the ground. The beast shrieked and tumbled backward.

Simcane pushed himself to his wobbly feet and staggered to the gasping, seizing ochrid as it flopped on its side. With a thrust of his sword, he ended its suffering. Then he looked toward the cave. He didn't see Thairen or the ochrids and hoped Thairen had found the crystals in time. If not, Simcane would soon find the creatures in the middle of a feast.

Simcane ran to the mouth of the cave and ducked inside. A dull blue glow lit the cave from deep within. Angry snorts echoed from different tunnels. Simcane raced to the glowing walls. Thousands of fist-sized, jagged crystals peppered the rock. He rubbed his fingers along the sharp edges of one of them. He pried one free with his sword, shoved it into his pocket, and dug out a second. That one he held in his palm. He started down the tunnel. He didn't have to go far before he saw Thairen leading Shelby toward him.

Thairen shouted, "Simcane, you're a genius." He was still laughing. Simcane didn't know whether the ochrids could hunt by sound, but if Thairen had his way, they were about to find out.

"How about you keep it down a bit?" Simcane whispered.

The two men met at the opening to another tunnel. Thairen shouted, "These crystals work great. We can walk right out of here."

Shelby's saddle was lined with so many bright blue crystals that Simcane chuckled. The entrance filled with more scampering claws.

Thairen couldn't stop laughing. "Here they come again." Shelby started to dance nervously and grunt. In what might have been the first genuine act of kindness Simcane had ever seen in his nearly invulnerable friend, Thairen caressed Shelby's muzzle and pressed his cheek to the horse's neck. Then he ruined it by whispering into Shelby's ear, "Do you think they like horse meat as much as they do people?" Shelby jerked away as though he understood.

Simcane pressed against the wall beside Shelby while Thairen stepped into the charging ochrids' path. "Watch this," Thairen said. The ochrids parted around him as they charged by. From within their stampede, Thairen casually waved at Simcane. Toward the end of the nearly twenty-strong herd, three ochrids slowed and stopped with their snouts raised.

Simcane froze, wondering if they had gotten a scent.

Thairen continued laughing.

The ochrids crept toward them, sniffing the air. Simcane pried another crystal from the wall just in case.

"That's hilarious, Sim. They smell us."

It didn't seem so hilarious.

The ochrids perked their gnarled ears. Maybe they heard them as well.

Simcane snapped, "Shut up."

"Why?" Thairen asked. One of the ochrids turned toward Thairen's voice. Thairen jammed a crystal at its eyes and it turned away. He tapped its head. "They're stupid, Sim." He laughed some more. Who needed a jester when the threat of death was so funny?

The three ochrids snorted and then ran to catch the rest of the herd. As vast as the tunnels were said to be, the ochrids could be searching for hours.

The men led Shelby deeper into the tunnels, the glowing crystals lighting the way. At the first serpent-tongued split, they went left. At the next, right. And then another left, just as Logan had said. Soon, they found a Lith soldier covered in crystals and guarding some kind of entrance.

Simcane regarded his overabundance of caution. "Not taking any chances, are you?"

The soldier shook his head fervently. "No way."

"Good thinking."

"Mr. Simcane? We've been expecting you." The soldier stepped aside.

Simcane and Thairen continued into a sprawling, open cavern filled with dozens of Lith soldiers. A large hole in the ceiling sucked up smoke from a fire in the center of the cavern. Multiple boar carcasses rotated on skewers over the flames.

Seeing his old friend, King Logan hurried over. "Simcane, great to see you. Are you hungry? We were just about to feast."

"I could eat. A little late for a meal, though, no?"

"That I can't argue. But the smoke is less likely to be seen at this hour."

"Ah." He looked around at the small army. "Are you sure you can trust all of these men?"

"Most definitely. They're from my Royal Guard. They would die for me and my wife. In fact, many did as we journeyed through Muél. The ochrids are indeed vicious."

Thairen marched down the steps to one of the roasting boars. Without being invited, he reached over the intense flame and tore off a hunk, singing his arm hairs and probably his arm in the process.

Logan asked, "Who's your brash companion?"

Simcane rubbed his forehead and sighed. "You'll have to ignore his rudeness. His name is Thairen."

"I've heard of him." Logan leaned close and whispered, "Is he as crazy as I've heard?"

As Thairen tore into the meat, a Lith happened too close and he growled at him.

"I don't know what you've heard, but I would wager he's crazier. But when it comes to fighting, he's unmatched."

Simcane and Logan found a seat on a rock formation and accepted slices of wild boar served on slabs of rock. "So, what was the meeting about?" Logan asked.

Simcane recounted Fice's speech, adding, "It wasn't worth a dragon's shit."

"Do you have any suggestions for how to deal with King Fice?"

"Maybe. First, we need to find a Gildonese I worked with during the Tek War. His name's Eldon and he lives in New Arc. Perhaps he can give some insight into how to defeat Fice." He paused and then added, "And if Rasi isn't already dead, we'd do well to locate him."

Logan nodded.

With Thairen off eating somewhere by himself, the two men feasted and discussed their pending travel to Eldon's home.

CHAPTER 26

DREAMS OF YESTERYEAR

In the newly renamed Castle Fice, King Fice lay on the hard floor of King Logan's chambers. He had ordered Ulrac, his second-in-command, to stand guard outside. It was time for his monthly sleep which would see the suns rise and set and rise again before he awakened.

Ulrac leaned his head into the room and announced, "The castle and surrounding areas have been evacuated, King."

Fice nodded. He didn't like mere mortals to hear his uncontrolled shrieking while he dreamed, and it was just easier to send them away beforehand than to sway them to forget after. Ulrac closed the door.

Josilyn stepped from behind a folding partition while tying her pants and readjusting her blouse. "Are you ready for your sleep, my love?"

Fice nodded.

She sat beside him and began caressing his hair. She sang an ancient Gildonese song in his head. Her doubled voice overlapped itself in harmonic waves to ease him into his twisty, violent dreams. Her warm, soothing breath gently brushed his ear. Before he was even asleep, his eyelids started to twitch. His clenched and shaking fists cramped. He moaned as he fought against his slumber.

It wasn't that Fice didn't know when he started dreaming, because he was acutely aware of the fact; he just couldn't control what played out in his mind. For at least the ten-thousandth time in the last thousand years, he found himself at the final massacre of the Gildonese-Epertasian war, once again helpless to alter its violent course. The Gildonese lost, as they had in each previous nightmare, and his pack of twelve was down to five. With the arrows raining like hail, he needed to escape or, like most of the other packs, they would be down to none.

The Gildonese had fought hard, slaughtering thousands of Epertasians along the way, but the sheer numbers of their enemy were too grand. Fice scanned the killing ground. He'd never seen so many lifeless Gildonese bodies, many with Epertasian arrows embedded in their skulls or hearts, or all three.

Wave after wave of arrows launched from the eastern hills and battered their shields as they held them above their heads. The assault was relentless and had been for days. There were more arrows than space on the face of Fice's shield, and each new assault added more. The sounds of battle pounded his sensitive ears. *Tink. Crack. Thunk.* And the screams. Damn, the screams.

Fice's reduced pack, as well as the rest of the Gildonese packs near him, could not advance, nor could they retreat, for they had been surrounded. It seemed every male Epertasian and Lith had joined the fight.

Closer to the front lines, Gildonese warriors met the overwhelming Epertasian forces and fell to their swords, though they made their enemies pay dearly.

This battle was different from the previous battles of the year-long war. The Gildonese had gained ground in each of the previous battles and were nearing the capital city of Thasula. This was King Thadius's desperate last stand, and the bastard was winning.

Near the rear of the Gildonese army, Fice's supreme commander and his hundred-strong pack faced a similar fight against the Liths.

Against every Gildonese instinct, Fice ordered his own pack not to help the supreme commander. Fice mentally barked orders to stay put while he planned. A barrage of arrows felled his longtime friend Kasartha beside him.

We must retreat, he screamed in their heads. *Syphis? Where are you?*

His most loyal follower struggled to his side, arrows pounding his protective shield and exposed legs. "Yes, my master," he answered without flinching as another arrow plunged into the meat of his thigh.

We must flee. Where should we go, Syphis?

"Lithia?" Syphis suggested.

Fice shook his head. "Lithia hunts us as well. They have secretly allied with Epertase and are battering the supreme commander as we speak. It's no safer there than it is here."

"The mountains near Pataska?" He pointed to the visible tips.

"They would hunt us down. We need an army … or a country." A powerful wave of nausea swept through him and was followed by the grandest rush of strength he had ever known. He cried, "Syphis, the supreme commander has fallen."

Syphis stood emotionless.

The war is lost. There will be an immediate struggle for the supreme commander's replacement.

"Are you feeling the pull?" Syphis asked.

Fice nodded; it was strong.

"Should you take his position?"

"Whoever assumes that role will be dead by morning. We are far enough from where he fell that we can flee the pull. Recitar. We will hide in Recitar until the day we exact vengeance on Epertase."

A packless Gildonese wandered past aimlessly. He held neither shield nor sword as he staggered over the battlefield among the raining arrows. Either by luck or the will of the gods, the arrows had thus far missed his flesh. He was leaderless and confused.

He turned back as if drawn to Fice's sway. The Gildonese stranger stumbled toward him. His eyes were glossy and bewildered.

Cover him with your shields, Fice ordered his remaining pack. As the stranger approached, Fice asked his allegiance.

At first, he answered that he didn't know anymore. But Fice swayed him. Then the stranger shook off his confusion and answered, "To you, of course, my liege."

What is your name?

"I am Ulrac of the pack of Fice."

Fice smirked. *Very well, Ulrac. Join us in our escape.*

As an accepted member of Fice's pack, Ulrac's senses quickly flowed back to him. He lifted a discarded Gildonese shield from the blood-drenched ground.

While the scattered Gildonese army charged headlong into the endless wave of Epertasian soldiers, Fice and his pack knifed through their sloppy ranks toward the northern Epertasian border. He knew he'd have a fight there as well, but if he could get to the mostly untouched Recitar, he might have a chance. Thadius's strength was undoubtedly weaker in the north.

While he and his pack fled, he was filled with another rush of nausea and pain as another Gildonese took the supreme commander's role only to lose his life in that very instant. He was smothered again and again with those same ominous and sickening feelings. When would his brethren learn? When would they realize the war had been lost and their thirst for power would end with their deaths?

The front lines echoed with screams of Gildonese and Epertasians alike. Swords and shields and armor collided in a symphony of deadly cries. Fice and his pack ran as if gliding across the battlefield, their large shields held above their heads. Fice's legs bled from the arrows that had painfully found their marks.

Most of the other Gildonese raced blindly toward the fight, while he and his pack continued to cross northward through their ranks. With the grace of angels and the hatred of devils, they hurdled the dead and dying Gildonese along the way. More Epertasian soldiers advanced from the north. Their ranks were not as thick as those protecting Thasula, and Fice and his pack prepared to meet them head on.

He screamed, "We must pass through them to escape."

Fice and his pack outran the rain of arrows from the east and hurled their shields to the dirt. As Fice ran, he bent at the waist and his fingers skimmed the ground to snatch two discarded Gildonese war hammers. His pack found weapons of their own.

The Epertasians shouted the order to charge.

Fice extended both hammers at his sides. He roared and lulled the first of the Epertasian attackers into slowness. Then he filled their heads with static, a skill used by only the most powerful of Gildonese. They swung their swords and shields, but his war hammers came too fast to elude. Their heads smashed; their bones snapped. And Fice continued swinging with every ounce of his vengeful hate.

His pack leaped into the fight, equally violent and almost equally skilled. Fice was drenched in blood by the time the relentless Epertasian mass took their first pause. He looked to the skies and roared again, blood dripping from his chin and his matted hair.

A different Gildonese presence swarmed his senses and he looked to his left as a fire-haired female joined his fight. His powers of sway were strengthening, he felt it, and a female joining his pack only proved as much. And this female was skilled, swinging a sword with devastating grace.

The brave Epertasians attacked again. Fice smashed his hammer into Epertasian heads, cracking their helmets and shattering their skulls. His next upward swing took the jaw off another soldier. They continued coming, and Fice and his pack continued releasing their souls from their mortal bodies.

As Fice fought surge after surge, Syphis drifted farther away in the press of bodies. Even as Fice wielded his hammers against more soldiers, he watched his friend with a cautious eye.

Syphis laid waste to his attackers almost as effortlessly as Fice until he stood alone as the Epertasian soldiers backed away. The reason for their quasi-retreat quickly revealed itself when they parted to make way for a long-haired warrior in a blood-smeared breastplate. Fice recognized the subtle powder-blue symbol of a backward "C" adorning the man's thigh plate.

An overwhelming surge of fear for Syphis rushed through him. He started toward his friend, plowing through the Epertasian masses, but they were too thick and Syphis too far away. Syphis laughed at the lone warrior's gall.

Fice shouted in his mind, *Syphis.* He thrust the butt of his hammer into an Epertasian nose. *Fall back, Syphis. Do not fight him alone.* By the time Fice freed himself from the mob of soldiers, Syphis's head lay in the dirt with his dead, soulless eyes staring back at him.

"Nooooo," Fice cried. He pounded his hammers into Epertasian faces with speed and fury until he stood within a horse-length of Syphis's murderer. "What is your name, warrior, for I must know it before your head joins my friend's."

The warrior answered with an unimpressed smirk, "Mallard."

"You were taught by the Ciliac tribe and took an oath never to use your training against the Gildonese."

"Well, that was before I killed Ciliac and his pack."

"You are a traitor to the Gildonese who took you in."

"You brought war to my countrymen."

Fice lifted his hammers. "Now I bring war to you."

Mallard lifted his sword.

Even with Fice's sway working to perfection, Mallard avoided his deadly hammers while delivering flawless strikes with his sword. Fice groaned and concentrated, but Mallard was gifted and eluded his blows. Fice looked to his pack for an advantage, but his Gildonese brethren were being swarmed by Epertasian soldiers. A small slice of Fice's flesh just below his ribs flew into the air. Fice grunted and gnashed his teeth. This warrior may be too skilled after all.

Then Fice saw the fire-haired female Gildonese break away from the fray and creep toward Mallard's back. Some of the Epertasians shouted warnings, but Fice filled Mallard's head with screaming static.

Mallard laughed. "You cannot distract me with petty mind screams. Ignoring them was the first lesson Ciliac taught me."

Fice didn't intend to distract him, only to prevent him from hearing the warnings. Mallard poised for his next attack. Fice drew back, hoping to keep his attention. Then, in an explosion of glorious violence, the female's blade burst from Mallard's chest. Fice soaked in the delight the warrior's stunned expression gave him as the female removed her sword and Mallard fell to his knees.

Fice lifted Mallard's chin. "I hope Syphis is waiting for you on the other side. He will have more pain for you there."

Mallard spat a mouthful of blood onto Fice's thigh. Fice glanced at the devastated Epertasians to make sure they were still watching. He smiled. With an effortless swing, he removed Mallard's head. While the Epertasians watched in horror, he retrieved Mallard's head and placed it next to Syphis's as he had promised. Now, the only promise he had left to fulfill was vengeance on Epertase, which he knew would take patience and time. He asked his new female companion her name.

Josilyn, she answered with pride.

Fice grinned. "You belong to me now."

"I am honored."

The Gildonese continued fighting through the thinning Epertasian forces until they were able to break through their lines and run from the battle. The Epertasians gave chase, but Gildonese speed all but guaranteed their escape.

Fice's nightmares of the war continued through his retreat and into his escapes from the many Epertasian kill squads later sent to eliminate rogue packs.

After a bloody fight with one such group, Fice and his pack reached the dense, overgrown border of the primitive country known as Recitar.

As he stood on a large boulder in the center of the wall of brambles, he stared at a distant city. Though it was the ugliest, most decrepit city he had ever beheld, it was the most beautiful as well.

He turned to his pack, his family. As he stared at them and his dream world faded, everything grew brighter until the light swallowed their images completely. The brightness was followed by a sudden darkness.

And then he was again in the center of the Epertasian battlefield, cursed to relive the final battle in his dreams for eternity.

After reliving the horrors of that day at least a dozen more times, the scene flared to whiteness and ended yet again.

This time, he sat up on the castle floor and scanned the room to get his bearings. The desk and nightstands were overturned. The covers had been ripped from the bed and lay on the floor. The pictures had been torn from the walls and their frames smashed to pieces. His senses slowly returned, and he remembered he was in the Lith castle. He felt rested, yet his muscles ached.

He wiped blood from his lips and sweat from his face and gathered his composure. His knuckles ached and the blood-stained stone walls revealed the painful reason why. He opened the door to see Ulrac standing guard.

Ulrac smiled. "Good sleep, King?"

"Wonderful. I am prepared for another moon cycle or two. Were my dreams hurtful to your ears this time as well?"

"Deafening."

Fice looked up and down the halls. "Where's Josilyn?"

"I'm not sure."

"Find her and send her to me, as I am in need of company and I much prefer her soothing voice to yours leading me from, as well as to, my rest."

Ulrac bowed before taking his leave.

CHAPTER 27
TRAINING TO DEFEAT

Rasi grunted from Eldon's blow, the sting still burning in his jaw.

"Again," Eldon ordered.

Rasi lifted his fists and stalked forward. Before he threw his next strike, Eldon jabbed a finger into the soft flesh of his shoulder, shooting numbness down his arm.

"Again."

Rasi tried a kick, but Eldon struck him in the groin before he could draw back his foot.

"Do you see why you lose with each advance?" Eldon shouted.

Rasi shook his head.

"Because even though you are a skilled combatant, you still think, even if only for an instant, before you strike. The reason I appear so slow to you when I attack is because I am lulling your senses into thinking I am. I hear your muscles contract and your reflective thoughts before you ever launch your attack. When you struck my arm on that first day, you were concentrating on your initial assault. Though I was likely diverted by your overwhelming tentacles and the intentions of your coming strike, you were able to get your other fist to where my arm was going to be instead of where my arm was. It is much like the way I attack you. You mustn't attack where I am but make me go to where you are attacking. Either by thinking it or telegraphing it.

"That first day, you didn't punch at my arm, you punched where you thought my arm was going to be. And you did it by instinct. If you planned such a tactic, I'd have read your intentions. But you didn't. You improvised at that moment and I was unable to avoid your blow. You must overwhelm me, distract me, and then attack on instinct. If you think you will skewer me, I already know before you try. Do you understand?"

Rasi shook his head. *Not really.*

"You'll get it … Again."

As Rasi stepped into Eldon's makeshift fighting ring for another beating, or what Eldon loosely referred to as a "lesson," his Gildonese trainer added a new element. Rasi's head filled with a low hum that built into a loud static. Eldon attacked. Rasi was on his knees before he felt the first blow. Eldon backed away, the static fading until it was gone.

What did you do? Rasi rubbed his jaw.

Eldon grinned. "That's called a mind scream. It will not harm you; it is only designed to distract you. Mind screams are a difficult skill to master and can only be used in short bursts as they cause incredible mental fatigue. I do not know whether Fice is able to perform them, but you must assume he is and be prepared."

Eldon bent his fingers back and cracked his knuckles. "Again."

Rasi continued absorbing blow after blow until Eldon grew more tired of striking him than he was from being struck. He imagined the pain he would feel had Eldon not been holding back.

Alina announced lunch from the front door. The two warriors agreed on a break and hurried inside to eat. Getting an ass-beating all morning made Rasi quite hungry. She dabbed with a rag at the trickles of blood from Rasi's nose, mouth, and small lacerations on both cheeks while he ate. Rasi ignored her as his strategic mind refused to slow; he had plenty more questions for the Gildonese.

What if I get a hold of you?

"Ahhh. Very good question. You would need to be exceedingly strong, like that Simcane fella, and endure an infinite amount of punishment to do so, but if you were somehow able, you could neutralize some of my advantage." He paused for a moment before adding, "I don't think I would advise such tactics."

What about long-range attacks? Rasi asked. *Arrows?*

"They are effective. Though I am quick enough to catch arrows if I see them, I cannot read your subconscious thoughts or hear your contracting muscles from so far away. I believe long-range attacks were Epertase's greatest strength in the war against my people."

Rasi was careful not to overindulge, knowing a full stomach would slow him even more, if that was possible. After lunch, the two returned to the ring and continued the training.

Rasi was still unable to land a single blow, but Eldon insisted he was getting closer.

During one particularly painful training session, Rasi grew frustrated and asked, *Would there be any benefit to killing Fice's females before meeting him? After all, I'd enjoy making him suffer, as he has caused me much pain.*

Eldon was momentarily speechless as he rubbed his chin. After a long silence, he answered, "If you could pull off such a task, Fice would probably go into a rage and he might become careless, which would be good for you in theory, though the pummeling you would likely take at his hands would be fatal."

Teach me what I need to do.

Eldon smiled.

Before turning in for the night, Rasi asked Alina to join him for a walk. His entire body ached from the day's lessons, but he wouldn't let that stop him from doing something he'd wanted to do since reuniting with his love.

Alina happily agreed, adding, "You mean I get some of your attention for a change?"

He scoffed. *You get all my attention.*

She rolled her eyes. Rasi took her hand and led her to Eldon's barn.

"This isn't much of a walk," she said.

He pulled the barndoor open. Inside, a blanket sat in the center beneath a lantern hanging from a post. There were two glass goblets leaning against a wine bottle.

"What's this?" she asked.

He tugged her hand toward the blanket. While still holding her hand, he knelt and looked up. *Alina, I love you and have since the day we met. I don't want to ever be without you again. Will you marry me?*

Her free hand went to her heart. "Oh, Rasi." She let go of his hand and touched his cheek. "Of course, I'll marry you."

He stood up and hugged her.

She kissed him. They sat on the blanket and shared the entire bottle of wine before they eventually fell asleep in the barn. Rasi's straps kept them warm.

Rasi was sound asleep when the screeching of crows woke him. He sat up quietly, his head throbbing from too much wine. Eldon's hurried footsteps sounded from outside. The straps around Alina slithered away, careful not to wake her. He folded his side of the blanket over her. She stretched and moaned and went back to sleep. Rasi crept from the barn.

Eldon was just outside the door.

What is it, Eldon?

His Gildonese host stared toward the sky. "Look," he said, pointing upward.

The squawking continued from four crows, black as night, crossing in front of the light of the moon.

Eldon whispered, "Four people approach. These are the friends that told me when you and the queen first arrived."

How do you know there are four coming?

"Because there are four crows, of course."

How far away are the intruders?

"I cannot be sure. I do not know how long I meditated through their warning."

I'll grab my sword.

"No," Eldon snapped and touched his arm. "You stay with the queen. I can more than handle a few wayward travelers."

Rasi hated to admit that Eldon was right. Eldon flowed across his land with speed and grace.

Rasi waited. Alina slept. The moon crossed the sky.

And then Eldon's unmistakably gangly silhouette appeared in the distance. He accompanied four others on horseback. It didn't appear there had been a scuffle. As they neared, Rasi didn't need to see the largest traveler's face to recognize Simcane's unique physique. He met his friends in the yard.

Simcane's grip almost hurt Rasi's hand. "What happened to your face?" the big man asked, referring to the different shades of purple from Eldon's "lessons."

Rasi shook his head.

Eldon grinned.

The other travelers lowered their scarves from their faces.

Simcane introduced Rasi to Lona, Thairen, and Logan. The scarred man continued past without acknowledging Rasi's extended hand. Rasi turned to the king and queen and bowed. Though he had met them once before, it had been many years when he was but a lowly soldier in King Cecil's army, inconsequential enough to not make a lasting impression. Logan watched Rasi's straps, fascinated, as they floated in the air. Rasi wouldn't be as easily forgotten this time.

Thairen disappeared beyond the house. Rasi turned to Simcane, who shrugged and said, "Don't even ask. He's probably looking for goat's blood to drink or something."

Alina appeared at the barn door. At first, she didn't see her old friends on the lawn as she squinted and rubbed her eyes in the early morning brightness. Once she did see them, she raced to Simcane and embraced him. "How is Thasula?" she blurted before any pleasantries could be exchanged. "Have you heard anything?"

Simcane responded with a false smile. "We don't bring much in the way of news. We were fortunate just to escape Lithia. I'm afraid my home country is lost forever."

Alina shook her head. "I refuse to believe that. We'll get to Fice." She looked to Rasi with hopeful eyes. "Rasi will get him."

King Logan said, "We've heard rumors, though vague, that a small rebellion has begun outside of the Parsons warehouse district, but we've not been able to confirm it."

"Homer's land," Alina whispered.

Logan shrugged his shoulders, having no idea who Homer was.

"Is Thasula as far gone as Lithia?" she asked.

"The Lith people are not the same people I once ruled. While I don't believe Fice controls all of Thasula, the word is your army has imposed a curfew over your people. It seems it's only a matter of time before Fice rules Epertase as well. I don't understand how Fice came to be so powerful so quickly. If he had such power, why didn't he invade years ago?"

"I believe he was waiting for an opportunity, and because of the Tek invasion, I unknowingly gave him the invitation."

"Nonsense, Alina. Do not torture yourself over the actions of a madman."

Rasi listened with half an ear as his mind wandered elsewhere. Strategies for getting to Fice occupied his thoughts much of the time already, but with Logan's news he was more determined than ever. He needed to forget about taking back Epertase and instead focus on Lithia and Fice. Without Fice's sway, if his hopes proved true, Epertasians would welcome Alina's return to rule. And he could easily handle Jarrah's coup if, after Fice's fall, it came to that.

Eldon invited his guests into the house. As they started up the porch steps, Rasi grabbed Eldon's arm and held him back. *Any word from your messenger?*

Eldon nodded. "Yes. He found your friend. I was going to tell you over breakfast."

And he's coming?

"He should arrive in two days. Did you ask her yet?"

Rasi smiled.

"Did she say yes?"

Rasi cocked his head. What kind of question was that? *Of course.*

Eldon's face brightened. "Oh, Rasi, that's wonderful news."

That only leaves one other issue. Rasi's eyes drifted toward the door. *And I think the solution has just arrived.*

Eldon's eyes followed Rasi's.

Do you think King Logan would—

Eldon interrupted, "Oh, yes. I'm quite sure he would be honored to officiate."

Rasi grinned. *Well, I guess I'm getting married in two days, huh?*

"I guess you are. We should go in and celebrate." He slung his gangly arm over Rasi's shoulder. Rasi's pounding headache didn't like the idea of more celebrating.

CHAPTER 28

REBELS

A mid all the chaos, Dillon and his mother, Chloe, were lucky to escape Thasula with their lives. They fled to the small town of Tiffin, hoping to get as far from Thasula as possible. There they found a friendly couple to take them in.

But Dillon wasn't satisfied with merely hiding; he'd always seen bigger things for his future. Unwilling to sit idly by, he had spent the time since their escape building a small group of what some might call rebels outside the city. Like the good leader he aspired to be, he had gathered thirty men who shared his desire for Thasula's freedom from the traitorous Epertasian army that now ruled large chunks of the country. Though Dillon's rebellion against Fice's revolution was in its infancy, it was growing by the day. Just the night before, he received word of two dozen more men coming from the south to join his cause.

The townspeople supported him and his fellow rebels with food, supplies, and encouragement. He quickly became a hero among them and worked tirelessly to keep from disappointing them. Planning ways to fight back kept his mind occupied and his sleep scattered. He tried promoting men to lessen some of his burden, but they were mostly farmers or shopkeepers and had no more experience in being or leading soldiers than he did.

He prayed someone among the new arrivals, who were rumored to be four days away, had leadership skills. Without someone who knew what they were doing, his budding rebellion could wilt before its first battle. But it wasn't all stress. He'd had one significant accomplishment three days prior when some of his men successfully hijacked an Epertasian supply wagon. The grain and rice alone was worth the risk, because it meant he could provide for his men as opposed to being provided for by the townspeople for a change. It meant his idea was growing.

Surely by then the Epertasian army had heard that one of their supply wagons had been intercepted. He imagined their anger as they pounded their fists on the table, shouting, "Who dares interfere with our supplies?" That gave him a smile. When his rebellion was larger, he planned to attack an actual troop deployment.

That afternoon, Dillon's tireless work was rewarded by the townspeople inviting him and his men to a special celebration at the town hall in honor of what he was building. At the outer edge of a farm where Dillon and his men camped, Dillon walked from cooking fire to cooking fire. He told each man about the invitation and the coming reinforcements. The news gave them smiles and put a little extra bounce in his step.

Dillon gave his scouts a single night off so they, too, could enjoy the festivities. He figured the odds of the enemy learning the whereabouts of his rebellion and choosing that same night to attack were slim at best.

When they packed up to head for the celebration, his mother decided to stay behind, claiming she didn't feel well. Dillon knew it was really because she didn't like seeing him drink. He let her be because he indeed planned to drink. A lot. When he arrived at the town hall, the people of Tiffin had already started and the celebration was in full swing. Before he could officially release his men, most of them blended into the crowd with fresh tankards of ale and other beverages likely much stronger. He followed their example, and by the time the moon could be seen he was far from his senses.

Dillon danced with a woman named Suzie. He was pretty sure men were supposed to lead in the dance, but since Suzie's grip was the only thing keeping him upright, he had no choice but to go wherever she wanted. He was so drunk that he even leaned in for a kiss.

She turned her head and gave him her cheek instead. "Not yet. We just met."

Something in Dillon's pants told him their short acquaintance wasn't as much of a deterrent to him. He started to take another drink and she guided it away from his mouth. "I think you've had enough."

Dillon was ready to protest when the town hall doors burst open and a young boy rushed in. His face blanched and his eyes bulged. "Mr. Dillon."

The partygoers went quiet. The band stilled their instruments. All eyes went to Dillon.

"What is it?" he asked.

"Soldiers are coming," the boy answered.

Dillon smiled. "You mean the volunteers. They are early."

"No. Epertasian soldiers. Wearing war fatigues."

"That doesn't seem right. Where are they now?"

The boy pointed in the direction of the farm where Dillon had set up camp. Where he and his men had left all their weapons. He followed the kid into the street. His men joined him.

In the distance, Epertasian soldiers scrambled to block the road. There were dozens of them, at least. Dillon's stomach turned. His farmers-turned-soldiers panicked and started to scatter. Dillon stood in the center of the road and watched a ball of fire light up the evening sky. They had brought a catapult.

What have I done? The adrenaline coursing through his system quickly sobered him. He followed the fireball's trajectory until it struck a store behind him.

"Fight," Dillon shouted to his panicking men, and raised his fist.

The man closest to him cried, "With what? We have no weapons."

Another fireball slammed into the town hall, igniting it and collapsing the left wall. Dillon ducked away from falling debris.

Seven of his more sober men joined him and pledged to fight, but they were braver than they were smart. The rebellion was over. Surely they saw it. They were only farmers a few weeks ago, and being true patriots didn't suddenly make them skilled soldiers.

Dillon and his seven brave men watched the Epertasians march toward them and saw something dreadful: two men on horseback who towered over the others. The sight of the Gildonese leading the march stole his breath. Dillon had doomed everyone who had trusted him.

"Run," he whispered.

His seven men turned to him in disbelief.

"We can't win. Save yourself."

They knew he was right. They turned and ran. Dillon stumbled back a drunken step.

For the briefest of moments, he considered charging, because what else could he do? Then he thought of his mother finding his dead body after the massacre, and he couldn't do that to her.

He ducked into an alley and ran as fast as he could to the friendly couple who had taken him in. That's where his mother said she was headed before he left for the celebration. He blew through the door and into the room where she was asleep.

"Mom, get up."

She nearly fell out of bed. He grabbed her hand and pulled.

"What's going on?" she asked, panic creasing her face.

"They've found us. We've gotta go."

He ran to the window and peeked out. She started to empty her clothes chest into a bag, and he grabbed her again. "No time. Get a robe. Let's go."

They looked to the town as they ran from the house and saw nothing but flames. It was the worst day of Dillon's life. They headed westward, away from the fray. He prayed the townspeople escaped as well, though the lack of people he encountered on his retreat made him fear the worst.

CHAPTER 29

THE MOST
BEAUTIFUL DAY

The day of Rasi and Alina's wedding arrived on a brisk, cloudless morning.

It was a special day.

It was a day without training, or worrying, or planning for wars. It was a day that kings planned for their daughters and mothers planned for their sons.

And it was the first day in many weeks that Rasi allowed himself the luxury of sleeping in. He had been working hard, nearly to the brink of exhaustion, and the extra rest left him feeling spry. He sat alone with his straps on the edge of his bed while the suns peeked through his window.

Alina had left a note on the bedside table. She, Eldon, and the others had gone to town early. Everyone except Thairen, it said, because Thairen hadn't returned from his hunt the day before.

Rasi stared at the fancy, knee-length kilt draped over his dresser. Hanging from the wall next to it was a dark pair of leggings and the fanciest cloak he had ever seen. He chuckled when he thought about how long it had been since he'd dressed in such gentlemanly attire and realized it might have been for his first marriage.

Eldon had outdone himself. Rasi dared not imagine the number of coins Eldon had parted with to purchase such gifts, but he would be sure to thank the Gildonese another hundred times once the day had ended.

He gathered his clothing and carried it into Eldon's washroom where a bath awaited. He wondered how everyone's trip into town was going. After lowering himself into the tub, he bathed in absolute peace. He even closed his eyes for a bit. No thoughts of war or hate or Gildonese tyrants to bring down his mood. He almost fell asleep again.

Once he toweled off, shaved the whiskers from his chin, and dressed in his fancy attire, he made his way into the kitchen where Eldon had prepared a magnificent feast of eggs, bacon, and some of the most decadently soft bread Rasi had ever bitten into.

His stomach felt bloated by the time he finished, so he leaned back in his chair and rested for a bit. He realized he hadn't thought of his sword in his contented daze and had left it leaning against his bedroom wall. Though he felt naked, he didn't retrieve it.

The front yard revealed how hard Eldon had worked while Rasi and Alina had slept, and again he felt undeserving. The melting snow had been cleared from the front of the house and he was amazed he had slept through the racket of his host's nighttime preparations. At the far edge of the clearing stood an oak trellis arch that Eldon must have spent weeks building, if not longer. Ten wooden chairs sat before the arch and he wondered who else was expected besides Atticus.

Rasi walked toward the amazing trellis in awe of Eldon's hard work and magnificent carvings. Rasi's name alongside Alina's had been etched into the honey-toned wood in fancy, centuries-old script. Rare lavender tulips adorned the sides and arch of the trellis while flowers of every color littered the ground as if each petal had been meticulously placed. Again, he worried over the cost. Flowers were rare that time of year. He sat in a chair at the front in disbelief that the day had actually arrived. The morning passed while he sat and dreamed of a better life.

He gazed at the cloudless sky as he imagined what his son might be like. He couldn't wait to hear his voice for the first time or see him take his first steps. As he watched the sky, lost in thought, four crows appeared overhead. He held his hand above his eyes and looked to the forest. Four figures approached with horses in tow. Rasi slowly rose to his feet when he saw his friend. He started toward the figures, first jogging and then in a full sprint. Eldon's messenger deserved an award. It was Atticus, Celia, Homer, and Irene.

When he reached Atticus and Celia, he embraced them in a powerful group hug. If not for their physical touch, he'd believe he was still daydreaming.

Irene touched his shoulder. "Congratulations, Rasi. I'm so excited for the both of you."

Homer bobbed his head in agreement. Celia wiped her wet eyes and then laughed, embarrassed that she couldn't control herself.

Rasi led them into Eldon's home and gestured to the plush chairs in the main living space. Once they were settled, Rasi asked, "How did the messenger find you?" repeating himself a few times until Atticus understood.

"I'd been secretly gathering resistance fighters, though I suppose in hindsight I wasn't as secretive as I thought. He told us your plans to marry, and we wouldn't dare miss it. We've been traveling the back roads ever since.

Atticus leaned back in his chair and locked his fingers behind his head. "We met Alina and the others in town. They said they'll be back soon." He shook his head with a slight whistle. "I must say, you're a very lucky man."

Celia interrupted, "Oh, Rasi, she's stunning. Wait till you see her."

Rasi served his guests some of the ale reserved for the celebration. He poured himself a glass of tornment juice.

Atticus scooted to the edge of his chair. "So, what do you say? Do you need a right hand for the ceremony?"

Of course. He nodded.

Atticus asked him to step outside for some fresh air and the two friends excused themselves. Atticus sat on the porch step while Rasi leaned against the post. "I'm happy for you, Rasi. You're a good man and you deserve good things. But I've known you for many years and I see a measure of sadness on your face."

Rasi turned away. He didn't have to speak for his friend to know what was troubling him.

"What happened to Edonea wasn't your fault."

Rasi lowered his head.

Atticus stood up and placed a kind hand on Rasi's shoulder. "I knew Edonea. I'm not hesitant in saying she would want this for you. Alina is a special person and Edonea would have loved her if she could have known her."

Rasi bobbed his head in reluctant agreement.

"Today begins a new stage of your life. Take today and never look back."

Rasi turned with wet eyes and embraced his old friend. Those were words he needed to hear. Neither man said much more as they sat on the porch stoop and waited.

It was evening when Rasi found his way to the trellis with Atticus standing at his side. Logan wore a midnight-blue, ankle-length robe purchased in town as he faced the two men and looked past them toward Eldon's home. The guests—Celia, Homer, Lona, Simcane, and Thairen—sat in the wooden chairs. Eldon stood off to the side. Thairen's head bobbed in a constant battle against sleep and boredom.

The door to Eldon's home opened. Irene came out first before stepping to the side.

The suns appeared to stop their descent just above the horizon, as if waiting for the big event. Rasi couldn't picture a more glorious day for his wedding.

Then Alina stepped through the doorway. She was the most stunningly beautiful sight he had ever seen, more than eclipsing the gorgeous landscape. She wore a white dress that exposed her shoulders and trailed behind her like a wave of the purest snow. Her hair was coiled at the back of her head and adorned with a large lavender feather. Rasi wore a matching lavender flower pinned to his cloak on his chest.

Alina paused to take in the moment before continuing forward.

Irene moved to stand next to Homer as everyone rose to their feet. Alina continued to the trellis, and Rasi took her hand. She smiled shyly up at him.

You look beautiful, he told her.

Her cheeks reddened and her dimples showed.

King Logan stood at the front. He began. "Thank all of you for attending. You may have a seat. We have gathered here today to witness the fullest extent of a woman's love for a man and a man's love for a woman. I am honored to be here to share in this queen's marriage to this honorable hero of the people." He looked to Alina, whose face bore happiness unmatched in this world or the next. "Alina, never have I met a person more giving and more deserving of the title Queen. I am in awe of your presence and honored to be performing this ceremony today."

"Thank you."

He looked to Rasi. "I see an honor in you unmatched by anyone who has ever stood before me. Your legend grows by the day. I see a warrior. A protector. A husband. And soon, a father. I admire you and have the greatest respect for you."

Rasi nodded, touched.

Logan addressed the small group again. "Distinguished guests. Welcome to the joining of two hearts. Commander Rasi and Queen Alina have chosen this moment to bind themselves for an eternity of love. Through all the hardships of this world, these two have found each other, and this world is a better place because of it."

He looked back to Rasi and Alina. "Day in and day out, the gods above struggle to recreate the excellence that can be found in the two of you. A more perfect union I have never seen. Alina, every breath that comes from your lungs is a blessing to this world. I ask that you take Rasi's hand and know that no matter how good this world is, it will never truly be worthy of you.

"Rasi, everything you have done has brought you to this place, and I only ask that you enjoy and savor this moment.

"Alina, Rasi, you may speak your words to each other."

Alina turned from Logan to her true love. Rasi faced her and locked his gaze with her dazzling green eyes. He smiled, and she smiled back.

"Rasi, in you I have grown to find love that is stronger than any I have ever known and that grows stronger each day. You are kind and gentle and everything to me. I love you now and forever. Thank you for being you."

Alina, I will forever protect you and love you. I am only happy because of you. I vow to be the best husband and father I can possibly be. Thank you for being my world. I love you.

Logan asked, "Alina, do you take Rasi as your husband?"

"I do."

"Rasi, do you take Alina to be your wife?"

Rasi had been practicing for weeks. He paused between each word, struggling to get them right. "A'ena ... I ... 'ou."

She smiled and her lower lip quivered. Her eyes filled with tears. "It was perfect, Rasi."

He couldn't imagine a better day.

Logan ended the ceremony with, "I now pronounce you husband and wife."

Rasi smiled as he and Alina walked past their friends to receive their warm congratulations.

The day ended with a wonderful celebration inside Eldon's home before the revelers made their way to the front porch. It was inevitable that talk of strategy on how to return Alina and Logan to power would trickle into the conversations.

Atticus described his budding army as strong and getting stronger. He recommended using trusted messengers for monthly correspondence from Homer's farm to Eldon's, and everyone agreed.

Alina spoke for Rasi. "Do you believe, as we do, that eliminating Fice and restoring order to Lithia first will make it easier to deal with Jarrah and his coup?"

Atticus nodded. "Absolutely. In fact, we believe your castle has been mostly abandoned. Fice has gone back to Lithia. Occasionally, our spies have seen Jarrah visit your castle for only the gods know why. The joke around camp is that he is so thirsty for the throne that he pretends to be Epertase's king when no one is around."

Simcane quietly took everything in. Then he said, "I will focus on gathering my team. With Thairen here …," he looked around, "… well, somewhere around here, I need only contact Willum and Gillian, which shouldn't be a problem. And then I'll figure out where BJ the Keen is currently wooing the ladies, though I hear he's in—"

Alina dropped her gaze.

"What is it?"

"I'm afraid BJ may not be with us any longer. The Elder Three confirmed it."

Simcane sat, puzzled. "You mean not with us as a team or not alive?"

"Not alive."

Simcane rubbed his whiskers. "That is a shame. I rather enjoyed his company." After a pause, he added, "Thairen and I will gather Willum and Gillian and meet Atticus at Homer's farm. Rasi, I will see you again on the steps of Lithia's castle." Rasi shook his hand and Alina hugged him. He turned to Eldon. "We will meet you at the church in Pataska where we first met when it's time." He scanned the field and mumbled, "Damn it, Thairen. Where the hell are you?"

Atticus chuckled. "Good luck with your companion."

Simcane grunted with a backward glare at him, and then left in search of Thairen.

Logan and Lona, Celia and Atticus, and Homer and Irene said their goodbyes shortly thereafter and took their leave as well, but not before Logan gave Rasi a few secrets about his beloved castle—most importantly, how to get into it undetected.

CHAPTER 30
SET IN MOTION

Alina's belly continued to swell as winter threatened to break into spring. Rasi and Eldon had practiced day after day after day through the long winter while Atticus worked building a small army far away. Eldon had left a few weeks earlier to meet up with his team and prepare for his part in the rebellion. By the time he had left for Pataska, Rasi was landing sixty percent or so of his strikes. While sixty percent was good, it wasn't nearly good enough against a Gildonese as deadly as Fice. At least, that's what Eldon kept telling him.

Rasi was sitting on the porch, mentally running through the plan as he often did, when a single crow flew overhead. While Rasi expected to see Atticus's most trusted messenger, a young soldier named Coen, with an update on the war preparations, he was surprised to see it was actually Atticus himself. It could mean only one thing: the plan was in motion. Knowing the challenges ahead, Rasi's stomach fluttered at the sight of his old friend.

Alina? he projected from the front stoop.

She appeared in the doorway, drying her hands on a rag. The sight of Atticus approaching pulled her smile downward. One of the easiest ways to keep from dreading the coming war was to quietly pretend it was still a long way away. Seeing Atticus crushed those illusions. Each clop of his horse's hooves was an inevitable nail in the scaffolding of the plan.

"Rasi, can we wait a little longer? Please."

He reached back and took her hand. *We knew this day was coming.*

"What if we waited until after the baby's born? You want to meet him, don't you?" She squeezed his hand, hopeful.

More than anything. But my child will not be born into a world that's not free, if I have any say. Prolonging it would be much worse.

Atticus dismounted and walked solemnly to the porch. "Rasi. Alina."

Alina covered her eyes and hurried back into the house. The two men shook hands.

"It's time," Atticus said.

Rasi simply nodded.

"Simcane and his team, along with a hundred men, have met Eldon in Pataska and are moving into southern Lithia. If all goes well, they'll be in position on schedule. Aidric and Christopher are leading their forces into position as we speak. How has your training gone?"

Rasi shrugged his shoulders.

"Are you ready to beat Fice?"

The number sixty percent, combined with Eldon's subdued tone when he said it, stuck in his mind. He glanced at the door to make sure Alina wasn't there and then shook his head.

Some of the optimism drained from Atticus's face. "Should we abort?"

Rasi shook his head again. It was probably too late even if he wanted to call it off.

"Then we should head out soon."

Rasi nodded. He held up a finger and went into the house where Alina stood by the table. With red, puffy eyes, she said, "I don't want to do this anymore."

We have no choice.

"I just can't."

You're the strongest woman I've ever met. You can do this. You must.

She raced into his arms. "I'm worried."

I know. I am, too. But it's time to leave.

She nodded and rubbed her eyes. "You go out there. I'll be out as soon as I gather myself."

Rasi rejoined Atticus on the front step, carrying two tankards of ale. They clinked them together before Atticus took a swig. "Ahhh," he sighed. "This warms my gut."

Alina soon exited the house, the redness and puffiness around her eyes mostly gone. Rasi smiled.

"I'm ready," she said.

They gathered their supplies—water bladders, food rations, and some extra clothing—let Dog out of the house, and started their walk to the eastern shore of Lowland Lake. Dog tried to follow, but Rasi shooed him back to the house.

No one spoke much during the long walk. Once they arrived at Lowland Lake, Atticus led them to a small boat stashed within some cattails and hidden beneath a cowhide tarp. He removed the tarp, scooped a stowaway snake into the water, and climbed in.

After Rasi's straps pushed them from the shore, Atticus motioned his head toward the north and what was left of the Great Dam, destroyed during the Tek War. "Maybe one of the greatest strategies ever devised, Rasi. You should be proud."

It was Rasi's first look at the damage, and while he was indeed proud, it meant nothing going forward. Atticus lay back and took some time to catch up on sleep with a shirt covering his face. With nothing but calm waters and the setting suns around them, Alina guided Rasi's hand to her distended belly.

What is it? he asked. *Are you all right?*

She grinned. "Just wait."

The single most incredible feeling he'd ever felt pressed briefly against his palm. *Is that ...?*

"Yes. That was your son kicking."

Rasi missed a breath. Alina turned and leaned against his chest, and he wrapped his arms around her with his hands on her belly. For the rest of the night, she slept cuddled in his arms while he sat awake, longing for the next kick. But his son must have fallen asleep as well. Eventually, the boat reached the western shore.

Atticus scuttled the boat then turned to them and said, "Not far to the safe house." It was less than an hour's walk. Enough fit young men patrolled the field around the unassuming cottage that Rasi knew he was in the right place.

One of the men approached Rasi with his head respectfully bowed. Rasi gripped his sword just in case. The man stopped. "Commander Rasi, Atticus, Queen Alina, we've been waiting for you. Right this way." He escorted them to the front of the house and then departed to stand watch at the edge of the field.

Atticus faced Rasi. "This is where I take my leave. It's time for me to join up with my soldiers south of Lithia. You need to be in position when the fighting starts." He turned to Alina. "These men will take you to the Tunnels of Eiger to meet King Logan. They have crystals for your safe passage."

Alina hugged him. "Are you sure Fice will take his sleep soon?"

"Quite. His sleep schedule has been very regular according to our spies. They say he empties the castle of people before he sleeps." Atticus turned to Rasi again. "As promised, if our plan fails and you are unable to return for Alina, I will see to her safety. If not me, then Simcane or Aidric will come for her and take her far from here."

Alina's sad face filled with defiance. "What do you mean, if Rasi is unable?"

Rasi glanced over his shoulder. *You know what he means, Alina.*

"Atticus, I won't listen to such talk."

"I'm sorry, Your Majesty. I should have chosen my words more carefully."

A soldier stepped out of the cottage, gave Atticus a glowing blue crystal, and ordered two horses be brought around from the back. Atticus said his good-byes, mounted a beautiful, white-speckled mare, and rode toward Lithia.

Now it was Rasi's turn to leave. He took Alina's hand. *You two mean everything to me.*

"I don't want you to go."

And I don't want to go.

"There's no other way? Simcane can't beat Fice?"

Simcane has his own role to play in the coming fight. I'll come back for you when it's over.

"Do you promise?"

Of course. He loosened his grip, but she held tight.

"I just can't seem to let you go."

He wiped a tear from her cheek. Being strong for her and his son was all that mattered. He bent over and kissed her distended belly. *There's nothing I wouldn't do for both of you.*

"Coming home safely is what you can do for us."

If everything else fails and we're forced to take to the wind, I will find you where we had our first kiss.

She nodded.

He looked away, hoping to hide his weakness. He couldn't bear leaving and quietly cursed Fice for making him. Painful images of his burned mother and father steeled his resolve and gave him the strength to pull his hand away. *Never forget our first kiss, Alina. I'm always near you as long as you have that.*

"I love you, Rasi."

I know you do. And I love you.

As he climbed onto his horse, he let his eyes linger. He would lock away the pain so he could use it when doubt inevitably set in. With Alina now openly sobbing, he turned away and rode toward an impossible fight. Part of his heart stayed on the stoop with her.

By hiding during the days and traveling under the cloak of night, Rasi reached the eastern edge of Lithia's capital city of Reigal. He made his way north, circumventing the city to the Danduke River. He was right on schedule. After unsaddling his horse, he set him free in the open countryside.

A quick brush of his forearm against his sword assured it was secured to his hip. He dove into the cool, refreshing water, ever hopeful that the churn, those slimy underwater parasites, wouldn't find him. His straps stretched down his back and worked in concert with his arms to propel him quickly through the water like an ocean squid. Years of hunting in the river by Shadows Peak had made him an expert swimmer, and he knifed through the harbor like he was born with gills.

The long swim hardly winded him. Once he reached the pier, he quietly treaded water beneath where two Lith guards stood watch. They were complacent in their duties. That Fice only kept two guards at the pier was evidence of his overconfidence.

Rasi pulled himself under the pier where he would wait for the violent sounds of Fice's sleep. One of the straps anchored him to the pier while the others hovered above the surface to avoid pruny skin and hungry churn. So far, neither had afflicted him, and he hoped his good fortune would continue. The calm, rhythmic bobbing in the water would have soothed him to sleep if not for the adrenaline giving his hands the shakes. The guards joked and smoked weed sticks and talked about their families while Rasi floated beneath them.

It was late into the night when a haunting moan finally left King Logan's third-floor chamber window. A hideous, high-pitched scream soon followed. It sounded as though someone else had gotten to the Gildonese king ahead of schedule, and a small, vengeful part of Rasi hoped it wasn't so.

"Well, I guess he's asleep," one of the soldiers said.

"I guess so."

"What do you think he dreams about?"

"I have no idea."

Two straps slithered silently along a piling and onto the wooden planks behind the soldiers. Rasi floated closer to give them the reach they needed. Loosely, they coiled around the soldiers' legs, unnoticed. Once in place, they waited for Rasi's command. When he gave it, they cinched tight and yanked the soldiers into the water.

At first, they held their breath as they kicked at the straps holding them down, but then they panicked and their lungs filled with water. They reached toward the surface, desperately hoping someone might pull them free, but there was no one to help them. Slowly, they weakened and then went limp.

Rasi used his straps to pull their faces close to his. As he looked into their lifeless gazes, he channeled his guilt over killing them into rage at his enemy. Fice had turned him into the man he feared, and he hated the bastard for it. He burned the soldiers' faces into his memory to live alongside the many others he had killed over the years.

Damn you, Fice.

He was ready.

His straps released the soldiers, allowing them to drift into the depths of the harbor while he pulled himself onto the pier. The straps shook away the water like a bunch of wet dogs. Rasi scanned the pier in search of his prize. With no other guards in sight, he snatched one of the torches that lined the pier and ran to the circular stone well King Logan had told him to look for. After his straps found anchor points around the outside, he dove into the well. Just as Logan had promised, rocks protruded from the wall like a ladder. He grabbed hold with one hand while holding the torch with the other. His straps slithered down alongside him and helped him the rest of the way. Just above the water line was the tunnel in the well wall that Logan had described.

Rasi slid the cover aside and crawled through the webs and bugs and dirt. The torch revealed a long, narrow tunnel. He shoved the torch at a couple of curious rats to scare them away. One that he missed bit into a strap, which sent all seven of them into an angry frenzy. They thrashed and pounded it into mush.

Rasi waited patiently for their temper tantrum to end. *Feel better?* he asked. One of the straps smacked the flattened rat one last time as if to make a point.

It was a long, tight crawl to the end of the tunnel. *"Look for a false ceiling,"* Logan had said. *"It'll be heavy."*

Rasi traced the stone ceiling until his fingers found the outline of a trapdoor. He set his torch aside and maneuvered onto his back with his feet pressed against it. With a grunt, he kicked with both feet. The jolt jarred the trapdoor loose. He pivoted until his shoulder was firmly against it and heaved. Once he had it open, he grabbed his torch and climbed out into a large closet with an overturned shelf. Rasi lowered the heavy trapdoor back over the opening and righted the shelf over it. By genius craftsmanship the handle of the trapdoor hid within the framework of the shelf. Rasi slipped a rug that had shifted back over it.

The closet door opened into a large room. Rasi placed the torch in a sconce and cracked open the door to an empty hallway. Following Logan's instructions, he turned right and followed the hall until he found a staircase to the third floor.

The halls were vacant as the spies had promised, but as Rasi reached the door to Logan's chambers, something didn't feel quite right. He listened close. Where were screams? They were supposed to last for days, yet it was quiet inside. Had Fice already left? There was only one way to find out. The door was unlocked, so he pushed it open.

Standing by Logan's desk with his back to the open balcony was the Gildonese king. He looked over. "And who might you be?" he asked. He had heavy bags under his eyes. "Are you the one who caused me to wake so early?"

Rasi nodded.

"Are you the one who brought the soldiers who attack from the south?"

Rasi nodded again.

"Well, I was just about to join my army to defeat them, but I suppose I can deal with you first since you have found your way in here and deserve at least that much."

I'm going to kill you, Fice.

He chuckled. "I'm sure you believe that, but better men than you have tried." His tired eyes brightened. "Maybe, after I embarrass you a bit, you can be my personal jester with those funny hunks of meat hanging from your back. Let me ask you something. Can you dance?"

Rasi stepped inside and closed the door.

CHAPTER 31

ELDON

The strategy was multipronged. Eldon sliced through the deserted back alleys of Reigal while Atticus led men into battle against Fice's Lith soldiers south of the castle. The rebellion used the buildings and narrow streets to nullify some of the advantage Fice enjoyed with his superior numbers. If all went well, Aidric was to lead a second force to attack from the northeast.

Eldon reached the castle's perimeter wall in short order. Since Fice wasn't concerned about lone soldiers getting near the castle, he'd posted few guards behind his engaged army. As Eldon marched along the wall, he easily dispatched anyone he stumbled upon.

It wasn't long before he saw his two targets ahead. They sat on horseback. Gildonese generals. Eliminating them would give Atticus his only real shot at victory. Eldon only hoped the others were having as much luck reaching their targets as he was.

Surprise, he figured, was the best approach when facing two Gildonese. As Eldon jogged toward them, he saw that one was a female with long, dark braids draped over her thin, sickly shoulders. She would be his first target. The other was a male—muscular, with dark, patchy hair that revealed scars from many battles.

A Lith soldier ruined the surprise when he noticed Eldon's approach and pointed. The female straightened, nudged her partner, and turned her horse toward him.

Eldon charged in a full sprint. Immediately, his mind went fuzzy, filled with a dull hum. He'd expected as much. The mind scream muffled a constant, almost inaudible voice within it. Eldon had never felt such a strong sway. He tried to shake the voice out of his head, but it persisted. It was a male's voice repeating over and over, *We do not know you, but we are your family. You must join us.*

Concentrate, Eldon told himself. The unexpectedly effective mind scream brought on a wave of dizziness unlike any he'd ever felt. As he ran, he wobbled and vomited to the side. A dull ache began at the base of his skull and radiated through his brain until it rested behind his eyes. Fice's pack was more powerful than he'd ever imagined.

The female heeled her steed toward him and drew her sword. Eldon closed his eyes and breathed deeply, concentrating on the sounds around him to clear his thoughts. The clops of her charging horse. The clanging of swords and shields from the battle in the streets. The voice that wouldn't shut up in his head.

"I won't join you," he screamed.

She was upon him in a flash. She whirled her sword with a shrill battle cry that nearly drowned out the voice.

Eldon dove away from her lightning attack. *Join your new family,* she projected. Her horse looped around for another strike. Eldon righted himself and waited with his sword extended at his side. He sent a mind scream into her head and she smiled.

You belong with your family, she insisted.

Eldon cocked his head to the side as he curiously watched her approach. Maybe she was right. There were few things more enticing than being part of a family again. Her sword drew back.

It was almost as if she planned to hit him with it, but why would she do that to family? *Wait ... No.* He shook away the trance as her blade swung at his neck.

He dropped to his knees. Her sword nicked the top of his scalp. Though his thoughts were sluggish, he could still fight. He swung around as she passed and snapped her horse's front leg with his fist. She and her horse tumbled to the ground with the mare landing atop her chest.

The male's voice returned, stronger and more deliberate. *You could be king. You could rule these pathetic Epertasians.*

He had a good point. Eldon imagined himself in a throne with lowly Epertasians at his feet. Something trickled from his left ear. He touched it. Blood. He thought about how bad the static hurt. He wondered …

The male Gildonese grunted, suddenly right beside him. Reflexes pushed Eldon's sword in front of the strike. Both of their swords fell to the ground. Eldon drove his foot into the male's chest, knocking him to his back. That was his chance to even the odds as the female struggled beneath her horse nearby. Eldon scooped his sword from the ground and raced to her side while the mare tried to stand with only three good legs. Eldon plunged his sword through the mare's chest, collapsing her back onto the female before she could wriggle free. She stared up with pitiful, begging black eyes. *Join us,* she said in his mind.

Behind him, the male bounced to his feet with a blood-curdling wail and raced toward him. Eldon's brain rattled with the volume of the male's mind scream. An image of Rasi flashed through his thoughts and reminded him of his true family. He drove the blade downward. With ungodly speed, the female shifted away from its point. But Eldon was a Gildonese too, and he adjusted mid-thrust to pierce one of her hearts. Her eyes went wide, and she released a beastly screech. Eldon wished he had time to pierce her second heart so her death wouldn't be a long, agonizing one, but the male slammed into his side with the force of a mule kick.

Eldon tried to fight back, but the voice in his head told him how wrong it was to do so. A fist met his cheek, the blow stinging like fire. *You are ours,* the voice screamed. Drool dripped from his enemy's lip. Or was it his friend's? Eldon hesitated. His mouth exploded into a volcano of crimson, but still he couldn't fight back.

Do not fight your family, the voice implored. Another eruption of pain in Eldon's nose made him see a flash of white for an instant.

The Gildonese on his chest raked fingernails across his face. The burning from the fresh gouges, along with the constant beating from the fists, weakened his will to refuse the voice. All he could think was how much he wanted his family to stop hitting him.

Finally, after pummeling Eldon's face into a bloody, broken mess, the male stood up. Eldon lay in a spreading pool of his own gore. Blood choked each of his breaths. He looked up at his conqueror through swollen eyes. The fuzz in his mind faded or was masked by the burning and throbbing of his wounds.

The male cocked his head as his feet straddled Eldon's chest. "What are you thinking, friend?" he asked.

Eldon looked around at the fighting mortals in the streets. Then he looked back up to the Gildonese, wondering why he was where he was and how he had come to be so injured.

He mumbled through broken teeth and bloody lips, "Why did you hit me, brother?"

The Gildonese smiled. "Because you were out of line. But you are back with your family now. You are part of a pack."

Eldon felt as though something seemed out of place, like there was something menacing about his fellow Gildonese's words, but he couldn't place what. Something else told him to follow along, since a pack was stronger than an individual. "What are we doing here?" he finally asked.

The male offered his hand and helped Eldon to his feet. "We are killing the invaders."

Eldon pointed to a dead Gildonese female beneath a dead horse. "What happened to her?"

"She was your sister. And these men we fight slaughtered her."

Eldon didn't remember having a sister, but he didn't remember coming to that place, either. He felt unimaginable rage. *How dare anyone hurt my family?*

"To whom do you belong now?" the male asked.

"I am Eldon of the pack of Fice."

"Very good, Eldon."

Eldon tilted his head. "And you, brother?"

"I am Ulrac, also of the pack of Fice."

The fuzz in Eldon's head receded, though it never completely went away. Ulrac ordered Eldon into battle and Eldon couldn't wait to kill Epertasians.

CHAPTER 32
THAIREN

Thairen hated waiting.

He knelt next to the rubble of an old barber shop near Reigal's main drag where he could see Eldon talking to another Gildonese. Eldon shook the bastard's hand, turned, and raced into the battlefield, not to fight Fice's Liths, but directly toward Aidric's men. Thairen shook his head, disappointed. Eldon being unable to fight the sway was Simcane's greatest fear and the reason he'd secretly sent Thairen behind enemy lines. Just like the old days, Thairen got the shitty clean-up jobs that no one else could handle. Though he didn't want to kill Eldon, he wouldn't falter if that's what was needed.

But first, the Gildonese generals needed removing from the battle. That was the most important part of the plan. Adding sweetness to the shit was the fact that his mission gave him a shot at the one who'd broken his arms.

And hanged him.

And kicked him in the face.

And buried him.

As he crept closer, he caught himself licking his lips. A fight against a Gildonese was, perhaps, the greatest challenge a man could ever face. Knowing what he was about to do to the arm-breaking bastard gave him a warm, fuzzy feeling.

As he waited for just the right time to engage, he noticed something warm trickling down his arm. He looked closer. His forearm was red and raw. He had nervously dug it open with his own nails. *Not again.* After the last time this had happened, he'd had to force himself into self-isolation after killing a dozen people who may or may not have been his enemies. It had taken months of meditation to calm himself and right his angry brain enough to safely be around people again.

His daggers rested in his waistband and he rubbed their hilts to keep his fingers from his own flesh. He hated waiting.

Just as he thought he might explode in anticipation, the towering Gildonese joined the fight behind Eldon. He ripped through Aidric's advancing soldiers like a madman. Blood spurted into the air, drenching his sick, smiling face. He flung Epertasian soldiers over his head like they were weightless, their necks snapped before they hit the ground.

The rebellion hadn't a chance if they had to fight the Gildonese on their own. Luckily, they didn't. Thairen cracked his knuckles. It was time. He charged the Gildonese warrior, knifing through the fighting soldiers on his way. Behind them, he noticed a dead horse atop a female Gildonese who wasn't moving. Barely able to contain his excitement, he found himself laughing out loud and compulsively digging at his arms again.

When the Gildonese saw him, he discarded the Epertasian soldier he was killing and grinned. *I know you,* he said in Thairen's head.

The Lith and Epertasian soldiers continued to fight around the two as if they'd been commanded to stay out of the way. Thairen stopped short and gnashed his teeth. "Tell me your name so I can brag for all eternity about the Gildonese scum I defeated."

"I would be glad to. I am Ulrac of the pack of Fice."

"We're gonna kill you and your leader today."

Ulrac laughed, which really got under Thairen's skin. Thairen decided to tweak him in return. "Where's your girlie friend to help you this time?"

Ulrac's laugh quickly darkened.

Thairen tilted his head. "Is that her lying back there? She doesn't look so well."

Ulrac snorted like an angry bull.

"Ahhh. Did I touch a nerve?"

There was no more laughter from Ulrac's lips. "Though you have proven terribly difficult to kill, warrior, I rather look forward to the game."

Thairen tried to shout that he was ready, but only garbled sounds passed his lips. There was no more planning or mercy or any of that boring shit; it was time for the fun part.

A dull hum filled his head and he wondered if it was from the Gildonese or his own craziness. He leaped forward, fearless.

Careless.

He swung his daggers in staggered horizontal arcs, first the left and then the right. Ulrac ducked the left and plunged his sword into Thairen's gut before Thairen could connect with the right. Without pause, Thairen pulled himself farther onto the blade, so he could get closer to his foe. As with most of his opponents, his recklessness caught Ulrac off guard. It was hard to predict what Thairen was going to do since even he didn't know. He jammed his dagger into the soft flesh below Ulrac's collarbone.

The Gildonese shrieked and pushed him away, leaving his sword in Thairen's gut. Though Thairen's stomach hurt like he'd swallowed acid, he couldn't stop laughing. "Abu caush sew," he shouted, spraying spittle, and even he didn't know what he had said.

Ulrac pressed his hand against the bleeding hole in his chest. Thairen grimaced as he yanked the sword free from his gut. His body wanted to double over for a breather, but his anger wanted him to attack again. The anger won, as it usually did.

The Gildonese seemed slow in Thairen's eyes, but every blow of his fists connected with stinging accuracy. Thairen cursed while Ulrac's fists pummeled his face into a swollen, bloody mess. But still, Thairen didn't give any ground.

After what seemed like a lifetime, Ulrac stopped battering Thairen and stepped back with two winded breaths. Thairen grinned.

Ulrac glanced toward his bloody sword on the ground. Thairen nodded, inviting him to reach for it.

Ulrac took a third breath and then lunged, striking Thairen between his blurry eyes. Thairen wobbled. While Ulrac went for his sword with the gracefulness of a calm breeze, Thairen dove at his back with the awkwardness of a tornado. Again, Thairen was impossibly one step behind.

Ulrac snatched his sword and whirled around.

Thairen drove both of his daggers downward. His blades pierced the soft flesh of the Gildonese's chest, one beneath each of his nipples. He'd never felt such euphoria as he did when Ulrac's eyes went wide. But it was short-lived as Ulrac's blade continued around, its momentum barely slowed.

For the last instant of Thairen's life, he was happy, even as Ulrac's sword struck his neck. He watched the Gildonese fall backward, his daggers lodged into both of Ulrac's black hearts. For the briefest of moments, Thairen couldn't get air to his lungs. He dropped to his knees. His eyes continued forward to the dirt and the world spun until he stopped, staring up at his own headless body.

And Thairen would never have to wait again.

CHAPTER 33

ADVANCE

C hristopher rode to the edge of Reigal's main drag where he could see Atticus's men engaged in battle. He was joined by a third wave of Epertasian rebels under his command. Atticus's plan appeared to be working flawlessly as his men had already made a solid push into the Lith defenders.

Having never witnessed war as a soldier before, Christopher took a moment to take in the awesome sight of Atticus's fighting men. He had become friends with many of them. The splattering blood and dead and dying bodies in the streets racked him with worry. His hands shook and it took everything he had to not vomit.

Just ahead, he saw Atticus on his horse, swinging his sword madly at the Lith defenders. As Atticus's men pushed closer to the castle, Christopher wondered how different things would have been had Atticus enjoyed the full might of the Epertasian army at his command.

Christopher looked around at the soldiers who awaited his command. It was the moment Atticus had groomed him to embrace. Christopher had been secretly practicing what he would say for weeks. The nervous chatter of his men silenced as he prepared to speak. He swallowed hard. "Men of Epertase. As you look to the streets of Reigal, you see your Lith brothers defending a castle that has been stolen by the evil Gildonese. I know you will feel guilt fighting our Lith brothers, as I do, but know this: today, these men are not the men you once knew. They are not our Lith brothers after all. They are no more than puppets of King Fice, and they are here to bring you death. If you hesitate, they will kill you without remorse."

His horse danced from foot to foot as he fought with the reins to keep facing the men. "You are the only chance the Lith people have for freedom from the spell Fice has cast on them. By winning this war, you will in turn save many of the very men we fight against. With Fice's spell broken, these men will welcome us with open arms instead of steel. This will be a hard day for all of us, but it is a necessary day. Atticus needs you. Queen Alina needs you. I need you. And Epertase needs you."

The soldiers roared their approval.

Excitement thickened in the air. Christopher felt the rush of adrenaline surge through his veins as he prepared to overwhelm an enemy already being driven backward. His hands trembled and he no longer tried to hide them from the others. He was ready to fight. He was ready to die.

"We have fewer numbers than our enemy. We have fewer weapons. But what we have that they do not is a choice. We can live out our lives as slaves to the Gildonese. Or we can fight here today. When we win, we will have our freedom once again. And our families will welcome us into the Epertase we love. I choose to fight for my family. If I am to die in the streets of Reigal to give them what Fice has taken away, then I am here to die." His voice cracked as he shouted, "Will you fight with me?"

His men roared again. Trying to hold them back now would be futile.

"Will you die with me?"

They banged their weapons against the ground with a roar loud enough that King Fice himself could probably hear.

Christopher spun his horse and drew his sword. "Long live Queen Alina," he screamed. He pointed his sword toward the enemy and cried, "Attaaaaack."

Christopher whipped his steed into a gallop. He was near the front of his charging men when Atticus disappeared down one of the streets.

Christopher's men joined Atticus's and slammed into the Liths. Christopher swung his sword at every Lith he met. The first soldier's helmet flew off, splattering Christopher's face and lips with blood. The taste of rusty coins filled his mouth and he spat it out.

He pushed his steed into the swarm of Lith soldiers that had started surrounding him. They appeared confused and hardly fought back as he swung his sword. But not all of them were wilting.

Christopher's horse reared and screeched, sending Christopher tumbling from his saddle. He landed badly and jolted his back out of place. His horse collapsed with a sword jutting from its chest. The steed struggled to get back to its feet, but flopped to its side again.

A few of Christopher's men pulled him away from the Liths. Two of them died in the process. Christopher scrambled to his feet and pushed forward. Standing straight was painful. He held his lower back and groaned. Ignoring it was his only choice. Between the clashing metal, dying screams, and war cries, the noise was was deafening. A glance down an alley revealed the same scene on the next street over, and probably every street throughout Reigal.

Liths historically had always been skilled fighters, but some of the men he fought that day moved as if in a trance. Their strategy appeared to be overwhelming Christopher's men with sheer numbers rather than fighting prowess. They fell by the hundreds. But when one soldier fell, two more would take his place.

Christopher's men fought through the town without remorse, the other captains and their men hopefully doing the same in the other streets. Christopher shouted, "Do not give them time to regroup," as they pushed the Liths back toward Atticus.

During a momentary lull, Christopher slowed for a breath and a chance to gather himself. His men were winning. He put his hands on his knees and looked toward the castle walls where the heaviest fighting took place. They were too far away to see faces, but he could see shapes. One of those shapes drained his optimism. A single warrior towered above all the others. It was a Gildonese. And that Gildonese plowed through Atticus's men with merciless speed, flinging some of them through the air like gnats.

Christopher's shoulders drooped. *If that's who we have to fight, we haven't a chance.*

But just as all hope appeared lost, the fighting soldiers around the Gildonese parted and allowed a single soldier to advance. Though Christopher couldn't make out the warrior's face, he recognized his strut and his reckless, dual-knife attack. Thairen.

Christopher climbed onto the porch roof of a saloon. He wanted a better look at the progress his men were making. Also, who else could say they'd seen a Gildonese bested in battle? By the time he reached the porch roof, both combatants appeared battered and winded. When Thairen attacked and jammed his blades into both of the Gildonese's hearts, Christopher had just enough time to open his mouth to cheer before the dying Gildonese's blade took Thairen's head.

Without their Gildonese commander, the Lith soldiers suddenly appeared lost. One of Atticus's men thrust his fist into the air. "Hail to Thairen," he screamed.

The Liths backpedaled, lost and confused. Christopher's men pushed them into retreat toward the castle. Christopher felt proud and excited and powerful all at once.

They were winning. Maybe they had already won. Hopefully, Aidric's men were having the same success.

CHAPTER 34

HATRED

Rasi scanned Logan's room and saw a second Gildonese sitting up in the bed with her legs hanging over the foot. She was a fire-haired female with anger simmering in her glare, the type of woman who didn't take kindly to intruders. She rose from Logan's bed.

He remembered Eldon's training. *"Ignore the female,"* he had said. *"Let her know you're not concerned with her presence."* Rasi scoffed at her and then glared at Fice.

She removed a sword from a hook on the wall, but Rasi didn't look over.

"She will move to your back," Eldon had said. *"Let her. Make your straps ignore her, too."*

The female cautiously moved behind him. Two of Rasi's straps tried to follow her, but he called them back.

A low static filled his mind, as expected. He drew his sword. Fice smirked, confident, his sword still at his hip. When he spoke Rasi somehow heard him over the static—a trick even Eldon hadn't mastered. "Your name is Rasi, no? I've heard you're called a god among the creatures of the volcanic regions."

Rasi tilted his head.

"I, however, have my doubts." Fice placed his finger against his lips. "I wonder, will taking your head make me a god as well? Hmph. We shall see, I suppose."

Rasi felt the female move closer to his back, but continued ignoring her. *"She will be overconfident,"* Eldon's words echoed through his mind. *"She will not use her powers of sway to attack because your disrespect will make her want to prove herself to her master by killing you without it."*

Rasi lifted his sword toward Fice. The static rose to a painful level. He concentrated on recalling Eldon's words. *"Wait for Fice to attack. She will use him as a distraction. You must accept Fice's initial assault and, instead of defense, focus your first attack on her. You must be precise, as you will only get one shot."*

As Rasi had practiced with Eldon so many times before, he focused on Fice while carefully spinning his sword in his hand. It had to be automatic and without thought. He pressed the cold blade against the side of his chest beneath his armpit. With both hands around the hilt, he plunged it blindly behind him. He needn't feel her soft flesh giving way to his steel to know he had hit his mark; her painful grunt told all he needed to know. He drove the blade upward through her gut and into her chest.

Fice lunged.

Eldon's words rang in his mind. *"Twist your blade side to side to hit both of her hearts."* And that's what he did. He felt her go limp on his blade.

In mid-air, Fice's eyes bulged.

Rasi ripped his sword free as Fice swung his sword. Knowing he couldn't avoid the blow, Rasi leaned forward to meet the hilt instead of the blade. His jaw shifted from the impact. He sprawled to the ground and his sword slid out of reach. He might have even gone unconscious for a flash.

Though Rasi was still dizzy from the blow, his warrior instincts pushed him back to his wobbly feet. He staggered and tried to shake away the fuzz. The mind scream that filled his head ceased so abruptly that he feared something had broken in his brain. The room slowly came back into focus.

A pained breath stuttered across Fice's quivering lips as the Gildonese king cradled his female companion in his arms. On his knees, he rocked back and forth.

Rasi rubbed his jaw as he staggered to his sword and picked it up. Fice didn't attack.

"Anger him as much as you can," Eldon had insisted.

Rasi smirked. *What's her name, Fice? I mean ... what* was *her name?*

She coughed blood into Fice's face. He licked it, ignoring the taunt. "Josilyn, I'm sorry," he moaned.

Rasi crossed the room with a strut and twirled his sword as if he were on a stage. It was hard to pull off because he wasn't a showboat by nature.

Josilyn gasped and choked until she eventually drew her last breath.

Fice lifted his coal-black eyes and stared through Rasi's soul. Rasi antagonized him with a cold, bloody smile. *That should do it.*

The Gildonese king released a scream so primal, so deafening, Rasi pressed one palm over his ear and his sword hilt over the other. A glass ornament on the wall above the bed shattered. Fice gently lowered Josilyn to the floor and rose to his feet. "You will suffer for all eternity," he said, his voice cracking with pain. A thin stream of drool leaked from his lips and ran down his chin. He wiped it away with his arm. The static screamed in Rasi's head again.

And then Fice charged.

As planned, Rasi plunged his sword forward, knowing Fice would disarm him. He hated to lose his sword so early in the fight, but he had to sell his attack. Like Eldon had done many times, Fice sidestepped his plunge with ease.

A strap reached alongside Rasi's attacking arm. Fice punched Rasi's wrist, knocking the sword from his hand. Eldon's plan was perfect. The strap caught Fice's lightning-fast wrist.

If Fice was surprised at Rasi's success, his face didn't show it. His fury boiled out of him in a barrage of unrelenting punches from his free hand. As slow as the strikes appeared, Rasi couldn't avoid them. One of the blows shattered his nose. Another loosened a front tooth. His straps flailed to defend him, but Fice avoided them with ease.

Rasi realized his own strikes were mere guesses, like his early days with Eldon, but he couldn't help himself. The strap around Fice's wrist tugged and pushed, trying to knock Fice off balance to no avail. Fice was unbelievably faster than Eldon and, even with his right arm restrained, his strikes were far more potent.

The unoccupied straps attacked wildly, but Fice effortlessly shrugged and bobbed away from each blow. Rasi considered retreating to catch his breath, but he didn't dare allow Fice to break free of his strap's grip. With his face throbbing, he attacked again. Fice ducked beneath his wild punch and drove a fist into his side, snapping two ribs and sending the last bit of air from Rasi's lungs.

Ignoring Rasi's mental pleas, the strap released Fice's arm to defend him while he tried to catch his wind. He stumbled backward. His every attempt at taking a breath caused a wave of grunt-inducing pain. Something was wrong inside his chest, something far more serious than broken ribs.

Fice laughed, a furious sound. Instead of finishing Rasi, he backed up to Logan's desk where two war hammers rested.

Rasi coughed and doubled over. His mouth filled with blood that leaked past his swollen lips. He'd seen enough men die of punctured lungs to know he would suffer the same fate if he didn't retreat soon. His mission had been a failure, and the speed at which it had fallen apart was staggering.

Fice collected the two war hammers. The wooden handles were stained red and the stone heads were chipped, scuffed, and lopsided. It was obvious many men had died because of those weapons, and Rasi was next.

He remembered Eldon's words. *"He will be slower with his weapons."* That would be helpful if Rasi had the strength to do anything about it. He'd never dreamed he would be bested so fast and so decisively.

Fice licked the head of one of his hammers. "I will break every bone in your body before I end you by crushing your skull."

Rasi believed him.

CHAPTER 35

WILLUM AND GILLIAN

Gillian squatted on the partial roof of an abandoned two-story blacksmith shop near the southern front where some of Atticus's men engaged the Liths. She scanned the streets until she spotted her husband, Willum, entering the fray. She had twenty-seven arrows in her quiver and was determined to use every one of them. Willum cut through the fighting men, careful not to engage anyone in combat unless forced. His ultimate target, a lone, horseless Gildonese, barked orders to the Lith soldiers in the distance.

Gillian wanted to save her arrows for that Gildonese, but the Liths were too thick for Willum. Gillian helped to clear him a path with her arrows, mentally keeping count as she used them.

With eleven arrows still poking from her quiver, she left her husband at the mercy of his own skills. The sinking realization that she should have done so five arrows earlier gnawed at her gut. She watched, both helpless and hopeful, as he fought closer to his prize.

The Gildonese saw Willum coming long before the mercenary got close. Willum readied himself for the fight with his bloody sword in hand. The Lith soldiers parted as if commanded without words. The Gildonese lifted his sword. As planned, Willum hesitated, waiting for the first of Gillian's arrows.

The Gildonese took an aggressive step forward, but stopped suddenly, lifting his eyes to the rooftops. He smiled and winked at her. She drew her arrow back. The Gildonese nodded as if coaxing her, and then laid his sword on the ground.

At first, she thought it was an odd move and released her arrow. It shot toward its target with brilliant aim. With her first arrow flying, Willum leaped forward. The Gildonese twirled, snatched the arrow from the air, and jammed it into Willum's shoulder in a flash. And then she understood why he'd left his weapon on the ground. She didn't waver, sending another arrow just as they had planned. Willum swung his sword, ignoring the arrow that protruded from the meat of his shoulder. The Gildonese smacked the second arrow from the air. Before Willum could land his blow, the Gildonese slammed a fist into his jaw. Willum's sword fell to the stone road. He staggered. Another arrow whizzed past his ear, but the Gildonese deflected it with ease.

Willum regained his footing and his senses and attacked again. Gillian launched another arrow, and another, only to have them both effortlessly batted away. Willum took two more blows for his trouble, but fought onward. For the first time since the fight began, the Gildonese took a backward step. Gillian released her next two arrows as fast as she could.

Willum charged, his face taking the punishment for his aggression. One of the arrows clipped his side, redirecting its path enough to elude the Gildonese's defensive swipe and land in the bastard's thigh. Both Willum and the Gildonese winced. While the Gildonese stumbled backward, Willum grabbed the arrow in his thigh and jerked it side to side. The Gildonese howled in pain and swatted another arrow from the air.

A Lith soldier pulled away from his own battle and charged Willum's back. Gillian used one of her last three arrows to send the soldier sprawling face first to the street. The Gildonese took advantage of the interruption to grab Willum's hand and yank it away from the arrow in his gushing thigh. But Willum was close and recklessly lunged. Gillian's next arrow plunged through the back of

Willum's hand and pinned it to the soft flesh above the Gildonese's waist.

Willum pushed forward, his momentum spinning his foe away from Gillian.

Gillian aimed with her last arrow—her last hope.

With the Gildonese's back momentarily to her, she released. The Gildonese wailed loud enough for her to know she had struck her mark. Willum gripped the arrow that pinned his hand to the Gildonese and ripped it free. The Gildonese dropped to his knees.

Willum retrieved his sword. The Gildonese reached for the arrow that lodged between his shoulder blades, but it was out of reach. Willum, with sword in hand, stood before him. Even with the Gildonese on his knees, Willum had to look up to meet his eyes. Gillian wished for one more arrow for his other heart. The Gildonese cursed in defiance. With one powerful, arching swing, Willum lopped off his head.

He tore part of his sleeve away, wrapped the hole in his bleeding palm, and cinched it tight with his teeth. Then he turned and waved to his wife. She blew him a kiss.

CHAPTER 36

PAIN FOR A FRIEND

T he battle also waged from the northeast where Aidric led his men against the Liths. Simcane used the battle to sneak himself, Coen, and thirty other men through the alleys, avoiding the bulk of the fighting as much as they could. For all the Gildonese's skills in combat, Simcane questioned their ability to lead men in war.

In addition to weapons, Coen and his men carried wire nets and led seven riderless racing stallions. Their mission was to find the Gildonese generals who led the northeastern front against Atticus's men.

Simcane reached the rear of the battle where the Liths were fully engaged with Atticus's men. Three Gildonese generals fought among the Liths. Simcane cursed. They had expected two Gildonese at that post, not three. Though their numbers were only greater by one, a single additional Gildonese was as dangerous as another army altogether.

Two of the Gildonese were strangers, as expected, but when the third member of the pack turned and Simcane saw his bloodied face, his stomach turned. "Damn it, Eldon."

"Are you ready to attack?" Coen shouted.

Simcane didn't answer, only stared at his Gildonese friend.

"Sir?" Coen asked again, and shook his arm, breaking his trance. "Are you ready to attack?"

Simcane paused before answering, "Eldon's there."

"Where?"

Simcane pointed.

"What's he doing with them?"

"He's been swayed."

"What should we do, sir?"

"Continue with the plan, but don't harm him. Is that understood?"

"I understand, sir, but how do you propose we handle him without harming him? I'll not let my men die to protect the very Gildonese who's trying to kill them."

"I will face Eldon myself," Simcane snapped.

"What will you do?"

"I'll convince him of his errors."

"And if you cannot?"

"Treat him as you do the others, I suppose." Simcane sighed and looked away.

Coen turned to his men. Simcane dismounted and started the long, ugly walk toward his Gildonese friend.

"Eldon," Simcane shouted.

Once their eyes met, Eldon tossed his current foe aside and marched toward Simcane. There was nothing left in Eldon's black eyes that Simcane recognized as his old friend. Eldon tossed several more of Aidric's soldiers over his head to clear a path to Simcane. Then he charged, death in his eyes.

"Eldon," he shouted again. "Listen to me."

"I do not listen to the enemy any more than I hear the gods' whispers, and you shall have your larynx removed for even speaking my name."

Simcane kept his sword sheathed even as Eldon raised his own.

"Eldon. You don't have to do this. You're not one of them."

Eldon swung his sword. Simcane flinched as the blade bit into his flexed shoulder, not stopping until it met bone. He grunted and winced, but stood his ground. Eldon yanked at the embedded sword, but Simcane grabbed the blade with his other hand and twisted it from Eldon's grip. He tossed it aside. "Eldon?"

Eldon scowled. "I needn't a sword to finish the likes of you." *Tap. Tap. Tap. Tap.* His fist pummeled Simcane's face. The big man stumbled backward.

Simcane covered his face with his thick forearms, but Eldon kept punching. It hurt, but it was better than taking the shots to his face. Unable to see past his arms, he didn't notice Eldon drawing back his foot. An explosion of pain in Simcane's balls sent him to his knees.

Eldon stepped back and sneered at him. "A man as large as you should be a much more worthy adversary than you have proven to be. No matter. By the way you bleed, I am certain that you die the same as any man half your size."

"I was your friend, Eldon." He spat blood and a tooth onto the stone street. He wanted to stand up, but the twisting pain in his groin told him no. As much as he didn't want to fight his friend, he was out of options. He couldn't stall any longer.

Like a hunter, Eldon strutted to the side, searching for the best angle for a killing blow. He smiled. "How about I break your pathetic neck?"

"Don't do this, Eldon. You're a better man than that."

Eldon cracked his knuckles. "I am no man. I am a Gildonese of the pack of Fice."

Simcane looked past Eldon with a half-smile. *Just a little longer.*

"What are you looking at? Your pathetic friends can't help you now."

On horseback, Coen closed in from Eldon's rear with another soldier riding beside him.

Eldon shook his head. "I hear your friends coming. Do not think they could possibly get near us while keeping their lives."

Simcane swallowed hard. "Heh. They don't have to get near." He lifted his fist into the air. Coen peeled off to Eldon's side while his partner rode to the other. Eldon leaped at Simcane.

Simcane drove his fist to the ground. A blast of air and stone and dirt slammed into Eldon and knocked him to the ground between the two charging horses. Simcane fell to his rear, exhausted from using such a large blast of his gift.

Eldon scrambled to stand, but not before the two riders rode past, their wire net dragging between them. The mesh swept Eldon off his feet.

Simcane stood up with a hand over his aching crotch. He watched as they galloped past. Coen and the other soldier leaped from their horses and rolled to a stop. Their horses galloped along the front lines toward the west with Eldon thrashing within the tangled net between them. If the racing horses did what they were trained to do, Eldon would be dragged far away before they stopped. Hopefully, it would be far enough away to break Fice's sway.

Simcane took off his shirt and tied it around the gash on his arm until the bleeding slowed to a trickle. With the adrenaline of the fight subsiding, he squeezed a fist. His fingers tingled and he worried that Eldon had done more damage to his shoulder than he originally believed.

Coen pulled Simcane's hand away from the laceration for a better look. "Nasty cut you have there, sir."

"I'll be fine. You worry about the mission. Where are the other two Gildonese?"

"Though we lost a few men, we managed to deliver a similar fate to them."

"And you sent them in opposite directions?"

"Yes, sir. One south toward Pataska, and one on track to be swimming in the Lowland Lake if the horses stay their course. Also, we've just received word that the Liths are falling at every front. The battle appears to have been won."

"Very good. As long as Rasi can kill Fice before the other Gildonese can return, we will be on our way to victory. Any word from Masera and his men?"

"Not yet."

"That's a good thing, I suppose. It means Fice didn't send soldiers to flank them." Masera and his men were the final wave, waiting behind the battlefield in case they were needed.

"Fice isn't much of a strategist, is he, sir?"

"Thankfully, it doesn't appear so."

CHAPTER 37

THE WORST DEFEAT

The taste of blood in Rasi's mouth wasn't as crushing as the knowledge of why it was there. His chest felt as though a constricting band had been wrapped around his lungs, and he grunted with each breath. Fice advanced on him with both hammers raised.

Rasi's straps occupied Fice enough to slow him, though they couldn't keep him at bay. Fice swung a hammer; Rasi ducked his head and lifted his left arm in defense. That was his first mistake. Eldon was right that Fice was slower with the extra weight of his weapon, but as Rasi's forearm snapped, that knowledge seemed of little use. Rasi fell to his rear. The broken bones in his arm painfully scraped against each other with each movement.

In one fluid motion, Fice drove his other hammer downward. Expecting such an attack, Rasi rolled to his side. The hammer hit the stone floor, sending chips of rock flying. Fice lifted both hammers above his head.

Rasi's straps snaked along the floor past his head and grabbed one of the bed posts. Fice swung his hammers. Rasi flinched, but his straps yanked him out of the way in time.

Fice didn't let up as he jerked his hammers from the broken stone. He pounced, landing next to Rasi's legs, and swung one of the hammers. Pain exploded in Rasi's foot. It must have shattered every bone. Rasi pressed his face to the floor to keep from screaming.

Fice laughed and drew back again, more focused on causing pain than on defense. One of Rasi's straps lunged at Fice's leg and wrapped around it. Fice stumbled, his next hammer swing whiffing past Rasi's smashed forearm.

The two straps still around the bed post tightened and strained while the strap around Fice's leg quivered. Fice's femur snapped so loudly that the noise echoed through the room. The Gildonese king crumbled to the ground with part of his bone jutting through the flesh of his thigh.

Fice ripped the strap from his thigh and scooted backward in retreat. His face was filled with pain and rage.

Rasi reached for the bed post with his good arm while pressing his shattered forearm tight against his gut. The agony of his broken ribs was unbearable. He pulled himself to the bed and rested with his back against the wood frame.

Fice sat a couple of horse-lengths away with both hands pressed against his bleeding thigh. His hammers lay on the ground just out of reach.

It was Rasi's chance, but he was too weak—too injured—to take advantage of it. His straps pulled at the bed and forced him onto his good foot. Though he could barely get air into his lungs and the pain of his broken bones was excruciating, he dug deep and hobbled toward Fice. He had to kill the bastard, no matter what. The Gildonese king hissed and retreated along the floor.

Fice pushed himself up onto one leg. The break was complete, shortening his other leg enough that his foot brushed the ground. One of Rasi's straps whipped around, stiffened, and struck Fice's cheek. The strap's momentum threw Rasi's balance onto his shattered foot, and he and Fice both tumbled to the floor.

Rasi's body wanted to surrender, but he couldn't waste this chance while Fice was so vulnerable. With his uninjured arm, he pulled himself across the floor. Each scrape of bone against bone in his forearm brought fresh waves of nausea, yet he continued to claw his way forward.

Fice grimaced with his hands tight against his bleeding thigh. Rasi reached out with one of his straps and coiled it around Fice's neck. His other straps danced in the air.

The Gildonese king let out a forced chuckle. "You think you've won?" His voice was strained from the pressure of the strap around his throat. He gasped. "You haven't won anything."

Rasi snarled. *Maybe not. But I'm going to kill you just the same.*

"And ... Epertase ... will still ... be lost."

I'll deal with Jarrah in due time.

Fice tried to pry his fingers beneath the strap, but it was too tight. "Jarrah? Heh, heh. You fool."

Rasi's strap tightened, sending a wheeze from Fice's throat. *Goodbye, Fice.* And then the hair on the back of his neck stood on end; his stomach turned.

They weren't alone.

CHAPTER 38

THE END IS THE BEGINNING

Outside the Lith castle, Atticus looked over his men from the town square as they met Aidric's men in the streets among hundreds of surrendering Lith soldiers.

Shouts of "Long live Queen Alina" rose throughout the ranks of the victors. Men embraced their fellow soldiers in celebration. Atticus watched with pride as Aidric rode to his fore. They nodded to each other and shook hands. "Well done," Atticus said.

Aidric smiled. "I can't believe we've won. Any word from Rasi?"

Atticus shook his head. "Nothing yet."

Then they turned to face the celebrating soldiers. Because of them, Reigal was now liberated and would soon return to the rightful leaders. Christopher approached with a smile the size of Havens Ravine.

Atticus nodded proudly at the young man. "You did well." He turned to the troops. "Men," he shouted. Shushes carried through the streets until, slowly, everyone had quieted. Atticus took a swig from a water bladder before addressing them. "You have accomplished a great victory for Epertase and Lithia today, but we are not finished. We must take the castle, and if Rasi has not succeeded in removing Fice, then we must do it ourselves. Your courage and skills will surely make our queen proud once the word travels to her. You will be the men to help rebuild what Fice has destroyed."

The soldiers erupted into cheers. He hoped if Fice still drew breath that the bastard could hear what was coming for him. He waited for the soldiers to calm before attempting to continue, but their celebration didn't end quickly.

Before Aidric could step forward to congratulate the men, a low rumble lifted from the rear, different from the celebratory buzz. He squinted to see what was causing the commotion. Nervous chatter spread through the ranks toward the front. He looked to Christopher, who shrugged.

"You want me to go check it out, sir?"

Aidric nodded.

Christopher rode into the crowd as the men created a path for him. He wasn't far when the spreading word reached him. He twisted his upper body around, the color drained from his face. "Commander Atticus," he shouted in a suddenly shaky voice. "Word from Masera's men is that another army approaches. They are wearing Epertasian colors."

Aidric turned to Atticus. "What do you think that's about?"

"It's probably Jarrah. Send riders to inform him of our victory here. Tell him we have secured a pathway toward the restoration of power to Epertase's ruling family. And then arrest him."

"Yes, sir."

Though Atticus couldn't imagine Jarrah continuing the wrong that had been done to Epertase, not with his powerful Gildonese alliance all but broken, he also didn't want to leave any doubt of his army's intention. He shouted, "Hold on, Aidric. I'll join you." If Jarrah's choice was to continue the struggle for whatever power Fice had promised him, Atticus should be there to deal with his former compatriot himself. Feeling many pairs of nervous eyes on him, he felt he should address their concerns. "Fear not, men. Epertase has likely heard of our movement and has sent soldiers to reinforce our victory. I am confident we will be greeted with praise, despite Jarrah's treason. I will ride out to meet them and—"

As he spoke, a fireball soared through the sky and landed somewhere near where Masera's men should have been staged. Panic filled the streets. More fireballs traced the sky. He looked back at Aidric and then to Christopher, who sat paralyzed on his steed.

Aidric's forehead creased. "You don't think Jarrah's attacking, do you?"

Atticus half shook his head, not completely sure. "Come on, Aidric. Let's go check it out." Aidric, Atticus, and Christopher hurried toward the now constant barrage of fireballs. When they reached the edge of the city where Atticus could see Masera's forces, his heart sank. Arrows blotted out the suns as Masera's men redeployed to face the new enemy charging from the south. It appeared to be at least one Epertasian battalion, if not two. Masera's men would have no chance.

"What do we do, sir?" Christopher cried.

Atticus stared at the growing massacre. It couldn't be.

Aidric grabbed his arm. "Atticus?"

Atticus looked at his friend, his hope draining. There was only one thing they could do. He swallowed hard. "Announce our surrender, Aidric. It's the only way we'll survive." Even fresh and prepared, their numbers would be too small to fight multiple Epertasian battalions.

"What about retreat?" Aidric asked.

Atticus shook his head. "There's nowhere to go. They'll run us down from behind."

Christopher shook his head and stared back at the battlefield. "Atticus, we can fight."

"No. We must surrender. It's our only choice."

Atticus moved between Christopher and the pending slaughter. "Christopher, look at me."

Christopher pulled his gaze from the battlefield to Atticus's eyes. "But—"

"We will surrender, Christopher. When they cease their attack and accept our surrender, we'll speak with their commanders— explain what we have done here. They will free us once they see

Fice's reign is over. Jarrah doesn't have enough influence without his Gildonese master."

Christopher bowed his head. "If those are your orders. Let me do it. Let me lead the surrender."

"Why you, Christopher?"

"If I do it and it doesn't go well, you can flee and find the queen. Make sure she's safe." He grinned, though the look in his eyes betrayed him. "Come and free me one day if they take me to prison."

Atticus hated the idea, but he knew Christopher was right. After much consternation, he conceded. "I will not allow you to rot in prison, Christopher. I promise. Send Masera back here. I doubt he will accept surrender without hearing it from me."

Christopher nodded. Then he rode toward the battlefield.

Atticus watched him with just as much pride as guilt, which was to say an ocean full. Christopher met Masera beneath a barrage of arrows. Masera's eyes instantly shot to Atticus. He kicked his steed into a full gallop toward Atticus at the edge of Main Street.

He shouted, "What is the meaning of this, Atticus? You dare call me away from my men during battle."

"It's over, Masera. We've lost this one."

"Nothing's over until my breath is gone."

"We have to think bigger than this."

Masera glanced at Aidric. "Are you on board with this dragon shit surrender as well?"

Aidric reluctantly nodded and then looked away.

"Unbelievable. Explain to me why, Atticus."

"Just hear me out."

Masera's upper lip curled.

"I understand you're angry."

"You don't know the half of it." He looked out over the battlefield where his men laid down their weapons. "I can't believe this is happening."

"Hear me out."

Masera steered his horse away from Atticus. Then he turned back. "If it was anyone but you, Atticus, I'd have ignored those orders and removed my soldiers from his command for even suggesting surrender. You have until my patience wears thin. And I must warn you, it is like paper already."

"Jarrah has the weight of the entire Epertasian army. We can't even come close to withstanding their full might. You as well as anyone know what that means. We cannot win. If we die stupidly here, Alina is lost." He rode to Masera's side and put a hand on his shoulder. "Old friend, we need to get to Alina. I need you to trust me. It's our only move now."

Masera spurred his steed toward his waiting men as if ignoring Atticus's pleas. Then he slowed, turned back, and said with calm resignation, "Damn it, Atticus. What is going on here?"

"I'm afraid Jarrah is more dangerous than we gave him credit for. I think he wants Lithia as well as Epertase and allowed us to defeat Fice for him. That's all I can figure."

"I cannot leave my men. You know that."

"You must. Your allegiance is to Epertase and our rightful queen. If you are captured—or worse—you will be no good to that cause."

Masera bowed his head and then nodded.

Atticus took one last look at the battlefield where the Epertasians had surrounded Masera's men. Then he turned to his own men. They looked like children waiting for their parents to tell them everything would be all right. But it wouldn't be all right. "Surrender, men. We will come for you. I vow it."

Aidric volunteered to lead the surrender of Atticus's men along with his own.

Atticus shook his hand, followed by Masera. "Long live Queen Alina," Atticus said.

"Long live Queen Alina," Aidric repeated. He started toward the Epertasian command post far off in the distance. Christopher was already headed there, having relayed the surrender to Masera's men.

Atticus nodded to Masera and kicked his horse into a gallop toward an alley. Masera followed.

Once they reached the wall outside Lithia's castle, Atticus said, "Go to Homer and Irene. Make sure they're safe. After I gather Alina, King Logan, and Queen Lona from the Tunnels of Eiger, we will go to Eldon's as planned. If Rasi makes it there, we'll bring him and meet you at Homer's farm to regroup."

"What if Rasi doesn't make it?"

"I'll worry about that later. Right now, getting to Alina is all that matters."

"You have a crystal?"

Atticus patted his waist pocket.

"Good." Masera shook his hand, and the two separated and raced away.

CHAPTER 39

THE TRUE ENEMY
REVEALED

Rasi's straps helped him onto his good foot again and he stood over Fice. All he needed to do was snap Fice's damn neck and the fight would be over, Fice's grip broken. But something felt wrong. Something tingled in his bones and held him back.

He thought about the pain Fice had caused him. He envisioned his parents and their last moments of suffering. He wanted this death. His straps wanted it. Fice had stopped struggling, but before Rasi allowed his straps their glory, he loosened his grip enough to let Fice answer the one question that was eating at his gut.

Why aren't you fighting back?

Fice gasped for air. "I've failed," he answered between breaths. "If you … don't kill me now … he surely will."

Rasi grit his teeth. *He? Who's pulling your strings?* That prickling feeling of not being alone intensified.

Fice's lips blanched; his skin blued as he struggled for air. Even with the air barely getting past Rasi's swollen, broken nose, a faint and somehow familiar stink of decaying teeth assaulted his senses. He ignored the smell, focusing solely on Fice. He wanted to snap Fice's neck, but he couldn't, not without learning who "he" was.

Despite his reservations, he lifted Fice's head enough for their eyes to meet. The distinct smell of rotten teeth grew stronger. Again, his strap loosened enough for the semi-conscious Fice to take another breath.

In his tunnel vision, Rasi hadn't noticed the creature that had landed on the balcony until a familiar taunting "Raasiiieee?" reached his ears.

He spun toward the balcony. The smell suddenly made sense. A hylock. The creature grinned. Rasi uncoiled his strap from around Fice's neck. The room fell silent, save for Fice's gasping. *Who did you mean when you said "he," Fice?*

The pieces didn't add up. The hylocks didn't seem like Fice's game. This was bigger than the Gildonese. As a soldier, Rasi had trusted his instincts. When had he gotten so sloppy?

The door bulged like a bloated stomach. Rasi cocked his head. Fice turned away. The door pulsated like a beating heart before it exploded. Rasi recoiled and covered his eyes with his forearm. Splintered debris peppered his flesh.

Fice scooted away until his back met the wall. He gagged and hacked blood-tinged sputum onto the floor. Rasi stared at the empty doorway until a familiar woman stepped into the room.

Cyn? He glared at the symbiot. *Have you come to defend this trash?* None of it made sense. The symbiot leader, Scorne, wasn't strong enough to control Fice and orchestrate an uprising.

Cyn shook her head and moved out of the doorway.

Rasi clenched his good fist while his other hand dangled uselessly.

A stranger with straggly gray hair covering his face like a tattered curtain stepped into the doorway where Cyn had stood. He parted the hair from his eyes and tucked the strands behind his ears. There was something about him, though Rasi couldn't immediately place the face behind the beard. But it wasn't the beard that Rasi had seen before. It was the eyes.

"Rasi," the man said as if they were longtime friends. "I have waited for this moment since you were banished many years ago."

His voice stirred faint memories, though Rasi still couldn't place him.

The stranger tilted his head. "Has it been so long that you have forgotten me?"

Then it hit him. He stumbled back, accidentally putting his weight on his injured foot. Though he had been through every possible angle in his planning, nothing could have prepared him for this.

The man said, "You killed my closest friend. You and that whore daughter of his took his life and kingdom."

Rasi shook his head, stunned. *Tevin? How?*

Tevin dusted off his shoulder and then stroked his beard. "What's wrong, Rasi? A little tongue-tied?"

Rasi stared in disbelief. How could he have missed Tevin?

Tevin turned to Cyn and grabbed the back of her neck. He crammed his lips onto hers with passionate fury, which she returned. Then he yanked his face away. "If you love me, you will not return until you find Alina and bring her to me. I want her Light."

Cyn stared into Tevin's eyes. "I will bring her, my love. I promise."

Tevin's next words shattered Rasi's heart. "They hide with King Logan in the Tunnels of Eiger."

No, no, no. How could he know where she hides?

An evil smirk split her face. "How should I handle Lithia's former king and queen?

As cold as a mountain blizzard, Tevin answered, "Have your fun." He yanked his hand from the nape of her neck and turned back to Rasi.

CHAPTER 40

REGRET

From high atop a hill on the outskirts of Reigal, Jarrah surveyed Atticus's failed rebellion with pride. Andon sat on a horse at his side with his head hung low. He couldn't look at Aidric as his friend and Christopher were led away in restraints.

"Cheer up, Andon. We've won."

Andon's eyes fell to the ground. "I don't feel like we have. I feel like all we've done is kill our fellow Epertasians."

"Nonsense. They were a cancer. You will be rewarded greatly under my brother-in-law's rule. Epertase will have a new future, free from the lies of Alina and Rasi."

"I never expected so many of our countrymen to die."

"Unfortunately, that's what this victory called for. But take solace that the killing is over now. We've won. All that's left is to bask in our glory. If it's any consolation, I'll try to convince Tevin to spare the lives of these men."

Andon looked up with hopeful eyes, which made Jarrah laugh.

"I can't promise anything, though."

Andon looked back to the ground.

Just as Jarrah turned his horse away from the field of victory to start the long ride back to Epertase, someone shouted his name. He turned back.

Simcane, Gillian, and Willum approached, surrounded by Epertasian soldiers. Their hands were bound behind their backs.

The lead soldier said, "They were determined to speak with you, sir. It was the only way we could get this big one here to stop breaking jaws and cooperate."

"What do you want, Simcane?"

"What are you doing? We had victory for Epertase in hand. You can't possibly believe life under Fice would be better than under Alina."

"What makes you think I give a shit about Fice?"

Simcane shook his head. "Jarrah, listen to me. Fice has been all but defeated. There's no good endgame for you here."

Jarrah laughed. "Simcane, you fool. Fice was never in charge. It's been my brother-in-law, Tevin, all along."

"Tevin? Tevin's a coward. How does he wield enough power to pull off something like this?"

"When the Light left King Elijah for Alina, the fire in the sky awakened a gift buried deep within him. Now he will use that power to take Alina's Light once and for all. He will be invincible. And I will be his right hand."

Andon looked away.

Simcane lunged with his hands still bound behind his back. Two soldiers crowded between him and Jarrah as Jarrah backed his horse away a few steps.

"I will never allow that," Simcane snapped.

More soldiers grabbed Simcane to hold him back. His veins bulged from his forearms and neck and his face grew red. Andon wondered if the restraints would hold and what would happen to him if they didn't.

Jarrah chuckled. "You have no choice."

Simcane looked to Andon with beseeching eyes. "Andon. You mustn't let this happen. Order your men to stand down. They'll listen to you."

Andon's stomach turned. "I cannot, Sim. It's too late for that now."

Simcane grunted and the ties around his wrist fell broken to the grass. He slammed his fist to the ground, sending a thunderous blast against his captors. Jarrah and Andon scrambled away from the blast. Simcane fell to one knee, wheezing. Another wave of soldiers swarmed him and pulled him to the ground.

His pleading eyes met Andon's again, and Andon turned away, ashamed. The first soldier to recover cracked Simcane's skull with his sword hilt. "Should I kill him, sir?" the soldier asked.

Before Jarrah could answer, Andon shouted, "You will not."

The soldier looked to Jarrah for confirmation. Andon crowded Jarrah's horse and gave him a look. "I will not tolerate you killing him, Jarrah."

Jarrah rolled his eyes. "Don't be so dramatic, Andon." He turned to the soldier and shook his head. "Just take him to Thasula's prison with the others."

Simcane spat on the soldier and got another crack to the head. He collapsed.

Jarrah caught Andon's glare. "What? I did what you asked, you softy. Now, come with me. Let's see what territories Tevin will give you."

Andon had never cared about territories. He only cared about Dru, and he feared what his brother would say about what he had done when they met again on the other side.

CHAPTER 41

HOPELESSNESS

A thousand strategies rushed through Rasi's mind, any one of which might have some success if his body wasn't so broken. He searched for something to say as he limped closer. *Cyn, wait.*

As Cyn walked toward the door, a strap reached for her. Tevin stepped in the way, so the strap grabbed his arm instead. It strained to shove him aside, but it was as if his feet had grown roots. The whites of his eyes turned as black as Fice's. His arm trembled and glowed orange beneath the strap. Rasi ordered the strap to release Tevin's arm, but it held on as if permanently melded.

Tevin smiled and eyed the strap. It stiffened briefly before dropping limp from his arm. Rasi staggered backward, his chest, his arm, his foot, seemingly every part of his body aching and throbbing. His other straps hovered defensively in front of him.

As if bored, Tevin waved his arm, sending a blast of intense heat at the straps. The impact hurled Rasi against the farthest wall. More blood poured from his shattered nose. Burn blisters lifted on the straps that had absorbed the brunt of the attack. They writhed on the floor. Rasi scrambled to his rear, grunting with each worthless gasping breath. His eyes blurred.

The hylock on the balcony cackled so violently that it almost tumbled from its perch.

Rasi pressed his back against the wall.

Tevin scoffed at him and went to Fice, who still sat on the floor. "You have failed me, Gildonese king," he said.

Fice pushed himself up onto his good leg. Tevin glared up at him, and he wilted like a dog who'd misbehaved. "You have made me reveal myself before I was ready. Now I will be forced to proceed without the Light." He winked at Rasi. "But only temporarily, huh, soldier?"

Fice hobbled backward. "Tevin, please. While it is true I failed you this time, and for my failure I apologize, we have easily taken Lithia and are well on our way to taking Epertase. We didn't need this so-called Light to do it, either. You still need me to finish our plan."

Tevin seethed at the interruption. "Need you? Your powers of sway are weak without my magic amplifying them. Epertasians are not weak-minded Recitarians, you fool. It took you generations to obtain complete control of those feeble-minded savages. You never could have secured Lithia so quickly, if at all, without me. You were merely a tool to get me where I needed to be." Tevin closed the gap between them. "With the Light, no one will dare rebel against my rule. But since you've allowed Rasi and his friends to conquer you, my hand has been forced. You are wrong. I do not need you. I used you."

Tevin planted his feet and drew back his hand. Fice tried to avoid the strike, but some invisible force seemed to hold him in place. Tevin's open hand smacked Fice lightly across the jaw.

Fice dropped to one knee with his broken leg awkwardly extended in front of him. He stared up in horror and whispered, "What did you do to me?"

Tevin grinned. "Just something I've been working on."

Deep, pitting cracks formed in the flesh of Fice's jaw like the lines of a puzzle. A chunk of skin hardened and crumbled away. He pressed his hands to his jaw, and another chunk crumbled beneath his fingers.

"You promised me Lithia," he pleaded while he still had a jaw to speak. "You have Epertase. You can't be stopped now." His jaw disintegrated through the gaps in his fingers as he spoke.

Tevin rolled his eyes. "When my ancestors created the so-called Gildonese Syndrome, they intended it to kill you creatures in moments, not years. Where they failed, I have succeeded. Your rein has ended. Members of your pack have been scattered or killed. You have proven yourself to be weak. Besides, I don't really trust you. Now, for your failures you must pay with your life." Tevin, no longer concerned with Fice, turned to Rasi.

The Gildonese king tried to speak, but his lower jaw had fallen to dust, and he could only moan. As he stared at his long, tapered fingers, they fell away one by one, stirred by the breeze from the window.

His left ear crumbled. Then his right arm did the same. Sheer terror filled his eyes. He dropped to his back. As he twisted in pain, his leg crumbled next. His moans slowly softened as his hearts suffered the same fate as his body. The agonal rise and fall of his chest repeated one more hopeful time. When it fell, a death rattle escaped from his exposed windpipe.

Tevin stood over his deteriorating body and admired his work. "To be quite honest, I wasn't entirely sure I'd really perfected the syndrome. I'd say I've succeeded, wouldn't you?" He leered at Rasi and shrugged his shoulders. "Now then. Where were we?"

Rasi lay in a heap against the wall, too injured and weak to fight back.

"I will be sure to tell Alina about your heroic fight before I take her Light and her life."

No, Tevin, please. Rasi silently begged the gods for just a little more time to gather himself before Tevin attacked. Tevin's pet hylock continued cackling on the balcony.

Rasi took a shallow breath, swallowed the pain, and used the wall to help him stand.

Tevin grinned. "You have heart, I'll give you that. I see why the soldiers respected you during the Heathen War."

Rasi stumbled along the wall toward the balcony.

Tevin watched, amused. "And where are you gonna go? Just give up, Rasi. It's all over."

Rasi ignored him and dragged his dead strap closer to the balcony and the hylock. Tevin smirked, intrigued by Rasi's gall. At first, the hylock cowered, but then it lunged forward to intimidate him. Just as the creature lunged, Rasi sent a strap for its leg. The hylock recoiled, its wings extended.

Rasi snagged the creature's leg as it retreated. It dragged him over the edge of the balcony behind it. The sudden addition of his weight was too much for the hylock's wings to get any lift.

Tevin raced to the balcony. Annoyed, he shouted, "Bring him back here."

Another strap reached up and ripped away the hylock's left wing. Both the hylock and Rasi spiraled toward the ground. The straps released the creature, and all but the dead strap enveloped Rasi in a cocoon of sorts, flexing just before he struck the dirt to absorb some of the impact. It was a battle within Rasi's body to see what hurt more. Probably his ribs, he ultimately decided. The hylock landed with a thud beside him. By instinct, the straps snapped the creature's neck. Rasi looked to the balcony above.

Tevin peered over the edge and sighed. Then he waved his arm in a circle above his head, whistled, and looked west.

Rasi squinted to follow his gaze to where a swarm of what appeared to be insects filled the sky. He knew it wasn't insects at all, but more hylocks. And he also knew he would be dead soon.

He clawed at the ground with his undamaged arm, refusing to surrender. If he could just make it into Danduke Harbor, he'd have a chance. He willed himself to his knees with thoughts of Alina and his unborn child. His straps pushed him to his good foot.

Tevin applauded from above. "You continue to amaze," he shouted.

Rasi pulled his dead strap behind as he limped across the courtyard. The distant swarm grew closer, the thunder of their wings louder.

The hylocks merged into a single-file line above as Rasi neared the harbor. They dove toward Tevin's perch first, and Tevin pointed to Rasi.

The creatures blew past Tevin toward the ground, swooped at the last moment, and closed in on their prey from behind. Rasi's every step sent knifing pain through his foot; his every clumsy bounce sent jolts of agony from his broken arm and ribs. He had little air in his working lung, but he pushed harder. The thunder of hylock wings increased in volume as he reached the docks.

At the edge of the pier, he smelled their stink. He spun to face them. The lead hylock's wings shot out, stopping it in mid-air. It swiped at Rasi's chest with its razor toenails just as Rasi fell backward barely out of reach.

Rasi's back struck the Danduke with another wave of agony. The hylocks dove at him as he struggled for a shallow breath and held it. His straps dragged him down just as the hylock's fingers broke the surface. He only hoped they couldn't swim.

The swarm of hylocks circled above like vultures waiting for him to resurface for a breath. Rasi would rather drown than give them the satisfaction of taking him back to Tevin.

Even injured, his straps made him a skilled swimmer. Blood filled his mouth and seeped from his swollen lips into the murky water. Every thrust of his straps took him farther from the hylocks. He just needed to hold his breath long enough to lose them.

The straps slithered like water snakes through Danduke until he couldn't hold his breath any longer. The straps lifted him to the surface for air. When his head finally broke the surface, he took a shallow breath and scanned the sky. They'd underestimated how far he could get. He floated on his back, his straps propelling him farther away. With enough distance between him and the hunters, the straps guided him from the harbor, into the river, and to the embankment. They pulled him onto the bank. Exhausted and likely dying, he sprawled on his back while pulling short, excruciating bursts of air into his good lung.

His vision was going dark, but he fought unconsciousness with everything he had. His right lung had collapsed—that much he knew—and his only hope for it to inflate was to remove the object piercing it. He wasn't looking forward to what he had to do next. He felt his ribcage. With his eyes closed, he bit his lip and dug his fingers into the soft flesh beneath his displaced ribs. A short, horrible yank shifted a rib outward. Somehow, he muffled his scream. His time in the Heathen War had taught him that as long as the bleeding around his lung wasn't severe, he could survive, though the misery that accompanied it would make him wish he hadn't.

His head throbbed from his thrashing and the concussion he'd surely received. Though he wanted to rest, he had one more unbearable act to complete before he could sleep. And if his sleep never ended, he took solace in the fact that he had done his best.

He strained to lift his head. The riverbank had plenty of rocks. He selected one no bigger than his hand with a sharp, flat edge. He sat up, his body hating him for doing so.

First, he set the rock next to his shattered arm and reached over his shoulder. *I'm sorry,* he whispered in his mind. Then he ran his hand along the ground until he found his dead strap and pulled it taut, securing it beneath his foot. His other straps lifted cautiously into the air, one of them curling slightly around his neck.

I have to do this. We have no choice.

He gripped the rock and began to saw. Though the strap around his neck tightened slightly, he didn't waver. Slowly, he sawed at his dead appendage. It stung as though he cut through his own arm, but he didn't relent. He muffled another scream when his tool finally ripped through the last strand of muscle. Blood sprayed the rocks. The strap around his neck loosened and it, along with the others, draped the embankment as if in mourning.

And then he was done.

He laid his head back on the rocks. The wheeze in his chest grew louder. The sky blurred as his eyelids grew heavy.

He pictured Alina in his mind. *Endure, my love. If I survive, I'll come for you.*

CHAPTER 42

RESET

Pain racked Eldon's body with shockwaves deep in his muscles and bones. *I'll kill all the Epertasians,* he screamed in his own fuzzy mind. *They dare hurt my family.*

He covered his head with his arms, leaving his ever-bruising body vulnerable to the rough terrain the horses dragged him over. "Stop," he screamed to no avail. One needn't be an expert on horses to know that these were racing stallions and, short of tugging on the reins that were far out of his reach, they weren't stopping until they tired. And when they did finally tire, he would go back and kill …

The static hum in his mind faded. Who was he going to kill again? The constant thrashing the ground was giving him no longer seemed of concern as he struggled to clear his thoughts. He was going to kill those … those … No matter how hard he concentrated, he couldn't remember who he wanted to kill.

Peering through the net that held him and between the horses flashing hooves, he searched for some clue as to where he was or where he was going. Why were the horses dragging him anyway? He strained against the odd net. Who could have done such a thing? If only he could remember why he was so angry and who should get the brunt of it.

Eventually the stallions did tire and slow to a stop. Dizzy, Eldon sat on the hard dirt to gather his wits, though everything was still foggy in his mind. After the world stopped spinning, he wrestled with the wire netting until he got free. He stood next to the horses. The suns were blistering and the thick, heavy air made sweat drench his hair. His tattered clothes exposed raw purple and red rashes that oozed tiny drops of blood from his arms and legs and back and sides. In a daze he climbed onto one of the horses, grabbed the lead of the other, and patiently watched the movements of the suns to get his bearings.

He was thirsty.

CHAPTER 43

OUT OF THE PAN

Rasi hadn't slept long; the suns' positions told him as much. His straps lay exhausted at his side. The severed stump on his back had mostly clotted, reducing the bleeding to a trickle. Too weak to sit up, he concentrated on breathing. His ribs hated him for each shallow attempt, and he hated his ribs for everything else. *Just a little more rest,* he lied to himself. He couldn't stay there long. Alina didn't have the time.

And that's when he saw them along the top of the embankment. Though there were only three stray hylocks about to stumble upon him, in his condition three might as well have been a hundred. They sniffed the ground until they were directly above him. One of them stopped and lifted its nose.

I'm sorry, Alina.

The other two stopped and lifted their noses as well. They licked their slimy lips. Cautious, as if they feared he was luring them into a trap, they climbed down to the river. Rasi lay still, saving any energy he might still have for one last fight. All he could do was watch them crawl closer.

The nearest one lifted a limp strap, shook it, and then dropped it back to the ground. Another one crawled closer and sniffed Rasi's neck, while the third scraped its nails along the rocks as if sharpening them.

Rasi thought about his parents, remembering back when they were healthy and strong. They would have been proud to see how hard he had fought to make the world a better one. As the hylock that was sniffing his neck dragged a poisonous nail along his spine just gently enough to not penetrate his skin, he thought of Alina. He loved her and was willing to give his life for her and for their unborn son. Knowing that's what he was about to do gave him peace. He was ready. *Do what you must.*

The next sound wasn't the hylocks' victorious screeches as their nails raked his flesh, but a low growl from above. Rasi shifted his head to better see.

The hylocks froze and perked up their ears. Then they spun toward the embankment. One hylock cranked its neck back and released a scalding cry to the sky. Maybe it was a call for help. Then all three crouched and spread their wings. But before they could take flight, a wave of bodies leaped from above and slammed into them. They kept coming over the edge.

Rasi blinked the blurriness from his tired eyes. The hylocks shrieked and clawed and tumbled through the grass, the other creatures smothering them with sheer numbers. One hylock fell into the water, but the other creatures dragged it back to shore. Rasi watched as the attackers dug out the hylocks' eyes with their scoop-like claws. What little air Rasi could get through his swollen nose burned and stank of sulfur.

Oh shit. Fishers.

One of the fishers turned to Rasi. "Raaasiiiee," it crooned from its perch atop its kill.

A chill ran up Rasi's spine.

After slaughtering the hylocks and consuming their eyes—despite them being not much better than their own—the fishers crowded around him. The outer circle turned outward and stood poised to defend their prey. Six of the fishers moved in. Each one dug their scoop-claws into the ends of each of Rasi's limp, weakened straps. With coordinated heaves, they dragged him up the embankment where a hundred more of the creatures waited. Helpless to stop them, he wondered why he still had his eyes.

The raw tearing of his flesh along the hard, cracked ground only added to his misery. His lips were dry and split. Buzzards circled overhead, and he wondered if they circled for him. The desolate terrain told him where he was; he'd seen the Wastelands enough during the Heathen War to know. And he also knew enough about the fishers to know where he was going. His thoughts faded until he went numb and closed his eyes.

CHAPTER 44

DEFEATED

The night was moonless. Atticus abandoned his horse and crept through the Lands of Muél, his blue crystal providing the only light. *"Enter near the break in the bush,"* Logan had said. *"Feel for my mark at the base of each tree. Once you find the last tree before the open field, walk straight until you see the glow."*

Despite the protection of his crystal's dull blue glimmer, the constant hissing and skittering of the surrounding ochrids filled him with unimaginable dread. It wasn't lost on him that Rasi had probably died and he was Alina's last hope. His heart hovered above the open pit of his stomach.

When something brushed against his thigh and snorted, his heart dropped the rest of the way. He squeezed the crystal with one hand and his sword with the other. Although Logan had promised the crystal would protect him, having one of the hideous beasts so close that he smelled its rotten stink and felt its scaly skin against his leg was almost more than he could stand. No matter how hard he tried, he couldn't stop his hands from shaking. Step by terrified step, he marched on until he saw a slight blue glow coming from the ground.

He approached the fabled Tunnels of Eiger. The faint stench of burning wood met his nostrils. Two members of King Logan's

Royal Guard stood at the entrance. "What's the word?" one of them asked.

Atticus solemnly shook his head.

"Damn." They escorted him into the illuminated bowels of the cavern where soldiers quickly gathered in anticipation of his news.

King Logan rushed to meet him. "You bring word of victory?" he asked.

Before Atticus could say a word, Logan saw the answer in his eyes. Atticus's head drooped forward. Logan covered his mouth with his hand. "By the gods. We failed?"

Atticus nodded once, the words stuck in his throat.

"How?" Logan asked, stunned.

Atticus tried to collect himself. "We secured a victory over Fice's men, but at least two Epertasian battalions arrived and forced out surrender."

Alina approached through the crowd of somber soldiers. She wore a hopeful smile. Atticus looked to the ground.

"What's happened, Atticus?" she asked, her smile fading.

Logan turned away.

"Atticus?" she asked.

"We failed, Your Majesty."

She raised her hands to her face. "Failed? Where's Rasi?"

Atticus shook his head. "I don't know."

Logan stepped toward his gathering soldiers. "Men, get to your posts. Our cause is not lost as long as we have our breath. We must prepare to absorb whatever comes next. In a fight, both sides get to throw punches." With a glance back, he asked Atticus, "Did anyone follow you?"

"No."

Logan turned back to his men. "No one enters these tunnels except Rasi or Simcane. Anyone else is to be captured or killed."

While Logan barked orders, Atticus said to Alina, "We must go, Your Majesty."

"Go? Where?"

"To Eldon's. If Rasi survived, he'll go there."

She choked at the word "survived." She tugged on Logan's sleeve. "You and Lona must come with us. We'll regroup."

Logan shook his head with stoic defiance. His mind had obviously been made up long before he saw Atticus. "No, Alina. We'll regroup here. It's time to regain Lithia or end this whole nightmare altogether."

"That's suicide."

"I'm done hiding, and running has gotten us nowhere."

Alina wanted to argue, but Atticus touched her shoulder and whispered, "No one knows they're here. This is as safe as anywhere for them. We must follow our plan."

Alina lowered her head.

Atticus gently grabbed her arm. "We must go now, Your Majesty."

With tears filling her eyes, she conceded. They gathered dried rations, water bladders, and more crystals, and said their goodbyes.

Atticus shook Logan's hand. "Good luck to you, Your Majesty."

"You just worry about Alina and getting her safely away from all of this. You've been a good friend."

"You have been, as well."

Atticus led Alina through the tunnels and into the dark night.

CHAPTER 45

THE DEADLIEST ASSASSIN

C yn crossed into the Lands of Muél with a torch and little else. The protecting crystals from Eiger would have been nice to have, but not having any hardly gave her pause. If Tevin wanted Alina, no men or creatures, ochrids included, could stand in her path.

King Logan wasn't the only one who knew how to find the entrance to Eiger. Scorne used to speak of hiding in the tunnels if the heat around him ever grew too hot, and he demanded his symbiots know how to reach it as well. Read the stars, the legends said. While Cyn was no astronomer, she had learned how to find Eiger by connecting the various constellations. She never dreamed it would ever actually come in handy.

The hissing, grumbling sounds around her only heightened the thrill. She cleared the tree line before a single ochrid had closed in. The sky was awash with thousands of stars, but she knew right where to look. All that was left was to run and watch for the magic blue glow. The ochrids kept their distance at first. Maybe they were leery of her torch. Or maybe they knew a killer when they smelled one.

A deafening roar filled the darkness. She ran faster. Her metal skin slithered along her torso in a panic. She soothed her symbiotic friends with reassuring thoughts. The metal along her forearms rose up like knife blades.

She was ready long before the first ochrid leaped into her torchlight and slung a leech from its tail. With lightning speed, she severed the slimy creature in the air with her forearm blade.

The ochrid pounced.

Cyn met the beast head-on, the impact knocking her torch to the ground. As they tumbled, she sliced at the creature frantically, hoping to hit something vital. The ochrid landed on top of her, dripping putrid blood from its many superficial wounds. It snapped at her shoulder, shattering several teeth on her living armor. The ochrid recoiled. Cyn drew back beneath its chest. It lunged again. Cyn made a fist; metal extended into a point from her knuckles. She plunged her weapon into its gullet, spearing the back of its throat. The ochrid reared back. She sprang to her feet, ready for the next comer as the ochrid scurried away to die. More creatures surrounded her.

Another ochrid attacked. She sliced at the creature as her metal skin defended against each of its slashing assaults. A leech slapped her cheek. She ripped it free before it could inject its toxin and squished it beneath her metal-coated foot.

Cyn ended the second ochrid with a swipe of her blades across its scaly throat. Winded, she gasped for air as a seemingly endless horde of ochrids closed in. She scooped her torch from the ground and raced through the void left by the creature she had just felled.

Yet another ochrid intercepted her. The creature flicked its tail at her. Cyn sliced at the leech and missed, and it hit her throat. She reached for it, but it scurried away from her grasp and bit into her flesh. A wave of nausea made her wobble. Without stopping, she blindly jammed a metal spike through the leech with such zeal that she pierced her own flesh. With a shake of her hand, the dead leech smacked the ground. The nausea faded as quickly as it had come. The ochrid attacked. Cyn leaped at the charging creature, braced her hands on the top of its head, and hurdled it. Her glowing blue goal appeared in the distance.

The ochrids gave chase, but she was fast and had a head start. She reached the entrance before they could catch her. Once inside, she dug out a crystal from the wall. When the line of ochrids passed by, she jabbed some of them with her metal spike just for fun. *Stupid beasts.*

Once they were deep in the tunnels and out of sight, she turned to the path ahead. With the blue glow of the walls sufficient to light the way, she set her torch down and stepped forward.

Distant whispers from the left tunnel gave her a direction. The whispers grew louder as the whispering men walked obliviously toward her. She backed against the wall into a dark space between the crystals and waited.

Three Lith soldiers grumbled about their watch duties as they walked. She smelled the sour breath of one of them as they passed. Then she stalked them from behind like a lioness after an unwitting deer. Before they heard her, she jammed her fist spike into one soldier's back just below his rib cage while slicing a second soldier's throat in a flash. The third soldier dropped his crystal, spun, and drew his sword as he backed away.

"Who are you?" he asked. He held his weapon defensively across his chest.

Cyn looked down at his crystal on the floor and then back to his square-jawed face. Something moved behind him. She grinned and lifted her own crystal close to her heart. A low growl from behind froze the soldier. His eyes bulged and darted toward his crystal.

With a flirty smile, Cyn waved goodbye. Before he could reach for his only protection, an ochrid clamped down on his shoulder and dragged him kicking and screaming deep into the tunnels. Soon after, his screams ended abruptly.

Covered in both ochrid and human blood, Cyn continued through the tunnel the three soldiers had come through. Along the way, she killed two more guards before she reached the entrance to King Logan's cavern. A single soldier stood with his back to her.

As quiet as a shadow, Cyn slid her bladed forearm around his neck and touched his Adam's apple. "Shhhh." She looked over his shoulder into the cavern. King Logan and Queen Lona mingled with more soldiers near a fire in the center. She promised herself the joy of hunting them down once her mission was done, but finding Alina was the only thing that mattered at that moment.

She dragged her captive away from the cavern entrance.

"King Logan," he shouted.

Cyn sighed. She should have cut his miserable throat when she had the chance, but she was hoping for answers first. To show her seriousness, she stabbed him in his flank just deep enough to elicit a painful groan. Soldiers crowded the entrance with swords drawn. The narrowness of the tunnel minimized their advantage. She kept them in front of her.

"Who are you?" one asked.

Cyn eyed them one by one. They waited cautiously, probably hoping to save their friend's life. They were fools. "Where is Alina?" she asked.

Her captive's eyes shifted to the others.

"Don't look to them for approval. It's not their throats I'll cut."

One of the soldiers stepped forward with his hands up. "Easy now. Don't hurt him."

Cyn's captive swallowed hard. "What should I do, boss?"

He smirked. "Just tell her what she wants to know. She's not getting out of here alive." This one was cockier than he deserved to be.

She had already heard the scurrying feet of sneaky guards somewhere behind her, but it mattered little. She let her forearm blade break the skin of her captive's throat. "You heard the man. Little ol' me ain't long for this world."

The soldier stammered, "They're going somewhere in New Arc. I heard them say something about a Gildonese named Eldon."

"Ah. Now that wasn't so hard, was it? Thank you."

The "boss" said, "All right, lady. Now let him go."

Cyn licked her captive's ear and tilted his head back by his hair.

"Please, don't kill me. I gave you what you wanted."

She whispered into his ear, "You should have negotiated before you had nothing left to offer."

"Wait," he cried just before she slit his throat to the stunned horror of his friends. She turned and ran. They gave chase. The men sent through other tunnels to surround her tried to block her path with swords raised, but she ducked and dodged and sliced as she plowed through them. She wasn't able to kill them all, but the ones who lived would definitely remember her.

A new day had dawned by the time she found her way through the tunnel maze to the outside. Being able to see the ochrids grazing from so far away, combined with her remarkable speed, gave her the advantage. She tore off toward the trees. At first the soldiers gave chase, but she was too fast, so they retreated for their horses. They would never find her. Soon she was clear of Muél.

By the time she had crossed Lowland Lake with a stolen raft and reached New Arc, her blood was boiling with rage and she couldn't wait to find Alina and whoever protected her. She killed two people before she found someone who knew where the Gildonese lived.

The house sat quiet with only the flicker of a single candle shining through the curtained window. A crow circled above.

A predator pure and simple, Cyn crawled through the high grass to the edge of the porch, using the candle as a beacon. The front door was open.

The metal on her arms slid over her elbows and rose to points. She took a deep breath and then ran through the door. Those moments just before the kill were her favorite moments in life.

She tore across the main room and crashed through the closed door to the lighted room like it was a curtain rather than wood. Her momentum carried her to the floor. She rolled over her shoulder and bounced up onto the bed, ready for anything. She was alone. The candle was little more than a stub with a puddle of melted wax on the dresser surrounding it. A dog barked madly on the porch.

Cyn turned to face it as it stood snarling in the doorway. It pounced. She grabbed it in mid-air and heaved it across the empty bed. It scrambled up with a growl. Cyn crouched and egged it on with a growl of her own. They lunged at each other simultaneously. The dog yelped a single time before it was over.

CHAPTER 46

AN ASSASSIN COMES
FOR THEE

Alina scrambled from her straw bed, Eldon's barking dog stirring her. Atticus was already awake, leading two horses to the barn door. His finger hovered in front of his lips.

Alina ran to him. "Who is it, Atticus?" she whispered.

"I don't know."

"Is it Rasi?"

"It's not Rasi."

Eldon's dog yelped and then went silent.

Atticus helped Alina onto her horse. "Someone's found us. We need to leave. Now." He pulled open the barn door and smacked her horse's rear. Then he mounted the other steed and followed her from the barn.

As the horses carried them past Eldon's front door, the sight in the doorway sent a chill through Alina's soul.

By the gods, no. It can't be.

Her eyes met the eyes of her nightmares. She went weak and almost fell from her saddle.

No, no, no.

Atticus shouted, "Keep going, Alina. Don't look at her."

Cyn stood in the doorway with a cold, hateful glare. Alina couldn't take her eyes from her. She kicked her horse into a full gallop.

Cyn jumped from the porch and gave chase.

Alina screamed at Atticus, "She's catching up."

"Face forward, Alina. Keep pushing and don't look back, no matter what." He spurred his horse until he was alongside her. "She won't catch us," he yelled, though his voice lacked confidence.

Cyn grunted with each stride as she ran. She slowly fell behind until she disappeared altogether. Alina's heart pounded through her chest. Atticus looked back. "All right, Alina. Slow down. Give your horse a rest. She's gone."

Terror still twisted Alina's gut. She didn't want to slow. "She'll follow us. We have to keep moving."

"We will. But we're pushing our horses too hard. We need them ready if we need to run again later. I won't let her catch you."

She knew Atticus would do all he could, but she wasn't convinced it would be enough. They trotted for a bit until they found a stream to water their horses. They drank as well.

Alina's eyes darted around her the entire time. "We need to make more distance, Atticus."

"I know. We will."

"We need to go to the southern mountains. We need to find Rasi."

"It's not safe. If Rasi indeed goes back to Shadows Peak, he will need to defend himself until we can get to him. Right now, we need to stay far away from Thasula."

Against her every wish, she knew he was right.

With refilled water bladders, they rode through the night and into the next day with very few stops for rest or food. Mostly they "borrowed" from farms, which allowed them to keep moving without making friends. By the third day Atticus wondered aloud if Cyn could still possibly be on their trail, and Alina answered, "I'm not willing to take that risk."

They avoided towns as much as they could. Any locals they happened across nodded and waved but kept to themselves. At some point during their travel, Alina grew nauseous, though she didn't tell

Atticus. She hoped it was just nerves from constantly needing to look over her shoulder, but nerves didn't persist and get worse like her current pains were doing.

It was late at night when a sudden cramp wrenched her stomach and she pushed her face against her horse's neck.

Atticus grabbed her horse's reins and slowed to a stop. "Alina? What is it?"

She didn't want to tell him, hoping somehow not acknowledging it might make it go away. Every motherly instinct told her to stop and rest, Cyn be damned, but she was terrified of the assassin. After the wave of pain lessened, she righted herself. Beads of sweat formed on her forehead.

"Alina? We need to stop."

Regardless of whether they needed to or not, stopping meant suicide as far as she was concerned. Maybe Atticus could beat Cyn, but she wasn't willing to stake their lives on it. She sat up straight, ignoring the tightening in her stomach, and focused on the road ahead. "No, Atticus. I'll be fine. Let's keep moving."

The moon was bright, reflecting the two sleeping suns and forming a rare hourglass of shadow down the center. By the time it had reached its peak, Alina's cramping had passed again, and she didn't know if that was good or bad. Every time she looked at Atticus, she saw his concern, so she looked away. The more distance between her and Cyn, the better for all of them. They should be at Homer's within a couple of days. She could rest then.

The soporific bounce of her horse attacked her eyelids. After the third time her head started bobbing, Atticus cleared his throat to wake her. "That's it, Alina. We're making camp." She was asleep on the grass before he returned with wood for a fire.

When she opened her eyes again, she was nestled within her magical heating blanket next to a fire with her head resting on a wad of clothes. The very tips of the suns cast a dull glow on the undersides of the clouds. She felt rested for the first time in a week.

"Atticus?" she whispered. He was nowhere to be seen. "Atticus?" she said again, slightly louder. She started to get up, but the pain in her stomach returned with a vengeance. She pulled her knees closer to her chest and felt something wet and sticky where her thighs rubbed together.

With a trembling hand, she lifted the blanket. *Oh no. Blood.*

"I'm so sorry," she whispered to her unborn son. "If you have any of your father's strength, please fight."

"Alina?" Atticus whispered from behind, startling her.

She clutched the blanket to her chest so he wouldn't see the blood.

He squatted next to her and shoved dirt over the small fire. "We have to go. The assassin still follows and she's getting closer. I saw her crossing the field about a mile back."

"I don't know if I can ride anymore."

"I know. That's why, while you slept, I returned to that farm we passed earlier and borrowed a wheeled cart for the rest of the journey. Can you take a few steps if I help you to your feet?"

"I think so."

Atticus lifted her arm around his neck and hoisted her to her feet. She tried to be strong, though he carried most of her weight. As they walked, the pain in her stomach faded again, allowing her to stand straighter. Before they reached the cart, she stopped and smiled.

"What is it, Alina? We must keep moving."

She put her hands over her belly and said, "He kicked."

"What?"

"He kicked, Atticus. My son kicked."

Atticus nodded. "That's good."

He put his hand behind her knees and lifted her into the hay-filled cart. When he stood back, he stared at the blood smeared along his forearm. "Oh, Alina," he said, his eyes wide with concern.

She sat silent.

He wiped his hands on his leg. "I'm sure it'll be fine."

She wondered if he was lying or if he had simply convinced himself of the truth of his words. He placed her blanket beside her as she lay on the hay, tied the reins of her horse to the back of the cart, and then climbed onto his horse to restart their journey.

After much of the morning passed, Atticus leaned back and pointed east. "Look, Alina. Parsons. It won't be long now."

She was almost too weak to smile.

When the town of Parsons was finally behind them, a new kind of cramping grabbed hold of her. "Atticus," she shouted.

He looked back with concern. "More cramps?"

She nodded.

"We're almost there."

"Atticus, I think I'm going into labor." Her contractions came and went, came and went, but the time between them remained fairly consistent. Atticus asked her a hundred times if they should stop, and she told him a hundred times "no." She knew she would have no choice but to stop soon, yet she saw making it to Homer's first as an absolute necessity.

When Homer's farm finally appeared in the distance, some of the weight of her dread was lifted. With Doc Eckels, her baby would have a chance. Masera and two soldiers hurried out to greet them.

"Get Doc Eckels," Atticus shouted.

Masera raced back to the house. Celia, Homer, and Irene came out first, followed by Doc Eckels, who was drying his hands. He wiped them on his pants and sprinted to the cart.

"The baby's coming, Doc," Atticus shouted.

Doc Eckels reached the cart. "Your Majesty? How long between your birthing pains?"

"About a hundred heartbeats."

"Have you passed the water?"

"I think so. But there's been a lot of blood."

"All right. It won't be long now." He reached into the cart. "Someone help me get her into the house."

Atticus touched his shoulder. "We can't, Doc. We're being chased by a most lethal assassin and we can't stop."

"But … I can't deliver a baby in this …" His eyes drifted to Alina's. Then he nodded. "If that's what we must do, Your Majesty."

Beyond Doc Eckels, Atticus hurried to his wife and embraced her. "If you have anything you absolutely need from the house, get it now."

"Where are we going?" she asked.

"To the Islands of Torick."

That was the first time Alina had heard Atticus's plans beyond getting to Homer's. Doc Eckels climbed into the cart. "Irene, can you get my bag and some water?"

She nodded, and she and Homer hurried into the house.

Masera joined Atticus. Atticus spoke low, hoping Alina wouldn't hear, but she did. "The assassin Cyn is close behind. I don't think it's safe here anymore. If she knows where we are, then Jarrah soon will."

"We should fight her together."

"We can't beat her. She survived Rasi, for gods' sake."

Masera looked around with a twisted scowl as if contemplating something grim. Then, with determination in his eyes, he said, "I'll stay behind and slow her down."

"Masera, no. You go with Alina. I'll stay behind. I'm honor bound to do what's needed for her and her kingdom."

"And I'm not? You're honor bound to care for your wife. I will not be looking at her each day knowing I let you face Cyn. I'd rather deal with an assassin than do that." Masera gripped Atticus's shoulder. "I'm the head of the Elite Guard anyway. This is as much my duty as yours. In fact, it is more so."

Atticus put his hand atop his friend's. "This will be a fight you cannot win."

Masera chuckled. "It seems like all the fights are fights I can't win. But I'm still here."

Homer and Irene returned with some supplies and the doctor's bag. Homer turned to Atticus. "Do you want the wagon from my barn? It's bigger and far more comfortable."

"Is it tied to horses already?"

"No. But it won't take long."

"We don't have time."

Seeing the worry on his friends' faces, Atticus softened his tone. "Homer, Irene, I'm so sorry for what I have to ask of you now."

Homer shook his head. "Nonsense. We are happy—"

Atticus lifted his hand. "You need to leave with us."

"I have no desire to leave my—"

"Homer," Atticus snapped. He didn't have time for protests. "You don't understand. Your lives are in grave danger if you don't come with us now. I can't make you leave, but I can warn you that the assassin who tracks us will show you and your wife no mercy."

Irene put her hand to her mouth. Homer reached for her other hand. He looked into her wet eyes and then back to Atticus. "I suppose you're right." Irene started sobbing.

Atticus nodded. "Homer. You understand that you will probably never be able to return?"

After hesitating, Homer nodded with a sigh. "Let me release our animals from the barn and gather our horses." He looked to Atticus again. "Are you sure we haven't time for the wagon?"

It broke Alina's heart to ask him to give up everything they had for the dangerous road ahead, but she knew they were no longer safe there. She muffled a cry with her next contraction. Doc Eckels held her hand and wiped the sweat from her brow with a towel.

Atticus scanned the road they had come down. "Homer, we're wasting precious time as it is. We need to start on our way. Don't be long."

Masera said, "You get started. I'll see that they get on the road safe."

Homer headed for the barn while Irene went into the house.

Masera stuck out his hand. Atticus looked at it and then pulled his old friend in for a hug. "You be safe, Masera. Kill that bitch and then come find us."

Masera nodded. "I'm looking forward to it."

Atticus climbed onto his steed and pulled Celia up behind him. With Alina's horse pulling the cart, they headed south. The last Alina saw of Masera he was running toward the barn.

"How close are we, Doc?" Atticus asked.

Doc Eckels leaned over the edge and held up his first finger and thumb a sliver apart. "Close."

The cart hadn't gotten far when Irene and Homer caught up to them. Irene climbed into the cart next to Alina and tied her horse to the side. She held Alina's hand. "You will do fine, child."

Alina groaned with another contraction.

CHAPTER 47

AN UNWINNABLE FIGHT

Masera sat alone in Homer's house. Though he had been through many battles and had the scars to prove it, he didn't remember ever being as confident of his impending death as he was at that moment. Except instead of nausea, which was what he expected to feel, he felt overwhelming peace in the knowledge Alina would survive another day, and he was proud that he was part of the reason.

He carried a glass of wine to the porch. If she was as good a hunter as he'd heard, he expected her to search the house before continuing along the road. After a final swig, he tossed his glass into the grass. It was time to get ready. A solid shake of the porch post revealed how strong the roof was. He climbed onto the porch railing and pulled himself up. A decorative ridge at the edge of the roof made the perfect cover. He lay flat on his stomach and waited.

It wasn't long before she appeared on the road in the distance, casually riding a no doubt stolen horse. She was a pro, confident and unconcerned with how long her mission took. As Masera took in her long black hair and pale skin, he realized she was the most beautiful and lethal killing machine he had ever seen. He used those last quiet moments to push away the fear and replace it with anger and determination.

Cyn looked around before dismounting. The metal blotches on her skin crawled and slithered as if anxious for the next challenge.

Instead of using the stairs, she climbed over the rail beside them and disappeared onto the porch beneath him. He heard her walking through the house. Quietly, he climbed over the decorative ridge and waited just above the porch stairs with his sword in hand. Patience and surprise were the only advantages he had. He asked his gods for protection, or at the very least a swift end.

Inside, Cyn overturned furniture and shattered windows. Finally, she stepped onto the stoop directly below him and spit into the grass. Masera moved his sword point downward, leaned forward, and quietly let his feet slide off the edge.

He was nearly perfect.

Nearly.

Cyn shifted to the side at the last instant. Masera's blade rode her metal-coated arm to the ground. She stumbled down the steps. Masera's momentum carried him into the yard beside her horse. Though he hated to do it, he jammed his blade into the horse's chest. He'd never killed a horse in cold blood before, and the guilt ravaged his gut before the mare even hit the ground. Cyn may kill him, but he took solace in the fact that he'd just slowed her pursuit greatly.

Cyn slammed into him with untold speed and power. With his sword, he fended off the first of her wild blows, but she was too frantic in her strikes to stop them all. She sank a metal blade protruding from her fist into his side. He let out a shrill cry. He froze. His sword thudded to the ground.

She paused with her blade still in his side. He stared into her cold, shallow eyes. Her strike wasn't a killing blow and she knew it. The sickest grin stretched her lips.

Unwilling to concede defeat, Masera drove his head against her skull. He must have caught her off guard because his forehead connected with her unprotected nose. She staggered backward, her blade ripping from his side. It hurt almost as much coming out as it had going in.

He bent over for his sword, but she kicked his jaw with a metal-coated foot. His vision flashed white and then black.

When he woke up, he was lying on his back on the porch. His pelvis burned with pain. He lifted his head to assess the damage. It almost made him vomit. His lower legs were wrapped unnaturally around the porch post. He tried to move his left foot and it did nothing.

Cyn sat on Homer's rocker, admiring her work. "Gooood, you're awake. It doesn't look like you'll be running to catch up with your friends anytime soon. I'm terribly sorry about that."

He strained to move, but the piercing pain in his legs stopped him cold. The broken ends of his leg bones ground together with a sickening din.

"I'm pretty good at tying knots, huh?" she mused.

He was in too much pain to answer.

She stood up. "I sure hope you feel like talking." She straddled his chest. "Actually, I hope you don't."

Masera told himself not to give her the satisfaction of a scream, even as she slowly pushed the metal spike extending from her knuckles into the soft flesh just above his collarbone. He tried to push her away, but he was too weak. The strain of holding back the scream rolled his eyes into his head. His clenched fists shook at his sides. He held his breath and bit his lower lip until his mouth filled with blood. Then he spat it onto her chest.

Worse than the pain, worse than the knowledge of what she was doing, was her damn disgusting grin. He would give anything to smack it from her face.

She pulled the blade from his throbbing flesh and licked the blood from it. "I will show you mercy if you tell me where that whore queen went."

"I'll never tell you anything." He just wanted the end to come soon.

"Very well." She dragged her blade along the side of his face, filleting his skin like a surgeon. Judging by her happy expression, she clearly enjoyed her work.

Three broken fingers and plenty of carved flesh later, Masera passed out from the agony. She was standing over him with a glass of water when he woke again. She drank from the glass with an orgasmic moan. "So refreshing." Then she tilted her head and looked down at him. "Thirsty?"

He was so thirsty.

She held the glass out to her side and slowly poured it onto the porch. Masera watched it splatter near his head and licked his lips. She tossed the glass aside and moved to his disfigured legs.

Her firm grip on his left knee made him cry, "I'll tell you whatever you want to know. Please. Just stop."

She tilted her head, almost as if disappointed.

"If I tell you, no more torture?"

She crinkled her nose and hesitantly nodded.

"I'm so sorry, Alina." He stared up at her.

"Go on."

He closed his eyes and took a deep breath. "They're hiding in the town of Parsons, in an apartment above the general store."

She tapped her upper lip with her finger and stared quizzically at him. "I don't believe you." She pressed her knee against his crotch. Her metal skin slid down her thigh, over her kneecap, and poked his groin.

"Wait, wait, wait. They *are* going to Parsons."

"Hmmm." She stared into his eyes as if searching for deceit. "I don't know. Why would they go to Parsons?"

"I have no reason to lie. Rasi will be there to protect her. And he'll kill you."

"Rasi?" She stood up and stared northward with a chuckle. "Your savior, Rasi, is already dead, you fool. I saw his broken body just before Tevin killed him. You've betrayed your friends for your own pathetic life, and Rasi's not even there. No one is there to save her."

"Just finish me. Please. I can't live with myself now that I've betrayed her." He expected his death to come swiftly, but Cyn simply stood up and walked away.

As he watched her leave, he whispered, "Stupid bitch." He almost choked on his own pained chuckle.

CHAPTER 48

THE LIGHT
AWAKENS

Alina's party reached the majestic southern beaches of Epertase without incident. Someone had been there before them, possibly Jarrah's soldiers. The shoreline was littered with abandoned boats, most of which were either burnt-out husks or rotted with holes.

Celia, once again riding with her husband, whispered in Atticus's ear, "Do you think Masera will make it?"

Atticus didn't answer. He stopped the horses and cart short of the shoreline. "Homer, come with me. We need to find a boat that we can work with."

Homer scanned the damaged pickings. "From this mess?"

"It doesn't have to be perfect, just repairable in short order."

Atticus headed east while Homer went west. By the twelfth worthless boat Atticus came across, the nagging voice in his head screaming reminders of Cyn's imminent arrival was getting frantic. Just when he was considering whether the cart itself could be made seaworthy, Homer shouted, "Over here."

Atticus raced to his side. Homer stood over a small but salvageable vessel. The hull on one side was charred as though the fire had been snuffed before it really got going. Some leftover japsy weed lay in the sand beside it. Atticus scavenged a set of oars and called for Celia to bring the cart.

Celia eyed the boat skeptically. "Will that really make it past the tide?" she asked.

Atticus gave a less-than-confident nod.

Alina cried out in pain, and he hastened his pace.

Together, he and Doc Eckels carried her from the cart to the boat where Homer had spread a blanket along the bottom. Doc Eckels stayed at her feet while Celia, Irene, and Homer squeezed in near the front. Irene sat at Alina's side. Atticus pushed the boat into the shallow water and hopped in.

He and Homer paddled against the waves. The going was slow and strenuous, but they eventually made it past the tide.

As the partial moon rose, Alina's birthing pains increased in frequency and intensity. Doc Eckels announced he could see the baby's head and that it was only a matter of moments. Alina bit down as another pain took hold. Irene held her hand and brushed her sweaty hair from her face.

"Push, Alina," Doc Eckels said.

She strained and squeezed Irene's hand until Irene pleaded for her to let go before her bones cracked.

Doc Eckels looked over her belly with a comforting smile. "You're doing well, Alina. Stop pushing and breathe for a moment."

Another contraction sent stabbing pain through her womb. Something was wrong.

"All right, push," Eckels said.

She strained and groaned.

"Your baby's head is free."

She lifted her head to see Doc's concerned face.

"What is it?" she cried.

"Your baby's lifecord is around his neck and very tight."

Her heart fell through her back to the bottom of the boat. She knew enough about medicine to know this was bad. How bad, she wasn't sure. "What does that mean?"

Irene caressed her forehead.

"It means you must let me work, Alina. I need you to listen. No matter how badly you feel the need, you mustn't push. Atticus, give me your knife. Quickly."

Atticus passed a blade from his waistband to Eckels.

Calm and steady, Eckels said, "Homer, I need something to tie around the cord. Rip thin strips from your shirt and come down here to help."

Homer started toward her feet and then hesitated. "I'm sorry, Your Majesty. I'll avert my eyes the best I—"

Eckels snapped, "No time for that, Homer. Get down here. Tie that cloth as tight as you can right here."

Alina wanted to watch, but hadn't the strength to hold up her head. She lay back, exhausted. Irene rubbed her sweaty cheeks and forehead with a piece of cloth ripped from the blanket beneath her. "It'll be all right, dear. Doc is very good."

Alina wanted to cry, but held back for her son. Or maybe she was too tired.

Eckels worked frantically. "Tie the other cloth here, Homer. All right. Give me the knife. You're doing great, Alina. It's time to push again."

"I'm too tired. I—"

"You can do it. Push."

With every ounce of strength, she pushed one last time and felt her son leave her body. She stared at the stars, waiting to hear his cry. She was too weak to move and asked Irene to hold her head up so she could see.

Irene looked away. "I don't think it's a good idea just yet."

With a weak yet determined voice, Alina snapped, "Do it."

Irene lifted Alina's upper body and supported her back. Doc's grim face told her the news was bad, but she wouldn't accept it without hearing for herself. "What is it?"

Eckels turned away with her baby cradled in his arms. "He's not breathing, Alina. I'm doing what I can."

Her tears blurred their faces. "Please," she begged everyone, including the gods.

Irene squeezed her shoulders. "He's doing everything he can, dear."

Doc Eckels seemed to work for ages before he turned back with a somber tear glistening on his cheek in the faint light of the moon.

"Please, keep working," she pleaded.

He nodded and turned away again. Alina looked to Atticus and he looked away.

Irene caressed her sweat-drenched hair.

Doc Eckels turned back, the lifeless, blanketed bundle in his arms. He could barely get out "I'm sorry" before he choked on his words.

Alina had never felt such pain before. Irene lowered Alina's head back to the pack that she had been using as a pillow, turned toward the sea, and wept.

Celia held Alina's hand and rubbed her arm. Even as Alina had friends near, she felt lonelier than ever before. Though she'd only had her baby for moments, she already loved him more than anyone could ever love. "I wanna see him."

"Of course," Doc Eckels answered. He held the limp bundle out toward her and Celia helped her to hold him.

Though he was pale and lifeless, he was beautiful. She saw Rasi in the shape of his eyes and wished he was there with her. As she held her son against her chest and cried, the night turned eerily silent, shattered only by her broken sobs. The ocean settled, as if the gods themselves had suddenly stilled the waves. Atticus stopped rowing and looked around the boat. The air grew thin like they were near a mountaintop. The world seemed to stop. Alina choked back her sobs. A cool breeze brushed her cheek and she shivered. Atticus covered her with the last of their blankets.

"What's happening?" Celia asked.

"I don't know," Atticus answered.

A low rumble filled the air. Alina stared at the heavens where one star grew brighter than all the others. Clouds formed and streaked across the sky with unnatural speed.

The boat started to rock as the waves returned. The slight breeze grew into a whistling gust. Alina protected her lifeless son with her body. The waves crashed violently against the hull, threatening to capsize the boat, but somehow it stayed upright. When the whistle faded, a slow, steady hum replaced it. The hum built into a roar like an all-encompassing battle horn ten octaves too low.

Atticus screamed something to her, but she couldn't hear him despite how close he was. Celia pressed her forearms over her ears with pain etched into the creases in her face.

And then it all stopped. The crashing waves, the darting clouds, the roar, everything ceased as quickly as it had started. At first, no one moved as they sat in stunned silence. Alina stared at the unusually bright star that had caught her eye. She lifted a shaky hand and pointed. Everyone looked to the sky.

Atticus whispered, "I've never seen a star so bright."

It appeared to grow as if it were hurling toward them until it was nearly as big as one of the suns. Then it exploded in blinding light, turning night into the brightest day.

Alina closed her eyes and recoiled, but the brightness surrounded her, seeping through her eyelids. She wondered if she was in the clouds during a lightning storm. She braced for a burn that never came. And then the light vanished as quickly as the roar had before it.

She blinked away the spots until she could focus again. The star had retreated, once again nothing more than one of a thousand pinpricks of light within a sea of black.

Alina felt a slight nudge against her chest. She looked to her son's face. He drew in a deep breath and loosed the most beautiful cry she had ever heard. Alina looked to Doc Eckels, who sat motionless with his mouth agape.

"Doc?" she asked.

"I have no words, Alina."

Her son cried and stretched and writhed in her arms. She stared into his dark blue eyes. He seemed to recognize her even though his eyes weren't yet focused on his new world.

Irene leaned closer for a better view. "My goodness, Alina. He's beautiful." She was right.

Alina couldn't take her eyes from her screaming son. She wanted to squeeze him and never let go. Her tears flowed like rain, and they were the happiest tears she'd ever shed.

Irene wiped her sleeve across her own wet eyes. "What is his name, dear?"

Alina looked at her and then back at her son. She thought about it for a moment before answering, "Cridon."

"Cridon?"

She nodded.

"Is there meaning to that name?"

She nodded again. "I'm naming him after Rasi's parents. His mother's name was Criya and his father's name was Donis."

Irene smiled. "I think Cridon is a perfect name."

Alina stared at her son throughout the night. Though she was exhausted and growing weaker, she never wanted to look away. Irene leaned in and whispered, "You look so tired, dear. Let me hold him for a bit."

Though Alina didn't want to let go of her son, she was too weak to argue. Irene lifted Cridon from her arms. Alina's eyelids fell heavy. Day was just dawning. Before she drifted off, she heard Doc Eckels say, "She's still bleeding. We need ..."

Alina wasn't sure how long she had slept, but it was daytime when she opened her eyes.

Irene smiled when she caught Alina's groggy gaze. "Your mother's awake," she whispered to the bundle in her arms. She held Cridon out to Alina, but Alina was too weak to lift her arms.

At the head of the boat, Celia leaned over the edge and washed the shirts-turned-diapers in the ocean. Homer and Doc Eckels quietly discussed something urgent at her feet and repeatedly looked to her with concern as they spoke.

"What's wrong?" she asked. Her voice was weak, and she worried they wouldn't hear her. She was dizzy. Irene reached down and squeezed her hand.

Homer scooted to her side and whispered, "We're almost there."

"Why do you look so worried?"

Homer looked to the others as though seeking approval. Doc Eckels nodded. "It's just that ... well ... they're waiting for us." His tone frightened her.

"Who?"

Irene lifted Alina's head so she could see past the prow of the boat.

The shoreline of the Torick Islands was a castle-high, jagged cliff that overlooked the water. The scenery would have been breathtaking if not for the army of Tek soldiers standing in wait along the top.

CHAPTER 49
THE FISHER KINGDOM

Rasi opened his eyes. The air was thick and hot and rumbling, almost suffocating. The ground was covered in gray ash and mud. In the distance, he made out the only foliage that could grow in such a desolate place: an endless line of blue wheat-like plants, standing as high as a man was tall. He needn't have ever seen the Bluefields of Sorrow in person to know what awaited him. As far as he knew, no creature had ever survived a journey through the fields, and he couldn't imagine the fishers were an exception.

When they cleared the ash from a large, flat rock and slid it aside to reveal a dark tunnel, he realized he wasn't going through the Bluefields at all, but under them.

When they finally pulled him from the total blackness of the tunnel, they headed for an army of their waiting brethren at the base of a mountain. Once they saw them coming with Rasi in tow, a few of the waiting fishers strained to push a boulder that rested against the mountain face. Then the mountain rumbled, and Rasi understood it wasn't a mountain at all, but a volcano. The fishers rolled the boulder aside, exposing a dark, cavernous entrance.

The six fishers with their hooks embedded in Rasi's six straps heaved and dragged him toward the hole. Panic filled him and he struggled against them. But he was too weak to put up much of a fight. The light of the suns dimmed behind him as the boulder rolled across the entrance.

He forgot about his pain and took in the deepest breath he was able. He would have screamed if he could.

The world around him went black.

Except for the thousands of glowing eyes.

To be concluded in The *Rise of Cridon* on sale now.

ABOUT THE AUTHOR

Douglas R. Brown is a fantasy and horror writer living in Pataskala, Ohio. He began writing as a cathartic way of dealing with the day-to-day stresses of life as a firefighter/paramedic in Columbus, Ohio. Now he focuses his writing on fantasy and horror, where he can draw from his lifelong love of the genres. He has been married since 1996 and has a son. He has had four books published to date, including his werewolf tale with a twist, *Tamed*, and his fantasy series, *The Light of Epertase* trilogy. Though the publishing company ultimately closed its doors, Douglas has given his work a new home under his own imprint, Epertase Publishing. Visit Douglas at www.epertasepublishing.com or email him your thoughts at epertase@gmail.com.

ALSO FROM EPERTASE

LEGENDS REBORN
THE LIGHT OF EPERTASE, BOOK 1

THE RISE OF CRIDON
THE LIGHT OF EPERTASE, BOOK 3

TAMED

DEATH OF THE GRINDERFISH

www.ingramcontent.com/pod-product-compliance
Lightning Source LLC
Chambersburg PA
CBHW020639030726
47498CB00002B/286